RENEGADE LEGACY

STAR BANDITS: UPRISING
BOOK 4

JENNIFER M. EATON

Renegade Legacy
Star Bandits: Uprising, Book 4
© 2023 Jennifer M. Eaton

Published by Galactic Razor
Cover design: Covers by Julie
www.coversbyjulie.com

For E—
When you feel like your ship is crashing,
Your crew will always be there to save you.

CHAPTER 1
CAL

CAL HISSED as sparks shot from the wires in his hands. He sat back in his command chair on the *Star Renegade*'s bridge and shook his fingers to ward off the sting. He should really be better with simple wiring projects.

Drawing in a deep breath, he got back to work. He'd never be as good at repairs as the rest of his crew, but Cal needed to find a way to pull his weight and be good for more than just cooking great meals.

Over the past month and a half, thanks to Stanley's hospitality, the *Star Renegade* had gone through a major overhaul. The people of Kirato were generous with their time and helped with what supplies they could, but Cal tried to avoid taking anything from their adopted home world.

Since the colony had been cut off from trade due to the Cartek War, every resource the people of Kirato had was precious to them. Of course, many of the colonists insisted on helping. They'd pointed out how the *Star Renegade* had brought them food and supplies, daring to travel so close to enemy territory with no regard to their own safety, when all other traders had written Kirato off as a loss.

Still, Cal didn't like to take charity from people who probably needed the supplies more than he did.

He crimped the wires together and sparks shot out again. He winced, dropping the tool. Why was he so bad at stuff like this?

To be honest, fixing this light beside his station was more of a convenience repair than anything else. Since they'd had so much concentrated time to work on the *Star Renegade*, they'd been able to take care of minor repairs like this—things that were more of a nuisance than an actual problem.

Another pop sounded, and a puff of smoke wafted up from the wires. He sat back. Thank goodness Ethan had gotten pretty good at assigning Cal repairs that couldn't harm any of the major systems.

The door slid open. Doc shifted left and right as he rubbed the back of his neck before he walked onto the bridge. "Hey, boss."

Cal taped off the last of the wiring. "You have that: *'it's not good news'* look on your face."

Doc dragged his fingers through his dark hair. "It's been really quiet since Rachel decided to move out into the colony. So I've been filling her chaotic void by tapping into the intergalactic comms as background noise while I'm working."

Monitoring long-distance chatter was nothing new. Doc kept an eye on everything. His penchant for hacking into restricted comms wasn't entirely legal, but it had gotten them out of jams more times than Cal could count.

Cal sat back. "I guess you heard something?"

"It's not good. I had to try to piece it all together, but from what I could tell, the Banes have heavily fortified all of the outer rim planets to protect them from the Carteks."

"Every planet except this one."

"Yeah, although we still can't tell why they're ignoring us, other than the fact that Kirato is sitting right on top of the enemy border."

Cal cringed. It seemed the Banes had forgotten about Kirato long before the Cartek threat had become so bad. These people deserved better.

Doc's gaze remained on the floor, but his thoughts seemed elsewhere.

"I have a funny feeling you didn't come all the way up here to tell me about fortifications."

"No." He looked up. "Again, it's long-range chatter, and it's hard to decipher sometimes, but to me, it sounds like the Carteks know which worlds are fortified. They passed right by those planets and started attacking the inner circle.

A chill ran over Cal's skin as he stood. "Earth?"

It seemed unthinkable. Even before humanity signed the alliance with Keveron and the king drove the Carteks back, the fighting had never gotten close to the Earthan cradle.

Doc shook his head. "It doesn't look like they've gotten that far, but the inner circle colonies are reporting massive casualties. It sounds like three of them have already surrendered."

"Surrendered?" He grabbed the back of his chair. "That's impossible."

"I would have thought so, too. The only thing that I'm sure of is that the Banes are en route. The king is pissed."

Cal didn't doubt it. But why had it taken them so long to act?

Cal eased back into his chair. "I can't believe that three colonies surrendered. Do you know which ones?"

"That part came from Cartek chatter, and I had to translate it. I can't tell."

"This isn't good."

"No, it's not. This information is already weeks old, though. Anything can be going on out there."

It seemed crazy to think that there was war raging so close to the Earthan cradle, while Kirato—the closest planet to the Cartek home world—sat abandoned by both sides, untouched.

This could be the break they'd been looking for, though. Cal needed to keep Dania away from that star-blasted prince. If they had to hide for months or even years, they could definitely find worse places than Kirato, even if they had to start eating rat as a major staple of their diet.

Doc shifted his weight, his gaze trailing over the nav station. He pursed his lips and looked down again.

"I hope you're not telling me this in hopes that we'll run back there and join the fight. We barely got out of the last skirmish with the hull intact."

"Hell, no. I think we're all aware how lucky we were to get to a safe port in the condition we were in." Doc looked at the wires Cal had been repairing—such a tiny thing compared to the larger repairs they'd gone through in the past few weeks. "It's just insane. I mean, living under Bane law hasn't been the best for humanity, but at least the majority of the colonies were thriving. I can't believe we're at war again."

Cal nodded. Humanity had been living in relative peace

for years. The fighting the *Star Renegade* had gotten wrapped up in was mostly their own fault.

He looked out the window to the desert-like terrain. Kirato wasn't much, but it was peaceful. "I'm thinking of staying put for a while. If no one is willing to come here, Kirato is going to need us to bring them supplies. We can stick to the outer rim colonies to get what we need. It will take longer, but it will keep us away from the fighting."

"Is that the notorious Calvin Espinoza, saying he wants to play it safe?"

"You know I always want to play it safe. We're smugglers, not mercenaries."

It was just that things tended to go wrong for them more than Cal would have liked. So far, they'd been lucky not to get blown to smithereens.

Not being chased for the past few weeks had been nice. He'd gotten full nights of sleep. He'd been happy. Out in the outer rims, they might be able to avoid theCarteksand the pirates. It may seem like hiding to some, but he didn't care.

Over the past few years, Cal had been racking up enemies, and he didn't like it. For the sake of his crew, they needed to lie low for a bit, at least until the ship was completely repaired. With any luck, the galaxy would fix itself. This wasn't his battle, anyway.

CHAPTER 2
ALEXANDER

STANDING BENEATH THE SHIP, Alexander held two wires steady as Alanna melted the edges together with a small torch. The scent of liquid metal mixed with the dull tinge of sand particles in the air.

"There we go!" She removed her goggles and attached them to her belt. "This old girl is going to look brand new before we're all done."

Alexander pursed his lips. This ship looking ten years old, let alone new, was highly unlikely.

She started walking toward the next landing leg. "Do you think we can get another support repaired before lunch?"

"Possibly, if I use my powers to heat the wires."

She spun, pointing the torch at him like an extension of her finger. "No way. Doctor's orders. You are on light duty, mister, and I won't be your accomplice."

Alexander folded his arms. "You do realize it's more taxing to do all of this manually."

"Nope. A little manual labor never hurt anyone." She

continued walking, taking out her goggles again. "Like my mom always says, *a little sweat is good for the soul.*"

What sweat had to do with one's soul, he couldn't fathom. "If we finish faster, we can start the modifications to the shields we've been discussing."

She hesitated, and Alexander smiled.

The woman had a penchant for systems modifications that rivaled his own. Many of their discussions on how they could use some of the rarer components in Kirato's storage facilities had them both dreaming of tinkering. However, they'd have to wait for the repairs to be done first.

Alanna shook the torch at him again. "You're trying to distract me into letting you use your magic mojo, aren't you?"

"It *would* expedite the repairs."

She poked him with the back of the canister. "You, sir, are what my mother used to call *an instigator.*"

Alexander smiled. "Is that good or bad?"

"I haven't decided yet."

Footsteps sounded from above, and Dania stepped off the newly installed cargo ramp. Her light brown hair hung limp at her shoulders, and her eyes had lost their primordial luster, now faded to a color neither green nor blue. Alexander would never get used to her looking so plain, so *human.*

She shielded her eyes, looking over the crumbling buildings before shaking her head and walking beneath the ship toward them.

"Hey, girl." Alanna placed the torch canister under her arm. "Care to help?"

Dania eyed the torch. Alexander doubted she'd ever held a maintenance instrument in her life.

"I'd love to, but Ethan asked me to tell you that he can't get into the anterior flexing shaft."

Alanna blew a hair out of her eyes. "Again?" She handed Dania the torch. "Sometimes I swear he drops stuff down there just so I have to go help him." She pointed at Alexander. "No powers." Then to Dania, "Make sure he acts like a good boy."

Dania saluted her. "Aye aye, captain."

Alanna kissed her own fingertips and tapped the upper shaft of the landing gear before she headed for the cargo ramp.

Alexander folded his arms. "You do realize Alanna is not the captain."

Dania laughed. It was an odd sound that suited her. "No, she's nowhere near as broody." Her smile faded as her finger ran over a scorch mark in the outer shielding of the landing leg. The ship held many scars, but this one was fresh. "That was quite a battle."

"I know. I was in a fighter craft in the thick of it, if you'll remember."

When the high prince's ship had arrived, Alexander had projected himself into space between the cruiser and the *Star Renegade* in a futile effort to protect his general. Pitting himself against Geron's brother had been reckless. He could have died, but he at least would have sacrificed himself doing his duty.

She turned toward him. "Cal tells me that the fighting has moved closer to the Earthan cradle. Things don't look good."

Alexander lowered his eyes. This wasn't all that unexpected. Every intelligence they'd studied over the years told them the Carteks still desired many of the planets colonized by Earth. She shouldn't have looked so surprised.

Then again, she had been spending excessive time with the humans. He'd hoped coaxing her to return home would be an easy task, but she'd become far too attached to the *Star Renegade*'s larcenous crew.

He leaned against the landing leg. "This war is illegal, and all enforcers will be called to protect the innocent."

She nodded. "I realize that."

"Geron'senforcers will be severely disabled without you. You can't possibly be planning to stay here."

The wind whipped up, jostling her hair. Too bad it did nothing to fight off the desert heat.

"Geron's enforcers are perfectly lethal without me. Did you see how well Shivana and Miguel fought? None of you need me. They just need to get used to tapping into their own potential."

It was true that some enforcers had come into their own in the battle, but many more fell into confusion. It was a sad truth that many of them simply weren't trained enough to act on their own.

He gripped her shoulder. "They are doubly lethal when they are connected to their prince by their general."

Other enforcers had several generals ready to take command in case their primary general fell, thus keeping a brigade of enforcers strong. Geron never felt the need to create another leader, and now his enforcers were paying the price.

She shrugged him off. "I'm not going back."

He sighed, looking at the bottom of the ship above them. "I know you must feel the same pull to return to

Geron that I'm experiencing. How can you stand it? How can you just ignore the need to feed?"

Her eyes darted to the side. "I do feel it. But I know what will happen to me if I go back."

"He will make you whole. He will make you powerful again."

She parted her lips and looked down. "Don't you like having the ability to choose? Don't you like making your own decisions?" She returned her gaze to his. "I'm not only talking about enforcing the law, but doing what you want, rather than running home for orders after you finish a mission."

A light breeze whisked particles of sand over Alexander's boots. "I find it disconcerting. At times, I have found myself arguing right and wrong inside my head."

"I remember that stage. It's hard, but you'll get through it."

Heat flashed over him as he stepped back. "I don't want to *get through it*. I want to go home."

"Do you?" She held up the torch. "It looks to me like you're enjoying helping with the repairs."

Alexander looked back at the wiring in the landing leg he and Alanna had just secured. "You know I've always loved to fix things."

"And this crew will welcome any improvements to the ship's efficiency." She stepped closer. "If you return to Geron, you'll be back to following orders again. You won't be doing any of this kind of work. You know that. The king has engineers to make repairs for him. Fixing things is…"

"An inefficient use of my time." He grimaced. "I know." That didn't mean it didn't give him joy.

She placed her hand on his arm. "I can see you're

conflicted. All I ask is that you think it over. If you don't go back…"

Alexander shrugged her off. "If we don't go back, we'll die." She had to know that. Every enforcer did. When your power begins to wane, you return to your sponsor. There are no choices. You do what is expected of you.

"Do I look dead to you?" She cocked her head. "What Geron did to us is wrong. The doctor healed me."

"He didn't heal you. He gave you a synthetic replacement for what your body really needs."

She held her hands to her chest. "And it's working. I'm fine."

"Well, you look horrible. And you're weak. How can you stand it?"

She closed her eyes and took a deep breath. "You just need more time to understand."

His eyes narrowed. "I understand perfectly well." What she wanted was for him to spend more time with the crew, allowing them to poison his mind against his prince, as she'd allowed them to do to her. He would not succumb so easily.

"Are you telling me you're ready to throw it all away?" She tossed the torch on the ground. The canister bounced once before it rolled across the sand and clanged against the landing gear. "You're ready to give up the right to do what you love?"

The canister lay against the foot of the ship, a useful tool, discarded like trash. Her point was well made but still inconsequential.

"In order to do my duty to my prince? Yes. I would give this all up in an instant."

Alanna came back down the cargo ramp. She stopped,

adjusting one of the new rigs the locals had installed. The breeze blew through her hair, the pink-tinted strands tangling with the brown and lighting up in the warm Kirato sun.

Alexander shivered and closed his eyes. The truth was, he did like doing repairs. And he did enjoy time spent with the crew. Some more than others.

Alanna touched the ship like a lover, dragging her palm along the landing gear as she descended.

Dania leaned closer. "If you go home, repairs aren't all you'll have to give up."

He glared at her. "Meaning?"

"Meaning, you'll have to leave the crew behind, too." She looked back to Alanna. "All of them."

Alexander's stomach sank as the ship's navigator reached the ground and turned toward them.

"Did I miss something?" Alanna frowned, her gaze trailing to where the torch lay on the sand.

"Alanna!" Doc called from within the ship. "Can you give me a hand with this?"

She glanced at Alexander and Dania, back to the discarded cylinder, and then ran back up the cargo plank. "Coming!"

Alexander walked toward the rear landing gear, avoiding Dania's gaze as he picked up the torch. It was true that some things on the *Star Renegade* would be harder to forget than others.

But he wouldn't forsake his prince. And in time, he'd find a way to bring Dania back to her senses.

Dania bounded up the cargo ramp. She loved Alexander dearly, but he could be so stubborn. He thought he was right, though, which made it even harder to get through to him. Maybe if she waited a little longer, he'd start to question the stark line between right and wrong that the Banes had drilled into their psyches from the time they'd woken up on Keveron.

"Your boy isn't getting any better." Cal leaned against the rim at the opening of the cargo deck. His thick arms stretched the sleeves of his white T-shirt.

Dania kept walking. "Isn't there a proverb or something in your culture telling you eavesdropping is bad?"

"Not when it concerns the safety of my crew." He grabbed her arm. "And especially when it concerns you."

Why did he always single her out? Was he really that concerned that she would turn on the crew? On him?

He softened his grip, his thumb trailing across her skin. "I don't trust him."

"This isn't news to me, Cal." She shrugged him off.

"And as I keep pointing out—but you refuse to remember for some unknown reason—you didn't trust me, either."

"No, I didn't, but my crew believed in you, and the weaker you got, the more I saw the hope of humanity in you." He pointed down the cargo ramp. "That one is not getting weaker. And if I'm being honest, I'm scared to death. Not just about you. Not just about my crew. But also, about Kirato."

Dania closed her eyes. It was true. Alexander was far too smart to not notice all the hidden alcoves and tarps thrown over illegal goods. But this world was getting by with whatever means possible. Alexander had to respect that. At least, she *hoped* he would.

"Alexander is a healer. He's coded to protect people." She turned to Cal. "I don't think even time away from Geron can take that out of him. He believes the people of Kirato are innocents. I can see it in his eyes."

"And the crew?"

Dania lowered her gaze. They both knew that the crew, including Dania, were a different matter entirely.

The overhead comm pinged. "Boss," Ty called. "Stanley is looking for you. He wants you and our beautiful flying lady to meet him in the center square as fast as humanly possible."

Cal tapped the comm. "I'm on my way."

"That sounds mysterious." Dania followed him down the cargo ramp.

"Yeah, Stanley is rarely in a rush."

Dania looked over her shoulder at the base of the ramp. Beneath the ship, Alexander paced, dragging his fingers through his long, platinum hair. He stopped, his gaze fixing on Cal before he grimaced.

"What's his problem?" Cal paused beside the landing gear. "Oh, wait. He's an enforcer."

Dania nodded. Hopefully, he was an enforcer having a deep inner conflict deciding between his duty and what he really wanted.

She turned, grabbing Cal's arm and tugging him away from the ship. "Let's go see what Stanley needs."

As they entered the U-shaped courtyard attached to Stanley and Amelia's home, their host ran out to meet them. His robes billowed behind him, and the wrappings on his turban-like head covering had started to unravel.

"My friends, my friends, what took you so long?" He waved them forward. "Come, come. You must see."

A group of colonists mulled about a large, black saucer-like ship, shimmering in the Kirato sun.

Cal held out his palm to a man in his early twenties wearing loose, faded gray coveralls. "Regan, it's been a while."

Regan smiled, shaking Cal's hand. "Captain Espinoza, good to see you." He pointed his chin at the ship. "It's something, huh?"

Human pleasantries continued to baffle Dania, but she had to agree with the man's assessment. The sleek, shiny exterior of the ship took up almost the entire center courtyard and seemed out of place hovering a few feet above the ground among the dusty, pockmarked machinery normally housed in the yard.

Cal whistled. "Wow. That's some serious tech."

Dania stepped toward the craft. "Stealth. State of the art."

Stanley nodded. "That's what I thought. Very expensive, no?"

Regan snorted, folding his arms. "Keep your shirt on, old man. It's not salvage. Someone's gonna be looking for it."

"Where did it come from?" Cal asked.

"It just appeared." Stanley pointed up. "It came out of the sky, hovered, and then slowly came to the surface."

"Didn't you pick it up on radar?"

Regan wiped the sweat from his brow. "Not even a blip. Even when we could see it with our own eyes, the scanner saw nothing."

Dania circled the craft. "Tech like this doesn't get lost."

"Have you seen anything like this before?" Cal asked her.

"Once. It was part of a shipment of supplies sent directly to the king." The contents of that ship had been classified and could only be opened by a rank of general or above. All these ships were locked with special coding to make confidential deliveries possible.

She placed her hand on the side of the ship, and the hull lit up. The deep, black wall beneath her hand swirled red until the lights joined into a twisting spiral symbol.

Cal looked over her shoulder. "Royal markings."

"So it would seem." Dania touched the center, and the insignia split apart into a mix of Kever symbols.

Regan stepped back. "Should we be touching that? I mean, this thing looks built to kick ass."

Dania raised a brow, and Cal smiled. "You'll have to excuse Regan. He's an old friend of Ty's." He turned to the colonist. "With tech like that, if it came to kick ass, it would have already done it."

Dania leaned closer to the mechanism, looking over the jumbled symbols.

Cal inched closer. "Can you read that?"

Read random letters? No. But she did understand the mechanism's purpose. "It's a lock."

Her fingers hovered over the keys. Could it be so simple?

Taking a deep breath, she typed in her personal pass-code for critical transmissions between her and Geron. The numbers winked out.

Regan took a step back. "Umm, is that okay?"

Cal moved closer to Dania. "Please tell me this thing won't blow up if you guessed wrong."

She stared at her reflection in the shiny hull. The truth was, she had no idea. Still, if a lock had been personally coded by her sponsor, she had no reason to fear. Geron would never hurt her.

She blinked, her eyes widening. *Geron would never hurt her.* Those were not her own thoughts, but thoughts implanted inside her. They were what she was *supposed* to think, not what she *should* think.

Gasping, Dania pulled away as a small hole formed in the surface of the ship. Two black bands shot out, circled her wrist, and yanked her down.

"Yo!" Regan stumbled back.

Dania cried out as the bands constricted, drawing her wrist tight against the hull.

"Dania!" Cal gripped her arm, tugging.

People shouted and Regan appeared beside her with a long, metal rod. "Hold her head back!"

Cal pulled her toward him as Regan slammed the pipe down on the metal bracelet. The clanging sound filled the square.

"Stop!" Dania shouted. "That's reinforced plating.

You're just going to hurt me."

Cal released her and wiped his brow. "Well, I'm sure as stars not leaving you attached to a demon ship."

The hull flexed again, and a rectangular vial the length of her thumb rose out of the ship and pressed into Dania's palm. The container warmed in her grip and the crimson liquid inside began to swirl.

Her heart clenched as the significance of the contents dug at her soul. It was difficult and painful for a sponsor to create an emergency feeding. As far as she'd known, Geron had never made the sacrifice before.

Until now.

A chill settled into her core as she gazed into the priceless gift from her sponsor—one she would have been thrilled to see just over a year ago. But now the contents promised nothing but a life of automatous servitude.

"What is that?" Cal asked.

It was...*everything*. The most precious gift a sponsor could give their enforcer. But Cal wouldn't see it that way. She knew she shouldn't see it that way, either, but still, tears welled in her eyes. After everything, Geron continued to love her. He wanted her back, and she ached to see him one more time.

She blinked, shaking her head to push away the invasive thought. Geron knew that any enforcer away from their sponsor this long would be desperate for the contents of that bottle. He probably figured she'd break it open, scrambling to get to the sweet oblivion held within. Of course, Geron had no idea that Peter's artificial pathogens had placed her on the trajectory to freedom. Dania would never take this willingly. She'd come too far to go back to her old life without a fight.

The top of the vial shifted, and a wisp of red smoke wafted into the air.

"No!" Dania leaned back as far as she could. "Everyone, get away. I don't know what that will do to you!"

Regan backpedaled toward the house as the colonists ran. Stanley stepped back, but Cal held his ground.

Tears burned her eyes. "Cal, please. Leave me."

"You know me better than that." His gaze centered on hers. "Tell me what to do."

But there was nothing he *could* do. Kile must have told Geron there was a chance she wouldn't open the vial, so he'd made sure the container would open on its own. If even a trace of that gas reached her, she'd be under Geron's control again. Then Cal, and everyone on this planet, would face her wrath.

The vial warmed in her grip, pulsing. Her skin itched, her eyes growing heavy. One whiff and it would be over. No more worries. No more choices. No cares whatsoever. She wanted that oblivion. Needed it like air. She leaned closer, licking her lips.

"Dania."

The voice seemed distant. It didn't matter. All she needed was Geron.

Cal grabbed her shoulders, pulling her back from the smoke. "Dania, tell me what to do!"

She blinked, startled to see him. Had he been standing there all along?

Another puff of smoke left the bottle as tears streamed from Dania's cheeks.

"I'm sorry." And she was. This was her fault. She'd convinced Cal to trust that Kile would return to Geron and send Kirato help, and now they'd all pay with their lives.

CHAPTER 4
CAL

CAL DRAGGED his fingers through his hair. There was no way he was going to stand there while Dania watched that red smoke like death was knocking on her door.

Dania yanked harder, leaning away from the crimson plume. "I'm sorry!"

She obviously wasn't thinking clearly, so he needed to step up, even if she wasn't able to verbalize how to help. He knew the smoke was bad. So all he needed to do was stop it.

Should be easy, right?

Maybe not.

Her first reaction was to get everyone way. The others were right to run, but he'd never abandon her, even if that was what she'd insisted she wanted.

Cal turned away from the smoke and took a deep breath, holding the air deep in his chest. Doing his best to avoid the red vapor, he got close to the vial.

Dania yanked against the binding again. "What are you doing? Get away!"

The vial was firmly in her grip. Her knuckles were

white, and her hand shook. Could the movement be what was releasing the smoke? A tiny bubble formed on top of what appeared to be a pin-sized opening. *Could it be so ridiculously simple?*

Cal placed his hand around hers, moved her thumb over the opening, and pressed down, sealing the container. He stared at the demon tendril of smoke hovering in the air. It seemed so unassuming. Why was she so afraid of it? His lungs began to burn, and he released his breath in a single directed puff, scattering the smoke. A light breeze picked up as Kirato gave a gentle assist and whisked the rest of the smoke away.

Cal stood, a small laugh escaping his lips. The immediate problem was over, but there was probably a lot more red stuff in that bottle waiting to do whatever horrible thing it was meant to do.

Dania let out a deep breath of her own. She blinked and looked up at Cal, obviously stunned.

Cal steadied himself, pointing at the container. "What's in that bottle?"

"A gift from Geron." Dania gulped. "An emergency feeding."

That sounded like something they wanted absolutely none of.

Cal's skin flushed. "Pathogens?"

She nodded. "Yes."

Stanley moved closer, frowning at the vial still in Dania's grip. "What are these *pathogens*?"

"It's what makes enforcers what they are," Cal said.

Stanley grimaced. "It makes them fly, or it makes them mean?"

"Both," Cal said. "Now we have to figure out how to get her untied without spilling the rest of that bottle."

Dania looked at her hand. "I have an idea." She leaned closer to the bottle.

Cal grabbed her shoulder. "What are you doing?"

"Trusting in the vanity of the Banes." She placed her head down, pressing her chest against the ship.

"Don't you dare move that thumb." With her that close, she'd get a full breath of that stuff.

"I won't."

Still, he reached over her and held his hand over her thumb, just in case.

She took three slow breaths, the breeze shifting through her hair, making her look ominously like a fully fed enforcer. Something clicked, and the bands shifted, lifting into the air like wild octopus arms before slipping back into the ship. The black, metal hull closed over, leaving no signs the wild shackles had ever existed.

"What just happened? Why did it let you go?" Cal asked.

Dania stood, holding the vial away from her like it might come to life and bite her. "These ships are integrated with AI. The ship already had my arm, and it placed the vial in my hand. Once it felt my body move closer, and my head near the vial, it could naturally assume that I'd drunk the contents."

Cal glared at the red fluid. "That seemed almost too easy."

Dania shook her head. "It wasn't. If you hadn't been here, I would have done exactly what Geron wanted me to do. Every ounce of my programming screamed for what's in this bottle. My mind thought I needed it."

"How do you feel now?"

She raised the bottle. "Confused? Embarrassed? Afraid?" She shook her head. "Pick the emotion. I feel them all." She twisted the bottle, and it made a soft, electronic sound.

"Careful with that!" Cal said.

"I closed it."

Regan stepped beside her. "It has a lid? Why didn't you do that sooner?"

Dania lowered her eyes. "It's hard to explain. My thoughts were so overcome, I couldn't think of anything but the contents. I was so scrambled, it never even occurred to me." She gazed into the red fluid inside the vial. "Geron knows the strength of this gift. He must have figured one whiff, or even seeing the smoke, would have been enough."

"Enough for what?"

"To make me want to drink all of it." She held up the bottle.

There was no way in hell Cal was going to let her take a whole dose of that. He reached for the vial, but she pulled it back to her, cradling it in her arms.

A chill ran over his skin. "What are you doing?"

Her lips started to form a word, but she seemed to think better of it. "I can't."

"You can't what?"

She took a deep breath as she stared at the vial with a longing in her eyes that made him want to grab the container out of her hands, fly toward a sun, and shoot the demon fluid out of a munitions tube right into the flaming core.

Her gaze turned defiant when it met his. "Peter will

want to see this. Maybe he can figure out why Alexander is still so strong, while I'm withering away."

"You aren't withering away. You're human. You're normal again."

She stared at him, and a grim determination passed over her features before she slipped the vial into her pocket.

Apparently, being human was no longer enough.

The ship hummed and lowered to the ground. The dust kicked up around the edges, and they stepped away as Kever symbols flashed across the surface again.

"That thing's not filled with pathogens, is it?" Cal glanced at Stanley. "Maybe we should evacuate?"

Dania moved closer. "I doubt it."

Cal reached for her. "Wait. It might grab you again."

"It won't. The Banes are too arrogant to think that I might not be under their control by now." Tears crested in her lashes. "No enforcer in their right mind would refuse a supplemental feeding." She smiled before wiping her eyes. "Luckily, I am *not* in my right mind."

But still, she wouldn't give the blasted vial up. Cal would have felt worlds better if that bottle was in his pocket and not hers.

She frowned, staring at the surface of the ship. "The security is disengaged."

The ship still hung, glistening in the Kirato sun. "What do you mean?"

"Watch." She tapped her fingers across the surface of the ship again.

A small crack formed in the surface. A hissing sound filled the courtyard as the crack widened, opening into a door. Stanley whispered something in his own language as cases upon cases of crates marked "Perishable" came into view.

"There should be a manifest. It's usually mounted on an interior wall." Dania reached inside and grabbed a data pad. She flipped through the screens and smiled.

"What is it?" Cal asked.

"Hold on. Let me translate it." She pressed a few buttons and handed the pad to Cal.

He read out loud:

"'People of Kirato: The Banes deeply regret recent events and lack of assistance to your colony. Within this vessel are emergency rations of food, water, vitamin supplements, and medicinal supplies. More will arrive within eight standard Kever revolutions. This message comes in trust of our king. Signed, Geron Bane, Prime Eighth, Keveron.'"

Cal wasn't sure what that fancy title meant, but that didn't matter.

Dania's smile beamed. "Kile made it home. He kept my promise."

Stanley grabbed her shoulders. "I never had a doubt." He pointed at her. "You, lovely lady, I have always had a good feeling about." He turned to Regan. "Get the others. We have work to do!"

Cal grimaced. Yes, the supplies were good, but they could have lost Dania in the process. Would the next shipment be covered in pathogens, just waiting for Dania to touch a crate? How hard would it be for that prince to poison her again?

They needed to be cautious at every turn because now the royal family knew exactly where she was.

The colonists started unloading and categorizing the

food. The ship had been packed so every cubic inch housed supplies with no wasted space.

Cal dragged his fingers through his hair as case after case of food appeared. "This is incredible. This cargo is easily worth millions."

Dania hugged herself. "I was thinking the same thing. Why would they send this without an escort?" She watched Regan unpack a crate of oranges. "Even a stealth ship would have been an easy target for pirates, had it been discovered."

Cal puffed out a breath. "There's only one reason: All possibleescortswere elsewhere."

"Could the fighting really be that widespread?"

Cal shook his head. They had no way of knowing, but he had a bad feeling that this shipment was great news for Kirato, but a bad omen for the rest of the galaxy.

CHAPTER 5
ALANNA

ALANNA GRABBED an energy bar from the lounge and headed down the stairs to the cargo deck. A sense of calm fell over her the closer she came to the open door. Kirato had become just as much home as Reglia had been, or any of the other colonies she'd lived on, and the fresh air from outside smelled like sweet freedom, even with the harsh heat.

She stepped off the cargo ramp onto the dusty surface and heard Alexander's steady pacing beneath the ship.

She leaned around the ramp's retraction gear. "You're still down here?"

"It's quiet. I find the pandering of your engineer distracting."

"Ethan is definitely an acquired taste, but you don't have to come out here to avoid him. I mean, it's a small ship, but it's not *that* small."

He looked at her for a moment before he continued to pace. His brow creased.

She shoved the remainder of her protein bar into her pocket. "Okay, what's really bothering you?"

He stopped pacing and stared at her. He seemed to study her face before he began walking again.

Alanna leaned against the side of the ramp. "You're going to wear a permanent trench beneath the ship if you keep that up."

He stopped, gazing out toward the buildings. "The galaxy is unsettled."

"That's not exactly news."

"Not like this." He turned to her. "It's wrong for us to hide here when we could be helping with the war against the Carteks."

She shrugged. "Yes and no. We tried to help, if you remember, and we nearly got our tushies scattered across the stars."

"We were ill-prepared."

"That's an understatement."

He closed his eyes and squared his jaw. "I cannot stay here. It's not right. I need to protect those in danger."

Alanna eased off the edge of the ramp. Dania had explained a few things about enforcers and coding, and that certain things wouldn't change no matter how long they stayed away from their prince. The trick was to use this to their advantage.

She folded her arms. "Well, now that the repairs are mostly complete, maybe we can find other ways to help?"

"Like what?"

"We're not exactly hiding here. Kirato is right on the border of Cartek space."

"Your point?"

"That this colony is still pretty much unprotected. If the Carteks decide to attack, everyone on this planet will be in big trouble."

"What are you proposing?"

"Maybe we can work together to see if we can come up with a way to protect them."

He looked down, and his eyes darted from side to side, as if maybe he was considering the possibilities. "That will be difficult. We'd be limited to the supplies available on this planet."

Alanna smiled. "It'll be like a puzzle. It sounds like fun."

He continued to stare at the sand beneath the ship before he looked up. "Being productive in any way would be more beneficial than wearing a trench under your ship."

"That's the spirit!" She tugged his arm. "Come on. I get my best ideas when I see what supplies I have to work with. Let's talk to Stanley and see what he'd be willing to give up for the cause."

At Stanley's courtyard, colonists were busy unpacking supplies from a shiny, black ship.

"What's all this?" Alanna asked.

Stanley smiled. "A glorious gift from the king."

Alanna elbowed Alexander. "I guess that means Kile made it."

Alexander gaped. "Geron actually helped?"

His gaze carried over the supplies—far more than the *Star Renegade* had ever dropped off. A slight edge of pink touched his cheek. Had he been concerned that the prince wouldn't send anything?

Stanley pointed to the boxes. "Would you like to help categorize the supplies?"

"I think our expertise could be used elsewhere," Alexander said.

Stanley clasped his hands behind his back. "Oh? How is that?"

"We have a few ideas to boost your defenses," Alanna said. It wasn't quite the truth, but she was sure between the two of them, they could come up with something after they saw the supplies. "We just need a few things from your coffers, if you don't mind."

Stanley chuckled, holding his stomach. "Today, I feel generous. Even more so if you can strengthen our shields." He motioned to the far end of the courtyard. "Be my guest. Whatever I have is yours." He headed back to the shiny ship.

Alanna couldn't hold back her giggle. "Did you hear that? We can use whatever we want!"

Cal waved them over as they walked toward Stanley's stash of supplies. He tapped Alexander on the shoulder. "Your prince really came through. This is amazing."

Alex nodded. "He's a good man."

Cal shrugged. "I'm not sure I'm ready to agree about that after what he almost did to Dania, but I'll certainly take the supplies."

Alex frowned. "What does that mean?"

Dania's hand moved to her pocket, and she took a step back. "It's nothing. I'm fine."

Cal frowned at her, and Alanna could feel the tension between the two of them. Whatever Dania was hiding was obviously a little more than nothing.

Alex opened his mouth like he was about to ask a question, but Alanna tugged him away. "We're on a mission, remember? Let's leave them to the supplies." This was obviously something between Cal and Dania, and she didn't want to get drawn into anything that wasn't her business.

Alex's gaze lowered to where Dania's hand still protected her pocket, but he didn't argue. Thank goodness, because Alanna wasn't sure she'd be able to make a six-foot-four man comply. Especially one with magic powers.

She smiled. It sure would be fun to try, though.

CHAPTER 6
DANIA

DANIA OPENED A CRATE, picked up an orange, and took a deep whiff. Citrus was such a decadent gift, even for the Kevers. She still couldn't believe Geron would have parted with any, if given a choice.

Two men laughed, lifting heavy crates from the ship and passing them out to people waiting in the staging area. Regan grabbed a smaller crate with a blue colonial medical symbol stamped on the side. His eyes widened as he reviewed the attached paperwork. His jaw dropped, and he stumbled before Stanley directed him to add the crate to the stack of supplies slated for their hospital building.

Regan set the box down and walked back to the ship, looking over his shoulder at the crate he'd just unloaded. What could have been in that box to cause such interest?

Cal placed a box of apples beside her. "If there's any cinnamon around here, I see a pie in our future."

A pair of insects circled above the container.

"What's pie?" Dania asked.

"Pie is like a wonderful dream come to fruition when made by the right hands."

Stanley's wife, Amelia, smiled and waved at them from an open window. The scent of fresh baked bread wafted through the air, the smell mingling with the fruit. While others unpacked the new supplies, the woman had taken it upon herself to make sure there was enough food for all the volunteers. Dania had to admit, her cooking smelled delightful.

Cal licked his lips. "I just might have to cheat and send a bag of apples to Mel."

He shooed away the insects, his arm knocking into Dania.

She flinched, grabbing her pocket.

Cal's smile faded. Many times, he'd overreacted to things with her and the crew, but this time, she understood his concern. The vial was meant to save her, at least from Geron's perspective. But for her and the crew of the *Star Renegade*, it could be the end of everything they'd built together over the past year.

He pointed to her pocket. "Do you want me to take that to Doc for you?"

"No!" She closed her eyes, wishing she hadn't answered so quickly. "I mean, no. I can take it to him."

"Why do I have a bad feeling you don't want it out of your sight?"

"That's not...what I said." She looked down. She'd wanted to say that it wasn't true, but the words refused to pass through her lips.

Was she afraid of the vial? Maybe. Just a few drops of the contents might make either her or Alexander into a living horror for the people of this planet, not to mention the *Star Renegade*.

She should give it to Cal. Let him destroy it.

But the thought of losing such a precious gift from her sponsor left a deep ache in her heart. Cal would never understand that this was a kind gesture and not a weapon. Geron still wanted her back, and a small part of her reveled in that knowledge, even if that wasn't what she wanted anymore.

Cal took both her hands in his. "Whatever is going through your mind, you need to focus on the fact that the stealth ship was programmed to contain you. You were shackled to the hull when that gas nearly shot in your face.

She nodded. Thank goodness for the light Kirato breeze, or she may have succumbed instantly.

Cal grabbed her arm. "He doesn't care about you, Dania."

Her heart clenched. "He does."

"He doesn't! Not more than he cares about one of his ships or a favorite pair of shoes." He pointed at her, fire in his eyes. "You're nothing but a possession to him."

She shook her head, but in many ways, he was probably right.

"You need to get it through your head that he's a spoiled prince and a sore loser. He doesn't need you. He just doesn't want to give you up."

He was certainly right on the last part, but saying Geron didn't need her wasn't entirely accurate. Geron's poor planning made her invaluable to him in the current war climate. He needed a general, and he'd only created one. The war might be over before he'd be able to properly program, let alone train, another.

Cal moved closer, his voice softening. "I just want you to consider that he just proved that he wasn't opposed to playing dirty to get you back. I'd bet the next ship is booby trapped to drug you as well."

Drug her? An emergency feeding wasn't quite the same as being drugged, but maybe from Cal's perspective, it was. The Kever culture was too alien to explain to a human. Even the word *prince* was a human word. Yes, Geron's father was the highest-ranking Kever in the galaxy, in control of all. But the term *king* was one given to him by humanity. It was something familiar that made the people of Earth feel safe. The truth was far different, except maybe for the totalitarian control the king demanded.

Mel pushed through the doors of the house. Her long black skirts blew in the breeze as she stormed toward them. "Calvin Espinoza!"

His eyes widened. "Oh, boy. She used my full name."

The breeze blew Mel's graying black hair in her face as she slapped his hand from Dania's arm. "Is that how we treat a lady, young man?"

He held up his palms. "Mel, I was just trying to..."

She held up her pointer finger. "Shush!"

"But I..."

"I said, shush!"

"Shushing." He pressed his lips together, but his gaze darted back to Dania and then down to her pocket. His eyes seemed to plead with her.

Did he think that she was going to use it? Did he actually think she was that weak?

Amelia reached up and grabbed the back of Dania's collar. "You. Come."

Dania stumbled backward as the woman dragged her to the house. "But..."

"Shush!"

Dania pressed her own lips together. Cal's smile was broad, softening his features, before Amelia slammed the door, shutting Dania into her kitchen.

Tall, wooden cabinets lined the walls, and long counters led to three gleaming, metal sinks. Four metal doors reverberated with slight hums similar to the refrigeration unit in Cal's galley. Two pans of rolls lay atop the oven to her left, the aroma filling the room. Mel frowned at the markings on the pan, where it appeared someone had removed two of the rolls closest to the edge of the counter.

She growled under her breath before she turned, a pleasant smile appearing on her face. "So. How goes the unpacking? It is good. Yes?"

Dania stared at her, before the woman raised a brow. She had a feeling Mel wasn't used to not getting expedient answers.

"Yes, the unpacking is good. I mean, we have a lot of help, but there's so much. It's taking time to go through it all."

Mel's brow remained quirked. "The red smoke. That was not good. No?"

Dania shook her head. "No, it was definitely not good."

"Would it have hurt my Stanley? My Calvin?"

Dania pursed her lips. She wasn't sure it would have done anything to them. But she had no idea. Her body had been conditioned and changed at a cellular level to accept the Kever pathogens. If a human being breathed it in, it may have had an effect similar to acid, for all she knew.

"I don't think it would have been good," Dania admitted.

"Yet my Calvin did not leave your side."

It was interesting that she referred to him as *her* Calvin.

She'd raised Ty, so that made sense, but Cal had only hidden away here when he'd been on the run.

Mel continued to stare at her before the woman's chin lifted. "You need to cook for him."

Startled, Dania blinked. "What?"

"You need to cook." She grabbed Dania's arm and drew her farther into the kitchen. "The way to a man's heart is through his stomach. You don't want him to get skinny, now, do you?"

"I-I…"

"Of course not! Now we just need to find the right meal." She pointed at Dania. "What will get to his heart?"

Dania shrugged. "Mac and cheese?"

Mel guffawed, holding her belly as she chuckled. "That is funny." Her features grew stern. "No mac and cheese. Where would I find cheese, silly girl? This is Kirato. Do you know how much milk it takes to make cheese?" She shook her head like Dania might be completely daft. "What else?"

Dania looked around the kitchen. "Pie?"

Mel's eyes lit up and she clapped her hands. "Yes, yes! A girl after my own heart." She poked Dania's midriff. "We will make a good wife out of you yet."

"Wife?"

"Quiet! Pay attention. What kind of pie?"

Dania gulped. "Apple? But I think we need cinnamon for that, right?" At least, that was what Cal had said. The only thing Dania knew about cinnamon was that it was the wrong thing to add to tomato sauce, but it had given her accidental concoction a pleasant zing that the crew had seemed to enjoy.

Mel clapped her hands again. "Yes, yes, cinnamon is

lovely. And other spices that I may have lying around." She slapped the counter. "That is perfect for my Calvin. He will not know what hit him." She pointed at Dania again. "You. Stay here. Don't move."

The odd woman pushed through the door they'd entered from, and it slammed behind her.

Warmth still eddied up from the rolls on the stove. Three rolls seemed to be missing. Hadn't it been two before? Had Amelia grabbed one before she'd stormed out?

The door slammed open again. "Ha!" She plucked an apple out of the bag in her arms. "More than enough to win a man's heart."

Win a man's heart? "I'm not sure I understand."

Mel shook the fruit at her. "You will, my dear. You will."

———

Dania curled her fingers around a warm mug of a chocolatey drink Mel called "cocoa." It had probably been stolen, but Dania decided not to ask. The flavor wrapped her tongue in delight, and every sip warmed her from the inside.

Mel laughed, slapping the table. "My Stanley, he always bustles about, acting busy. Half the time, he has no idea what he's doing!" She wiped her eyes. "It's good, though. *We* are good."

The scent of cinnamon and apples filled the air, dancing alongside the cocoa. The smells were one of the joys Dania had learned about cooking. It was amazing how simple scents could make the world a better place, at least for a short while.

"It will be just as good for you when you bring my Calvin this pie. Yes?"

Did she mean the pie would make Cal not know what he was doing? What was the woman getting at?

Mel frowned, her gaze traveling down to Dania's pocket. She had been watching from the window. Had she seen everything?

Dania reflexively placed her hand over the vial hidden inside.

"That is a gift from your prince. No?" Mel asked.

Dania gulped. "Yes."

"It will do bad things to you?"

"Yes." *Very* bad.

"Then why do you keep it?"

"I..." Dania looked into her steaming cocoa. "I don't know." She just couldn't stand the thought of anything happening to it. But she would give it to Peter. At least, that was the plan. But even then, would she be able to give it up?

Mel placed her hand on the table, palm up. Dania stared at her palm.

"Hand it over."

Dania leaned back in her chair. "I'm going to give it to Peter."

Mel's eyes narrowed. "Why?"

"Because he's brilliant, and I think he can use it for good."

"Is that the truth?"

"Yes." And Dania realized it *was* the truth. Peter could use it for good. He also wouldn't destroy it. Not that Dania needed it or wanted it around. But just in case...

Mel folded her hands. "Men do not like it when other

men give their women gifts. Especially a man from her past."

Dania shook her head. "I'm not—"

"Shush. Are you making pie?"

"Yes."

"For whom?"

Was this a trick question? "Cal."

"Then shush." She continued to stare, as if trying to figure her out. "My Calvin. He makes you feel nice. Yes?"

"I suppose."

"You snuggle on the couch. You spend the night. You blush. You giggle. You hold hands."

"How do you know that?"

"Shush."

A laugh escaped Dania's lips. A year ago, she may have put this woman in her place. But now, she enjoyed this odd banter while they waited for the pies to cook.

Mel continued to stare. "You will bring him pie. You will sit on the couch again."

"Why the couch? Wouldn't the table be a better place to...?"

"Shush. Pie. Couch. Cuddle."

Dania raised a brow. "Can we have tea? Last time, we had tea."

Mel gave a curt nod. "Tea goes good with pie."

"Okay, then. At least that's settled."

Mel smiled. "You make good pie. This will work. Trust me."

Dania nodded, but she still had no idea what this odd woman was talking about.

CHAPTER 7
CAL

CAL GRABBED a bottle of water from a table beside the demon supply ship and took a long drink. His shoulders ached, but it was a good ache. All those cases of food were like a miracle for these people. Part of him still couldn't believe that the star-forsaken prince had sent help. But then again, he'd disguised a trap within that gift. That little trick had only proven that no matter what, they couldn't trust the Banes.

Regan approached and grabbed a bottle of his own. "Everything's been categorized. Stanley has already begun rationing emergency supplies, but we're going to start handing out basic supplies in the morning."

Two men stacked the last box of oranges on a row ten feet deep.

Cal wiped the sweat from his brow. "It certainly is a lot."

"Sure is. How long have you been friends with this prince?"

Cal laughed, choking on his water. "We're not friends."

"Well, sure, everyone knows you stole Dania from him,

but it's like a friendly rivalry, right?"

Was he serious? "Did you not just help me try to free Dania from the trap he set for her?"

Regan shrugged. "I guess you can't really begrudge a guy trying to get back their girl."

Why was he making this sound like Dania had left Geron over a lover's spat?

Regan looked over the containers lining the courtyard. "And he must not feel all too bad about everything if he's still sending food."

"*Still* sending food? When did he send food before?"

"Every other time you came. Isn't that where you're getting all the supplies from?"

Cal laughed. "I think you have a huge misconception of what's going on here."

Regan stared at him for a moment before a smile broke on his face. "Whatever you say." He looked in the direction of the landing platform. "You know, I haven't seen Ty since you've been back. Where's he been hiding?"

"I'm surprised you two haven't run into each other. He's been out to visit Mel in the kitchen every day."

"Lucky guy."

"I agree. She's quite a cook." Cal pointed his thumb over his shoulder. "I'm heading back to the ship if you'd like to visit."

Regan's nose flared before he smiled. "That would be great."

Cal waved to Stanley and started heading back to the landing platform.

How would anyone in their right mind believe that Cal had ever been in cahoots with a Bane? He supposed it had been a shock for the people of Kirato when the *Star Rene-*

gade had shown up with Dania on the last supply run. But they all knew what had forced Cal to hide out on Kirato in the first place all those years ago. A death sentence ordered by a prince was not commonly rescinded, if ever.

Regan stared ahead as they walked around the crumbled remains of what used to be the side of someone's house. "Do you think we can make requests for the prince's next supply run?"

Was he serious? "How would we even do that?"

"I don't know. I figured you could just call him."

"Regan, how many times do I have to tell you I'm not friends with Geron Bane?" The polar opposite was true. Cal couldn't imagine how these rumors had gotten started.

Ty and Ethan were tinkering with the *Star Renegade*'s landing gear as Cal and Regan approached the ship. The sun reflected off the sand, lighting up Ethan's red hair, white leaving Ty partly in shadow, making his blonde hair seem darker.

Ty smiled, seeing his old friend. "Regan! How are you, buddy?"

"The usual. Barely getting by. Hungry most days."

Ty frowned at him before looking at the ground. It took a lot to render Ty speechless. Regan's demeanor had changed since unloading the ship. The only question was: Why?

Cal walked toward the gear, hoping to divert the awkward conversation to something more mundane. "I thought Alanna and Alexander had finished working on the outer maintenance?"

"Yeah." Ethan wiped the sweat from his brow. "But you asked me to look over anything Mr. Perfect touched, right?"

Cal nodded. Alanna was more than capable of watching

over Alexander, but they'd been fooled by his kind before, and it never went well for them. "Everything seem okay?"

Ethan tossed a cloth over his shoulder. "Yeah, but I still don't like it."

Cal frowned. "You don't like what?"

"You know…the way Mr. Perfect walks around, all holier than thou. I hate it."

Cal tried to keep his expression neutral. Ever since Alexander had snapped and attacked Ethan over what was supposed to have been a joke, the engineer had been overly cautious and judgmental, even more so than he'd been with Dania. Cal supposed it was rightly so. Ethan had almost died. Cal harbored a lot of the same concerns.

Ty leaned against the side of the ramp. "Ethan thinks Tall, Blonde, and Beautiful is coming on to his girl."

Cal quirked a brow at Ethan. "You do realize that Alanna has never been *your girl*."

"Semantics. I was wearing her down." Ethan waved his hands. "I'm *still* wearing her down. It's only a matter of time before she realizes that I'm perfect for her."

One of these days, Ethan would stop living in dreamland.

Regan leaned against the landing gear. "So, Ty. You ever plan on coming home?"

Ty snorted. "No way. I worked too hard to make it to the stars."

"What, you're too good to be suffering down here like the rest of us?"

Ty gaped. "What do you mean?"

"Don't give me that crap. You know how bad it is here."

"Yeah, that's why we bring food whenever we can."

Regan shoved Ty. "You mean, whenever it's

convenient."

"Hey." Cal stepped between them. "Let's keep things civil, gentlemen."

Regan stared Ty down. "I'm here to get the money you owe me. Two hundred quara is nothing to keep civil about."

Cal gaped. "Two hundred quara?"

Ty held up his palms. "I had a little gambling debt. Regan bailed me out."

"*Little?*" Cal and Ethan said at the same time.

"That was all I had. You promised to pay me back." Regan pointed to the crumbling buildings. "If you haven't noticed, the people you left behind are suffering, pretty boy. You bring back food, they call you a hero, and then you leave, all nice and cozy on your spaceship while the rest of us starve."

Ty flicked a glance at Cal before returning his gaze to Regan. "I'm good for it, man. We just need to make a few more viable trades."

Regan pulled a gun from inside his coveralls and pointed it at Ty's head. "I'll take it now."

"Yo!" Ethan held up his palms and stepped back.

Regan's fingers shook on the trigger, the barrel swaying like the handle felt unfamiliar in his grip. Cal took a deep breath, keeping still so the guy didn't slip with a weapon he'd probably never even picked up before.

Ty's hands shot up. "I don't have that kind of coin on me." He glanced at Cal. "Anyway, money is almost useless here these days, right?"

Regan shook his head. "Your prince's ship had a ton of medical supplies in it. There was a full case of *etriptolilipane* in there—enough to save my dad."

So this wasn't really about the money.

Cal inched closer. "Just ask Stanley for the medicine. He'll give it to you."

Regan shook his head. "You think my dad is the only one who needs it? It's going to be rationed. I'll need to trade to get more, but we don't have anything left to trade with." He centered the gun on Ty again. "I need my money. I'll find someone still willing to use cash."

Ty lowered his hands slightly. "I want to help your dad, believe me, I do, but I just don't have that kind of coin."

Regan's eyes darkened. "I actually believe you, but I'm thinking your rich captain and his good buddy the prince are more than capable of covering your debt."

Seriously? "I told you we have no connection to that prince." Other than the fact he wanted Cal dead.

Cal glanced back toward the colony. Alexander and Alanna were walking toward the *Star Renegade*, laughing and talking amongst themselves. Cal needed to get this resolved before the enforcer looked up and saw a confused, desperate guy in the middle of a criminal act.

Cal lowered his hands slightly, keeping his voice steady. "Regan, you have the completely wrong idea about who we are."

Regan turned his gun on Cal. "What I think you are is the captain of a ship that brings a fortune in food every few months. That has to come from somewhere." His hand shook on the gun. "I just want what's mine."

"Regan, come on, this is dumb." Ty's voice quavered. "We've known each other forever. I can pay you a little bit now, and more next time."

The gun swung back to Ty. "That won't save my dad. You aren't one of us anymore. You…"

Cal grabbed for the gun. Regan grunted and they spun, struggling for the weapon. The guy was small but wiry, twisting Cal's shoulder.

As they spun, Regan's eyes widened. "Enforcer!"

A loud boom echoed beneath the ship and a sting lanced Cal's shoulder.

"Cal!" Regan's eyes got even wider. "Cal! I-I'm sorry. I didn't mean…"

Regan gasped as the gun flew out of his hand. Alexander slammed into Regan as the gun bounced off the landing gear and landed on the sand in a puff of gray dust. It was odd, how the dust seemed to hang in the air, like time had stopped.

"Cal!" Alanna screamed.

A high-pitched tone filled Cal's ears as his knees hit the ground.

Dania ran toward the ship carrying a thin container— but she seemed to float, barely moving at all. She stopped short, dust puffing up around her feet.

Why was everyone moving so slow?

Cal's heartbeat drummed in his ears. The shrill tone heightened as Alexander pinned Regan to the sand with one hand and raised a fist.

Voices arguing seemed distant, like they were underwater.

Regan screamed as the drumming in Cal's head overcame him, and his vision closed in on all sides.

Something…*hurt*.

Someone slid beside him and placed a cold hand on his forehead.

Alanna's concerned eyes came into focus. "Cal's been shot!"

A STREAM of ice rushed over Dania's skin as a ball of fire erupted in Alexander's fist, his hair alight and floating with primordial energy.

The box holding the pie slipped from her fingers, crashing to the sand. "Alexander, stop!" Dania leapt over the container as she raced toward him.

Ty's friend Regan was already at Alexander's mercy, screaming as the fireball scorched his skin.

Ethan backed away, gaping, the white fire reflecting in his eyes. His reaction was warranted. It wasn't too long ago that Ethan had been on the receiving end of Alexander's anger.

"Yo!" Ty held up his hands. "Alex, calm down."

Alexander's fist shook, fire dripping from his fingers and singeing the man below him.

Dania touched her friend's shoulder. He flinched but kept his grip on the man beneath him.

"Alexander," she whispered. "What are you doing?"

His arm trembled beneath her. "This man committed a crime."

Alanna sniffed somewhere off to Dania's left. "Cal needs help!"

A new chill coated Dania's veins. Cal lay on the ground beside Alanna. His eyes were closed, and a growing red stain spread over his white shirt. His breathing was ragged but steady.

Alanna's eyes hardened from fear to determination when she met Dania's gaze. "I got this." She pointed to Alexander. "You get that."

Dania nodded, but they'd be better off if their places had been exchanged. Alanna had proven much better at keeping Alexander's emotions at bay, and for some reason, Alexander had become nearly as crazed and bloodthirsty as a fully-charged enforcer.

Dania squeezed Alexander's shoulder. "I ordered you to stop."

He shook beneath her touch. "Stop enforcing the law? Stop a man from murdering another?"

"You stopped it already. Further enforcement is unnecessary."

"All crimes deserve death."

It was true. At least in the minds of a fully-charged enforcer. Yet the ball of energy wavered, as if maybe Alexander wasn't so sure, even though Dania was fairly certain the man was more than guilty.

She reached for the fireball, and the energy winked out before she touched it. Alexander released his grip, and Regan scurried back like a crab, blood from his wounds slicking the sand beneath the ship.

"I'm sorry." He looked at Cal and a sob broke free. "I'm so sorry!" Regan pushed up to his feet and bolted across the sand, disappearing behind the buildings.

Alexander's lips twisted as he watched the man's retreat. "He was guilty."

"And you're out of your mind!" Ethan said. "You can't just run around burning people's faces off."

Alexander frowned at him. "Are you daft? He was going to kill you all."

"Stop it! All of you!" Alanna wiped back her hair. "We need Doc!"

Dania moved to Cal's side and placed her palm on his cheek. His skin seemed cold despite the Kirato heat. His eyes fluttered open and fixed on her before they closed again.

Her heart clenched. Nearly every time she'd woken in the medical bay, Cal had been at her side. His presence had warmed her, but she had no idea how to do the same for him.

"I'm not sure how bad it is," Alanna said.

Alexander stood over them. His eyes narrowed as his gaze carried over Cal.

Dania breathed a sigh of relief. She'd seen Alexander heal wounds far worse than this.

He crouched beside her, reaching for Cal's shoulder. "The bullet went straight through. I need to..."

Alanna shoved him away. "I don't want your help."

Dania gaped. What was she doing?

"Wait." Alanna wiped her eyes and looked at Alexander. "Just stop the bleeding."

Alexander frowned at her before he placed his hand on the wound. "The bleeding has stopped. But he still needs..."

She swatted his hand away. "Doc will take care of the rest."

Alexander stood. "I can very simply…"

She pointed to the divot in the ground, where Alexander had held Regan. "If you insist on being an enforcer, and that's what the enforcer side of you is like, then I'm done with you." Alanna turned to Ty and Ethan. "Help me."

The co-pilot and engineer both ran to Cal, Ty taking his shoulders and Ethan taking his feet as they hoisted Cal from the ground and ran him into the ship with Alanna following after.

Alanna stopped at the bottom of the ramp, looked back to Alexander, then lowered her eyes as she headed into the ship.

Instead of following, Alexander stood and watched Alanna disappear up the cargo ramp. He blinked, but once their friends were gone, his gaze seemed to fix on nothing.

Everything inside Dania wanted to follow the crew into the ship, to stay at Cal's side and give him the same comfort he'd given her so many times. Cal had looked far too pale, even for someone wounded. For some reason, though, it seemed like her friend needed her more.

He rubbed his eyes, then turned to her. "I could have finished treating him if they'd have let me. Their reactions make no sense."

This was true. Dania had embraced her humanity, but some of their reactions still puzzled her. Her gaze drew to the cargo ramp. "It appears they're angry with you."

His brow furrowed. "For stopping a crime?"

It did seem ridiculous, even to her.

Alexander was a healer. Cal needed to be healed. They should have allowed Alexander to finish treating him.

However, every one of them had looked at her friend like he was someone to avoid… Like he was *an enforcer*.

Dania rubbed her face. That was exactly the problem. It wasn't that Alexander had helped… It was *how* he'd helped. "You almost killed that man."

"One less…" Alexander closed his eyes.

One less criminal in the world. These were words they'd all been taught by rote. Yet she'd rarely heard them from Alexander. Maybe his time as a prisoner had scarred him worse than she'd thought.

She pulled him toward the ship. "Come on. Maybe we can still help."

When they reached the infirmary, Alanna and Peter were already scanning Cal's injury. His complexion seemed even more milky in the bright med bay lighting.

This crew spent far too much time in the infirmary. Hopefully, that wasn't because of her being on board.

"I can seal the wound easily," Alexander whispered.

Of course, he could. What he didn't yet understand was the human desire to take care of their own.

She squeezed his biceps. "Stay here, just in case they need you."

Heat bristled off his skin. He was probably stewing about how horribly inefficient human medicine was, and he'd be right. But for now, it was better if he stayed back.

Ethan glared at Alexander as he handed Peter a silver cylinder with a light on one end and a small keyboard on the other.

"Your friend is a psychopath," Ethan grumbled to Dania as she approached. "Hopefully, now everyone can stop playing games and remember what he really is."

What he really is... Did they all think the same way about Dania?

Regan had certainly broken the law. Granted, Alexander's punishment may have been harsh in the eyes of a human, but it had certainly been justified.

Still near the door, Alexander folded his arms. He had softened some since Kile had left for Keveron. It was possible the crew had started to believe that Alexander had embraced his humanity. Maybe this incident had them worried they'd simply traded one irrational enforcer for another.

Ty wiped the sweat from his brow with the back of his sleeve. "I can't believe borrowing money so many years ago led to this." He closed his eyes and sighed. "I can't get over some of the things he said. He just seemed so desperate."

"Desperation quite often leads humanity to foolish and rash behavior," Alexander pointed out.

"You don't know what his story is." Alanna placed a damp towel on Cal's forehead. "His father has been sick for a long time. He's a nice old man. I took care of him once."

"Nevertheless, his son committed a crime." Alexander pointed at Cal. "He shot your captain."

Cal groaned, his eyes fluttering open as a machine in the back of the room beeped and shuffled test tubes.

Alanna sniffed and wiped her nose. "When you first came on board, and you attacked Ethan, I defended you. I trusted you. I thought you were different. But I think I was wrong."

Alexander parted his lips as if he were about to speak, then decided against it.

Peter leaned away from Cal. "Okay, good news. Our

beloved captain is going to be fine. The bullet went right through, and he only needs a little laser surgery."

"I can take care of that for you," Alexander said.

Peter held up his hand. "It's a simple enough procedure. I got it."

Cal eased up in the bed, holding his left shoulder. "Hold on. I get that I was shot, but then what happened?"

"Dania's buddy went ballistic again," Ethan grumbled.

Alexander's brow furrowed. "Would you rather I'd let him shoot you all?"

Ty shook his head. "Alex, you're not getting the problem here. You're stronger than a cave boar. You could have just punched Regan and he'd be unconscious. That's what we're upset about."

Alexander's head cocked to the right as he continued to gape.

Dania's heart ached for him. In his mind, he'd done the right thing. He wasn't capable of understanding their perspective.

Tears streamed from Alanna's eyes as she shoved Alexander. "Stop looking so surprised and listen! Yeah, Regan had a gun. Yeah, Cal was down. But I saw that gun go flying. You'd disarmed him before you even got close enough to grab him. You'd already diffused the situation, but you were still going to kill him." She shoved him again. "That's the problem, Alexander! You don't just kill someone when there's a less-lethal alternative."

It was a valid argument that even Alexander should be able to understand. Before he'd been taken prisoner, he'd always looked for a peaceful solution to things. This rash man prone to anger and violence was a stranger to Dania.

Ty rubbed his face. "I think what we're all trying to say

is that we've gotten used to you being on board. You seemed like a great guy." He shrugged. "Hell, I even liked you. But you scared me today. That wasn't the guy I've had drinks with in the lounge. You were an enforcer. Plain and simple." He looked at the rest of the crew. "I can't speak for everyone, but I don't like being afraid of my friends."

Alexander frowned at him, and Dania didn't need any special powers to read her friend's thoughts. Alexander *was* an enforcer. People were *supposed* to be afraid of him. In time, he'd realize that what they wanted was his friendship. But she wasn't sure Alexander was capable of understanding that, yet.

Ty tapped Alexander's shoulder lightly. "I think you need to cut loose a bit and have some fun. I think you're a little bit high strung, my friend."

Alexander swatted his hand away. "Saving people from their own foolishness is about all the fun I can take in one day."

Dania blinked. Was that…a joke? With any luck, this was the start of his powers waning. If he lost the desire to uphold the law, maybe he'd stop lashing out irrationally.

Ty held up both his hands. "I think everyone needs to take a deep breath and calm down. No one died. We got lucky."

"This time," Ethan murmured.

Dania rubbed her forehead. Was this their new reality? Would they ever be able to return to the relative civility they'd enjoyed just that morning?

"Ty's right. I'm going to be fine." Cal leaned back on the mattress as Alanna smeared a brown liquid around his wound. He blinked at her like his eyes hurt. "What were you and Alexander doing off the ship?" Cal, as usual, was probably trying to deflect the topic of conversation and give his crew time to calm down.

Alanna shrugged, not looking up.

Alexander folded his arms. "Alanna and I are working on a plan to construct an ion shield around the colony. We were returning to the ship to procure a piece of copper to use as a conductor."

Dania's lips parted, tasting the dry air. Ion shields were incredibly effective. They'd been known to thwart most larcenous attacks on small space stations. However, they did have their complications.

She tilted her head. "You do realize that ion shields are illegal." They hadn't been at first, until pirates and smugglers had realized that enforcers couldn't see through ion particles with the standard scanning equipment on their cruisers.

Alexander stared at the wall and looked like he was chewing the inside of his cheek. That was a very human habit, yet another odd quirk she hadn't seen in him before.

He looked back to her. "Yes, they are illegal, but in this case, they are a little less illegal, since it was the only thing we could come up with to help protect the planet."

Dania's smile broadened. "Less illegal?" For an enforcer, that should have been an inconceivable concept. Things were either legal or illegal. Right or wrong. There was no in between.

He nodded. "Until you come to your senses, I am stuck on this planet. I need to use my time wisely to protect you as well as the innocents in this colony. I'm doing so by the only means available."

"By creating something illegal?"

He stared at her for a moment. "Yes." A smile touched the edge of his lips before he looked down.

"It sounds like fun," Dania said.

He looked up. "Yes, I think it will be."

Around the room, the crew stared at him with varying levels of what appeared to be disdain, distrust, and concern.

Dania took a settling breath. Hopefully, they could see his admission was an incredible step in the right direction. If he could only learn to control this newfound temper, he may have a chance to be accepted by the crew. Then she'd have the best part of her previous life, and all the freedom of her new one. It was still a dream, but one worth fighting for.

Peter approached Cal with a syringe. "I'm going to give you a sedative while I close your wounds. You'll be groggy and probably sleep for a few hours."

Cal nodded and closed his eyes. Peter placed the needle in his arm and then pulled over a tray of instruments.

Ty and Ethan whispered farewells to their captain and left the room. It seemed that Ty's admission of being afraid and Cal's tactical change of subject had calmed things down some. In time, that would give everyone a chance to realize that despite the severity of Alexander's reaction, it had been warranted.

She shifted her weight, and the vial in her pocket pressed against her hip, a grim reminder of how close she'd come to losing everything.

Sweat beaded her brow considering all Geron's gift offered. All she needed to do was drink the contents and all the fear, all the uncertainty would disappear. Life would return to normal. She could take Alexander home to Keveron, and they'd be happy again.

She blinked, shaking her head. *No, that wasn't right.*

Her hand warmed, and she realized she'd taken the vial from her pocket. Her fingers began to tremble as Alexander left the room. She wanted so much for him. Freedom. Choices. Love. But she also wanted these things for herself.

This vial represented everything she hated in her past life, and everything she wanted more than life itself. She closed her eyes and bit her lip, holding her breath. She didn't need this vial. She didn't want any of the promises it offered.

So why did she want so badly to open it up?

Peter grabbed her shoulder. "Sweetie, are you okay?"

Dania took a deep breath. The air was cool and dry with a slight twinge of antiseptic. It was real. This place was real. And these people cared about her.

Peter swept a light laser over her forehead. "Maybe you should sit down?"

The vial continued to warm, beckoning.

"No!"

Peter took a step back. "No, what?"

Taking another deep breath, she pressed the vial into his hands. "Take this. Hide it from me. Don't let me have it no matter what."

He frowned, looking at the container. "Oh-kay."

She stepped back, her hands shaking. What was she doing? "I changed my mind. Give it to me." She reached for it.

Doc held the vial back. "Whatever this is, I don't think it's a good idea."

"I need it."

Alanna appeared at her side, placing her hand on Dania's arm. "Dani, are you all right?"

Dania's breathing settled. When she looked back to Doc, the vial was no longer in his hands.

Her gut twisted. Blood raced through her veins. "Where is it?"

He raised a brow. "You asked me to hide it. How about you come back in a few days and tell me what it is?"

Dania took in a staggered breath. The vial was gone, and Alanna's grip was sure and strengthening. This crew was her family now. They were all she needed.

But it would have been far too easy to accept the gift Geron had offered. She'd wanted it more than anything, despite knowing deep in her heart how much she'd lose. One sip, one taste and everything she'd worked for would be gone, and everyone she loved would be made to suffer, and that scared her more than anything.

CHAPTER 9
CAL

CAL SHIFTED to the edge of his gurney and rubbed the bandage on his shoulder.

"How do you feel?" Doc asked.

"Like I've been shot. If it was such an easy wound to treat, then why does it hurt so bad?"

"Do the words *'you were shot'* have any meaning to you?"

Cal guessed that made sense, but his wound was probably the least of their problems. He rubbed his eyes. "Too much happened today, and I need your big brain."

Doc tapped his head. "My noggin is your noggin."

Cal took a deep breath, trying to sort out everything in his head. "Prince Geron sent a shipload of food to Kirato, but it was really just a fancy trap for Dania."

Doc nodded. "Does this have anything to do with a small container with very live pathogens in it?"

Cal's heart lifted. "She gave it to you?"

"Kinda willingly. Kinda not. I wasn't sure what was happening at first, until she grabbed for it like a junkie. I tested it while you were sleeping and confirmed my suspicions."

Cal rubbed his eyes. "I'm just glad she gave it to you. I wasn't sure how to get her to give it up."

"After her reaction, I'm definitely keeping it under lock and key. I'm interested in running tests on it, though. The payload in that little container is ten times what was in her blood. That prince wasn't fooling around."

"Just be careful. That stuff started affecting her the second she saw it. I don't even want to think about what it might do if she ingested it."

"You got it."

Cal rubbed his shoulder again. "On to the next problem. Can you think of a way to get Palian Steel cuffs on Alexander?"

"Without dying? No."

Cal rubbed his face. "He's still a ticking time bomb."

"I don't think he is."

"Are you serious? He almost killed Ty's friend. Regan was desperate, but he's no murderer. We would have been able to talk him down." Cal rolled his shoulder, testing the ache. "Alexander was just as crazed as he was a few months ago when he attacked Ethan."

"It wasn't like it was with Ethan."

Cal frowned. "You weren't there."

"Neither were you. You passed out."

"I saw enough."

"I don't think you did." Doc walked over to the screen and tapped on a keyboard below it.

The screen came to life with a video of Cal and Regan struggling. A loud bang reverberated off the metal hull before the gun flew out of Regan's hand on its own. A second later, Alexander charged onto the screen with one hand raised.

So, Alexander *had* disarmed Regan.

Cal cringed, watching himself fall to his knees. Everything had looked and sounded so strange, like he'd fallen into a dream.

Alexander pinned Regan to the ground and a flaming ball appeared in the enforcer's fist. The faint sound of Dania's voice calling for him to stop sounded in the distance.

Doc pressed the pause button and pointed at the screen. "See that? He stopped."

"He stopped because Dania ordered him to."

"I disagree." He backed up the video a few frames. "Watch. The flames appear in his hands, and he holds it for two seconds before Dania yells to stop."

"So?"

"Two seconds is a long time."

"Your point?"

"It would have taken him less than a second to kill Regan, but he didn't. He hesitated."

"I still don't get your point."

"He questioned what he was about to do before Dania even screamed. What enforcer would question punishment for someone so obviously guilty?"

"They said he was arguing with Dania, trying to change her mind and let him kill Regan."

"I disagree again. I think he was arguing with himself. Part of him—the enforcer part—wanted justice. The other part was questioning what was going on and trying to decide if death was a valid punishment." He turned off the screen and looked at Cal. "I think Alanna has gotten through to him. But unfortunately, I also think our girl is pretty upset by what just happened."

"I think we all are. He just proved he could snap at any time."

Doc shook his head. "I don't think he will. He stopped himself from enforcing the law today when he was completely in the right to execute what was, in his mind, a criminal."

"Ty was right. He could have just punched Regan and it would have been over." Cal rubbed the back of his neck, wincing as pain shot through his chest.

"I agree, and I think next time, we'll see that punch instead of a fireball."

That was a heck of a statement, and the consequences of being wrong were just too high. "Are you willing to stake your life on that?"

Doc sighed. "No. That's just my educated guess."

Cal shook his head. "Normally, I'd take your educated guess as canon. This time, I'm not sure I agree." He stretched his shoulder. The ache was deep, but not unmanageable. He just needed to be careful. "Can I go?"

"Yes, but take it easy. No heavy lifting, and rest if you can."

Cal pushed off the gurney and left the room. Take it easy... Rest... Sure. All he had to do was pretend the Carteks weren't out there, and the enforcers didn't know exactly where the *Star Renegade* was, and that blasted prince wasn't going to send another care package to try to poison Dania again. No problem.

He headed to the bridge. Normally, staring out at the stars relaxed him. Today, he'd have to take comfort in the desert terrain of Kirato.

When Cal reached the bridge, Ty was seated at the co-pilot's station, staring out at the crumbling buildings.

"I guess it's nice to be home?" Cal asked.

"It *was*."

"*Was?* What's that supposed to mean?" Cal eased into his seat, careful not to jar his shoulder.

Ty rubbed his eyes. "I think today really got to me."

"Getting shot at does that to you."

"It's not that." He looked back out at the colony. "Regan hated me. He said I wasn't one of them anymore."

"The day we got here, the guys who picked us up on the skipper craft seemed chummy enough. You were talking to them through the whole flight."

His gaze seemed distant. "Yeah, I guess." He looked down. "I just can't get over the things he said. I mean, my dream was always to leave this place and never come back, but it's still home."

Cal could understand that. He hadn't seen his mom since he'd been accused of murder. He'd always been afraid the enforcers were watching her. The most he could do was send her packages with coded notes, hoping she'd understand.

Maybe that was what Ty needed now: to send a message that he was still a part of Kirato, even though he'd left.

Tapping his personal code into the lockbox beneath his station, he pulled out some of his emergency stores. It was supposed to be for life-or-death repairs, or if the food ran out. This wasn't that much of an emergency, but that money had been locked up for years and he'd never had to tap into it. That wasn't because Cal was a great planner. It was because he had a resourceful crew. For once, maybe he could do something to make one of their lives a little better.

He placed three hundred-quara coins on Ty's station.

"Whoa, boss, what the hell is this?"

"That's to pay off your debt, and maybe help out Regan's dad in the process."

"But I only owe two hundred."

Cal nodded. "I know. The rest is to spread around. These people need it more than we do."

Ty bit the inside of his cheek. "I can't take your money. It's my debt."

"Then pay me back. A quarter of your pay off each trading run we make."

"That will take forever."

Cal laughed, then winced, wishing he hadn't. He might need a few more pain killers to keep the ache under control.

Paying Cal back *would* take forever. For the most part, the crew were here for family and a free place to live. He only paid them a nominal amount for expenses, and many of them put their excess back into the coffers to buy more supplies for Kirato.

"As long as you don't jump ship, you'll pay it off eventually."

Ty took two of the coins and placed them in his pocket. The third coin he placed on Cal's station. "I'll give Regan back his two hundred, but the people of Kirato don't need money. They need trade. They've been bartering with goods among each other for a while now. With no one coming to buy and sell, money doesn't have much value."

"Do you really think Regan will be able to use that money to barter for more medicine?"

"Who knows, but I feel a little better knowing that I did what I could, and maybe clear my name if anyone else knew about this." He looked out the window again. "Kirato isn't much, but it would be a great place to raise a family someday."

Raise a family? "Are you starting to think about your mortality?"

Ty shrugged. "The last year has been more than any of us bargained for. I think we all are."

Cal gripped the back of his chair. "Are you thinking of staying here? Of leaving the *Renegade*?"

Ty's eyes sprang open. "Oh, hell no. You'd probably pilot her into a satellite or something. I'm not letting you crash my baby." He smiled, holding up the coins. "But thanks. I think I need to start clean and then stay clean. I was a kid when I left here with you. It's about time I started acting like a man."

Cal nodded, biting back the desire to say he was proud of him. Ty had always been his own person, but taking onus for his mistakes was something new. It would be interesting to see how long it lasted. And now, with the weight of an intergalactic war bearing down on them, Cal felt even more driven to keep this kid, and all of the *Star Renegade*'s crew, safe. He just wasn't sure how.

CHAPTER 10
ALEXANDER

Taking a deep breath, Alexander placed his hand on the panel to open the med bay door. The bright lights from within flooded the darker hallway.

He considered backing away and returning to his room, but that would leave him no closer to diagnosing the problem.

The doctor looked up from a table scattered with test tubes half-filled with red, blue, and clear liquids. "Are... Are you alone?"

Alexander stepped inside. "I am."

"Huh." The doctor placed a thin cylinder in his pocket. "How can I help you?"

An interesting question. Alexander wasn't sure someone with limited or no training would be able to understand what he'd been going through. However, Dania seemed to be physically fine, despite her depleted pathogens. So, this man must have had some sort of skill.

Alexander held out his hand palm down. His fingers shook.

The doctor frowned. "How long has that been going on?"

"For the past few days. Alanna has insisted that I not use my powers, and this incessant shaking has made manipulating small objects problematic."

"Okay. First: Good on Alanna. You need to save your energy. And two: I saw a little of this in Dania, at this phase. Hers was a lot worse, though."

"She never mentioned her hands shook."

"She may not have even noticed. Our girl had enough going on. I didn't point it out. I just added it to my notes." He walked to the refrigeration unit in the back of the room and returned with a small bottle. "I'd like you to scan this with your super-enforcer sight to prove that it's unopened."

Alexander perused the intact seal. The label noted it as an electrolyte solution.

The doctor shook the bottle. "I tried to give this to you once before, but you refused."

"That will help with my shaking hands?"

"It did with Dania. I can do an IV if you have time, or a quick injection that won't work as well. I also have a mix that you can drink, but you'll have to drink it every day."

Alexander looked at his palms. It seemed like more than an electrolyte imbalance. "What's causing this?"

The doctor sighed. "Withdrawal."

Heat shot through him. He should have known that the doctor would use this as an avenue to attempt to deceive him as he'd deceived Dania. "I'm not taking your manufactured pathogens."

"I'm not asking you to. Dania was in a lot worse shape, but you're starting to have some of the same symptoms.

The shaking hands might be related, it might not. I'm just not sure."

"How can you treat people when you are unsure?"

He held up his palms. "Hey, with you enforcers, I'm making all this up as I go along. I know it worked for Dania, so I'm guessing it will work for you."

Alexander stared at the vial. Intravenous was the best route, but that was how the doctor had poisoned Dania's blood with the artificial pathogens. The man was clever. He'd already given Alexander one infusion of the synthetics when Alexander had been unconscious. What if he used the electrolytes to administer more pollutants into his blood?

The doctor sighed. "You don't trust me, and I guess I can't blame you." He walked back to the refrigerator. "From your perspective, you think I'm doing Dania harm. But from my perspective, I'm saving her. I don't think you're quite at a place yet where you're capable of thinking differently."

"I've told you before, I will never be at that place."

The doctor returned with a smug smile. He obviously thought he would win this argument in the end.

He was wrong.

He handed Alexander a gallon-sized container. "This should help. Run a test on this and you will see that it's nothing but fluids, flavoring, and electrolytes. Drink this instead of water."

Alexander accepted the jug. He wasn't sure the treatment would be so simple, but it was worth attempting. He nodded and turned toward the door, but his steps slowed.

There were some things about the crew that he had trouble comprehending. Alanna had grown colder to him after he'd saved the crew from the shooter. This perplexed him, but he wasn't above admitting that even he was surprised by his reactions.

"There's more." Alexander turned and met the doctor's expectant gaze. "I seem to be making irrational choices."

The doctor quirked one brow. "Care to elucidate?"

Not really. Not to a human. But apparently, he had no choice. "My general is correct. My programming normally leads me to find an answer to situations that increase the possibility of a peaceful outcome."

"Are we talking about what happened between you and Ethan, or what happened with the guy who shot Cal?"

Alexander lowered his eyes. "Both."

The doctor nodded. "Okay. Well, I think you need to realize something, though." He walked around the table, toward Alexander. "If the events had happened in reverse, if you'd attacked Regan before the Ethan incident, the crew probably wouldn't have bat an eye. In fact, they probably would have understood."

"That makes no sense."

"Oh, it does. Personally, I think you defended the crew the other day. Yes, maybe a little more brutally than we would have liked, but you still defended them." He plucked the cylinder out of his pocket and pointed it at Alexander. "The problem is that we all have a preconceived notion about you that you're a little screwed up in the head, and that you can snap."

"I am not 'screwed up in the head.'"

"Really?"

The doctor shoved Alexander's shoulder, and the heat in the room increased by thirty-seven degrees.

The doctor held his hands out to the sides. "What are you doing, Alexander?"

Alexander lifted his palms and gaped, finding them both engulfed in flames. His breath hitched, and the fire winked out.

The room instantly cooled.

Alexander glared at him. "That was foolish. I could have killed you."

The doctor rubbed the back of his neck. "Well, yeah, but I was banking on you having spent some time with Alanna. She seems to level you out a bit." He pointed to Alexander's hands. "But if this is the kind of irrational choices you've been making, I think it's your mind going right to defensive mode." He walked over to a computer monitor. "I've been doing some research, and it is pretty common in soldiers who have seen heavy action."

"I've been an enforcer my entire life. This hasn't happened before."

"Alexander, you were kidnapped when you were too weak to defend yourself. You were placed in a vat of liquid to keep you alive, and you were let out only when they wanted to humiliate or torture you. I'll wager that was a hell of a lot more personal than anything you experienced enforcing the king's law."

Alexander's jaw tensed as he pushed back memories fighting to return to the surface. He wanted to forget that time. He wanted to move on. "How did you know what happened to me?"

"The guy who purchased you from the pirates was pretty sick in the head. He took video."

Alexander grimaced. It was bad enough that the past lived in his memories. "Has Dania seen these recordings?"

The doctor shook his head. "No. Just me and Kile."

Alexander placed the jug of electrolytes on the counter and rubbed his face. The last thing he wanted was his commander seeing him so weak. Alexander had been defenseless and only barely capable of understanding what they'd been doing to him. The pain had gotten through, though. The pain he remembered all too well.

The doctor slowly placed his hand on Alexander's shoulder. "Kile doesn't think any less of you, either. In fact, he was pretty damn pissed off. He killed a lot of people afterward. It was almost like he could feel your pain."

Alexander lowered his eyes. He wasn't sure what to think of that. "I don't want to dwell on what they did to me."

"I don't think you should, but I think you need to own it. That's the only way to get past the emotional scarring."

"How does one *own* an experience like that?"

"You survived. There was another enforcer there who wasn't so lucky." The doctor pointed the back of the pen light at his face. "You need to get it into that pretty little head of yours that you're a survivor."

"It's programming. We need to get out of any situation and return to our sponsor."

"So why didn't you go back to Keveron?"

A valid question. "My last directive was to protect Dania."

"Really?"

"Really."

The doctor shrugged. "I think maybe, just maybe, you're intrigued by Dania's recovery."

"She isn't recovered. She's ruined."

"The enforcer part of you thinks she's ruined. But the doctor part of you has to see how much better she is."

"She's weak."

"Her body's not weak. It's stronger. Less dependent. And I think, in time, your doctor side is going to overrule your enforcer side, and you're going to want to be just as healthy as she is."

Heat flushed through Alexander's core. How dare this man think an enforcer would want to be weak? "You are wrong. I will never allow myself to wane like that."

The doctor smiled. "I said it before, and I'll say it again: Game on, my friend. Game on."

ALANNA TRIED NOT to look at Alexander as the warm wind whipped through his long, opalescent hair. He shielded his eyes from the blazing Kirato sun as he gazed at the outermost buildings of the colony. He looked peaceful, and just as beautiful as he had the day she'd first seen him. But for all Alanna knew, he could be looking for another civilian to punish for some ridiculous crime.

Her cheeks flushed.

Okay, maybe Regan pulling out a gun and accidentally shooting Cal was not a ridiculous crime, but still... Why had Alex acted like that? He'd looked like a crazed fiend. A monster.

An enforcer.

She closed her eyes and took a steadying breath. Hadn't he been listening to her at all these past months? Didn't he understand that you couldn't just go around hurting people?

Alanna rooted through their tools, slamming the instruments against the walls of the metal carrying case.

His shadow fell over her. "Are you trying to break the tools?"

She glared at him. "Just stop."

"Stop standing here?"

She threw a wrench into the container and stood. "You don't have to be like this anymore."

He tilted his head. "Be like what?"

She closed her eyes and took a deep breath. How could she make him understand?

"When you first came on board, Cal asked me to keep an eye on you. I told him you weren't a bad guy. I mean, how could you be bad when you pulled a bullet out of Peter's chest and then got in trouble for helping a commoner?" She pointed at Alexander's sternum. "I told Cal he was wrong about you. I believed in you."

Alexander lowered his eyes.

After Doc had been shot on Midway Station, Alexander had appeared like an angel and helped without them even asking. She'd been overwhelmed by his kindness. Now, though, she wasn't sure what to think.

Alanna dabbed the sweat from her forehead. "Twice since you've come on board, you've freaked out and almost killed someone." She shook her head. "I don't like it. I really thought you were different."

"I'm an enforcer, Alanna."

She lifted her chin. "I don't care. Dania was too." She looked away. "You just don't get it, do you? You disappointed me."

He looked down. "I understand."

She cocked her head. "You do?"

"Contrary to what you might think, I *have* been listening." He returned his gaze to hers. There was a pain there, a deep emotion swirling inside, begging to break free. "I feel like three people, and they're all at war with each other."

"How so?"

"I'm an enforcer: strong and infallible. But I'm also a victim: helpless without any control." He held up his hands. "And now, I'm on this planet, and I'm somewhere in between."

A flutter whisked through her chest. She moved closer. "Well, that's good, right?"

"No, it isn't." He rubbed his face. "I need to regain my balance. I need structure back in my life."

"Maybe a *lack* of structure is what you need."

He shook his head. "I'm an enforcer. I need to help people."

Alanna bit her lower lip. Helping people was better than executing them. "Well, you kinda are helping people." She pointed to the junction box at her feet. "The outer perimeter we created the other day is working like a charm. We've added an hour to their early warning systems."

"An hour is not enough. It will only warn them if something is already here. With their limited defenses, that's not enough time to save them."

She shrugged. "Well, that's why we're creating the ion shield."

This was good. They were talking about machinery again. Machines, he seemed to understand and even enjoy. She just needed to weave human reality into the conversation wherever she could and maybe, just maybe, she could make him a little less like a crazed, rigid, law-enforcing madman.

She walked around the junction. "Do you really think we can build the ion shield off the perimeter shields?"

He nodded. "Yes. That's why we created such a complex web. It's not necessary for the perimeter warnings, but it creates a pre-existing network to build from." He adjusted the canopy, casting more shade on their work area. "Are you ready to begin?"

Yes and no. It seemed like he'd started talking about something pretty significant before—about struggling with being three people. It must have been hard for him, being so in control, and then losing so much.

Was he using work to steer the conversation away from that now?

Maybe he had second thoughts about feeling weak. These were good things, though. The more he thought about his new reality, and the more he considered the intricacies of right and wrong, the better chance she had of getting through to him. At least, she hoped so.

Right now, he seemed more like the Alexander whose company she'd grown to enjoy. Dania seemed to think that the key to Alexander accepting humanity was in his love of tinkering with machines. If Alanna could help him create an ion shield, he might learn that he could save people with his smarts, rather than his magical powers. Then, if they were really lucky, he'd give up on going back to his prince, just like Dania had.

It might have been a stupid dream. Maybe saving Dania had been a one in a trillion success story. But Dania believed in Alexander, and despite his enforcer-like regressions, deep down, Alanna did, too. She was still angry. It was never okay to kill people. But giving up on him wasn't the answer, either.

She took a deep breath, steadying herself. "I'm ready if you are." She handed him a calibration tool. "Are you ready to break a few rules?"

"If you are asking if I am ready to *bend* a few rules to save a loyal colony from possible attack, then yes, I am."

Good. It was a start.

Sand whisked across the desert terrain, painting waves in the dunes as they worked throughout the day. The sun beamed down, relentless and demanding. Even the shade didn't give much respite from the heat emanating off the scorched ground.

Alanna sat back, grabbed her water jug, and chugged four gulps. The cold water soothed her parched throat. She loved this planet, but the heat was hard to get used to.

Taking one last gulp, she choked and spilled a few drops. Her chest clenched as the water created dark circles on the shaded sand. The people of Kirato had been so generous with their supplies, it seemed wrong to waste anything. Even a drop.

Sweat dripped down Alexander's temples, and he frowned, adjusting something on the panel that she couldn't see.

"Take a break before you faint from dehydration." She handed him his water jug.

He nodded, sat beside her, and tipped the bottle back, pouring a green liquid into his mouth.

"What is that?" she asked.

He replaced the cap. "Electrolytes. Apparently, I'm deficient."

"I think everyone is, from time to time."

He opened and closed his palm. "My hands have been shaking."

Interesting. He probably thought he was sick. That would mean he'd gone to see Doc to get the electrolytes. Kile would have dropped dead before asking Peter for help. That was a colossal step in the right direction.

He took another gulp and looked past the rolling waves of sand to the colony in the distance. "Are you still angry with me?" he asked.

A slight smile touched her lips. "I thought enforcers didn't care what people thought?"

"I shouldn't, but I do."

Once again…*interesting.* She'd chip away at this big, bad enforcer's resolve for months if she had to. "I said you disappointed me. That's not the same as being angry."

"Well, then, I didn't like you being disappointed in me."

She let that sink in for a moment. "Really?" For an enforcer, that was another huge admission.

He set his jug down and stared at the sand between his feet. "You've been avoiding me. I don't like it." He met her gaze. "I've enjoyed our conversations. I found your absence…disconcerting."

If she were being honest, she'd missed their conversations, too. She'd been willing to forgive what he'd done to Ethan as PTSD, but the animal that he'd turned into the other day had been pure enforcer…like all the horror stories she'd heard.

She'd been scared, plain and simple. In some ways, she was ashamed that she'd kept to herself. In her mind, it was almost like he hadn't existed anymore. But she knew that he was very much a living, breathing person, and maybe the last few days he'd needed her more than ever.

The sun started to warm her side, and she shifted until she was under the shade again. "You just really upset me. I started to think of you as a friend, and when I saw you go after Regan…"

He leaned his head back. "Why do none of you understand that he'd committed a crime?"

How could she explain that Alexander had turned into a crazed killing machine, and that he had scared the dickens out of her? Would he even understand?

"Killing is never okay," she said.

He opened his lips to speak, but she held up her palm.

"My mom always taught me: Two wrongs don't make a right."

He laughed, looking at the sand again. "She sounds like a wise woman."

"You bet that pretty, long hair of yours she is." And her mom also would have told Alanna she was insane for even sitting here and talking to an enforcer.

Yet here they were.

A dune crab scurried over the sand, stopped where Alanna had spilled the water, and then moved on, leaving dry sand in its wake.

Alexander watched the small creature, but his mind seemed worlds away. "So, your mother is wise. What about your father? Did you know him well?"

Alanna frowned. Why this sudden interest in her family?

Could he be missing his own parents—the ones the Banes had taken him from to make him an enforcer?

"My dad was a good guy. He died when I was young, so I don't have a lot of memories of him."

Alexander turned to her. "Where did you live when you were younger?"

"Reglia." Warm memories surfaced of her mom planting

flowers by the creek running through their yard, and her sister splashing in the water. "It's pretty much the farthest you can get from the industrial colonies. It's way out there."

He nodded. "Fairly close to Bane space."

"Yeah, I guess, if you call a few gazillion miles 'close.'"

He frowned, staring at the sand again. Something about what she'd said had bothered him. Were his memories resurfacing? Did he remember his own childhood?

She inched a little closer. "How about you? Were you close with your parents?"

He closed his eyes and shook his head, as if waving off a fog. "Enforcers don't have parents."

"Well, you did, right? Dania said you knew that you were human before." According to Doc, all enforcers were once human. The Banes handpicked young children, paid their families astronomical adoption fees, and then took the children away. There was no record of any families declining the offer, which probably meant none of them had a choice. She doubted that any of those families knew that the Banes would twist their children's minds and turn them into all-powerful law-enforcing killing machines.

He looked out over the dunes again. "I have no memory of the time before waking up and seeing my sponsor for the first time. But my childhood was good. I grew up with Dania, so we weren't alone."

Alanna nodded. Dania always spoke of him like a brother. It was sad, though, that neither of them could remember their actual parents.

It might be too soon to ask a risky question, but she saw an opening and decided to take a chance. "Have you ever thought of looking for your real parents?"

A tone sounded from the equipment beside them. Five short, high-pitched beeps. Alexander shot to his feet.

"What is that?" Alanna asked.

"The perimeter alarm is going off."

"How is that possible? We only just turned it on yesterday."

He pressed a button, and a four-inch square monitor rose from the base of the machine. Alexander tapped on the screen.

His eyes grew wide. "Several ships just breached the outer perimeter of the planet."

"It has to be a malfunction." She looked to the colony. "All of Stanley's alarms would be going off."

"Not if it's stealth technology."

"Could it be another ship with supplies?"

"No. They're coming in too fast."

Alanna looked up but could only see blue sky dotted with a few wispy clouds. It was beautiful and quiet, like any other day on Kirato.

Alexander grabbed her arm, pulling her to their transport. "Don't be fooled. We're under attack."

CHAPTER 12
DANIA

Dania took a deep breath, settling herself before she knocked on Cal's door. Maybe she'd get lucky and he wouldn't be there. Then she'd be able to avoid all this ridiculousness.

The door slid open, and Cal's cool, blue eyes sparkled when their gazes met. "Hi." His eyes widened. "What is that amazing smell?"

It…smelled good? Dania's eyes carried over the box in her hands. "I made pie."

His head tilted to the right. "You did?"

She nodded. "Apple."

His smile broadened. "Well, then, please come in."

She fingered the dented container. Dust still encrusted the corner where the box had hit the ground. "I'm afraid it might be a little crushed. I dropped it when you got shot."

"It's all right. It's the thought that counts." He took the box from her. "Come on in. Let's share a slice." He walked toward the table.

"Can we sit on the couch?" Dania asked.

His brow furrowed as he looked back to her. "The couch?"

She gulped. "We're supposed to sit on the couch."

"Says who?"

"The very pushy lady who likes to cook."

Cal laughed. "Ah, Mel. You gotta love her."

Dania looked down. "She seems to think that it's significant that I feel warm when I'm near you. So, she thought I should make pie."

Cal's lips parted and his eyes grew wide before his expression softened again.

She shook her head. "I don't understand human customs, and I'm sure I'm messing this up."

He placed the pie on the table. "Not at all." He stepped closer. "So, I make you feel warm?"

She nodded. "Yes. Warm and nice."

He smiled again. "Warm and nice?"

She nodded again. "Is that okay?"

"Yeah." He pressed his lips together. "You make me feel warm and nice, too."

"Amelia seems to think that's why you stood at my side when the transport seized me, despite the threat to your own wellbeing, and also why you wanted to cook with me. But I seriously don't understand how cooking or eating food has anything to do with the way a person makes you feel."

He took both her hands in his. "Cooking is a way to express yourself, like I cook for the crew to let them know I care."

Dania lowered her eyes. "Oh."

She hadn't thought about it like that. Deep down, she

knew this, but him speaking the words made it all seem so much more personal.

Dania gulped. "Do you…want to try my pie?"

He stared into her eyes for a moment. "Very much so."

He walked back to the table and opened the box. Dania cringed. The crust was cracked in several places, and the pie was smashed to one side of the container.

"Interesting presentation," Cal said.

"It's ruined." She closed the box. "Just forget it." Why had she even allowed Amelia to talk her into this? How could cut-up apples in a hardened crust make anyone feel anything?

"Hey." He rubbed the center of her back. "I'm sure it's fine."

"It's not."

He grabbed both her shoulders and leaned down, looking into her eyes. "Dania, I was just kidding. I don't care that it's crushed."

"You don't?"

"Not at all." He grabbed a fork, opened the box, and took a scoop from the center. He seemed to roll the pie around on his tongue. His eyes started to water.

"It's horrible. Isn't it?"

He shook his head. Swallowing. "No. Not at all." He huffed out a laugh. "Did Mel make that?"

"No, I did. Well, she showed me how to do it, and she told me to get a little creative. She laughed about some of my spice choices, but she thought they would be okay. Do you hate it?"

"No. It's actually amazing."

Amazing? "Even crushed?"

"I think the crushed part makes it even better. Who needs a perfect pie, anyway?"

Dania's face flushed. "You're doing it again."

"What?"

She placed her hand on her midriff. "That strange feeling in my stomach when we're alone."

He moved closer, placing his hands on her hips. "Am I making you feel warm, too?"

"Yes."

"Warm and nice?"

She nodded. The swirling intensified in her stomach. "Does that bother you?"

"No. That's *very* okay." He tilted his head toward her. "As a matter of fact, I'm feeling a little warm myself."

The air about them seemed to heat slightly, but it was probably her imagination. Her hands trembled. Why did she always feel so odd around him?

He leaned closer, his lips a fraction of an inch from hers. "Is *this* okay?" he asked, his breath warm on her lips.

Dania's own breath hitched as his hands tightened on her hips. She parted her lips and leaned her head back as he…

The comm pinged overhead.

Cal jerked back, growling at the ceiling. "Ty, someone better be dead."

"Sorry, boss. But we got incoming."

His head jerked toward the comm. "On Kirato? Are you sure?"

"Yeah, you better get up here."

CAL PUSHED through the doorway to the bridge. Why the blazes did something horrendous always happen when he was alone with Dania? "Tell me this is some sort of sick joke."

Ty spun toward him. "I wish it was."

"How many?" Cal sat at his station and called up the information.

"Four. One big cruiser and three escorts, but nothing identifiable beyond that."

Dania slipped onto the bridge behind Cal. "Could it be more supplies?"

"The movement doesn't look pre-programmed," Ty said. "In fact, they're flying worse than Cal."

Cal glared at him, then checked the monitors. The ships were descending fast. Too fast. "That's attack speed."

"I agree, but it's a weird angle."

The exterior comm pinged.

Ty pressed a few buttons. "It's Stanley."

The old trader's face appeared on the screen. "Do you see them?"

"Yeah," Cal said. "I'm not sure what to make of it."

"Your enforcer friend warned us of the attack, but we have no long-range defenses. A ship that size could hit us before they were even close enough for us to fight back."

"Let's not jump to conclusions. They're not firing yet." Cal shut off the comm.

Ty turned to him. "Did you just hang up on Stanley?"

Yes, he most certainly did. He loved Stanley, but the old man talked too much, and Cal needed to think.

He gripped the edge of his chair, focusing on Ty. "Can we protect this colony?"

Ty blanched. "From four ships? I'm usually running away. The last time we actually tried to fight, we got our asses kicked."

Cal took a steadying breath. He'd known the answer. He'd just hoped the kid had one of those crazy ideas that shouldn't—but always did—work.

The comm pinged again.

"It's Alexander and Alanna," Ty announced.

"Put it through."

They appeared on the screen. Alanna's hair stuck out to the sides, like she'd been pulling on it.

Alexander met Cal's gaze. "The trajectory of those ships will fly right over the colony."

"Can you do anything to shield the buildings?"

Alexander grimaced. "I may be able to protect them from one volley."

"Just one?"

His eyes darkened. "As you've all been pointing out, I'm much weaker than I'm accustomed to."

Alanna reached over and grabbed the enforcer's hand. "Can you do *anything more*?"

Alexander turned to her. His gaze swept over Alanna in a way that made Cal want to jump through the screen and pull him away from her. Cal was a guy. He knew that look, and it meant nothing but trouble. He didn't want that kind of trouble anywhere near Alanna, but at least that meant the enforcer would keep her safe.

Alexander turned back to Cal. "I'll do what I can, but once I collapse, it will be up to you."

Dania grabbed the back of Cal's chair. "Alexander!"

Alanna met her gaze through the screen. "I got him. For what it's worth. I got him."

The comm winked out.

Ty's breath hitched, and his face reddened as he rubbed his eyes.

"You okay?" Cal asked.

The pilot raised his gaze, looking out the window. "I spent my entire life trying to get off this planet. I hated it here. But that doesn't mean I want it destroyed."

Cal reached over and gripped his wrist, squeezing hard until Ty turned to him. "Kirato has become home to all of us. We'll do everything we can."

Ty nodded, wiping tears threatening to fall.

"Let's get in the air," Cal said. "You okay to pilot?"

"Yeah. Retracting the cargo ramp."

Cal hit the comm. "Ethan, Doc, we're lifting off. I trust you know what's going on."

"You got a plan, boss?" Ethan asked.

"Not yet. As usual, be ready for anything."

The buildings sank out of view as they hovered over the colony.

Ty took in another deep breath. "Why do I have a bad feeling that was the last time I'll ever see home?"

"Don't think that way. It's just us and Alexander, but that colony has a small footprint. We've got a chance."

His face twisted in anguish. "Against a cruiser?"

Cal gritted his teeth. The odds weren't in their favor, but they never were.

The comm pinged. Ty frowned. "It's Mel."

He pressed a button and Amelia appeared on the screen. "My Stanley says that what little ground forces we have will cover you."

Cal nodded, but their range would be pretty short. Cal didn't want to let those ships anywhere near close enough to where the ground forces could do any damage.

The colonists were survivors, though. They didn't have much, but they'd protect it with their lives. He had to respect that. "Thanks, Mel."

She turned her gaze to Ty. "My sweet Tyler. You are a good boy. I am very proud of you, you know?"

Tears filled his eyes. "Mel, I need to tell you something…"

She held up her pointer finger. "No. You tell me tomorrow."

"Mel…"

"You tell me tomorrow."

The comm winked out.

Ty lowered his head, sniffing. "I love you, Mel," he whispered.

A ball lodged in Cal's throat. Amelia wasn't Ty's biological mother. She'd plucked seven-year-old Ty out of the ashes of the accident that had killed his parents and walked him right into her kitchen. Ty had lived with her and Stanley until he'd left Kirato with Cal a few years ago.

Cal reached over and squeezed his pilot's shoulder. "She knows."

Ty nodded, took a deep breath, and released it. A grim determination swept over his features. "I'm going to hover in a sweeping pattern until we have a set attack vector."

"With four ships, we may have to defend from multiple angles."

"How can I help?" Dania asked.

Cal glanced at the navigation station. He'd feel more comfortable if Alanna had been here. "Do you know how to run nav?" He knew the answer, and it broke his heart. She hadn't shown an affinity for anything technical and hadn't taken the time to learn any of the stations.

Dania blanched, looking down.

This wasn't something he could protect her from. She was a general without an army to lead. And in this battle, there was nothing she could do.

CHAPTER 14

DANIA

D ANIA GLANCED at Alanna's station. "I-I..." She lowered her head. "No. I don't know how to navigate."

She clenched her hands into fists. If she lived through this, she would learn how to operate every station required to run this ship. She was used to being in control of everything. Being helpless when so much was at stake made her want to scream.

The door slid open and Doc ran inside. "I figured I'd be more help up here."

Cal breathed a sigh of relief. "You're on Nav."

Dania backed away. "I-I guess I should get off the bridge."

"No way!" Doc said. "One thing I can't do is multitask like Alanna." He tapped a few keys at the station he normally stood at and waved Dania over. "I need you to watch these four blips and tell me if they cross the red line."

Dania narrowed her eyes. She wasn't sure if that was really necessary, or if he was just giving her a job to do.

Either way, she appreciated doing something, even if it was small.

Dania nodded. "I can do that."

"Perfect." Doc exchanged a curt nod with Cal before the doctor took Alanna's chair and started moving his hands over the keys. He wouldn't be able to jump the ship, but in a close battle like this, that wouldn't help them anyway, not unless they needed to cut and run. That would mean abandoning Kirato, though, which she doubted any of them would be willing to do.

Alanna and Alexander's skipper craft shot across their screen.

"Welcome to the party," Ty said.

"They're accelerating," Alexander said over the comm. "I've tried hailing, but there's no response."

That wasn't good. Not that Dania would have expected them to respond. Radio silence was standard when a ship had no intention of negotiating, or no desire for the other side to surrender. With a ship that size, it would simply be easier to wipe the colony off the face of the planet than deal with formalities.

"They're breaking the atmosphere!" Ty said. "The big one's coming in with attitude. The smaller ships are riding shotgun on three sides."

Cal turned to Doc. "Can you tell how big the cruiser is?"

Doc blanched. "Just your average super-sized death machine. And the little ones are heavily armored."

But why attack now? This was supposed to be the planet everyone forgot. Dania tapped a few keys, trying to tap into the long-range sensors. If she could just figure out who was attacking…

"What are you doing, sweetie?" Doc asked.

She continued inputting commands, trying to clear up the scans. "I want to get a better look at the ship."

"Wouldn't we all? I'd love to know why the three smaller ones are flying so erratically."

Which was concerning, in and of itself. That wasn't a Cartek attack pattern. In fact, it didn't look like *any* familiar attack pattern.

Alanna's voice came over the comm. "I'm taking the controls. Fingers crossed, everyone."

The skipper started to wobble.

"Why is Alanna flying that thing?" Cal asked.

A bright light flashed above them, and Alexander appeared, hanging in the air. The Kirato sun lit up his shimmering, white hair like a crazed halo.

"I guess that answers that question," Ty said.

It certainly did, but this attack stance hadn't worked well for him lately.

A light tone sounded from Dania's station. She spun back to her screen, just as a large circle touched the line Doc had placed on the screen.

"Peter!" Dania shouted. "The ships are crossing the red line!"

"Here we go!" Ty said. "Shields are up."

"Where are they?" Cal leaned closer to the glass. "I'd be a hell of a lot more comfortable if I could see something to shoot at."

The broken yellow light on Ty's panel started to flash. Ty slapped the light three times and the flashing stopped.

Cal leaned closer to the window again. "Even if they're stealth, wouldn't we be able to see them with our eyes?"

Ty looked toward the sky. "Not until they break the cloud cover."

Dania moved toward the main screen and placed her hand on the back of Cal's chair. A deep emptiness settled in her gut. Something about this seemed so *wrong*.

Two small ships breached the clouds.

Outside, a light erupted around Alexander. He held up his palms and a wall of yellow light formed and shot toward the incoming ships.

Lightning crackled across the sky, bending and surrounding a massive, saucer-like form emerging from the clouds. The light flashed and dissipated, revealing a black Kever warship racing toward them. The room spun slightly, and Dania clutched the back of Cal's chair. That ship was not unlike her sponsor's.

A tone sounded, raking through the hull and rattling the floors. Cal covered his ears as the vibration lashed through him.

"What the hell?" Ty's voice seemed far away, mottled by the tone.

Outside, Alexander punched his fist at the oncoming ships. A bolt of light exploded from his hand and charged toward the cruiser. Was that a mistake? Had he not seen it was one of their own?

A poof sound followed by a dull hum rumbled the hull, as something they couldn't see slammed into Alexander. He flew back like he'd been punched and started falling toward the planet.

"Alexander!" Dania cried.

His head fell back, and his body went lax.

"No!" Dania reached out and punched her power out to catch him, but nothing happened. A shiver ran over her as she lowered her hand. She had no power coursing through her veins to protect him.

Alanna's skipper spun and shot straight up into orbit.

"What's she doing?" Ty asked. "She can't fly in space."

Dania ran back to her station and frowned at her screen. "I must not be reading these instruments right, because it looks like her ship broke the atmosphere, but there's no one on board."

Both Cal and Ty looked at her. "What?"

A purple glow surrounded Alexander's falling body, and Dania's heart leapt into her throat as Alanna burst into the sky just in time to grab Alexander. Glowing gears already spun at the edge of her fingers before they both disappeared.

Dania gaped. She must have sent the ship into the atmosphere so it wouldn't crash, then used her odd abilities to jump herself out of the skipper. Dania didn't even know that was possible.

Doc whistled. "That's my girl."

"Woohoo!" Ty punched a fist in the air. "Grab and go... Just like when we first picked her up."

"Yeah, but where did she jump him to?" Cal asked.

Doc rubbed his forehead. "Ouch. They landed hard. Just to the north of the colony."

"Are they okay?" Cal asked.

"I have no idea. I'm just picking up Alanna's wrist comm."

Ty pulled up the weapons controls on his screen. "They're out of the way. Now it's time to do some damage."

"Wait!" Dania stood.

"For what?" Cal turned toward her. "Alexander was our

best shot of defending Kirato, and they just attacked him." He turned to Ty. "Give it all you got."

"But they *didn't* attack him." She sprinted to Cal's station and tapped the screen, zooming in on one of the smaller ships. "Look." She pointed. "Royal insignias."

"I don't really care who's attacking."

"They didn't attack Alexander. If they had, he'd be dead. That's an enforcer craft. Those markings belong to Geron's brother, the high prince."

"Don't we hate this guy?" Ty asked, his hands hovering over the weapons controls.

"Don't you see? They didn't hurt Alexander. They just wanted to stop him from hurting them before he could see who they were."

Cal gaped at her. "They knocked him out of the sky."

"I'm picking up weapons' discharge from the ships," Ty said. "Preparing counter-maneuvers."

"Hold on," Doc said.

"They're firing!" Ty said.

"Yes, they're definitely firing, but the three smaller ships are firing on the bigger one."

Cal looked down at his screen. "What?"

"I'm telling you. They're firing on their own ship. Short-range bursts. Low-grade artillery."

Dania's gut clenched. They hadn't intentionally knocked him out of the sky. They'd *pushed him out of the way*.

"It looks to me like they're trying to slow that ship down," Doc said.

Dania gaped as the ships flew closer, becoming larger in the viewscreen. One of the smaller ships moved in front of the larger one, sending out a short burst of munitions. Simple, usually ineffective rounds, nothing that would break through the shielding of a ship that size. But they *could* slow momentum.

Peter was right. They *were* trying to slow it down.

"They're not attacking," Dania whispered. "They're crashing."

Cal and Ty looked back at her, gaping. She didn't need magical powers to read their thoughts.

That ship was still headed for the colony at high speed. And there was nothing they could do about it.

CHAPTER 15
CAL

THE SHIPS FLEW PAST THEM, and Cal grabbed the controls, keeping pace.

Ty grabbed the edge of his console as the *Star Renegade* started to shake from the G-force. "What are you doing, boss?"

Wasn't it obvious? "That ship is still heading for Kira-to." There was no way Cal would give up on them while he was still breathing.

Ty's face paled.

"This is not good!" Doc said.

This, Cal already knew. "Options?"

"Can we try shooting them, too, like the other ships were doing?" Ty asked.

Fire at a royal cruiser? Right now, the escort was ignoring them. Cal was fairly certain that wouldn't be the case if they started firing.

He looked at Dania. "If those are enforcers, why aren't they using their powers to stop the crash?"

She gazed out the main screen. "It's moving too fast. If

they projected themselves into the sky, they wouldn't have time to use their power before the cruiser passed them."

Cal supposed they were built more to kill people than to save them.

So they couldn't add the *Renegade*'s firepower to the rescue, but maybe the enforcers would understand if they tried to help in another way.

He hit the comm. "Ethan, hook the alien tech to the shields and give me a hundred percent on zone one."

Ethan's voice came over the speakers. "Please tell me you're not going to hit something on purpose."

Cal grimaced. That was exactly what he was going to do. "Give me the shields, Ethan. Now."

Ty's eyes were wide. "Are you really going to ram a ship ten times our size?"

Cal stared straight ahead. They didn't have a choice. If that ship stayed on its current trajectory, everyone inside the boundaries of the colony would die.

"We've got five minutes to impact," Doc said.

Dania darted to the nav station. "Open a channel to those ships."

Doc frowned. "We already know they're not answering."

"Maybe they *can't* answer. Open it anyway."

Doc nodded. "There we go. You're on."

Dania stood tall, hoping to channel the sound of her former self. "Royal ships, this is General Dania DuBane onboard the *Star Renegade*. We are en route to assist. Do not engage. Repeat: Do not engage."

Ty flicked off the comm. "Are they going to listen?"

Dania shook her head. "I don't know."

"Four minutes!" Doc said.

Cal throttled the ship toward the crashing megalith. "I need those shields now, Ethan!"

"I'm trying!"

"Try harder!"

"We're out of time," Ty said.

Now or never. "Hang on!" Cal punched the controls.

Dania sat on the floor and grabbed the sides of Alanna's station.

"Three minutes!" Doc called.

"Ethan!" Ty screamed as the base of the ship filled the viewscreen.

A yellow haze coated the glass a fraction of a second before the *Star Renegade* slammed into the larger ship's hull. The resounding *boom* echoed within Cal's skull. A calibration instrument slid off Ty's station and crashed against the back wall as the room shook around them.

"Point two-degree shift," Doc said. "It's not enough. We've got two minutes."

"We're going again," Cal said.

The *Star Renegade* slammed into the ship once more. The hull rattled around them.

"Ethan?" Cal asked.

"That's all we have. I'm not sure it'll take another hit."

"There's no need!" Doc called. "The trajectory will take them over the outskirts of the colony. They'll land just north."

Cal placed his head on the edge of his console, breathing deeply. They'd done it.

They'd *actually* done it!

"Wait," Ty said. "Didn't you say Alanna and Alexander had fallen just north of the colony?"

Cal lifted his head.

No. It couldn't be.

Doc cursed under his breath. "We've only got one minute!" He tapped on the comm. "Alanna!"

Her voice came over the speakers. "Doc?"

Cal hit the comm. "Alanna, can you get out of there?"

"Why?" A dull roar sounded behind her. She gasped. "Cal! The ship is crashing!"

"Dammit!" Cal punched the engines. "Ethan, give me everything you've got!"

"Alanna, get the hell out of there!" Ty called.

"I'm trying!"

Cal's hands shook on the controls. How many times had Alanna saved their asses? He wasn't leaving her there. But the larger ship was still picking up momentum.

Up ahead of them, two of the escort ships rammed the larger ship from beneath, probably trying to slow it down even more, but the behemoth still screamed toward the surface.

They were too late.

The boom was deafening, and sand shot into the atmosphere like a bomb had exploded. Static filled the viewscreen before the screen winked out, leaving a normal window behind. Dust filled the air.

"Visibility zero!" Ty called.

Cal gulped. The dust kicking up into the sky...it was like a massive cloud exploding from the planet's surface.

"I'm pulling up infrared," Doc said. "The dust is so bad, it's like looking through a blanket."

Alanna's voice came over the comm. "Cal!"

Cal breathed a sigh of relief. "Alanna, are you okay?"

She coughed. "Can't breathe!" The line sizzled.

"Alexander put a bubble around us." She coughed again. "But he's falling in and out of consciousness."

Ty cursed under his breath. He looked at Cal. "We can home in on her comm."

Cal nodded, relinquishing controls to the pilot. "Do it." He tapped the comm. "Sit tight, Alanna. We're coming."

Dania eased off the floor, gaping at the foggy dust outside. "Do you think anyone survived the crash?"

At the moment, Cal only cared about his own people. The Kevers could fend for themselves.

Doc ran his fingers over the nav console. "The people in that ship are not going to be happy, but it looks like they slid across the surface. I mean, they probably hit hard, but they might be okay."

And then there were the other ships, which, for all they knew, were lurking just out of the range of their radar, waiting to strike. The last time they'd run into this prince, he'd tried to kill them all.

Alanna's voice came over the comm. "I hear the *Rene-gade*." Her voice sounded raspy. "I can't see you." She coughed. "But I'd know those engines anywhere."

"We're right over you," Ty said. "We're coming down easy. Scream if I'm going to squash you."

"Roger that." She coughed again. "Believe me, I will."

Ty set the ship down then let out a deep breath, dragging his fingers through his hair.

Ethan came over the comm. "I'm engaging the evac system in the lower cargo hold. It won't keep all the dust out, but it *will* keep the ship from getting inundated with sand particles until we get them on board."

"Do it." Cal rubbed his head. All they could do now was

get Alanna and Alexander on board and wait for the dust to settle—literally. Hopefully, those enforcers weren't waiting in that cloud, just looking for a clear shot at them.

CHAPTER 16
DANIA

DANIA STOOD at the base of the *Star Renegade*'s landing platform and stared at the wreckage of the royal cruiser. Even an hour after the crash, a slight haze hung in the air. It might be days before all the sand and particles settled back to the ground.

They hadn't heard from Kirato yet, other than a green 'all clear' beacon, which they took as a sign that they hadn't suffered damage in the crash. With any luck, the dust cloud wouldn't cause more problems for the already struggling colony.

Cal stepped off the platform behind her. "Are you okay?"

She nodded, but seeing that ship lying in the sand, incapacitated, sent a shivering dread through her core. One of the smaller ships, the one with the high prince's insignia, hovered between the *Star Renegade* and the crashed cruiser, spinning once before landing a few hundred feet away.

Cal tensed beside her. "I hate to say this, but I wish Alexander were here."

Dania nodded. He and Alanna were still in the med bay,

117

both being treated for particle inhalation, and Alexander being treated for overexertion again.

Up until now, she'd hoped he'd drain his primordial energy enough to understand her way of thinking. Now, faced with enforcer ships, she wished her friend, and his considerable power, stood at her side.

The door to the ship opened, and a single enforcer nearly as tall as Alexander disembarked and strode toward them without even pausing to take in his surroundings. His opal-white uniform seemed to slice through the haze, and his shimmering, white hair flew in short, swirling waves about his head as the power of his prince pulsed through him.

Dania shivered, feeling the intensity even from the considerable distance between them as his gaze latched on to hers.

Orion… One of the high prince's commanders. And he was fully charged.

He stopped a few feet in front of them and narrowed his eyes on her. "Your assistance in downing the cruiser safely does not erase your crimes."

Cal shifted his weight, agitation filling the air about him.

Dania took a step forward to keep herself between him and the commander. "You're not here to inflict judgement, or I'd already be dead."

His lips thinned. "No, I am not."

Interesting. That meant that executing Dania would be in direct juxtaposition to his orders.

Cal's temperature steadied as he moved beside her, probably displaying a show of solidarity, although he, too, was marked for execution.

Her gaze carried over the fallen ship. It was one of the largest in the galaxy, but not the largest she'd seen. "Whose ship was that?"

Orion looked over his shoulder. "Zindiria's."

Dania flinched. She wasn't the worst of the Banes, but she definitely wasn't the best.

Cal glanced at her, raising a brow.

"Zindiria is Geron's older sister, Prime Four."

He cocked his head, as if questioning that information.

"She's the fourth-most powerful Bane, which makes her third in line for the throne." She turned to Orion. "Should I trust, by the way you were protecting that ship, that she's still on board?"

He glared at her. "If you had taken your place at your sponsor's side, you would know that Zindiria is missing."

Dania frowned. How could one of the King's children be missing?

"I was charged by the high prince to find her." Orion turned back to the wreckage. "Instead, we found her ship."

"Just the ship?" Cal asked.

"I will not speak to you, smuggler."

Cal glared at him. "We've been through this before. No one ever wants to speak to the smuggler until they realize they need his help. So how about you drop the enforcer attitude for a second and tell us why you're here?"

Dania gaped. Cal stood tall, his temperature rising, rather than cooling. He was actually angry and not even moderately anxious.

Heat rose off Orion, and Dania prepared to step forward, but Cal held out his arm, stopping her.

"Don't," Cal said, not breaking Orion's gaze. "I'm not afraid of this guy."

A soft glow shimmered around the commander. A warning. Cal didn't even flinch.

An amused smile crossed Orion's lips. "You do not disappoint, Mr. Espinoza." He looked down. "It is unfortunate that I will have to execute you when this is all over, because I do appreciate your assistance with stopping the ship from a more serious crash."

Cal folded his arms, continuing to stare the commander down.

Apparently, killing Cal would also be contrary to Orion's mission. *Even more interesting.*

Dania cocked her head. "Did Kile tell you that we could be trusted? Is that why you're here?"

He turned to her with all the speed and pointedness of an enforcer. "You *cannot* be trusted. You've made that more than apparent, not only to your enforcers, but to your sponsor." He scowled. "Unfortunately, I had no other choice."

Cal sighed. "So, are you going to keep talking in circles or tell us what you want?"

"What I want is inconsequential. My mission, however, has led me to a debate in priorities."

Dania lifted her chin. "A debate? How so?" For a fully charged enforcer, the mission was the priority. Nothing else mattered. Being unsure of your priorities was nearly impossible.

He looked back to the crash site. "When we found the ship, it was not empty. A contingent of her enforcers were inside, some badly injured, and all of them dangerously depleted." He turned back to Dania. "They fought with all their strength. Our understanding is the princess made a last effort to protect the ship by projecting herself into space with a contingent of her strongest guards." His cheek ticked. "Their attackers were obliterated, but she did not return."

"Leaving all her precious enforcers in a dead ship," Cal said.

Orion nodded, but to Dania, not to Cal. "We were able to get the ship running and endeavored to transport them back to Keveron, but the propulsion system was too damaged to get past the blockades."

Dania frowned. "Blockades?"

"As I said, if you were at your sponsor's side, you would know what's going on in the galaxy." He sneered. "All our generals are at the many battlefronts, fighting to retain our king's hold on the Earthan colonies." He grimaced. "I heard you were here, and my hope was that you'd have enough power to keep the princess's enforcers alive."

Dania's eyes widened. "Keep them alive? Are they really that depleted?"

Orion lowered his gaze. "Many are close to death."

Cal huffed out a laugh. "So, let me get this right. You're calling a temporary truce so Dania can heal your enforcers, and then when she's done, you're going to execute us?"

He blinked, like this was a ridiculous question. Maybe to an enforcer, it was. "Yes, that is correct. Your ship will be confiscated and Dania and Alexander will be returned to their sponsor."

Cal shook his head. "You've got to be kidding me! Go back home to your little prince. Maybe he'll give a damn."

Orion's jaw tightened. "I can't."

"Why the hell not?"

Orion turned to Dania. "I've been tasked with finding the princess. My only chance is using her enforcers."

"For all you know, she's dead," Cal said.

Orion glared at him. "She is not."

Cal advanced on him. "How are you so sure?"

Dania grabbed Cal's arm and pulled him back a step. "Enforcers feel a draw to their sponsor. If she were dead, it would be very unpleasant. Every one of her enforcers would definitely know."

"So you want to keep those enforcers alive so you can use them like homing beacons to track the princess?"

Orion's expression remained stony. "Yes."

Cal laughed. "And here I thought maybe one of you had a soul."

The enforcer's eyes latched on Cal, probably calculating if his impertinence was worthy of speeding up his judgement.

Dania prepared to step between them again when Orion's attention returned to her. He looked her up and down, like sizing up a piece of new machinery and deciding its worth.

He finally met her gaze. "My intended plans for them are irrelevant, since you are obviously in no shape to help anyone in your current condition." His lips twisted. "How can you stand allowing yourself to wither away like this?"

Cal shook his head. "All you guys are starting to sound like recordings stuck on repeat."

A white ball of light appeared in Orion's hand and he threw it at Cal. Dania reached for him, but the ball exploded at Cal's feet, sizzling in the sand. Dania froze, afraid to move. At this close proximity, there was no possible way Orion had missed. That had been an unmistakable reminder of whom they were speaking to.

Yet Cal still stood, glaring at the commander.

Cal's breaths were shallow, his temperature steadier than any time since she'd met him.

Cal's chin lifted slightly. "I'm done cowering at the feet of enforcers. Do whatever the hell you want. But keep in mind, there are a few dozen very illegal and masterly-modified laser cannons pointed at each of your ships." Cal folded his arms again. "I think that means you're about to have a very bad day, Commander."

Orion snarled. "Impertinent to the last."

"You bet your ass I am."

They continued to stare at each other, their postures similar to the way Cal and Alexander used to try to intimidate one another.

Orion was fully charged, though. The energy rolled off him, fiercer than the Kirato heat rising from the sand.

Orion was one of the high prince's commanders. Just his name made humans run and cower. He'd probably never been faced with the likes of Cal, and the way Orion's eyes kept narrowing and widening, Dania was certain he was warring against himself—deciding the pros and cons of passing a quick judgement and facing the firepower of one of the most renowned smuggling ships in the galaxy.

His brow furrowed, and he turned. "Enough." He stormed back to his ship.

Cal opened his lips to say something, but Dania placed her hand over his mouth. "Don't test your luck."

A smile crept over Cal's lips as Orion disappeared into his ship. Dania took a deep breath and closed her eyes. That could have gone far worse, but she had a bad feeling that this discussion was far from over.

CAL BARELY BREATHED until he stepped back into the cargo hold and closed the door behind him.

Ethan stood at the top of the ramp.

"That was freaking awesome!" Ethan stuck out his chest. *"I'm done cowering at the feet of enforcers."* He shook his head. "And you say *I'm* crazy?"

Dania stepped beside Cal. "I didn't know you had that many laser cannons."

Ethan snorted a laugh. "Because we don't."

Dania gaped. "What?"

Cal rubbed the sweat off the back of his neck. "I may have exaggerated a little."

"You *lied?*"

Ethan beamed. "It's called a poker face. And the boss is damn good at it when he needs to be."

And today, Cal had certainly needed to be. Funny thing was, he hadn't been scared. Just pissed. They'd almost crashed that ship into a loyal colony and hadn't even mentioned it. It was too much like enforcers to be worried about their agendas and not the big picture.

"Do you really think there are a bunch of dying enforcers on that ship?" Ethan asked.

Dania pursed her lips. "Enforcers can't lie."

"Are ya sure?" Ethan asked.

She huffed out a breath, swiping back her hair. "I didn't sense a lie. However, I didn't notice one from Cal, either, so I'm not sure we can trust my judgement on that." She looked down and frowned. "It would make sense, though. If Zindiria's enforcers had been fighting hard, they would have depleted their energy stores and needed to be fed."

Ethan's brow furrowed. "Does it work that way? I mean, could you do the feeding-thing for them?"

"They're coded to Bane blood, so in theory, if I were fully charged, I may have been able to give them enough energy to keep them alive. However, each feeding would have weakened me more." She looked down. "I'm directly coded to Geron's enforcers, so I can share my strength more efficiently with them. The similar bloodline would make it possible, just not as efficient. So, even if I were at full charge, I wouldn't have been able to do much more than keep them breathing." Her brow furrowed as she lowered her eyes. "The only way to save those enforcers is to get them back to their sponsor."

Cal shook his head. "Well, that's what your buddy Orion wants, too. But not for the same reason. I have a feeling he's just going to use them to point him in the right direction until he finds his boss's sister. If they die along the way, it's collateral damage."

Dania nodded. "So it would seem."

Cal shook his head. This smelled like another impossible situation—and one he wanted to get out of as soon as possible. "I need to talk to Doc." He tugged Ethan's arm.

"Get up on the bridge and keep an eye on things. I have Ty working on something important, and I don't want him distracted."

Ethan beamed. "Can I sit in your chair?"

"Just get up there. I want to know if those enforcers so much as sneeze."

"On it, boss."

Ethan headed toward the ramp while Cal grabbed the rungs to the ladder that brought them to the upper midsection. One thing he had learned about enforcers was that nothing eclipsed their missions. If Orion really had that many enforcers on that damaged cruiser, that meant he'd flown the ship to Kirato, despite its condition, because the princess's enforcers wouldn't all fit in his smaller, undamaged ships.

Now they had crash-landed on a planet with few resources, except the planet just happened to have a smuggling ship on it built for carrying lots of cargo—even people. If the thought hadn't occurred to the enforcers yet, it was only a matter of time before they came and demanded use of the *Star Renegade*.

Cal grimaced as he reached the top deck and headed for the med bay. Under other circumstances, he'd have gotten the ship in the air and gotten out of there. But that would mean leaving Kirato at the mercy of the enforcers.

Once again, they'd landed in a no-win situation and luck wasn't going to weasel them out of this one.

"Cal!" Dania called from behind him. "What are you going to do?"

"I don't know yet." He reached for the access control beside the med bay door.

She stopped him before he tapped it. "You lied to Orion."

"We already established that."

"But how?"

Was she serious? "You open your mouth, and you say what you want the other person to hear."

"But it was a lie, and I couldn't tell. Obviously, Orion couldn't, either."

"Which is good. What's the problem?"

She looked at the walls, her brow furrowed. With everything she'd been through, this seemed to confuse her more than anything.

"Look," he said. "Maybe I just wanted it to be true so badly that neither of you picked up on it."

She continued to stare at the wall and her brow pinched further.

Obviously, this wasn't helping.

"Hey." He rubbed the back of her neck. "In case you didn't notice, I was pissed, and it was hot. Those are a lot of extremes to deal with. Maybe enforcer senses aren't infallible?"

She nodded. "It *was* hot outside."

For some reason, that seemed to make her feel better. Maybe her ability to sense lies was one of the few enforcer skills that she'd held on to. It might have been less about Cal's ability to lie, and more her holding on to a bit of her past.

Cal hit the door control.

Inside, Alanna sat beside Alexander's bed, holding a cloth on his forehead. Their skin and clothing were soiled, but they both turned toward him. Alexander tried to sit up, but Alanna pushed him back down.

Cal held up his palm. "I'll fill everyone in on what's going on in a moment."

On the other side of the room, Ty and Doc sat at tandem computer consoles tapping on keys, their eyes focused on their screens.

"You're alive." Doc glanced up. "That's good."

Ty kept typing. "Almost there, boss. Give me a few more seconds."

Cal nodded. He figured with Doc's brain and Ty's very illegal skills, they'd find a way to crack into the enforcer ships. In a few minutes, they'd find out what was really going on.

Ty punched the edge of the table. "Boom! Here we go!"

Doc's fingers swiped over the keys. "Downloading their data stores." He chuckled. "Damn, boy, you've got some skills."

Ty leaned back in his chair, lacing his fingers behind his head. "I know, I know. It's an art form."

Dania walked over to them. "Are you downloading data from the cruiser?"

Doc snorted. "The cruiser *and* two of the other ships. But the smaller ships are sending back duplicate data."

Dania nodded. "Yes, the enforcer ships would all have the same data stores."

"Download it all," Cal said. "I want to know everything they know."

Dania crossed her arms and rubbed her shoulders. "Do you realize how dangerous this is? You're committing a crime directly against the high prince's enforcers. The chances of them finding out are far too high."

Ty shrugged. "I'm already part of a crew that's wanted for smuggling, and I do believe I'm considered guilty by association for everything they think Cal did, so I'm kinda screwed either way." He smiled, the data from his screen reflecting in his eyes. "I might as well have fun before I'm caught."

Across the room, Alexander coughed, rubbing his chest like it hurt. "Are you going to tell us what happened?"

Dania turned to him. "We met with Orion."

Alexander sat taller. "Tell me that's pathogen depletion allowing you to lie."

"I wish it were. Apparently, Zindiria is missing. He's been tasked with finding her, but all he's found is a ship filled with dangerously depleted enforcers."

Alexander paled as he looked down. "They're lucky he found them before the slavers."

Lucky for the enforcers—not so lucky for the *Star Renegade*. Cal's goal had always been to stay away from enforcers. Lately, it seemed, he couldn't keep them away.

"But why come to Kirato?" Alanna cleared her throat. Her voice was hoarse, probably from breathing in so much dust when the ship had crashed.

Cal folded his arms. "They couldn't get back to Keveron. They came here hoping Dania could save them."

Alanna's eyes widened. "Can you?"

Dania shook her head. "With synthetic pathogens in my system? I don't think so."

"She's right," Doc said. "My treatments are only good enough to keep *her* going. The synthetics don't have any properties that would allow her to share them."

Alanna eased off the gurney. "So, if we can't share Dania's pathogen-thingies, can we give them the same treatments?"

Cal flinched. He knew it would come down to this question. But that didn't get either the *Star Renegade* or the enforcers off Kirato anytime sooner.

Doc grimaced. "I'll have to run some simulations. The last time we made a supply run, I only picked up enough goodies to keep Dania and Alexander going as long as I could."

Alexander frowned. "You can keep your supply of *goodies*. I will not be using any of your treatments now, or in the future." He started coughing again.

Alanna rubbed his back. "Even if it saves your life?"

He glanced at her, then looked away. "No enforcer would allow themselves to be knowingly polluted."

Dania cringed, looking away. That dig was obviously meant for her, and it looked like she'd felt the sting. Maybe her boy Alex wasn't the perfect best friend she'd made him out to be.

Alanna's shoulders sagged. She'd probably hoped, as they all had, that spending time on the *Star Renegade* would have the same effect on Alexander that it'd had on Dania. If they could only slap all the enforcers in Palian Steel to sap their energy, maybe this would all be easier.

Doc stood, tapping his fingertips on his lips. "The idea has merit, though. I'd have to know how many enforcers are on that ship, and how bad a condition they're in."

As much as Cal didn't want to interact with the enforcers, this might be a good idea. If the enforcers weren't about to dic, then maybe Orion would allow Kirato's artisans to fix their cruiser. The local economy could certainly use the boost, and that would get the *Star Renegade* off anyone's radar as a means of transportation. It was a long shot, but it might be the perfect solution.

"I'll find out exactly how many enforcers are in trouble," Cal said.

"No need." Ty pointed to his screen. "I'll know more about those ships than the people inside them do in the next couple of minutes."

Cal nodded. "Good."

Hopefully the information they found wouldn't make things even worse.

He turned back to Alanna and Alexander. "I need you two on the ion shield. I don't want any more surprises." And if they calibrated that shield correctly, maybe they'd still be able to keep those enforcers out of the colony.

ALANNA STARED at Stanley's back as he led her and Alexander through the tunnels below Kirato's operational facilities. The power generators were hidden somewhere down here, safe from sandstorms or aerial attacks.

The frayed edges of Stanley's robes dragged through the dust behind him. Each time the *Star Renegade* came to Kirato, Stanley's once-immaculate clothing showed more signs of wear. Mismatched stitching ran down his sleeve, probably repairing a hole.

Alanna grimaced at the stains on his elbows. It was ridiculous, but studying the soiled stripes of the older man's clothing was far less uncomfortable than meeting Alexander's gaze.

Alanna's heart had broken when Alexander had said he'd never take the synthetic pathogens. Every time she thought they had taken a step forward, he seemed to revert into an automaton again. It was driving her crazy, and she wasn't sure how much more she could take.

Stanley looked over his shoulder. "I think you two are

the only ones other than myself and my engineers who have ever been down here."

"We're honored," Alanna said.

"No, my dear. It is I who am honored. The work you have been doing on our shields is revolutionary. In times like these, when ships are falling out of the sky, we may need all the protection we can find."

They continued down the dark hallway. Their steps thudded on the stone floor, the sound mixing with beeps and hums of older computer components.

Alexander cleared his throat, then winced.

Alanna brought her hand to her own throat, fighting the tickle deep within. Doc had told them that they'd both be coughing for some time until their lungs could clear all the dust they'd inhaled at the crash site before Alexander had encased them in a bubble. Even after they'd been shielded, the air had been riddled with particles. It was bad, but nowhere near as bad as the dust storm that had slammed against Alexander's shield. They were lucky to be alive, and probably wouldn't have been if he weren't an enforcer.

But him being an enforcer still made her want to throw something.

They stopped at a juncture where a few dozen thick cables connected to what was, in essence, an engine meant to propel an intergalactic cruiser. She didn't want to know where Stanley had gotten it, and hopefully, Alexander wouldn't ask.

Alexander ran his fingers over the sanded-off serial numbers. "Are you sure drawing extra power won't affect any of the colony's essential systems?"

Stanley shook his head. "My engineers tell me we've only tapped into a quarter of its power."

Alexander's lips twitched into a slight smile. She had to admit, the engine was overkill for running a colony, but it was the ultimate in salvage, and they had more than enough power to spare for her needs.

Stanley gave them a slight bow before he backed down the way they had come, leaving Alanna and Alexander to get to work.

Dropping her bag to the floor, Alanna rooted through the contents, unpacking them beside her. Soldering gun. Crimps. Wrench. Black tape. Toy box. Pliers.

Finding her energy gauge, she started making adjustments to the power matrix as Alexander began rewiring. She had to admit that they made a good team. Sometimes it seemed like he knew what she was thinking, always staying a step ahead of what she needed without all of Ethan's snark and sarcasm to slow things down. It was refreshing, but if Alex was serious about refusing the pathogens, she couldn't get used to this feigned camaraderie. He'd have to leave, or he wouldn't survive.

She started shoving the extra components back into her bag. The worst of it was, if he did decide to leave, they all needed to make sure that he didn't try to take Dania with him.

Alexander rested his calibration tool on his thigh. "Are you angry with me or has your equipment vexed you?"

She shoved a wrench into her bag. "What?"

He tilted his head. "You've barely spoken to me all day, and now you're being unnecessarily rough with your tools."

She threw the tape into the bag. "I'm not angry!"

He raised a brow. "You didn't even make an attempt to hide that lie. The last time we had a complete conversation was before the crash. The only thing I remember doing was shoving you to the ground so I could effectively shield you from the dust storm. If I hurt you, I assure you it was an accident."

Alanna sighed, dragging her fingers through her hair. "You didn't hurt me." Not physically, at least.

"What is it, then? You're normally the most stable of the crew, and for the past day, I've felt more like I've been spending time with the captain."

Alanna gritted her teeth. Clueless must be a genetic state of male-ness. That was one of the few truths she'd learned since boarding the *Star Renegade*. "Why won't you take Doc's pathogens?"

He leaned back. "This is about pathogens? I thought I'd made my stance on this clear."

"You've made it clear that you won't take them. But it's a bad decision. They can save you."

"I don't need saving."

She picked up the soldering gun and slammed it into the bag, clanking it against the wrench. "Not yet, but you will. Don't you like it here? Don't you want to stay?"

He looked down. "Yes."

Her eyes widened. Had she heard that right? "You do?"

He shook his head. "What I want is irrelevant."

She inched closer. "It doesn't have to be."

He sighed, looking away. "I can't expect you to understand."

She looked to the ceiling and growled. "I am so sick of you saying things like that. You know what's making me mad? Your stubbornness is making me mad."

"I'm not stubborn. I'm dedicated."

"Dedication is going to make you dead." She shoved the

roll of tape into her bag and sniffed, wiping dampness from her eyes.

He reached for her. "Are you crying?"

"Leave me alone." She swatted his hand away. "You don't get to pretend you care."

"But I do care."

"No, you don't." She shoved the crimps in her bag and reached for the toy box.

He grabbed her wrist as she held the box over her bag. "What is that?"

She looked down at the small, shiny, wooden box. The corner was chipped. Why she felt the need to carry it with her tools was beyond her. She was surprised any of the original finish was left on the surface.

"It's just a toy," she said. "It was a gift from my mom."

He frowned. "You carry that with you?"

Her fingers trembled on the ancient wood. Her mother had told her to keep it safe, and most importantly, keep it hidden. The only thing she didn't know was *why*.

She gulped. "Is it illegal?"

"No, but it *is* odd."

The tension eased from her shoulders. If it had been illegal, what would he have done? The chilling truth was that she had no idea.

He glanced up at her. "Why do you keep this with your tools?"

This was a good question. She'd always figured her mother hadn't wanted her dad to know she'd purchased such an expensive toy. After Alanna had grown up, she'd always just continued the habit. As her thumb rubbed over the chipped wood, she wondered if the reason she carried it around was far more simple. "I like to keep it close. It reminds me of home."

His gaze returned to the toy. "Home?" His lips thinned and his brow pinched.

"You're scaring me. Is everything okay?"

He blinked and smiled, his gaze meeting hers. "May I see it?"

Part of her, deep down, screamed, *No!*

Her mother had been adamant about keeping her special present a secret, but Alexander had already seen the box, and he'd said it wasn't anything illegal. Settling herself, she placed it in his hand.

He flipped it over, testing its weight. "You called it a toy. Can you do anything with it?"

Alanna smiled. "Yes, I can. Do you want to see?"

He grew pale before he seemed to force a smile. "Yes. Yes, I do."

ALEXANDER'S HAND trembled as he handed the *demori* back to her. Part of him had hoped that she'd say she couldn't do anything with the energy-focusing tool, that it was simply an ornate box that possibly her mother had stolen from a Kever family. He closed his eyes and took a deep breath. How could he consider a crime a better option than the thought of Alanna being able to use it?

She placed the box on the floor and bit her lower lip before she looked up at him. "Mine is a butterfly box."

Alexander tilted his head. "What do you mean?"

"My mom picked this out for me. She got exactly the right one." She held her hand over the shiny, wood-like surface. "Watch this."

Alexander held his breath as the resonance in the air around them changed, pulsing slightly. An echo of power ghosted over his skin before an orange-and-black-striped butterfly crawled from beneath the box, spread its wings, and hovered a few inches above the swirls carved in the box's lid.

Alanna lowered her hand. "Isn't it great? I always loved butterflies. I used to collect books with pictures of them." She held out her hand, and the butterfly landed on her finger. "I've never seen one in real life, but this is exactly what all the pictures show."

Alexander smiled. Butterflies...such an interesting, innocent choice. It was fitting for her. "Can you do anything more?"

Her eyes sparkled. "I sure can. Watch this."

She held up both her hands, and three additional butterflies crawled out and took flight, followed by four more. Another two followed, one blue and one yellow, to add to the group of eight orange.

Alanna placed her hands on her thighs. "I used to sit there for hours as a kid, watching them. It was like having a little bit of Earth at my beck and call."

Alexander's eyes narrowed. She had a *demori*, and all she conjured were butterflies?

"Have you done anything else with it?"

She shook her head. "It only makes butterflies." She looked away from the yellow and blue insects circling in front of her face and met his gaze. "Have you played with one of these before?"

He released a breath slowly. "No. It was frowned upon." He and Dania had caused more than enough trouble on their own, let alone if they'd had access to a *demori*.

He held out his hand, and an orange butterfly landed on his palm. He believed it was called a 'monarch' on Earth. A lofty title for something so small.

But Alanna being able to use the *demori*, even in such a simple way, was anything but small. This answered many questions and asked countless more.

The larger issue was, though, should the rest of those questions remain unanswered?

Alanna pushed the box toward him. "Do you want to try?"

The child inside who had rarely been allowed to play twitched within. It seemed like such a decadent, illicit offer, although he'd seen adult Kevers use the boxes on many occasions.

He flicked his wrist, and the butterfly on his hand took flight again. "You do realize that you can do more than conjure butterflies with this, don't you?"

She frowned. "I've never done anything else. The way my mom talked, I thought it just made butterflies."

Interesting. Had this been a lie on her mother's part? Had she known what the *demori* was? If she had brought the box to her daughter as a test, conjuring butterflies would have been enough to prove Alanna wasn't like other children.

Alexander ran his fingers over the edge of the lid and glanced up at her. "Would you like to see what it can do?"

Her eyes sparked, just like Dania's had when he'd coaxed her into breaking into the queen's private kitchens in the middle of the night.

Alanna rubbed her hands over her thighs and nodded.

Alexander stared at the swirling pattern on the lid as his palms heated, sending a trickle of primordial energy into the center of the markings. He wasn't sure if this would excite or frighten her. In some ways, that didn't matter.

He'd seen the cubes used so many times and had always wondered what he'd conjure should he have the opportunity. His heartbeat quickened as he focused on the delight

in Alanna's eyes, and for some reason, all he could think of
was making her smile brighter.

CHAPTER 20
ALANNA

THE AIR about Alanna tingled as her butterflies flew up and circled in a ball a few feet above the toy box. Another yellow butterfly crawled up the side of the box, then a black pair of wings appeared, then red, yellow, and fuchsia.

A light flashed and Alanna fell back as the toy box exploded with flapping wings.

"Oh my gosh!" She covered her eyes, laughing as dozens upon dozens of soft wings fluttered across her cheeks.

If she'd ever released that many butterflies in the house, her mother would have fainted.

Alexander's gaze was fixed on her, his eyes amused but focused.

She trembled for a moment before she straightened. She didn't need to be afraid of him. He'd told her this wasn't illegal, and this time, he'd released the butterflies himself. Another burst of colorful wings erupted from the box.

She shifted her weight. "You're good at this."

He laughed. It changed the entire appearance of his

face, making his sharp features less intimidating. "You really have no idea what this device can do."

Alanna frowned. A sinking feeling filled her stomach, despite his grin. What was he talking about?

Alexander raised his other hand, and the butterflies scattered, flying up toward the ceiling and down the hall. The box trembled like the ground had moved beneath it before a flood of green erupted from the box and spread across the floor and under Alanna.

She gasped as cool, crisp grass tickled her palms and spread out across the room. A puff of swirling blue shot from the box, and the ceiling disappeared, replaced by a blue sky dotted with wispy, white clouds.

The walls and machines they'd been working on melted away, and trees sprouted from the grass, exploding up, extending branches that reached for the sky as green, lush leaves covered the bark.

Alanna leaned back, staring upward as a lush, rich forest landscape erased the last of the inner workings of Kirato.

Alexander lowered his hands and closed his eyes, letting the sun warm his face.

The sun… When a moment before, they'd been underground.

"Wh-What just happened? Where's Kirato?"

His eyes fluttered open, and he scanned the trees. He seemed oddly at peace. "It's still around us. This is an illusion, just like the butterflies."

Alanna took a deep breath, and the smell of wildflowers filled her nose as a cool breeze shifted her hair. "How can I smell and feel an illusion?" She stood. A staticky noise came from behind the trees…or maybe it was more like a roar. "What is that sound?" She squinted through the tree trunks. Beyond the verge, the sunlight sparkled, reflecting off water. "Is that what I think it is?"

Alexander stood, looking toward the trees. "It's water from the hills above falling into a lake."

"A waterfall?" There were few planets in the galaxy with enough water to pool, let alone fall. Alanna took a few steps toward the sound, but he stopped her.

"Remember, you're standing in an illusion." He pointed to a large rock at her feet. "See that? It's your toy box." He pointed to the large tree right beside them. "That's the engine and the console we were just working on. If you walk too far, you might slam right into a wall."

An illusion…right. She sighed. "That means we can't go to the waterfall?" That was another thing she'd only seen in books or pictorials on the information servers. There were so many things about Earth that she longed to see. Which was strange because she'd never even been there. "It all just feels so real."

Alexander slipped his hand into hers. It was warm, despite the slight chill in the air. "Would you like to see it?"

"Can we?"

He pulled her close and the trees and the ground sped past them in a blur. Alanna gasped as they stopped suddenly at the edge of the grass. Water cascaded down a rock formation jutting out of a hill above, splashing into a small lake with a drumming roar.

Water splashed onto her face, and Alanna touched her cheek, staring at her wet fingertips. "This shouldn't be possible."

Alexander leaned toward the water, cupped his hand, and flicked the droplets at her. "It can seem quite real."

Alanna crouched and ran her fingertips through the water. The coolness flowed over her skin until it no longer felt cold. "The water's warm." She stood, pulling off her boots.

"What are you doing?"

"Going for a swim." She stepped in. Her feet sank, and she gaped. "How did I sink? Isn't the floor still beneath me?" She spun toward Alexander. His hands were raised.

"I lifted you a little to give you the sensation of a real lake."

Ah... Enforcer power finally put to good work. "So, I can actually swim?"

"Yes."

A giggle burst from her lips as she waded into the water and started to float. Her uniform flowed around her like it was actually wet, but it didn't pull her down. Alexander stayed on the edge of the lake with folded arms and his lips pressed together.

She waved at him. "Aren't you going to come in?"

He shrugged.

"Oh, come on." She splashed water in his direction. "You know you want to!"

A smile burst across his face. He held up his hand, possibly doing some magic before he dove in, splashing the water around her. When he resurfaced, his hair hung saturated, clinging to his temples and flowing in the water around him while clear droplets ran down his face. He looked so innocent. So childlike, so *normal*.

Did she look that way to him? Not that it mattered all that much.

She looked up to where the water fell above. "How is it that we're soaking wet?"

"We're not. If I call off the illusion, we'll be dry."

She shook her head, treading in the water. "It doesn't seem possible." But for the moment, she'd allow herself to be lost in this amazing dream.

Kicking her feet, she swam to the falls and dove beneath. The drumming water on her head actually hurt before she was behind the streaming curtain.

Alexander appeared beside her, rubbing the top of his head. "Ouch."

She puffed out a laugh, placing her palm in the falling stream. "I've always wanted to jump through a waterfall."

Alexander held up his own hand, allowing the water to flow over his palm. "Me, too."

He'd always wanted to play in a waterfall? Was that why he'd made it come to life?

It seemed hard to imagine that one of the royal family's super soldiers could find simple joy in nature.

She splashed at the falling stream, but there was so much water, it barely shifted. It was like a wall of nature, hiding them.

But were they really hidden?

She turned to Alexander. "What happens if anyone comes looking for us? What would they see?"

He smiled again. It was starting to look natural on him. "They'd see trees and a waterfall. But they'd probably walk into a wall of butterflies first."

She laughed, imagining Stanley accosted by dozens of colorful, fluttering wings. "But they wouldn't be able to see us in here?"

He shook his head. "Not unless they dove in like we did."

Alanna closed her eyes and enjoyed the tingle of the water spray hitting her cheeks. "This is nice. It's like hiding within our own little world."

"It *is* nice." He leaned his drenched hair against the rocks behind them. "We could easily get lost here."

Did that mean he *wanted* to be lost?

Alexander closed his eyes and sighed. She wanted to move closer and place her head on his shoulder...but that would be bad. Very, very bad.

He opened his eyes, glanced at her, and his cheeks flushed a brilliant pink.

"It's quiet." His voice was barely audible above the roar of the falls.

"What do you mean? It sounds like a churning engine."

He shook his head. "No. There's nothing but the water. Do you hear it?"

She closed her eyes and let the drumming of the water fill her. It was loud, echoing off the stone wall behind them, but yes, it was also lulling, and quiet in its own way.

When she opened her eyes, he was looking at her. Droplets of water glinted in his long lashes. "Do you feel it? Do you feel the peace?"

The cool water sprinkled her cheek. They were alone in their own little world. There were no crashed ships, no hurt enforcers, no colony that needed protecting. It was just them, and despite Alexander's recent outbursts, she'd never felt safer.

She nodded. "I do."

He cupped her cheek with his palm and dragged his

fingers through her hair before his gaze dropped to her lips.

His attention lingered there, and Alanna's breath hitched as the pressure of the falling water seemed to intensify. Should she move? Say anything? Was she imagining this?

He released her and turned away.

Alanna blinked, startled. "Alexander?"

His brow pinched before he lifted his other hand. The water formed an upside-down "U" around his palm as he held his fingers in the stream. He smiled, staring into the shape.

Once again, he seemed so like a child seeing something for the first time.

What was going on in his head?

She held her own palm in the water falling from his hand. The chill tickled her fingers, but she warmed inside. She may have only imagined him looking at her lips, but that was fine. Right now, he was enjoying something so simple, so normal…and it had nothing to do with enforcing the law.

Alanna pulled her hand out of the water. "It's nice to see you smiling so much."

He nodded. "Places like this make it easy to forget."

She frowned. "What do you need to forget?"

He glanced at her and his smile faded.

A deep pain settled in her gut. She hated that his smile was gone and wished to the stars that she hadn't ruined the moment.

He looked away and dove back through the waterfall.

"Alexander?" She followed, but he was already sitting

on the shore. The water streamed from his clothing and trickled back into the lake rather than pooling around him.

She swam to the edge and sat next to him. "Are you okay?"

He stared straight ahead, looking into the falling water they'd been hiding behind. He seemed so distant, and once again, lost.

He took a deep breath, as if enjoying the smell of the trees around them. "I feel alive."

The statement hung in the air, almost as if it echoed off the drumming falls.

Alive was good.

Wasn't it?

He stood. "We need to finish our work." His clothing dried with each step away from the lake, and the roar behind them stopped. Alanna looked over her shoulder at a rocky wall where they'd once hidden inside the falls. The trees faded away, and the sky evaporated until the ceiling came back into view.

It was plain, nondescript, and very much Kirato.

She loved this colony, but a deep dread settled over her, like she'd lost something that never should have been found.

CHAPTER 21
CAL

CAL PUSHED his way into the med bay. The information they'd extracted from the enforcers' ships should have been analyzed by now. He'd done everything he could think of to at least *look like* he was being patient.

Unfortunately, as Ethan loved to point out, patience was not one of Cal's strong points. He'd mopped the cargo bay, filled the food service shelves in the lounge, and rearranged the tables twice. If Ty and Doc hadn't completed the analysis, Cal would threaten to do maintenance work on primary systems. That always managed to get their attention.

Doc looked up from his computer screen. "Hey, boss."

"You got anything for me?"

"Well, it seems our new enforcer buddy told the truth. There is a minimum complement of royal big brother's enforcers on the four escort ships."

"What's a *minimum complement*?"

"Seven. Two on each ship and Orion was in the main cruiser when we downloaded the data."

That meant seven fully-charged enforcers. It might as

well have been an army of hundreds. "How many on the cruiser are injured?"

Doc tapped on the keys. "The numbers have changed with each of the time stamps Ty grabbed. It looks like a few have died, but at the last download, it was thirty-eight."

"Can we tell how bad they all are? Are the extra thirty-eight a threat?" Not that the original seven weren't already more than they could deal with.

"They're not going to be causing trouble anytime soon. Half of them are in the infirmary hooked up to heart monitors. We have multiple injuries one might expect from being in an attack of that magnitude, and that's on top of the pathogen depletion. It looks like these guys and gals expended so much energy fighting that their bodies don't have the strength to heal themselves."

Good for the *Star Renegade*, bad for the enforcers.

Doc pointed at the screen. "Before they decided to head in our direction, our boy Orion had been pulling one injured enforcer at a time to their bridge, using them as bloodhounds to send them in the right direction to help steer them closer to that princess. Once that enforcer dropped, they'd send them back to their med bay and grab another lucky volunteer."

"So he used them to the point of exhaustion and then moved on to the next one."

"Exactly. They may have been able to heal themselves in time, but now they're all in severe pathogen depletion." He stood. "Dania explained that they'd need either their sponsor or a fully-charged general to get an energy boost, but it appears that their generals disappeared with their princess, and Orion is only a commander, so he can't help them."

The entire enforcer dichotomy was just so odd. Could they really have been so vain to think that they'd never be attacked in such force that they'd run out of all their supernatural power?

Cal looked at the ceiling. He wanted to think this wasn't his problem, but in many ways, it was. They'd come here for Dania—not just to take her home, but in hopes she could save the enforcers. If Orion only wanted to keep the princess's enforcers alive, Cal may not have worried, but he wanted to use them as tools, and they were the only tools he had to point him in the direction of that princess. Cal had a sinking suspicion that he wouldn't give up on the idea of Dania quite so easily.

"Can you think of any possible way for Dania to help them? I don't want to be blindsided by him coming for her in the middle of the night."

Doc grimaced, looking down.

"What?"

He sighed. "Well, there is that vial that Dania called an emergency feeding."

Cal gritted his teeth. "You mean the trap her prince set for her? Dania said that would turn her into a monster."

"Yeah." He looked back toward the glass storage shelves. "I could offer it to them, but I'd be too worried Orion would turn around and force it on our girl."

Cal's jaw started to hurt. "That is *not* happening."

"I agree. I already wiped any mention of it from our records, just in case." Doc tapped a few keys on his computer. "But other than that, I don't see any way she could feed them. There's no magical energy in her bloodstream. Just nice, natural human chemistry." He looked down. "That doesn't mean they won't try to take her. You know as well as I do that enforcers don't like to take *no* for an answer."

A round tray of test tubes dropped into a container at the back of the room, while another machine started to release a white fog. Beside that machine, four blue test tubes rose from the middle of a wide, metal cylinder with condensation dripping down the sides.

Cal looked into the container. "What are you working on?"

"Mass production of pathogens. You were right with your original concerns. If Dania can't help them, we need to find a way."

"I thought you only had enough for Dania and Alexander?"

"That's true, but our boy Alex is still refusing treatment. I'm making enough for Dania to get her through the next year and setting it aside. The rest I was going to offer to Orion."

"He probably won't accept."

"He might if they start dying. He may not care about them, but he cares about his mission. He needs those enforcers alive to point him in the right direction."

Which was why Cal needed to get the cruiser repaired as soon as possible.

Doc looked over the test tubes. "The problem is, even if Orion smartens up and accepts our help, I don't have enough supplies to help all of them. And you and I both know that if they start dying, Orion is going to start looking for someone else to blame."

Cal nodded. "I know you've got a lot going on, but start doing some tests on the live pathogens in the vial from that emergency feeding. If there's any way we can use it, I want to know."

"You got it, boss."

Cal tapped on the comm, and Stanley's face appeared on the screen.

"Interesting morning," Stanley said.

"Every morning is interesting when there's enforcers around."

The older man grimaced. "You would probably know better than I, my friend."

"Do you have a team ready to try to repair that ship? We'll all be safer once they're back in the air."

"We have fifty-six people already working on the hull. An additional hundred are training to work on interior repairs. The bossy, impatient one in charge seems annoyed but satisfied."

Cal nodded. "Good. Let me know how I can help."

"Keep your enforcer friends busy and encourage them to stay outside the colony. That's all I want."

"Roger that." Cal tapped the comm and stared at the button. The problem was, if the healthy enforcers tried to leave the ship and explore, there wasn't much any of them would be able to do to stop them.

Doc leaned back in his chair. "So, do I save some of these artificial pathogens for Alex, or do I use them on the people who are dying?"

"How long do you think Alexander has before he gets in trouble?"

"I can't even guess. His timeline is nothing like Dania's."

So they were playing a game that could cost lives no matter what they did.

Doc sat up and leaned his elbows on his knees. "Long story short: I need more supplies, Cal."

Rubbing his face, Cal growled at the ceiling. "I was afraid you'd say that."

The comm pinged. Doc frowned at the screen. "It's Alanna." He tapped on the controls. "Hey, girl. What's up?"

Static crackled before Alanna's voice came over the comm. "Well, it's been an interesting day, but most importantly… We just started testing the ion shield programming. It looks good so far, but we're going to run it overnight."

"That's great news," Cal said. "How long until it's operational?"

"Alexander is hoping for tomorrow, but I don't want to make promises until it runs through all the cycles."

Doc rubbed his hands together, a twinkle of excitement sparking in his eyes.

A tingle of exhilaration swirled in Cal's chest. This was definitely promising news.

He tapped the comm. "Okay, make sure everything is settled down there and then get back to the ship." He hated to admit it, but he wanted Alexander on board. Chances were, Mr. Perfect would side with the enforcers if things went bad, but at least there was a chance that Alex would try to stop Orion from doing anything irrational. Cal also wanted Alanna on board in case the shield actually worked and they had an opportunity to get out of there.

Doc pulled a bag over his shoulder. "I'm going to find Rachel and let her know we might be leaving."

Cal smiled. One thing he loved about Doc was that they were almost always on the same page. The ion shield was a solid way to keep those enforcers out of the colony, which would give the *Star Renegade* a chance to make a clean getaway. He hadn't considered Rachel being part of the equation, though.

He followed Doc toward the exit. "I got the impression Rachel wanted to stay on Kirato. I think something happened between her and Alexander."

"I noticed that, too." He shrugged. "It's up to her. I just don't want to face her wrath the next time we drop off supplies if we don't give her the opportunity to come with us."

Cal snorted a laugh. "I was getting used to the quiet."

"Me too, but to be honest, I kind of miss the chaos."

CHAPTER 22

ALEXANDER

ALEXANDER BOUNDED up the *Star Renegade*'s cargo ramp, Alanna close behind. They'd finished the modifications to the shielding, but saving this colony seemed secondary...maybe even tertiary to the countless mission parameters swirling through his mind.

If Dania were in her right mind, she'd tell him to focus on the enforcers and help find the king's daughter. Yet Dania didn't have the information Alexander did. Alanna's ability to use a *demori* might change everything.

"Will you please tell me what's wrong?" Alanna called from below him on the ramp.

At this point, he wasn't sure what was right, let alone wrong. He should have left as soon as Alanna had made the butterflies appear, but instead, he'd called up a haven for them to enjoy.

What had he been thinking? The butterflies had been more than enough to confirm his suspicions. Now he needed answers. He needed causes. He needed clarity. Only then would he know what was wrong and what, if anything, was right.

She grabbed his arm. "Alexander, please, talk to me."

He spun toward her. He did, indeed, want to talk to her. But he knew she didn't have the answers to the questions nagging within. "I'm not feeling well. I need some time to decompress."

It wasn't a lie. His stomach churned and his temples throbbed. It wasn't a true illness, but an emotional reaction that he needed to get ahead of. Hopefully, some research would give him a valid explanation why a woman from a small, outlier colony had the ability to skip space and make butterflies appear on a whim.

The pain in her eyes dug through him. "Did I say something wrong? If I did, I'm sorry. I had a really good time today."

"I enjoyed our day as well. I'm not upset or angry with you. I just need some time to make sense out of things."

Her frown turned into a tentative grin. "In a good way, I hope?"

He certainly hoped so because a bad way would be unthinkable, and he wasn't sure what he'd do.

Alexander nodded, looking down.

Her expression brightened. "Okay. So, I'll see you tomorrow?"

"Yes. I'd like that."

Thank goodness she seemed to accept his response. She headed for the lounge while he turned toward the crew quarters. The roiling in his stomach heightened with each step and only grew worse as he entered his room. Closing the door behind him, he took in the stark, gray walls, the tightly made bed, and the bathroom and shower doors in the rear of the room. It was all so simple. So perfect. He didn't want to ruin this space with the realities of the day, but he had no choice.

Walking to the wall, he tapped on the computer screen and started a connection to the archives. He knew Alanna called the small planet of Reglia home, so that would be a good place to start.

He rubbed his face, waiting for the connection. The small box Alanna had called a toy was anything but a plaything. A *demori* was a training tool to help young Kever children develop their powers. To a human, it should be nothing more than a wooden block.

He started to pace. The fact that she could use it shouldn't have been that much of a surprise. Her ability to skip space was an oddity in itself, but he'd hoped there would be a less troublesome origin.

The connection to the archives hadn't gone through yet, which was more than likely a result of their location, and not an issue with the blockade that Orion had mentioned to Dania. Still, Alexander would have to look into the information that Ty had extracted from Orion's ship to find more details about the conflict.

He flinched. How could he even consider utilizing illegally extracted information? It was wrong.

For some reason, though, he didn't care.

Was this a result of pathogen depletion? Or was it simply that the information was valuable, and he should use whatever was in their possession, even if the information was stolen?

He pinched his brow. Conundrums like these made his head hurt. Choices were hard. He didn't know how Dania lived like this.

He kept the forthcoming connection to the archives running and searched the *Star Renegade*'s databases, looking for anything unusual. The pilot kept odd data on galactic yacht racing. The engineer dictated ideas for possible engine modifications that seemed to have no basis in engineering principles whatsoever.

The doctor used an interesting and direct filing system for his notes and had an entire folder labeled *Unexplained*. Much of it had to do with Dania, but there had been a lengthy entry not long after Dania had boarded. According to the crew, the doctor had suffered an accident and they'd thought he'd died. The doctor's own scans after the incident had proven that his spine had been broken in several places, and miraculously repaired.

Interesting.

Alexander looked back further in the logs. Ty, Ethan, and the captain all confirmed that Alanna had been holding the doctor after the accident, begging him to wake up. The doctor noted that Dania had been outside the ship, unconscious. The doctor also noted that he had no idea how he had survived.

But Alexander *did*.

If Alanna had primordial energy running through her and she wanted something bad enough, it was a viable assumption she could make it happen. It was possible that she had healing power and didn't even know it. She would not have been able to bring a man back from death, but if he was *near* death, she very well could have willed his body to repair itself.

He scanned more records, looking for any other instances of miraculous healing. The doctor had noted several times that Dania had been in pain but had calmed when Alanna held her temples.

There were also two instances of Dania showing power after her pathogens had depleted. Once where Dania had created an air shield and saved the engineer during a radiation leak, and another that Alexander had witnessed himself: She'd shoved the crew, including himself and Kile, with primordial energy when she'd felt threatened. In each of these instances, any semblance of power was soon gone, as if it had never existed.

The doctor further noted that in Dania's depleted state, he could find no reason for sudden spikes in natural pathogens, or why she had short, unexpected bursts of power.

Alexander leaned back in his chair. Several times since boarding, he'd felt weakened and feared he may have to abandon Dania and return to Geron. He was still weak compared to before, but when he'd spent time with Alanna, he'd seemed to feel better. Stronger.

He sighed, rubbing his eyes. Alanna had also, on many occasions, seemed tired afterward—sometimes bordering on illness. The woman did tend to touch the people around her. Could she be unintentionally sending strength to him and Dania?

He covered his face completely. That shouldn't be possible, but neither were any of the oddities surrounding this woman.

A ping sounded when the archives connected. He cross-referenced the *Star Renegade*'s records of her mother, whom Espinoza had apparently relocated to protect from some sort of pirates. That was an interesting bit of information Alexander would have to look into later.

For now, he followed the records back on her mother and found that before she'd settled on Reglia, just seven months before Alanna's birth, she'd been a worker in the Bane household on some sort of exchange program. She'd spent a considerable amount of time withZemeanBane,Geron'scousin.

Alexander's stomach sank. That may be the link he'd been looking for.

He called up the ship-wide medical scanners and checked the heartbeat sensors. Both the doctor and Miss Quirky were not on the ship, which would leave the med bay, and its equipment, free to use without prying eyes.

He left his room and headed down the hall to the stairway leading to the upper deck. Luckily, Miss Quirky had been decidedly absent since he'd confronted her about her stowaway. If she had a modicum of intelligence, she'd find somewhere on Kirato to leave their unregistered passenger so they would stop making the crew believe there were systems issues. It would also be highly inconvenient to run into Miss Quirky in the med bay and deal with the myriad of questions that would follow. For now, he needed to keep what information he had a secret.

The med bay door was locked, but Alexander sent a short burst of power into the mechanism. When the door opened, a slight hum in the air told him they'd installed additional security, most likely to keep Alexander from interfering with his pathogen experiment.

Peter's caution was founded. Alexander should be doing everything in his power to thwart Dania's poisoning. However, the doctor had been right about one thing that gave Alexander pause. Dania's body was physically strong, and she was losing the need to return to their sponsor. While he still couldn't fathom not wanting her power recharged, the intellectual side of him was fascinated with the doctor's work. Peter had achieved something that shouldn't be possible. And while his work would eventually be deemed illegal, Alexander couldn't bring himself to stop the experiments from running their course.

He sent a small electrical charge through the outer boundaries, and the hum faded. He was almost disappointed. He'd expected a more formidable puzzle from the normally efficient doctor.

Accessing an unoccupied microscope, he called up a few of the Bane DNA codes he was aware of and centered them in the A side of the comparison display. Taking a deep breath, he pulled the piece of Alanna's hair he'd taken from her when they'd been under the waterfall and placed it in the B compartment.

The analysis took fifteen seconds. Several test tubes rose from a machine in the back of the room before the microscope beeped.

Alexander closed his eyes, not wanting the results now that he had them. But he needed to know the truth. Dania may have been satisfied that Alanna's abilities were nothing more than an oddity, but Alexander's coding demanded answers, even if those answers would make their current situation more difficult.

He opened his eyes and sighed.

Now it made sense why her mother had departed Keveron so suddenly, not finishing her exchange program.

It explained why she'd settled on Reglia, the closest planet to Bane space, and married a few days later.

She'd been hiding.

Seven months later, Alanna was born.

He sterilized the equipment, erased the records, re-established the boundaries, and headed back to his room.

He needed to tell Dania what he'd discovered. Human and Kever couplings resulting in offspring were rare, but not all that uncommon. Ones resulting in an exchange of primordial energy, however, were unheard of. In almost all cases, the children of these couplings looked human, which attested to the strong genetics of the human race. This was probably why it had been so easy for the mother to hide the child.

Once inside his room, he sat on the edge of his bed. Alanna had seemed so innocent when she'd called up the butterflies, and her face had held a wonder he couldn't help but admire as the forest had appeared around her.

Alanna was good, despite her smuggler background. She didn't deserve the attention this new information would bring down on her. Likewise, Dania was Alanna's friend, but this new information would force her to look on the navigator with new, critical eyes, and the thought made him clench his fists.

When he'd been unconscious after his ordeal with the trappers, his only tether to reality had been Alanna's voice.

It was the best of times; it was the worst of times.

Those words never held more meaning than they did now. He'd enjoyed their conversations, how she listened and seemed to understand, even if there was truly no way she could possibly understand what he'd been through. Maybe that didn't matter, though, because she *cared.*

Her skin had been so warm beneath the waterfall,

despite the slight chill in the air. Her temperature had spiked a few times as she'd looked at him, and his own body had responded in ways that surprised him.

He'd spent time with human women recreationally, but they had been interchangeable. A means to an end. Entertainment. Something to use temporarily, then discard.

Alanna was worlds different. He appreciated her selflessness and love of the crew, and her ability to think fast and come up with clever solutions to problems. In fact, her ability to tinker rivaled his own. He found he enjoyed spending time with her, something he'd never experienced outside of his relationship with Dania.

But his stray thoughts about Alanna were decidedly different than those he had for his general.

When he'd reached for Alanna's hair in the waterfall, his palm had lingered on her cheek. Her temperature had spiked and wavered expectantly. He'd wanted to move closer, maybe even taste her. But he'd regained his focus, procuring the hair sample he'd needed for the test. She'd remained in his thoughts, though, and he'd immediately regretted not taking advantage of their closeness. Now, maybe he never could.

If he told Dania about Alanna's parentage, his general would caution him away from her. And she'd be right. Even though Alanna was a bastard to a lower-ranking Bane, her blood was still royal. Any intimacy between her and Alexander would be frowned upon.

Still, he found these odd emotions stirring inside him were something he wanted to explore, even if he never acted on them.

Moving to the computer screen, he deleted his search

from the ship's records. He coded an algorithm and used royal encryption to erase his tapping into the archives. Within moments, all evidence of what he'd found had disappeared into the ether.

Hiding the truth was not illegal, as long as no one discovered what he'd done.

CAL MET Doc at the top of the stairs. "Did you find Quirky?"

"Yeah. Our girl is acting just as strange as ever. She was sure that Alexander had sent me to find her. I don't know what has her so spooked about him."

They started walking toward the lounge.

"Does that mean she's going to stay on Kirato?"

"Hell no. She started packing the second I told her."

"Packing what?"

Doc shook his head. "I can't even tell you. She had boxes everywhere."

Great. They barely had enough room on board as it was.

Cal pointed his thumb over his shoulder. "Everyone is waiting in the lounge to discuss our next moves. I want to make sure we're all on the same page."

"Do you want to wait for Rachel?"

Cal shook his head. "I'd like to avoid the insanity for a bit. We need to focus."

"Agreed."

Cal tapped the door control and they stepped into the

lounge. Ty sat at his normal place at the end of the table, talking to Dania on his left. Doc took his own seat as Alanna, Alexander, and Ethan sat huddled on the other side of the table in deep discussion.

"Everything okay?" Cal asked.

"Yeah," Ethan said. "I'm just getting an update on the ion shield."

"How's it going?" Cal asked.

Alexander sat back. "It appears operational. We haven't tested it from the air, yet, but simulations seem promising."

Well, that was good news. Until the enforcers found out about it. Their new friend, Orion, would undoubtedly blow a fuse.

Cal took a deep breath. They were about to find out where Alexander's loyalties lay. "I know we expect it to work from the air, but will it work for a ground assault?"

Alexander's eyes narrowed. "A what?"

"Ground assault," Ethan said. "You know, like if a ship lands and tries to attack the colony on foot."

The enforcer glared at him. "I know what a ground assault is." He switched his gaze to Cal. "Why the sudden worry about a ground assault?"

"You know why." Cal leaned on the table. It was time to go all in, and there was no sugarcoating this. "Will the ion shield stop an attack by enforcers?"

Alexander flinched and gripped the ends of the table.

This was it. Mr. Perfect was about to show his true colors.

Alanna placed her hand over one of Alexander's. "There are innocents in that colony. We're just trying to protect them. That's why we made the shield, right?"

Alexander glared at the table.

Alanna gripped his hand. "No one said anything about hurting or attacking enforcers or doing anything illegal. We're only talking about protection."

The enforcer closed his eyes and nodded.

Damn, Cal had to admit Alanna had some mad skills that had nothing to do with jumping the ship.

She turned to Cal. "Yeah, I think with a few more modifications, the shield will keep them out for a considerable amount of time. I mean, probably not forever. It's not a real ion shield. Just the next best thing we could come up with using the supplies we had." She glanced at Alexander, then back to Cal. "I take it you're expecting the worst?"

Cal righted himself. "No. Like you said, I want the colony protected in case we're not here to run interference."

Ethan perked up. "We going somewhere?"

"Not yet. I just want to be prepared."

Ty sat up and leaned on the edge of the table. "So, what's the deal? I'm getting a little antsy staring at that crashed cruiser all day."

"I think we all are." Cal sat at the head of the table. "We all want to get the enforcers off the planet as soon as possible. We're thinking if we can get artificial pathogens to at least some of them, we can speed up that process."

"They won't accept that kind of treatment," Alexander said. "That, I assure you."

"They might," Dania said. "If we can convince them that it would bolster the chances of finding the princess." She tapped her fingers on the table. "If the enforcers die, they can't help Orion, and they should also be programmed to live at any cost. If their last resort is pathogens, it might work."

Alexander stared at the table. He frowned, then grimaced. Would he take the pathogens, if he thought it was his only chance to get back to that star-blasted prince he seemed to love so much?

Ethan ran his fingers through his copper curls. "The only problem is running out of supplies, right? Because if we're worried about not having enough of Doc's magic bugs for Dania, I'm ready to vote *no* on this now."

Ty rubbed his face. "I have a bad feeling this is why you had me checking on trajectories to Sector Z8."

Cal nodded. "What did you find?"

"It's not good. There's enough static and communication blocks for me to think we'll either have to go through one of those blockades our new enforcer friend warned us about, or it's quite possible Z8 may be one of the areas under Cartek control."

"That doesn't sound good."

Doc leaned across the table. "I disagree. If Z8 had been attacked, the pirates would have scattered and everyone would know about it. To me, that's good news because word would have gotten this far. I think a blockade is a more plausible reason for the interference."

"That's just as bad though, right?" Ethan asked.

"Not necessarily. It just means we'll have to get past what will probably be a nearly impenetrable barrier."

"Is that a big deal?" Alanna leaned on her fist. "Can't we just go around it?"

Cal folded his arms. "I wish. From what we've gathered from Orion's datastores, we're looking at a wall that might take weeks to get around."

Alanna's hand fell to the table. "How could it possibly be that big?"

"We all saw firsthand the size of the cloaked cloud of ships that attacked Ephershia. They were well within our borders before we even knew they were there." The cloud had been massive—like nothing anyone had ever seen. "They've been infiltrating our space for far too long. I wouldn't underestimate anything at this point." Cal looked at each of them. They needed to understand what they might be up against. "No matter how big this thing is, we're going to have to get through it."

Ethan sat back. "And how do you propose we do that?"

Cal pointed at Alexander and Alanna. "That's where you two come in."

They both glanced at each other, sitting straighter.

"You got the ion shield up and running. So now, let's step up your game. I want you to cloak the *Star Renegade*."

Alanna jerked back. "Huh? What?"

Ethan rubbed his chin. "It won't work. Stealth tech fools radars, not eyes. A blockade will see us coming."

Cal locked gazes with Alanna, then Alexander. "I want more than stealth. I want to disappear."

Alexander cocked his head. "Cloaking devices on that scale are only theoretical."

Cal tapped on a computer screen. "It's theoretical because Earth and Keveron haven't figured it out yet, but the Carteks have." A simulation of the thousand or so Cartek ships they'd encountered near Ephershia appeared on the screen. "Remember that cloud? The only reason we saw it was because there were so many cloaked ships, but when they were flying in smaller groups, no one knew they were out there."

Alanna folded her arms and leaned on the table. "Okay, I get that you think theoretical isn't all that theoretical anymore. I agree that building real cloaking tech would be amazing, but I'm not even sure where to start."

"Simple. We have Cartek equipment onboard. Not just the spatial inhibitor, but the weapon they put on our synch navigator. I want you to study them, use them, and connect them if you have to. Somewhere inside that tech is the solution of how to cloak."

"It might take months to figure it out," Alexander said.

"We're leaving tomorrow as soon as Rachel gets back on board. You have as long as it takes for us to get to Z8 without traveling fast enough to call attention to ourselves."

The enforcer blew through his lips slowly, as if contemplating their chances at success. Alanna nodded as her eyes centered on the table. Ethan rubbed his face and then leaned his head back.

Cal got it. This was a big ask. They were used to running away from trouble, not stepping right into it.

"Are we sure we want to save these enforcers?" Ty asked.

Cal straightened, his gaze lancing each of them. "Let's be real, people. Orion wants Dania. If he gets desperate enough, he'll take her, even if she can't help him. These pathogens are the only way to keep her safe."

Dania curled in on herself. "I don't want to be the reason you all risk running a blockade."

"It's more than that." Cal leaned on the edge of the table. "If we get those enforcers mobile, there's a chance Orion will leave as soon as the ship is space-worthy, even if the repairs aren't done."

Ty rubbed his chin. "I'm with you. Kirato's people need the work, but they'll be better off if those enforcers are gone before Orion gets too nosey."

Cal nodded. "Right now, Orion is only concerned with getting that ship operational and keeping the injured alive so he can use them to get to that blasted princess, but that won't last."

Alanna beamed. "The more I think about it, I don't think it will take months to figure out the tech." She turned to Alexander. "We can do this. Ethan, you'll help too, right?"

The engineer perked up. "Hell yes. I've always wanted to disappear."

Ty covered his face with his hands. "This is crazy."

"Crazy is sitting here and not doing anything." Cal stood and leaned on the edge of the table. "Tomorrow, I'll meet with Orion and talk him into trying the pathogens on a few of the enforcers in the worst shape. Once he sees what Doc can do, he'll be more open to the idea of us leaving so we can get more supplies."

"This is so risky," Ty said.

"If anyone has a better idea, I'll listen."

They all looked at each other. Cal really couldn't blame them for hesitating. This was a sparse plan at best, and too much rode on technology none of them really understood. But even if the cloak didn't work, they'd find another way.

"My goal isn't to fight through enemy lines. We want to sneak in, buy the supplies, and slip out before anyone even knows we're there."

On the other side of the table, Dania frowned, staring at her hands. She was probably feeling helpless again, wishing she could use her powers to assist in some way. There were a lot of enforcers dying on that disabled ship, and the only possible way to save them was manufacturing a large supply of pathogens.

He had to admit this was a long shot, though.

Cal's stomach soured. Ty was right. There were too many things that could go wrong, even if they did figure out the cloak. But he had to try. He wanted to believe it was all about helping the sick enforcers and saving the colony, but he knew it had everything to do with a former general who'd become more a member of this crew, this *family*, than Cal had ever dreamed possible.

He'd save her, no matter what.

He just needed to make sure that *no matter what* didn't get them into even worse trouble.

A GLOW SHIMMERED in the dust particles floating in the air about Orion as he marched from his ship toward the *Star Renegade*. Like before, the commander came on his own. Cal wasn't sure if that was the enforcer's ego, or if none of Orion's people cared if their illustrious leader got shot.

Dania shifted her weight beside him. She hadn't said much about the enforcers, but her silence, in this case, was telling. She was just as nervous about their presence as Cal was.

Doc tromped down the ramp and stood on Cal's other side.

Cal glanced at him. "Welcome to the party, but you don't have to be here."

"Yeah, well, I figured Mr. Attitude would probably have questions that you won't be able to answer."

Problem was, Orion probably wouldn't want to hear the answers. Cal didn't expect this to go well, but it was worth a try.

The enforcer stopped about a meter from the *Star Renegade*'s cargo ramp. "I trust you are not wasting my time."

Cal kept still, doing his best to hold the power position. "That's up to you. How are the sick enforcers?"

"They are not sick. They are weak. They will be fine once we return them to their sponsor."

"Do you really believe that? It's going to take a while to fix your ship."

The enforcer looked past them to the *Star Renegade*. Cal blanched. The *Renegade*'s roomy accommodations were the last thought he wanted to put in the guy's head.

Dania stepped forward. "You've been using Zindiria's enforcers to triangulate her location. How close are you to knowing where she is?"

"We have a navigational direction. It is our belief that if we follow, we will find her."

"When you get within a few hundred thousand *hecten*, you'll need her enforcers to point the way again."

"They are all more than willing to do what needs to be done to find her."

"Even if they die in the process?" Cal asked.

"Yes. Any enforcer would be happy to give their life for their sponsor."

Doc held up his hand like a school kid. "How about if they didn't have to die? What if we could heal them?"

Orion's nose flared. "By polluting them, like you polluted Dania?"

"We saved her," Cal said.

Orion strode forward and leaned into Cal's face. "You ruined her."

"Gentlemen." Dania placed her hand between them. "This is not about any of us or any convoluted need for posturing." She pointed at Orion. "You have been tasked to find the princess. You need her enforcers to do that. I'm sure your healers have already told you that most, if not all of them, wouldn't make it that far."

His eyes narrowed. "How would you know this?"

She lifted her chin. "I'm a general. My lack of power does not change who I am."

Damn, she was beautiful when she took charge.

Orion shook his head. "Inconsequential. My top priority is to find her, no matter the cost. The loss of her enforcers is an acceptable risk to complete my mission."

"Is it?" Doc said. "I hear there's a war going on out there. If I were that princess, and you showed up and told me every one of my elite soldiers was dead, and you could have prevented it, I'd be pretty pissed." He turned to Dania. "Are there any laws preventing a princess from killing her brother's commander if she saw due cause?"

Dania smiled. "No, there's not. And I've met Zindiria. I'm sure there'd be a considerable amount of blood and screaming."

The commander paled, but was that fear of a possibly homicidal princess, or was he working through all that ridiculous programming that told him he always needed to do the right thing to complete his mission?

To Cal's right, Rachel dragged a rectangular luggage box through the sand. She waved at Cal, then gaped at Orion before jumping behind the landing gear. Hopefully, she'd learned enough about enforcers to stay where she was.

Doc took half a step forward, probably realizing they'd found a weakness in Orion's considerable defenses. "Let me ask you a question. Do you plan on bringing Dania back to Geron when this is all over?"

"Of course. She is Geron's only general. She's needed at his side."

Doc held up his pointer finger. "Okay, hold on to that thought. If she is polluted, and irredeemable, then why are you bringing her back and not just executing her? If she's free, he can't use her anymore."

Orion sneered. "There is no such thing as being completely severed from your sponsor. Once we bring her back, Geron will absorb her back into the fold, and it will be as if she'd never left."

Cal cringed, shivering. *Absorb her back…* It sounded like ancient vampire lore.

Doc nodded. "Okay, good. Stay with me here." He pointed at Dania. "If she can be reabsorbed—or whatever—then any of the princess's enforcers who we treat will be able to be reabsorbed, too."

Orion's eyes flicked to the left, as if contemplating that.

"So, we can help keep them alive, and then when you find your princess, she can do whatever it is she does to take them all back, good as new."

Rachel peeked around the landing gear, then jumped behind it again. The dust kicked up around her like she'd tripped on the sand, but her boots didn't appear to move.

Orion's gaze returned to Doc. "Let's say I was considering this. Why would you help them? Your fates are predetermined. You will all be executed one way or another, and Dania will return to her sponsor's side."

That was an easy question. Cal wanted them off the damn planet. He wanted them to leave Stanley alone. These people needed traders, not enforcers.

Cal would have to put a different spin on that truth, though. "At the moment, you're helping the local economy and they're going to fix your ship fast, since you're the only source of income on the planet. I'd hope that you'd spread the word that Kirato is still strong, and that her people are capable and should be placed back on the trade routes."

Orion's eyes narrowed. "Your last wish before your execution will be trade for this planet?"

If it got to that point? "Yes."

"You are an interesting conundrum, Calvin Espinoza." He turned to Doc. "However, this conversation is pointless because you only have the supplies for maintenance doses. Isn't that right?"

"How the hell did you know that?" Cal asked.

Orion glanced at Dania. "I am a commander. Tending to a crashed ship does not change who I am."

Doc shrugged, like he expected the question. "I probably have enough to save one or two of your people with what I have in stock, but we're going to head out and get more supplies. By the time we get back, we hope your ship will be fixed. Then we can treat the rest and send you on your way."

Orion's expression remained blank as he glanced up at the *Star Renegade*. "Your plan has some merit and is worth consideration. Nonetheless, I doubt any of them would knowingly take your treatments."

Knowingly…that was an interesting choice of words. "Would you be willing to force them? After all, that would help your mission."

"That, it would." Orion looked away from the ship. "But the thought disgusts me, so I'd rather let them die. However, that does not change the fact that I have a lost princess to find." He turned to Dania. "You will prepare your ship for our arrival. I will leave a small complement of enforcers here to overlook the repairs. The remainder of my enforcers will be housed in your crew quarters. They will cycle on and off duty between your ship and the star skippers." He looked back at the *Star Renegade*. "We will use your ship to find the princess and bring her back here to collect her cruiser."

Cal gaped. "Like hell you will."

"Your choices are limited, Mr. Espinoza. I need a ship to bring me to the princess."

"Use your own ships."

"I would, but the skippers don't have room for her enforcers, nor do they have medical facilities, or the myriad of legal, as well as illegal, supplies on your ship that we could use in cases of extreme emergency."

This guy had way too much information. "Keep out of my ship's records."

Orion smiled wryly. "Certainly, Mr. Espinoza. As soon as your pilot stops illegally breaking through the security on my ships' files."

"He's kinda got you there," Doc whispered.

Cal folded his arms. "I'm not letting you on my ship."

Orion shrugged. "Fine. Then I will instruct my people to find residences within the colony. Our skipper crafts are too cramped to live in until the ship is repaired." He lifted the comm device on his wrist toward his lips. "I will instruct them to enter the colony *now*."

Now? Had he found out about the ion shield? Did he know it would be operational by morning?

Cal stared him down, trying to connect the dots. How had this gone so wrong?

The enforcer stared at him with blank eyes. He knew very well that Cal didn't want them anywhere near the colony, and Cal had already put his cards on the table telling him that his dying wish would be to protect the people on this planet. They didn't need to discuss Stanley's questionable dealings. The enforcer probably assumed what they'd find.

Cal wiped the sweat from his brow. He'd been played. He'd thought he'd held all the cards, but he'd walked right into a trap of his own making, and he wasn't sure how to get out of it.

D ANIA HOVERED at the entrance to the med bay. In many ways, she didn't want to enter, but she knew it was her duty. She needed to face the fact that they were flying through space with a complement of enforcers on board.

She closed her eyes and steeled herself. As soon as Orion had boarded, the enforcers had moved into temporary sleeping compartments Ethan and Ty had set up in the back of the cargo deck. Orion had tried to insist that he and his healthy enforcers be given upper-deck quarters, even if it meant displacing the crew, but Doc had made a valid argument for the stronger enforcers to watch over those who were waning.

In reality, Cal had wanted the enforcers contained so they couldn't wander through the ship, which was understandable. Doc had created a large, spherical containment field to make sure none of them tried to walk through walls, as Dania had done that night she'd relayed the *Star Renegade*'s location to Prince Geron.

She lowered her eyes. That seemed like so long ago, and she still dealt with a deep ache in her stomach any time she thought about how easily her sponsor had manipulated her into telling him exactly what he'd needed, no matter the threat to the crew she'd come to care about. She wanted to consider herself free, but Orion's words echoed in her mind.

There is no such thing as being completely severed from your sponsor.

She wanted this to be a lie, or simply him repeating what he'd been taught to be true, but deep down, she wondered, or maybe *knew*, her days with this crew may be numbered. Her only hope was if this came to pass, that Cal would have the smarts to stay far, far away. Because General Dania DuBane had no friends and would show no mercy to smugglers.

She rubbed her eyes and shrugged off the thought. The truth was, she belonged in two worlds, and somehow, she needed to force both sides to be okay with this.

She took a step toward the med bay doors. Five of the sickest enforcers had been taken here to be placed under Alexander's care. Cal had agreed because there was no way any of them could get up and walk around the ship, let alone cause any harm. Unfortunately, three of them had already died, despite the crew's efforts.

Deep down, she'd wanted to avoid this place, but the two who'd survived were her kind, and she couldn't ignore them, no matter what they thought of her.

She placed her hand on the entry pad. Inside, Alexander tapped on a computer panel in the wall. Rachel handed the doctor a damp cloth while he administered to one of two male enforcers lying on gurneys in the back of the room. Their hair hung limp on their pillows—still, like a human's. Their eyes were closed and their breathing shallow.

Dania shivered. Had she looked so sickly before she'd recovered?

Alanna held up one of the enforcer's heads, trying to help him sip from a small cup. He choked on the water, and she whispered something to him as she eased him back to his pillow.

Dania gritted her teeth as she walked toward Alexander. "Haven't you tried to heal them?"

He tapped on the screen twice before turning to her. "No."

She gaped at him. "No? Why not?"

"Because as the doctor keeps telling me, my powers are finite. I should only be using them as a last resort."

Dania placed her hand on the forehead of one of the unconscious enforcers. His damp skin chilled her fingers. "This doesn't look like an emergency to you?"

Alexander closed his eyes and sighed. "I can't think of myself anymore."

In the back of the room, Alanna helped the enforcer lie back down. Alexander stared at her like he'd stared at those ancient engineering schematics he'd been drawn to at the space travel museums on Hitus.

His brow furrowed before he turned back to Dania. "I need to take into consideration how using my powers may affect others."

"What are you talking about?"

"Dania?" Alanna patted the shoulder of the enforcer in the bed. "This nice gentleman would like to talk to you."

Dania took a deep breath. She'd known the time would come when she'd be berated by their new passengers, but she'd hoped to avoid it as long as she could.

She moved beside the bed, and the enforcer grabbed her wrist.

His eyes seemed foggy as he turned to her. "General. It hurts."

She held his hand. "I know." There had been times where everything had ached, and she had never been as far gone as this man.

He closed his eyes, gasping for breath. "Will you help us? P-Please?"

Her chest tightened. Everything inside her screamed to hold her hands over him, to send energy from her own core, through his skin, and into his veins. But this was no longer an option. "I wish I could help you, but I can't. I have no more power."

He blinked hard, as if trying to clear up his sight. "But you're not in d-distress. You're s-standing like nothing's wrong."

The doctor moved to the side of the bed and ran a red light over the enforcer's forehead. "They're all waning pretty fast."

"What do you expect?" Rachel moved a stack of towels from the recycler to a table beside the beds. "Two of them were already dead when they were dropped off."

Dania's heart clenched. "There has to be something we can do."

Peter shook his head. "Our boy Orion made Alexander swear not to give them pathogens, so there isn't anything we can do but keep them comfortable."

Dania frowned. "Isn't that the whole reason they're here?"

Rachel placed her hands on her hips. "Apparently, we're only approved to use pathogens if more than half of them die. Commander Annoying said he only needs twenty of them to complete his precious mission. I'm telling you, the guy's got serious issues."

Peter nodded. "He's not even worried about the body count...as long as he finds that princess."

The man on the gurney coughed. A small bubble of red appeared on the edge of his lip and dribbled down his cheek. He blinked several times before meeting Dania's gaze again. "I can't die like this...in a smuggler's ship. I n-need to serve my s-sponsor."

Dania held his hand again. "You have, and you've served her well."

He pulled his hand away. "We failed her. We all failed her, and now we are being punished." He coughed again, and a spray of blood speckled the white blankets covering him.

"Alexander!" Dania cried.

He appeared beside her, while Rachel pulled up a metal frame with a bag of fluids attached to it.

Doc placed a needle in the dying enforcer's arm. "This is electrolytes."

Alexander nodded, but he still checked the bag before he allowed Rachel to start the flow. His brow furrowed, and he frowned. She could sense the inner war going on inside him... The doctor who wanted to help, and the enforcer who could not disregard a direct order.

She waited for him to raise his hands to help heal, but instead, he stood beside her, watching as the doctor started the electrolyte drip.

"Aren't you going to do something?"

Alexander glanced at Alanna, who bit her lower lip, looking at them as she attended to another enforcer. "I can't. He needs a feeding. This isn't something that can be repaired."

He was right, but it was unlike him not to at least try.

Alexander leaned close to her ear. "It's also unlike *you* not to try."

She closed her eyes and didn't meet his gaze. She needed to be more cautious with her thoughts. Still, he knew she didn't have natural pathogens, but he, like the others, would probably blame these enforcers' deaths on her inability to help. They'd be wrong, but at the same time, they'd be completely right. And she didn't know which end of the spectrum she stood on.

The dying enforcer gurgled a breath and reached for her. His gaze was weak but imploring. He may have hated her for what she'd done to herself, but he still looked to her, the only general available, to help him as only a general could.

She steeled herself, taking a deep breath. "I'm going to feed him."

Both Peter and Alexander gaped at her. "What?"

"I need to try."

Alexander turned to Peter. "What could happen?"

Peter shrugged. "Umm, my guess would be that nothing would happen, but I've done all I can by giving him fluids, so give it your best shot."

Dania placed her hands over the enforcer and took a deep breath. What pathogens she may have, she didn't need anymore. All she needed to do was to give them to this man. She couldn't save all of them, but maybe she could save one.

Alanna moved behind her and rubbed her palm on Dania's back. "You got this."

Dania certainly hoped so.

She placed her hands on the enforcer's chest and searched inside her. A slight warmth swirled in her stomach, both familiar and calming. The sensation filled her like a hug from an old friend.

No—not an old friend—from her prince. She didn't need Geron anymore, nor did she want his power. Maybe this was a way to get rid of whatever remnants of her sponsor might be left. She focused, concentrating his strength into a ball, and then pushed, gritting her teeth and shooting the energy through her palms.

The enforcer jolted, trembling as her skin started to chill.

There, it was done. She'd given him all she had. Her stomach roiled and burned, twisting and knotting. She grabbed the edge of the bed and a slight haze coated her vision.

"Dania?" Alexander gripped her arm, but his voice sounded far-off, as if he'd called her name from another room.

Her gut clenched, and bile burned her throat as the man in the bed started to scream.

"Dania!" Alexander gripped her face and his hands warmed, but his power didn't flood her with the welcome chill of his healing strength.

She fell to her knees and vomited. Alanna shrieked as the enforcer coughed and vomited from the bed.

Alexander ran to him, then backed away, looking from the enforcer to Dania.

Peter shoved him back. "Alexander, get out."

He shook his head. "They are supposed to be under my care."

Dania's stomach clenched again, and she retched. Her throat burned.

Peter shoved Alexander again. "Get the hell out." He turned to Alanna. "Get him out of here."

"Why?" Alanna's eyes grew wide as Peter grabbed several of the vials from the back of the room and Rachel replaced the enforcer's IV.

Alexander shook his head. "I can't let you give him pathogens."

Peter kept preparing the vials. "They're for Dania. Now get out."

Dania wiped her mouth as Alexander eyed the two vials. The enforcer in the bed coughed, and more blood sprayed across the bed and floor.

Alanna grabbed Alexander's hand. "Come on. We have to go."

Alexander grimaced. Dania could see him fighting his programming.

"Go," Dania said, her voice harsh and raspy. "That's an order."

He glanced at her and nodded, allowing Alanna to draw him from the room. He knew very well what Doc was going to do. If anyone asked him, he could tell the truth and say the Doctor had promised to only treat Dania.

Now the only question was, would the pathogens save the broken enforcers as they'd saved her?

CHAPTER 26
ALANna

ALANNA TUGGED Alexander from the room and slapped her palm on the door control.

"Wait!" Alexander took a step toward the med bay door. "I can't allow him to pollute their blood."

Alanna drew him away. "Doc said he was only treating Dania."

Alexander struggled, but only slightly. "He had two vials."

"Well, Dania looked pretty sick."

He snorted a laugh and shook his head. "I'm not a fool."

"No, you're not. You're also a heck of a lot stronger than me, so part of you wants to believe that both those vials are for Dania, or you would have forced yourself back into that room already."

Alexander rubbed his face. "It's wrong to infect his body with synthetics against his will."

"How do you know it's against his will?" She turned him toward her. "Did anyone tell him that there was a treatment that may help him live long enough to get back to his princess?"

Alexander looked down.

Alanna had arrived at the med bay with Alexander, so she already knew the answer to that question. Those poor guys had been dropped off by healthier enforcers like pieces of meat—or lost causes they'd expected to die. Alanna had known there wasn't much she could have done to help them, but she'd stayed to make those poor men as comfortable as she could.

She gave Alexander a gentle tug toward the ladder, and thankfully, he complied, but his arm trembled beneath her grip.

He stopped at the top of the stairs and looked back in the direction of the med bay. "I don't feel well."

"Don't be silly. You're fine. Anyway, Doc is a little busy right now."

He grabbed the rungs. "This isn't the kind of illness he can help."

That sounded ominous. She followed him down the ladder.

He held his head low as they walked toward the crew quarters. She knew this was an internal struggle, and something that he needed to get over on his own, but the whole idea of treating someone who was sick seemed like such a no-brainer. She wished she could help him see that.

He stopped at the doorway to his room and placed his palms on either side of the archway. His hands trembled on the steel frame. "It hurts. I can't."

"What hurts? What can't you do?" But that was obvious. The prince still had a hold on him, even after all this time.

He placed his right hand on his chest. "It burns. I'm being punished."

She placed her palm on his back. "That's ridiculous."

He swatted her hand away. "It's not ridiculous. You have no idea." His face turned red as he grabbed his temples. He growled, backing up against his door before a sob burst free. "This is wrong. It's not fair." He choked out another sob, then another.

Ethan passed by the window inside lower engineering on the other side of the hall. The last thing she needed was for him to see Alexander crying. Ethan being *Ethan* would only make this worse.

She pulled Alexander's hand from his temple and placed it on the door control. He looked over his shoulder again but didn't struggle as she pulled him inside.

Alanna shivered, but not from the cold. The walls were stark white. The tables and counters were empty, and the bed was tightly made, without even a pillow on it. How could an actual person live here?

"No." Alexander stumbled back to the door. "I can't do this. I need to go back."

"No, you don't." Alanna leapt to the panel beside the exit and keyed in a locking code.

He tilted his head, raising a brow. "You know I can break through that."

"You can, but you won't."

"I need to."

"No, you don't." She grabbed the sides of his face. "I need to speak to Alexander the doctor, not Alexander the enforcer."

"They are the same person."

"No, they're not, and I think you're starting to realize that. I need you to think like a doctor."

He blinked and looked away from her. At least he wasn't disagreeing anymore.

Alexander turned and held up trembling hands. "You cannot fathom what's going on inside me." He brought his palms to his face again and started to sob.

Holy heck, this guy was in the middle of a meltdown.

When Alanna had been fifteen, she'd freaked out when her boyfriend had broken up with her. Alanna had sobbed uncontrollably, just like this, until her mom had intervened. What she'd done had been so simple, and probably wouldn't work for a full-grown man, but it was worth a try.

"Come on." She drew him toward the bed and made him sit.

"I'm not tired."

"I didn't say you were." She walked across the room and opened the closet. Three blankets and two sets of sheets lay square on the shelves, looking like they'd never been touched since being removed from the recyclers. She grabbed two pillows from the top shelf. "Here." She handed him one and placed the other on the top of the bed. "Lie on that pillow and hug the one in your hands."

He frowned at her. "That is not going to change the fact that a crime is being committed."

Alanna narrowed her eyes and pointed at the pillow on the bed. "Lie down. That's an order, soldier."

He stared at her for a moment. His cheek twitched before he complied.

"Good. Now hug the other pillow tight."

He grimaced. "This is ridiculous. We're wasting time."

Alanna took a deep breath. She had said something

similar to her mother all those years ago, and her mom had done something unexpected. It had worked on her teenage self, but would it work on an enforcer?

If her mother had been there, she'd have cautioned against it, but Alexander needed help, and her mother had always taught her that it was okay to break a few rules if you have the right intentions. Hopefully, this wouldn't backfire on her.

Walking to the other side of the bed, Alanna sat on the mattress and then laid down behind him. Steeling herself, she spooned up against his back.

Alexander tensed against her embrace. "What are you doing?"

Alanna cringed at the outraged tone in his voice. Was the thought of her lying beside him really that disgusting to him? Was that why he'd drawn away from her at the waterfall?

She shook away the affront. It didn't matter. That wasn't why she was here.

Closing her eyes, she tightened her grip on him.

"Stop," Alexander hissed.

She shook her head. "Nope. I'm not letting go. You need to understand that you're not alone. There are people here who care about you and not because they were ordered to. You have friends."

He curled in on himself, hugging the pillow tighter. "You don't know what you're doing."

"I know perfectly well what I'm doing. You need help, and friends help each other."

"You don't understand."

"I understand perfectly. I get that you have a war going on in your head."

His muscles tightened beneath her grip.

How could she get through to him? "You're the only one who can win this, Alexander. You have to relax and let go. Deep down, you know what we're doing is right."

His long hair shifted against her cheek as he shook his head. "It's not right. I can't."

His body cooled beneath her hands...or maybe her own hands heated up. It was an odd sensation she'd also experienced holding Dania when she'd been sick in the med bay. Was it some kind of strange enforcer thing?

"Alanna, please let me go."

"No way. I'm not letting go until you relax."

"I don't want to hurt you."

Hurt her? What was that supposed to mean?

Could that stinking prince still have so much power over him that Alexander might hurt a friend to stop what he thought was a law being broken?

She tightened her grip again. It didn't matter. She wasn't giving up on him.

"I care about you, Alexander. You need to get that through your thick enforcer head and relax."

He let out a long, slow breath, almost like a sigh. Some of his hair started to float around her face, tickling her nose.

"I'm sorry," he whispered.

Her head swam a little, and her eyes grew heavy. She held down his floating hair with her palm. "There's nothing to be sorry about. I know all these confusing emotions are hard, but you'll get used to them. And I'm here for you, no matter what."

He huffed a slight laugh and shook his head again, but his muscles relaxed.

It had to be so hard for them. Both he and Dania had grown up believing there was only right or wrong—nothing in between. What she was asking him to do was change who he was deep down inside. If placed in the same position, she wasn't sure she'd be able to do it. Still, she liked Alexander—maybe a little too much. She wanted to help him, just like they'd all helped Dania.

His breaths became deep and rhythmic, and his grip on the pillow laxed. Alanna smiled. At a bare minimum, she'd at least gotten him to sleep. Hopefully, when he woke up, he'd see reason and know that letting Doc help that enforcer was the right thing to do.

Her hands heated up again and Alexander moaned in his sleep. His hair started to sway gently like a breeze had kicked up in the room. Did all enforcers' hair float when they slept? Maybe, since it seemed to drift about a lot when they were just walking around, and none of them even seemed to notice. She drew her hands along his chest, and his skin seemed to chill, then heat beneath her touch. So...*strange.*

He moaned again, and she drew her hand away.

How creepy could you be, Alanna—feeling a guy up in his sleep?

He'd made it more than obvious he wasn't interested. Why would he be? He was beautiful in every way...other than the standard enforcer pigheadedness. He could probably snap his fingers in the middle of a way-station and have any woman he wanted.

Alanna's eyes grew heavier, and she blinked, easing her hands off him. She needed to get out of there. She sighed, rubbing her face as she sat on the edge of the bed. The last thing she needed was to fall asleep here. How awkward would that be for both of them when they woke up in the morning?

She made her way to the door and held on to the wall as her head started to swim. Why was she so tired all of the sudden? Her legs felt leaden beneath her, as if the gravity had increased a hundred times.

Alexander muttered in his sleep. He was so handsome and looked so normal while he was resting.

Making repairs and spending time with him had been so easy, so *comfortable*. She looked forward to their time together in ways that she really shouldn't have, and she knew that was bad.

He'd made it clear that he would jump on the first transport back home at any given moment. Falling for this guy was a one-way ticket to heartache, but she wasn't sure how to stop this meteor shower after it had already started.

Taking a deep breath, she unlocked the door and stepped into the hall. She needed to get Alexander out of her head. As her mother had always warned her, she gave away her heart too easily.

She supposed that was why Ethan was in permanent friend-zone, despite his pleas for her affection. After the last man she'd loved had sold her out to pirates, she'd sworn off romance. After all, caring for someone that deeply only led to hurt. She'd wanted a family when she'd joined this crew, not another chance at heartache.

She placed her palm over the door control. Inside, Alexander's chest rose and fell in gentle cadence. He may not intentionally hurt her as the others had, but him leaving would be just as bad. She needed to cut this off before it turned into anything she'd regret.

She tapped the control and the door closed. Her chest clenched as she walked toward her own quarters.

Leaving him was the right thing to do.

He didn't want her anyway.

So why did it hurt so bad?

CHAPTER 27
CAL

CAL PLACED his hand on Dania's forehead. She breathed heavily in the low light, her eyes twitching like she may have been having a dream. From the pinch in her brow, he'd have to guess it wasn't a good one.

About an hour ago, Orion had sent Doc three more unconscious enforcers. The commander was like a crazed dictator, making demands of his people without any regard to their health. It wasn't right, but at the moment, Cal only cared about the woman lying beside him.

Rachel smiled at him as she checked the readings on a machine hooked up to one of the enforcers. "She's lucky to have you, ya know?"

Cal nodded, but he wasn't really sure what she meant.

Rachel patted his shoulder before she walked toward the rear of the room. "She knows you're here, even all sleepy-like."

Cal hoped so. No matter how many times she ended up in the med bay, he'd never get used to her looking so helpless.

Doc approached, wiping a flask with a white towel. "How's our girl?"

Cal wished he knew. "I was going to ask you the same thing."

"Well, as usual, I'm winging this. I gave her a shot of pathogens and something to stop the vomiting. Now she's just asleep." Doc placed the flask beside the recycler. "I won't know more until she wakes up, but for now, I think it's best to just let her rest."

Cal sighed, nodding. They'd explained to him that Dania had tried to share pathogens with an enforcer who'd been close to death. Part of him was angry that she'd even risked it, but he couldn't fault her for trying to save one of her own.

"Do you know why she got so sick?"

Doc placed the flask on the table beside Dania's bed. "For sure? No. My educated guess is that she tried to make her artificial pathogens do something they weren't meant to do. And it had negative consequences for both of them."

Across the room, the latest casualties of Orion's quest to find his sponsor's sister lay in their beds with white blankets pulled up to their chins, the rise and fall of their chests the only thing proving they were still alive. At this rate, Orion was going to fill the med bay with unconscious enforcers.

"Which one did she try to save?" Cal asked.

Doc walked over to the bed on the far right. "This guy."

"Is he going to make it?"

Doc nodded. "Looks good so far." He pointed to the enforcer in the bed beside him. "After I treated one, I accidentally on purpose treated the other one. They both stabilized pretty quickly. I think I'm getting better at this."

That was good news. "I'm glad. Dania would have been crushed if she woke up and either of them had died."

"Yeah, but we're going to have to fess up to Mr. Grouchy Pants and tell him what we've done. It's going to be hard to hide that they're getting better."

"I guess we'll just have to deal with that when the time comes. You did the right thing." Cal looked to the other beds. "What about the newcomers?"

"They're stable for now. I have pathogens slated for each of them if that changes."

Rachel returned and adjusted the drip going into one of the enforcers' arms. "You gotta tell him the exciting news!"

"What exciting news?" Cal asked.

"I don't know if it's *news*, exactly, but it's a fun fact." Doc pointed at the computer screen on the wall. "I did a little more research on the blood testing that was done on our girl when she was a kid, and I discovered in the records that she has a birthday coming up...in two days."

Rachel clapped her hands. "Can we have a party?"

"I'm not so sure a party is a good idea." Doc raised a brow at Cal. "At least not one with the entire crew."

"Boo!" Rachel folded her arms. "No fair!"

"We're kind of in the middle of an emergency here," Cal pointed out. "Enforcers and all. Remember?"

"All the better reason to have a party!"

Cal held up a hand. "Maybe I'll just discuss it with Dania first."

Rachel pushed out her lip. "No hiding and yelling, *Surprise!*? That's the best part."

"Not this year."

The comm on the wall pinged and Ty's voice came over

the speaker. "Boss, I'm bringing our illustrious guest up to the lounge. He's insisting on talking to you."

Great. Now what? "I'll be right there."

"Want a wingman?" Doc asked.

"When dealing with enforcers? Always."

Cal pushed through the doorway and headed down the hall toward the lounge.

"What do you think he wants this time?" Doc asked.

"I'm going to take a wild guess and say he wants to complain about something."

Cal tapped the access pad and the lounge door opened.

Orion's voice boomed from within. "You will do as you're told!"

Ty folded his arms. "I haven't done what I've been told since I was in diapers. I'm sure not gonna start now."

Cal stepped inside. "What's going on?"

Orion glared at him. "Your first mate is being insolent."

Cal bit back his grin. "Welcome to my world."

"Our *guest* wants me to change course." Ty walked over to the food compartments and grabbed a bag out of one of the storage containers. "I told him I don't have authority to do that without your approval."

That wasn't *exactly* true, but Ty and his silver tongue knew how to talk his way out of not doing things he didn't want to do.

Ty popped a snack square into his mouth and crunched it.

Orion's glare returned to Cal. "I gave him coordinates. We need to reach that location expediently."

"I guess that means you have the location of your princess?" Cal asked.

"We have a definitive direction and a possible location.

We believe this enforcer's link to her is stronger than the others'. We need to follow while we still can."

Doc inched forward. *"While we still can? Does that mean I can expect a new patient in the near future?"*

"Possibly, if he survives. His link is the strongest we've encountered, and we will draw on whatever strength he has until he can no longer provide a direction."

"Whoa there." Ty stopped crunching and swallowed. *"Until he can no longer provide a direction?* Three enforcers are already dead. You can't be pushing those people any more than you already have."

"Death is an agreeable outcome for any enforcer in the service of their sponsor."

Ty threw the open bag back into the storage container. "Yeah, in the service of *their* sponsor, not in the service of *you.* This is your mission, not theirs."

"I am seeking their princess. Our goals are the same."

"Are ya sure? Did you ask them what their goals were?"

"I am not arguing with you about this. If he dies, it is an acceptable loss to bring us closer to our goal."

"I doubt *he* thinks so."

Orion's nose flared. "What he thinks is irrelevant."

"You know what?" Ty advanced and pointed at the enforcer's chest. "You're an asshole."

The enforcer's hair lifted, and Cal moved between them. "Gentlemen, this isn't getting us anywhere."

"You know I'm right." Ty shoved Cal and crossed the room.

A trickle of light formed around Orion's fingers. Ty was farther away, but nowhere near far enough from a fully-charged enforcer.

Cal stood firm. "I need my pilot. I can't fly the ship

while I'm sleeping. If anything happens to him, it will slow us down."

The light fizzled away. Orion continued to stare at Ty before turning to Cal. "You will change course and order your crew to comply with any directions I give them."

Was he out of his mind? "That's not going to happen. My crew takes directions from me and only me. Send me the course change." As long as they were still heading in the general direction of Z8, he'd humor them as much as possible.

"If I may interject." Doc waved his fingers at them. "If you're going to be sending me a half-dead enforcer every day, my med bay is going to get really full, really fast. I don't have the supplies or the manpower to…"

"Our readings show that the first two I sent to you are improving."

"The first two who came to me *alive* are improving."

"Semantics." Orion's expression didn't change. "As soon as they are able, I will place them back in rotation to provide our course. This will give you room to treat more. You will continue to heal them and…"

"You want me to heal them so you can try to kill them again? I don't think so. And those two enforcers are on the mend, but that just means they're still breathing. It may be weeks or months before they can even stand."

"I don't need them to stand. I just need them conscious so they can point the way to the princess."

Doc gaped at him before his face reddened. "Ty is right. You're an asshole."

Orion turned to Cal. "Mr. Espinoza, you will control your crew, or I will control them for you."

Cal folded his arms. "No, you won't. You're going to

shut the hell up and be a more considerate passenger. Because I happen to agree with them. You *are* an asshole."

"There is nothing to stop me from taking over this ship. Your help, or even your presence, is not necessary."

Ty snorted. "It is if you want our doctor to help you. And do you actually think we'd let you on board if we thought you could take our ship?" He turned to Cal. "How's that faulty airlock in the cargo bay doing?"

Cal loved when Ty was quick on his feet. With nearly all of Orion's *disposable* enforcers in their cargo bag, they definitely had some leverage.

He folded his arms. "It's pretty bad. It could blow at any moment and shoot everything down there into space."

The enforcer's eyes darkened. "You wouldn't dare."

Cal leaned closer. "Watch me. And this ship, as you are aware, is highly modified. Without a member of the crew, the systems will shut down. It's a little trick we learned to make sure no one steals the ship when we land."

The tech existed, but not on the *Star Renegade*. Keeping the food and fuel stocked always seemed more important than security. The enforcers didn't know that, though.

Cal steadied his breathing, keeping his gaze locked with the enforcer's. All he needed to do was keep his temperature in check. Maybe he was already mad enough that Commander Grouchy Pants wouldn't notice the lie.

Orion's cheek twitched before he turned to Doc. "How are you treating the princess's enforcers? Can we give the others the same treatment to keep them from getting sick?"

Doc shrugged. "Maybe. But you're not going to like it."

He sneered. "You gave them an artificial feeding. I ordered Alexander...."

Doc held up his hands. "Alex wasn't there. Our boy has to sleep once in a while. This one's on me."

"You've committed a crime."

"Hey, I'm a doctor. Hippocratic Oath and all that. If I have the ability to save someone, I need to do it. That's the law."

"You are not a doctor. You are an illegally practicing charlatan experimenting with things you don't understand."

Doc held up his pointer finger. "I am an illegally practicing charlatan experimenting with things I understand better and better each day—and I have two very much living enforcers down there to prove it."

"Listen," Ty said. "Those coordinates you gave me are inside a hot zone. There's a good chance we're going to need to fight our way in, scoop up your princess, and fight our way out. Would it really be that terrible to have extra enforcers who can actually stand up when we get there?"

Orion sighed. "That would be preferable."

Ty held up his palm. "Then how about you tone down the superiority complex a little bit and give Doc a chance to work his magic?"

"What he's doing is hardly magic."

"That's right," Doc said. "It's science. And two people you dropped off and left for dead are getting better because of it."

Orion glanced at Cal and then to the floor.

That's it… Work it out. This is your only option. And maybe if they are all healthy, we can grab you a nice new ship so you can save your princess on your own.

The commander raised his gaze. "You will continue to

treat the enforcers as they weaken. It is preferable that they are alive when we arrive."

"That's the trick," Doc said. "I don't have enough supplies to keep them all alive if you keep running them to the ground like you are."

"We need to stop for supplies," Cal said.

Ty tapped on a screen. "There's a supply base not far off your coordinates. We can land, get what we need to keep your people vertical, and shoot back into space before you even know we stopped."

"I assure you, I'll know you've stopped."

Cal struggled to keep from rolling his eyes like a child. "The point is, no one will have to die. It's a good option. You might not like Doc's methods, but right now, he's your only option. As we pointed out when you first got on board, that princess is going to be pretty ticked off if you arrive and all of her enforcers are dead."

Orion closed his eyes and took a deep breath.

There you go... Just work all that through your enforcer brain. This will get you one step closer to your princess, and you'll have a better chance of her not killing you when you get there.

Orion raised his head. "Get your supplies. I will *not* allow you to pollute the blood of the conscious enforcers. However, I will allow you to treat those who are near death."

Doc rubbed his forehead. "Don't you get it? They don't have to get that far. There's no need to torture them."

"I will not need to make that decision for them. They will each be given a choice: vile, unnatural treatment, or death." He lifted his chin. "I, for one, would rather die, and believe me, they will, too."

"Then why are you even agreeing to stop for supplies?" Cal asked.

"Because, as you said, the princess will not be happy if her enforcers are dead. It will behoove me to make sure they are alive when we get there."

Cal's nose flared. "Wait a minute. You're saying that you'll keep them alive after you've worked them nearly to death, but you won't allow us to treat them early to keep them from getting to that point in the first place?"

"Correct."

"You *really are* an asshole."

"And you *really are* trying my patience. Get your supplies and get back on course, Mr. Espinoza. If it takes more than two days, I will be agitated."

Two days? Hopefully, that would be long enough for his team to come up with a plan for getting out of this ridiculously one-sided agreement.

ALANNA TIGHTENED THE WIRING, readying the tech to receive ultraviolet boosts from the reactor's solar stores. As exciting as it should seem, she couldn't enjoy the fact that they were working on creating a cloaking device. Two more enforcers had shown up in the med bay that morning.

One had died before Doc could treat him. And the two who had dropped them off had moved slowly and had dark bags under their eyes, which meant that even Orion's healthy enforcers were feeling the strain. There seemed like too much at stake to have fun.

Alanna sat back, wiping the sweat from her forehead. "I just don't get it. Those poor people are so sick."

Alexander closed the panel he'd been working on. "You're talking about the enforcers?"

"Yeah. Did you see them? They look ten times worse than Dania ever did. And maybe even worse than you did when we picked you up."

"Your point?"

"I just don't understand why they won't take the pathogens. I mean, it'll save their lives."

"I think they realize that, but they also see that Dania seems less dependent on her sponsor."

"But that's a good thing."

He folded his arms and leaned against the wall. "In your eyes, it is, but not in the eyes of an enforcer."

"How can getting well be a bad thing?"

"Any one of those enforcers is still dependent enough that they would see the artificial pathogens as a possible way to sever their link to their sponsor. They didn't defend that princess to the point of exhaustion out of duty. The link between a sponsor and an enforcer is incredibly strong. Like family." He pushed away from the wall. "In fact, the title Dania and I designate for our sponsor is *Ada*, which loosely translates to *father*."

He smiled slightly, and his gaze seemed far away. Could he really love that prince so much, despite knowing he'd changed them all at a cellular level?

Alexander lifted his gaze to hers. "No enforcer in their right mind would do anything that might possibly sever the link to their sponsor."

"Even if it means thinking for themselves and making their own choices?"

His brow pinched. "Making your own choices may be the hardest part. I know for you that seems easy, but it's not."

Her chest tightened. She remembered Dania struggling, but she'd seemed to work through all this so much faster. If there was anything she could do to help Alexander, Alanna would do it, but the reality was, it all came down to one thing. He needed to *want* to be saved.

"I've seen you looking at the pathogens Peter is making.

Are you having second thoughts? Would you ever consider trying them?"

His lips pursed. "To be honest, I'm not sure anymore."

Wait. *What?*

Alanna froze. Last time Alexander had started making a breakthrough, she'd said something dumb and ruined it. But every ounce of her wanted to jump on this...maybe even drag him to the med bay so they were already there in case he made the right choice.

His eyes met hers again. His gaze intent, searching... just like it had been under the waterfall. A tingle started in her tummy and shot straight down to her toes.

Hol-ee-mashed potatoes. That look in the waterfall hadn't been her imagination.

Her mother's voice rose to her thoughts. *If a boy ever looks at you like that, Alanna, you best be running in the other direction.*

But she didn't run. Her feet remained cemented to the ground as she stared right back. Could it be possible? Could *she* be the reason he was considering freedom?

He broke their stare and looked back to the panel he'd just closed. "I think with a little more work, we may be able to do a controlled test."

Test? Oh, yeah...cloaking device. The job of their dreams.

Her stomach sank, and she wanted to kick herself. She should have been excited about a systems test. Overjoyed. But like a little lost schoolgirl, all she wanted was for him to look at her like that again. What was wrong with her?

He looked over his shoulder. "Do you have trepidations about the testing? I'd never put anyone at risk if I thought it wouldn't work."

"No, no, that's not it. It's just…" Skies, his eyes were a brilliant, icy blue.

"Are you all right?"

Staring, Alanna. You're staring at him.

She blinked, clearing her throat. "Yeah, sorry. I'm fine. And yes, testing would be good. Great, even." *But those eyes…*

This was ridiculous! She needed to focus on the real stuff. The important stuff…like cloaking devices and Alexander considering the fake pathogens!

Maybe she just needed a break.

She grabbed her bag. "Do you want to grab a bite to eat?"

"Certainly. It's well past mealtime." He motioned to the ladder.

Alanna grabbed the rungs and headed to upper engineering. If he'd been Ethan, she'd have made him go first, thinking his intentions were less-than-gentlemanly, but Alexander barely looked up as he grabbed his own bag and followed.

Cal's voice carried into the hall as they neared the lounge. "I'm not giving you free run of the ship."

Orion's demanding tenor answered. "Why? I refuse to be stored in the cargo area like contraband."

"*You* refuse? So, it's okay for the rest of your people to be down there?"

Alanna sighed. It sounded like Cal was doing just as good as always.

She placed her hand on Alexander's chest, stopping his gait. "Let me get some food. We'll find somewhere else to eat." The last thing she wanted was for Orion to start spouting orders at Alexander. She wasn't sure if he'd have to listen, but avoidance was a perfectly acceptable way to make sure he was able to finish the project with her.

Alanna eased into the doorway and shuffled over to the food cubbies.

Orion scowled at her. "I see your navigator has run of the ship."

Cal huffed. "She's a trusted part of my crew."

"Are you saying that you don't trust me?"

"That might just be the most ridiculous question you've ever asked me."

Alanna bit back her smile as she shoved a few supplement packets into her bag, not even taking the time to check the contents. Orion knew she'd been working with Alexander, and it was only a matter of time before he asked where he was. Not meeting either of their gazes, she slipped back through the door.

"Are you actually going to let her get away with entering a room and not acknowledging you?" Orion asked.

"Why in Jupiter's moons would I need her to acknowledge me? She was probably trying to get away from you."

Alanna tapped the panel to close the door.

Alexander snorted a laugh. "Do you think your captain needs help?"

"Nah. Personally, I think Cal likes fighting with him. It's a heck of a lot safer to fight with words than artillery or magic mojo."

It would be interesting, though, to see if Orion ended up with one of the spare crew quarters while the rest of his people made do in the cargo hold.

She pointed her thumb toward the stairway. "Do you want to head down to the crew quarters to eat? It'll be a little quieter than the lounge right now."

"I don't have a table in my room."

"That's okay. I do. The guys were super accommodating when I came on board. I mean, my table isn't as big as Cal's, but it'll do for a simple meal and discussing the next steps to making us disappear."

She opened the door to her room and stepped inside.

Alexander wavered in the hall.

Placing her bag on the small table, she waved him in. "Are you coming?"

He took a deep breath before nodding. He looked at the walls, the floor, the furniture. "Your quarters are larger than mine."

"Yeah, the guys are all sweet. They said girls need more room, which is silly, but I guess they wanted me to feel welcome."

She motioned to the table, and they sat.

Alexander opened up a cereal bar. "I think after allowing the circuits to charge, we can run a few small bursts of electricity through the wiring to see how they hold up."

"Electricity isn't as strong as what we're going to put through that thing."

"No, but it will be enough to show the sensors any leaks or breaks in our system matrix before we flood it with power that might damage the ship."

Her eyes widened. "Good call. I think I'll have Ethan look at that with us."

He nodded. "Agreed. He seems to be the most familiar with the enemy's technology."

Did that mean Alexander had doubts about his own work?

"Hey." She reached over and covered his hand with

hers. "You did good down there. You had lots of great ideas, and you're fast with the technical stuff. Don't second-guess what we did. Ethan's just a safety net."

He didn't look up from her hand. "I know."

He seemed to study her skin. The edges of his hair lifted slightly before he pulled his hand away.

"Are you okay?"

"No. I'm not. This is wrong." He stood. "Everything is wrong."

"What do you mean?"

He rubbed his face. "I enjoyed working on the cloak with you. I enjoyed creating an ion shield. I enjoyed your…" He glanced at her. "This is all just wrong."

"Why? Why is it wrong to enjoy doing things?"

"We're supposed to complete our missions. We're supposed to return to our sponsors. Returning expediently ensures that this won't happen."

"Ensures *what* won't happen?"

His eyes seemed glassy when he looked at her. "The more time I spend with you, the less I think about my prince."

Holy molten transistor cores. "That's good."

"No. It's bad. I'm supposed to be stronger than this."

"You *are* strong, Alex. Even Dania says so."

He dragged his fingers through his hair, tugging at the roots. "Then why don't I want to go back?"

Wait… Had he decided to take Doc's pathogens?

She grabbed his hands again. "Alexander, I don't want you to go back there, either. None of us do. You're a member of this crew now. You're welcome here."

His hair took flight again as she gripped him. "I'm not strong enough."

"Yes, you are. You've proven it over and over."

He shook his head. "I've only proven that I'm weak." He pulled away again. "I can't keep doing this. I need to find a way to go back."

But he'd just said he wanted to stay!

"You don't have to go back. We don't want you to." She grabbed his hand again. "*I* don't want you to."

He looked down at their clasped fingers. "You have no idea what you're saying."

"I do." She gripped his hand tighter, tugging him farther into the room. "Forget about your past life." She sat on the bed and patted the mattress beside her. "Sit."

He stared at the mattress. "The seats at the table are fine."

She patted the mattress again. "This is even better."

He rubbed his eyes. "You don't know what you're doing."

She stood and grabbed his shoulders. "I do."

"No, you don't." He shrugged her off, but the agony in his eyes ran deep as he walked to the door.

A deep pain formed in Alanna's throat. If she let him leave, she might lose him forever. "Stop."

He looked over his shoulder.

"Do you really want to leave?"

He reached for the door control.

"Don't you dare touch that button before you answer. I asked you: Do you really want to leave?"

He took a deep breath and released it slowly. "No."

"Then stay."

He lowered his hand before he turned. "I'm an enforcer."

"I know."

"I've done horrible things."

She placed her palms on the sides of his face. "You've also done wonderful things."

He shook his head and looked down. "I shouldn't."

"Why? Because it's a choice? Because it's something you *want* to do?"

"Yes, on both accounts. You deserve better."

She narrowed her eyes at him. "How about you let *me* decide what I deserve?" She pushed upon her toes and kissed him.

His muscles tensed, and he pressed his lips together.

Men can be so stubborn. She continued the kiss until he relaxed, opening his mouth to her.

Alexander slid his hand behind her neck. His fingers twitched before he pulled her closer. Alanna's skin tingled where they touched, like every cell in her body yearned to reach for him.

He leaned away, but the fire had returned to his eyes. "We shouldn't do this."

"Oh, we should. We definitely should."

He only fought her slightly as she drew him back toward her bed.

DANIA PUSHED the partially rehydrated egg pellets around on her plate as Cal stared out the lounge window. Outside, Orion's small but lethal star skipper passed by the window.

Cal's lips thinned. "Every time I see one of those ships out there, I lose my appetite."

"You've sufficiently spooked the commander. He has his people running scans of the ship, trying to find out if he can circumvent your security. He's quite annoyed that they can't even figure out what kind of system you've installed, let alone how to thwart it."

He rubbed his eyes, leaning his elbows on either side of his barely touched plate of food. "We're getting closer to Z8. That's about as far as my plan goes. There's no way in hell I'm taking Orion into a war zone to help save that princess. I just don't know how to get out of it." He shook his head. "Agreeing seemed like the only way to protect Kirato, but I keep thinking about the enforcers Orion left behind." He rubbed his eyes again. "I may have screwed us *and* the colony."

"Ty said he was looking at available ships in the pirate sector?"

"Yeah. There are a few, but their firepower specifications are circumspect. I don't think there's anything there that we'll be able to convince Orion to go for."

"We'll find something. Orion just needs a ship, and he'd rather have a ship that was under his own control. Ty is resourceful. He'll find something."

"I hope so."

The comm went off. "Hey, boss?" Ty's voice said.

Cal stood and tapped the comm on the wall. "What's up?"

"I gotta admit, I'm getting a little punchy. I was going to call Alanna to take over for a bit, but Orion and his buddies are flying a little close. I think they're trying to piss me off."

"Yeah, I saw that. No need to stress her out with all that. I'll be up in a minute." He tapped off the comm.

Dania forked a few of the pellets and held them up. "You're going to miss out on all this rehydrated deliciousness."

Cal smiled. "I'm hoping to find some real eggs on our trading run. Those are barely worth eating." He kissed her cheek. "I'll see you later."

Her cheeks heated as he left the room. One day they'd be able to finish a full conversation without someone needing him. She supposed that was the life of a captain, though. Especially the captain of a ship flanked by an unwanted enforcer escort.

A bag of protein bars fell out of the storage compartments and landed on the floor. Dania frowned. That was odd.

She ate the last of her eggs and tossed both their plates into the recycler. Deep down, she'd known that Cal had no intention of helping Orion, but this was the first time he'd voiced it. Her stomach churned, considering that a Bane was out there, needing help, and she wasn't running to her aid. But Dania was no longer a general. This was not her problem anymore.

She headed toward the food storage to pick up the fallen protein bars and stopped.

There was nothing on the floor.

Had she imagined seeing something fall?

The door opened and Alexander stepped in.

His eyes scanned the room. "I was looking for you. Have you finished your meal?"

"Yes, I was just leaving. Is everything all right?"

"Yes, and no." He walked toward the window and looked out.

"That sounds ominous. What happened?"

He looked to the floor, then met her gaze. "I'm not sure how to feel. On one side, I'm deliriously happy, and on the other, I feel this all-consuming dread, like I've disappointed our sponsor."

Dania understood that all too well, but in her case, the guilt was founded. She'd forsaken her sponsor, given up everything she'd known.

He looked back to the window. "All these sudden choices, all these feelings… It's hard."

Dania joined him and rubbed his back. "I wish I could tell you that it will get easier, but it won't. Do you want to tell me what happened?"

"I'm not sure how you're going to feel about this."

"If it's something that gave you joy, I highly doubt it would upset me."

He took a very deep breath and held it before he released it slowly. "I have been with dozens of women. They were interchangeable. Meaningless."

Dania cringed. She'd only recently found out that her people frequently sought out human company at the end of a mission. Something about expending large amounts of power had allowed them to embrace human desires before they returned home to their sponsor to be fed. Even Kile had been involved in a strange relationship with Rachel. The woman had even stowed away on the *Star Renegade* to spend more time with him.

That had ended badly, though, as did all endeavors that didn't support their sponsor's needs.

A deep dread settled in her stomach. This was a very odd subject for him to be thinking about. Why was he bringing this up now? "Alexander?"

He raised his eyes. "Please don't hate me."

A chill ghosted over her skin. "What happened?"

"Alanna." He turned away and started pacing. "I haven't been able to stop thinking about her for some time. I get a thrill working with her, speaking with her, and last night…"

A hard ball formed in Dania's stomach. "What?"

He met her gaze. Countless expressions crossed his features. Confusion, fear, anxiety, excitement, dread.

Dania's chest clenched. "Alanna is my friend."

He walked toward her and grabbed her arms. "She's my friend, too, but now she's so much more." He released her. "Can't you understand? All the other women were meaningless. I can't even remember what they looked like. Not a single one."

That wasn't surprising. Geron had probably erased their existence from his mind to avoid any complications.

"Are you telling me you have feelings for her?"

"I think I do. It's frightening and thrilling at the same time." He laughed. "I think I understand now."

"Understand what?"

"Why you decided to stay. Why you would forsake your sponsor." He placed his palm on his chest. "If this is how you feel about the captain, it's almost as strong, if not stronger than our bond to Geron."

No, it wasn't. It just felt that way because neither of them had fed in some time. If Geron were here, standing in this room, it would be very different.

Still, it was odd how he'd singled out the captain. "Cal is my friend, but this whole crew, this family, the freedom they offered me... That's what I wanted."

He cocked his head. "You and Espinoza still haven't..."

Her eyes widened. "No!" She turned away, rubbing the panicked flutter in her chest. "I don't even think he thinks about me in that way."

Alexander huffed out a laugh. It brought a sparkle to his eyes and made him even more beautiful than he already was. "He does. Believe me, he does."

Her heart ached. Despite *knowing* what her enforcers had been doing after missions, for some reason the idea had never sunk in and taken root.

Maybe because Geron deemed this information unnecessary. She'd had a certain amount of time where she'd been required to bring her enforcers home. She'd followed this directive without fail, never wondering what they were doing after a mission, or even considering seeking human company herself. The idea had never even crossed her mind.

She closed her eyes and steadied her breathing. This had everything to do with the shunt Geron had implanted in her, keeping her focused on her missions, and nothing else.

Dania reached back and touched the small lump at the base of her neck. Alexander's gaze trailed her movement, and he blanched.

Was it possible? Could Dania still be lost in Geron's forced state of oblivion?

Dozens of conversations jumbled within her head. So many times she'd been confused or simply felt...bewildered? Naive?

Could she have missed something? Was it possible Cal thought of her in that way?

Dania rubbed the center of her chest, warding away a growing ache. "How would I even know?" *But wait...* "Does this have anything to do with pie?"

He raised one brow. "Have you kissed?"

She placed her hand on her cheek. "He kissed me here when he said goodbye this morning."

"That's it? Has he ever held you close?"

Yes, many times. "I think he almost kissed me once." She blinked. "Maybe more than once." She rubbed her face. "Either his duty got in the way, or I did." Alexander was right. Humanity, at times, was just too hard.

"He's a good man," Alexander said. "I hate to admit it, but he is."

"He's still marked for death."

"They all are."

"They don't deserve to die."

Alexander lifted his chin. "I know."

Tears welled in her eyes. Had he just said what she thought he'd said? "Have you decided to stay?"

"You know I can't stay. My duty is to Geron. Still..." He looked down. "For the first time in my life, I have something more to lose than you. The draw to stay is strong. It will hurt very much when I leave."

A sob burst from her lips and she hugged him. The admission that he wanted to stay meant Geron's hold was breaking. He'd taken the first steps to freedom. She wanted to tell him so many things, but all that came out were more tears.

He leaned away from her. "I'm going to do some research and see if I can remove your shunt."

Dania gaped. "You will?"

"You, above anyone else, deserve to be as happy as I am."

She touched the back of her neck again. "Do you really think you can get it out?"

His gaze traced to her hands, and he paled. "I don't know. For now, please accept that I'm willing to try."

He squinted, though, and his jaw tensed. She'd realized long ago that was a sign he was in pain.

Pain was another form of control, and if Geron wanted the shunt inside her, Alexander *wanting* to take it out may not be enough. Even thinking about removing it hurt her friend at a far deeper level than a battle wound. If Geron still had that kind of control, she needed to face the fact that they may never be totally free.

CHAPTER 30
ALEXANDER

ALEXANDER TOOK a deep breath before grabbing the rungs and climbing down to the cargo level. Acting as a liaison between Orion and the crew had become increasingly irritating. The more time Alexander spent with Alanna, the more he realized how often these *important meetings* weren't very important at all. Still, he needed to keep the appearance of a dutiful enforcer.

The commander waited for him below, just inside the security shield Doc had constructed to keep the enforcers contained.

Orion's gaze carried over the slight sheen of the shield. "I still find it infuriating that they allow you to walk freely, and we are forced to remain in storage."

"I've worked at great lengths to gain the smugglers' trust." It was true, although at this point, the crew should have no concerns about Alexander, even though he knew the captain and the engineer were still cautious in his presence.

Orion glared, most likely thinking that he and his

231

enforcers were also trustworthy. He was also smart enough to know that an enforcer's idea of trustworthy had an entirely different meaning for a smuggler.

"My irritation with the humans is growing. They lack respect for authority."

Alexander ground his teeth to keep from smiling. They were smugglers. What did the commander expect? "Their incongruities are less than agreeable."

The commander raised a brow but didn't question Alexander's odd choice of words.

An enforcer cried out in pain from the back of the storage compartment.

Orion didn't react. Had this become so common an occurrence?

The commander held Alexander's gaze. "I do not believe the captain intends to help us on our mission."

"What makes you say that?"

"His stance. His glaring disobedience. His argumentative nature."

"He's posturing. He's trying to hold what little control he still has on his ship." It wasn't a lie. Espinoza was smart enough to know what a precarious situation he was in.

"They are going to try to get out of our agreement."

Alexander steadied himself. He needed to choose his words carefully. "I wasn't aware there *was* an agreement. You simply told him you were taking his ship. And there was a veiled threat to the colony if he didn't comply, if I remember correctly."

"How we got here is inconsequential."

"Nevertheless, you are right. The princess is not Espinoza's concern. It would be foolish for him to put his ship in harm's way to save her."

"Any loyal citizen would do so to serve the glory of their king."

"The terms *loyal* and *smuggler* are rarely used in the same conversation."

Orion's face remained stony. "You will order them to take us to the princess."

Alexander held his breath to keep from laughing. "What makes you think they will listen to me?"

"I thought you had their trust. Advise them this is the best decision."

"And how do you suppose I do that?" It certainly *wasn't* the best decision, at least not for the crew.

"You will find a way. They must comply. There is nothing more important than finding the princess."

"There's nothing more important to you and her enforcers, but it's far from important to the smugglers. There's no way I could possibly convince them otherwise without lying." Which enforcers, of course, were incapable of.

Orion's eyes darkened. "You are not being reasonable. If this is what the doctor's experimental feedings do to an enforcer, I want nothing of it."

Interesting, that he took for granted Alexander had already taken the pathogens. True, the doctor had admitted to giving him one treatment when Alexander had first arrived on the ship, but he hadn't had regular treatments like Dania had.

"I see the rebellious thoughts running through your mind, healer. I would rather die than pollute myself."

Alexander had said the same thing not long ago. Had he sounded as robotic in his answers? "It is certainly your choice, but my programming directs me to inform you that you do not have the right to make that decision for all the enforcers under your command."

Orion sneered. "You will not stand there and criticize my command. You are weak…a fraction of the enforcer you once were. If you can even be *considered* an enforcer anymore."

"I am still loyal to my prince." It wasn't a lie. Deep down, he knew Dania would still serve Geron too, if needed.

"I find that doubtful."

"I am weaker than I once was, but the power of my sponsor runs through my veins. You know better than anyone that the link is not easily broken, nor do I *want* it broken."

Orion's eyes narrowed, no doubt testing Alexander's temperature. "Fine. It's imperative that I know the moment any of them are insubordinate. You will report anything out of the ordinary with Espinoza or his crew. We may need to circumvent any security measures they have in place and deal with them quickly."

Alexander bowed his head slightly and backed away. He smiled as he climbed the ladder and walked down the hall. He'd passed Orion's test for a lie because he hadn't lied. The power of his sponsor *did* run through his veins. He was weak, though, because that power was no longer Geron's.

Luckily for the *Star Renegade* crew, they were entirely predictable. They were always insubordinate, so the only time anything would be out of the ordinary would be if any of them suddenly decided to comply. So, Alexander found it unlikely that he'd have to report back anything to the commander anytime soon. He just needed to help this crew in any way he could before Orion made a more direct order that he wouldn't be able to circumvent so easily.

CHAPTER 31
CAL

CAL PACED in front of the long table in his private meeting space. He'd asked Dania to meet him here, but she didn't know why yet.

He tried to stop his hands from shaking. He'd hosted countless meals for the entire crew in this very room. He couldn't fathom why he was so nervous about serving one person.

He tapped the comm to the bridge. "Everything still okay up there?"

Ty snorted. "Come on, boss. You made me promise not to call you tonight. Don't ruin it by calling me. I'm fine, and I'll keep things fine, I promise."

"My luck in this area hasn't been the greatest."

"As long as our passengers stay in the hold, it should be clear sailing. If they get antsy, we'll make them wait. It's not like they can get out of there unless we drop the containment field. I got this. No worries."

Cal nodded to himself, taking a cleansing breath. When he'd explained about Dania's birthday, Ty had been more on board with the idea of a private dinner than Cal had expected. The kid had become an even better friend than first mate. "Thanks."

"You got it, boss. Now, have a good time." Ty tapped off the comm.

He wasn't all that worried about *himself* having a good time. He wanted to make tonight special for Dania. If this was going to be her first birthday party, he had to make sure it was great.

The door tone sounded. He swept back his hair, straightened his shirt, and tapped the panel, opening the door.

Dania smiled. "You wanted to see me?"

Cal stepped back to make way for her. "Yeah, come on in."

She walked inside, and her gaze fell on the place settings on the table. "What's this?"

"Dinner."

She spun toward him. "Dinner? Where are the others?"

"It's just you and me tonight." He held out his hand to the table. "Please, sit."

As Dania sat, Cal went to the kitchen and pulled two plates out of the warm oven and placed one in front of Dania.

"You...cooked for me?"

"Yes, I did."

She stared at the plate before looking up. "Did you make...pie?"

Cal pressed his lips together as he sat. "No. No pie. Sorry."

She frowned and lowered her eyes.

Cal placed his hand over hers. "But only because I

didn't have anything to make pie with. If I had the ingredients, I definitely would have made pie."

She didn't look up, but a smile peeked from the edge of her lips.

Cal picked up his fork. "So, how was your day? You've been working in engineering with Ethan, right?"

"If you call it working." She pushed the chunks of ham around on her plate. "He gave me several jobs, and I failed all of them horribly."

"I doubt that's true. Ethan has thrown me out of engineering at least three times and begged me to never help again. You must have done something right."

She frowned. "He had me clean the long cables in the back of the room. They were thick with grease and some kind of sandy grit."

That must have been the anterior propulsion cables. That would be why they'd dropped power for a while. "That's great. Maintenance is a really important job."

"Cal..." She closed her eyes. "He had me *clean the cables*." Her lower lip trembled slightly.

Cal wasn't familiar with Kever culture, but what he *did* know was this woman used to command a small army. Now she was in engineering, wiping up goo.

"Hey." He squeezed her hand. "Those cables are critical components. The cleaner they are, the more efficient the engines will run." At least, that was what Ethan had told him.

She looked up at him, but her brow was still pinched.

He needed to make her understand whatever job she did on this ship, no matter how small, had value. "If you weren't there to clean those cables, Ethan would've had to do it. That's not a job that can be ignored."

"Is that supposed to make me feel better?"

"It should. Since you were there to help, Ethan was able to calibrate three important systems. He was thrilled with his progress, and now he's enough ahead of schedule that he can help Doc increase the efficiency of the machines in the med bay."

She seemed to consider that.

"Every job is important on this ship, and he wouldn't let just anyone clean those cables. They need to be meticulous. If he trusted you, that means he knew you'd do a good job."

The pinch in her brow relaxed, and she took a bite of her meal. With each chew, her expression softened until a more pleasant countenance colored her features. "This is wonderful, as usual."

"It's a pretty easy recipe if you have the ingredients. I can show you next time we get to a food trader." Which would most likely be at the same time Doc was getting his supplies in Z8. They'd only get one stop, though, before Orion started to squawk, so they needed to make sure they chose the right place and shopped fast.

Dania placed her fork down. "That was delicious. Thank you."

Cal stood and collected their plates. "I hope you left some room. The best part is on the way." At least, he hoped it would be the best part.

He headed into the kitchen and placed the dishes beside the sink.

A big part of being human was coming to terms with your past. At least, that's what Doc thought. Hopefully, a nice meal would calm Dania and make her feel safe enough to accept who she'd been in her life before becoming an enforcer.

He placed a few metal wicks into the cake he'd made earlier, grabbed the medical laser Doc had given him, and headed back to the table, placing the cake in front of Dania.

Her eyes widened. "That cake is huge."

"Yeah, well, the crew made me promise to save them some. You should expect singing, but not from me. No one wants to hear me sing."

"Singing?"

"Yeah, it's kind of a tradition. People sing for you when you have a birthday."

She looked back at the cake. "I've never had a birthday."

"Well, you certainly have. The Banes just never celebrated it. But Dania Rain did." He checked the setting on the laser. The last thing he needed was to accidently blow the cake up. "From what Doc could find out, you lived in a colony on Trellis. He found a picture of you when you were about five years old with chocolate cake on your face." He adjusted one of the metal wicks. "This isn't a real chocolate cake, but I did my best to simulate the flavor with what I had."

Cal flicked on the laser and started lighting the makeshift candles.

She gaped. "What are you doing?"

"This is another tradition. You're supposed to make a wish and blow out the candles."

The firelight danced in her eyes. "Wishes are ridiculous. They have no basis in fact."

He laughed. "Maybe not, but it's fun. And it's tradition." He pointed at the cake. "You better make a wish and blow out those candles because they probably won't burn all that long."

She took a deep breath.

"Don't forget to make a wish!"

She glanced at him and shook her head. He knew it was silly, but enjoying something as simple as a wish—the impractical rather than the practical—was the type of growth Doc thought she needed. Cal hoped he was right.

She stared at the cake again, glanced at him, smiled, and then blew out the dancing flames.

"One breath! That's good luck!" Cal clapped his hands. "Now, this part is really important: You can't tell anyone what you wished for, or the wish won't come true."

"Surely, you don't believe that."

"Like I said. It's all in good fun."

She seemed to contemplate the small trails of smoke drifting from the makeshift candles. "You said I used to live on Trellis?"

Cal hesitated as he reached for the cake. He'd expected to have to wiggle more information about her past into this part of the conversation. Maybe it was a good sign that she'd brought it up on her own.

"Yeah." He pulled the cake closer and cut her a piece. "At least until you got sick, and your information hit the royal databases. Not long after, the Banes showed up on your parents' doorstep."

She shivered. "You said the Banes purchased me from my family. Who would sell their own daughter?"

"I have to admit, there's a good chance they didn't have a choice. We *are* talking about the Banes. The money was probably a nice perk, but I can't see the royal family taking *no* for an answer. Your parents were probably afraid for their lives."

Dania straightened. "I will never think ill of the Banes, no matter how hard you try!"

He held up his palms. "That wasn't my intent. I'm just stating facts."

She closed her eyes and took a deep breath. "I'm sorry. I didn't mean to react like that."

"It's okay."

"No, it's not. I still don't know if my reactions are my own, or programming, or habit." She rubbed her eyes. "I know I should hate them for what they did to me, but I don't. Maybe I can't."

Cal wanted to hold her and tell her that it would be all right. But that would be no better than the neighbors who'd tried to console him after his father had been murdered, telling him it would be okay, and things would get better.

It certainly wasn't okay, and it never got better.

Better was relative, of course. Cal stepping on board the *Star Renegade* and taking on this crew had changed his life. It still might not have been better, but it was, maybe, a little easier to live with the echoes of his past. He'd built something here. Something he was proud of. If anything, maybe his own hardships had paved the way to give his crew a place to call *home*.

Dania hugged herself, staring at the slice of cake. "I wonder what it would be like to have a family."

Cal's chest clenched. Why in all the stars did it feel like she'd just driven a knife into his chest?

He reached over and touched her hand. "I'll be your family, if you let me."

"You've all been so kind, but I still lie awake at night, wondering why, and if, I really deserve to be here."

"You deserve to be here as much as anyone else in this crew." Hadn't they all made that plain? Why was she still doubting herself?

She closed her eyes and shook her head. "I wish I believed that."

He took her hand and pulled her toward him. "Believe it. Dania, you mean so much to all of us." Cal took a deep breath. "You mean so much to *me*."

She blinked, and a tear ran down the side of her cheek. "All of this is hard. The friendship. The cake."

Maybe the birthday had been a bad idea. There was no turning back on that now, though. "It doesn't have to be hard."

Cal wiped the tear away with his palm.

She grabbed his hand. "I wish things were different."

"I don't. Everything that happened brought you here, to my ship. We've all had hard lives with parts we'd like to forget or just put behind us. But that's what makes us stronger. It's what's turned us into a crew. A family."

She sniffed, forcing a smile. "I guess every family needs someone to clean the grease off their cables." She grabbed her fork and pulled her cake toward her. "I'm ruining everything. I'm sorry."

"You're not ruining a thing." Although he wished the conversation had gone a little better.

Maybe Doc was wrong about talking to her about this alone. Doc was the one with the great bedside manner. He could tell you the worst news and put a great spin on it. Heck, even Ethan could have probably handled this better than Cal.

Dania's eyes lit up. "This cake is delicious."

"Thanks." He wanted to tell her that he'd made it special for her. He'd wanted to make her happy on her birthday, not feel worse. Damn, he'd screwed this all up.

She licked the edge of her fork. "You've always made me feel like a part of things."

"You *are* a part of things." How could he get this through to her? "Dania, what do I have to do to make you understand how much you mean to all of us?"

She placed her fork down. "But you're the only one who made me cake."

Umm…what was she getting at?

Dania nodded to herself. "Cake is just as good as pie."

"I don't know. That pie you made was pretty amazing."

"It was crushed."

"It made it easier to chew."

She laughed and looked at her empty plate. She pushed a crumb with her finger. "We made each other dessert."

"Yeah." Was she working something out in her head? Was this one of those times he was supposed to talk, or keep his big mouth shut and see what happened?

Dania stood and walked across the room. She looked over her shoulder at him before she sat on the couch. She frowned again as she rubbed her chest.

There'd been too much spice on the ham. He knew it! Now she was sick and…

"Cal?" She looked up at him. "This is all hard. But I'm happy. I want you to know that."

That sounded promising.

He walked over and sat beside her. "Good. I'm glad."

"I never dreamed I could feel like a part of something… that I could be with people who enjoyed my company.

People who stood by my side because they wanted to, not because they were *ordered* to."

That little voice in Cal's head told him to shut up. This was going well, and him talking would only ruin it.

She looked down again. "Thank you…for everything."

Why in the name of all the stars in the galaxy was this vibrant, strong woman looking down? Everything she'd said, she should be proud of.

"Hey." He lifted her chin. "There's no need to thank me. You boarding this ship was one of the best things that has ever happened to me."

"Really?"

"Really." He leaned closer to her, and when she didn't pull away, he brushed his lips against hers.

She tensed, and he leaned away.

He wished he could read her expression. "Was that all right?"

Her eyes were wide, and she blinked twice. "I…" She looked back to the table, her gaze carrying over the candles she'd blown out before a smile spread over her lips. "Yes. It's all right."

"Good." He placed a finger on her chin and gently turned her face back to him. "Because I'd like to try that again." He leaned closer and gave her a second to object—because hey, he'd been known to read the room wrong, and there was no way he was going to screw this up.

She inched closer to him, and he closed his mouth over hers.

She was soft and warm and everything he'd imagined as he pulled her closer. Dania put her arms around his shoulders and melted into him as he deepened the kiss.

Dammit, Ty was right. He should have done this sooner.

She tensed beneath his hands. A tight squeak sounded in her throat before she shoved him away. "Please don't." She flinched, holding her hands in front of her face.

She barely seemed to breathe, curled up almost in a ball on the edge of the couch with her hands held up to ward off...*what*? What in the galaxy scared an enforcer?

"Dania?"

She jumped, as if she were surprised to hear Cal's voice, then stared at him, her eyes wide, like she'd seen a ghost.

He held both his hands up where she could see them. "I don't know what's wrong, but whatever it is, I'm here."

She blinked, still gaping as she reached over her shoulder and touched the back of her neck.

Cal took shallow breaths, trying not to move as she drew her hand away and stared at her fingers.

"Are you okay?" he asked.

"No." She looked up from her fingers. "And I'm not sure I ever will be."

CHAPTER 32
DANIA

DANIA STORMED THROUGH THE SHIP. Cal had gone through so much trouble to make her a meal, and he'd made cake!

And he'd even admitted that he would have made pie, if he'd been able. Tonight should have been perfect, but it wasn't.

She stopped at the end of the hall that led to the crew quarters and took a deep breath. Tonight had been all she'd been dreaming of…a real human connection.

Stars! She'd even wished for a kiss when she'd blown out the candles, and it had actually happened.

Until she'd ruined it.

She took a steadying breath and continued down the hall. She'd never be human, and she'd never be totally free while she was being controlled by another.

She banged on Alexander's door. When it didn't open, she banged again.

The silver panel slid back, and he raised one brow. "With all the noise, I expected the engineer. Or possibly the odd med tech."

She pushed past him and walked inside, closing the door behind her. His room was oddly in order, very much like her own room when she'd first boarded. A ball formed in her throat as she turned toward him.

He frowned at her. "What's wrong?"

"Cal kissed me."

He tilted his head to the right. "Was it that displeasurable?"

"No... Yes." She covered her face. "No."

"Which was it?"

How was she supposed to explain? "It was nice at first. It felt warm and good."

"And something happened?"

She placed her hand on the back of her neck. "I need you to take this thing out."

His eyes widened. "I don't think I can."

"Of course, you can. You're the one who put it into me."

"I know that."

"You said you'd look into it."

"I did, but the more I researched, the more it..." He looked down. "The more it hurt."

"What do you mean?"

"The closer I came to figuring it out, the more pain I was in, until I decided not to try." He looked up. "The second I decided not to try, the pain stopped."

Dania gulped. "He's still controlling us."

"So it would seem."

"There needs to be a way, Alexander. It's not fair that he's still stopping me from being happy when he's not even close enough to emit his power."

"It was never meant to keep you from being happy. It's meant to keep you focused."

"By stopping me from even thinking about anything that might give me joy."

He lowered his eyes.

She grabbed his hands. "Please help me."

His gaze remained downcast. "I'm sorry. I can't take it out of you."

"You can't, or you won't?"

Alexander growled, rubbing his face. "Don't you understand? The chip is in your spine. It would be a delicate operation, and just thinking about removing it causes excruciating pain. I could paralyze you by accident."

Dania gritted her teeth. She wanted to tell him it was worth the risk, but if anything did happen to her, Alexander would never forgive himself. It was too much to ask of him.

The comm pinged, and Alexander touched the control on the wall.

"Alex?" Alanna's voice filled the room. "Ethan finished the links. We're ready to test the cloak."

He closed his eyes and took a deep breath. "I'll be there as soon as I can." He tapped off the comm and turned back to Dania. "You do understand that I want only the best for you."

Of course, he did. There was never a question in that.

From her earliest memory, Alexander had always been the one she could count on. They had always been on the same path, whether they wanted to be or not. He'd help her if he could, but in the end, as always, it wasn't up to him.

Dania blinked away tears burning in her eyes. "We're never going to be free from him, are we?"

"Maybe not totally, but I find how far you've come, even with the shunt, very encouraging."

The only question was: Would that be enough to save them, if faced with the unthinkable?

CHAPTER 33
CAL

CAL ADJUSTED the clarity of the main viewscreen as Ty blasted onto the bridge like someone had lit him on fire.

"Ready to disappear?" Cal asked.

"You know it." Ty took his seat. "I feel like a kid about to steal cake from Mel's kitchen. I haven't been this excited in ages."

Cal hoped their excitement was warranted. He'd stayed alive this long being cautious. Messing with alien technology was being anything but cautious.

The door slid open and Dania stepped on deck.

The excited flutter in Cal's chest sank into his stomach like a rock. He hadn't seen her since she'd run out of his room the night before. He'd decided against chasing her, but he'd been second-guessing himself ever since.

He stood. "Hey. You all right?"

Dania closed her eyes and nodded. "I guess. For now." She looked up at him. "I'm sorry about last night. You deserve better."

"I don't deserve anything."

"Yes, you do. I need to figure this out, and it might take time."

Cal mustered up a smile. "Take all the time you need. I'm not going anywhere."

Ty cleared his throat. "This is one of those times I'm kinda wishing I wasn't here." He spun his chair toward them. "Do you want me to leave?" He held up his palms. "And I mean that sincerely. I'm not trying to be a smartass."

Cal patted him on the back. "No, you're good. We've got a job to do."

Dania walked over to Doc's station and tapped the screen. Her expression didn't have her normal, stringent focus, though.

Cal slid beside her. "I want you to know I'm okay." He pointed between the two of them. "*We're* okay. I meant that when I said I'm not going anywhere."

She nodded. "I know. Thank you."

Ty's voice filled the room. "La la la la la! I'm *not* listening! I'm just over here, doing my thing. Ears are solidly turned off."

Cal snorted a laugh and returned to his seat. "All right. Let's do this." He tapped the comm. "How do things look down there, Ethan?"

The comm crackled. "Just doing a final check and we'll be ready to go."

"Is Alanna staying down there with you?"

"No, she's on her way up to the bridge."

Good. Cal always felt better when she was at the nav.

He turned to Ty. "Where's Orion?"

"Having a nice, leisurely cruise on one of our lovely

state-of-the-art escort ships. Do you want to tell him what we're doing?"

Cal stared out at one of the enforcer ships flying just ahead of them. The other ships were behind them, as usual. "No. If it works, they'll figure it out. If it doesn't work, we don't need them asking questions about the tech and where we got it."

The door slid open, and Alanna entered. "Sorry I'm late." She took her seat at the nav station. "Ready to make history?"

Ty's grin reflected in the viewscreen. "I'm always ready."

Cal opened a channel to the med bay. "Doc, are all your patients secure?"

"As secure as I can get them when I have no idea what's about to happen. We're just going to sit tight and hold our breaths."

Quirky giggled behind him. "You can sit tight all you want. I've never been invisible before. This is going to be such fun!"

Cal smiled. "Let me know if there are any problems."

"Roger that," Doc said.

Ethan's voice came over the comm. "Alex and I are ready to get this party started. You all good up there?"

Cal took a deep breath to steady himself. Too bad it didn't help.

He closed his eyes and counted slowly to ten.

These people were galaxies more talented than he was. He needed to have faith in them. If they said it would work, it would work.

He took another deep breath. "Okay, let's go."

Alanna looked out the main viewscreen. "The lights

should dim for a few seconds. It's nothing to worry about." Her fingers traced shapes on the screen in her console. "Here we go."

A slight hum filled the room before the lights dimmed.

"That's all good," Alanna said. "Just as expected."

The floor rattled.

"Was that expected?" Cal asked.

Alanna bit her lower lip. "I'm not sure."

The enforcer ship in front of them fired its engines and circled, heading back toward them. The two ships behind the Star Renegade blasted forward, passing the *Star Renegade* and meeting the other ship.

"What are they doing?" Ty asked. "One of them almost hit us."

Alanna touched her earpiece. "Lots of chatter. It seems like—" A smile burst across her face before she spun toward Cal. "They can't see us! They think we jumped!"

Ty cursed and banked the ship down.

"What are you doing?" Cal asked.

"Getting out of the way. They literally almost hit us." He evened the ship out, pointing their viewscreen at the three enforcer ships. "That's crazy. They were close enough to see us with their eyes, even if their sensors went down."

"Not anymore," Alanna said. "The mechanisms in the new tech reflect space. It's like we're covered with mirrors, and all they can see is stars." She looked at her screen. "If they matched us against a star map, they'd realize it was wrong, but to the naked eye and to the equipment, we just went *poof*." She snapped her fingers. "Disappeared."

Cal sat back, grinning as the enforcer ships spun, no doubt looking for jump signatures. "I'd say that was a successful test."

Ty snorted. "Orion must be having an aneurysm."

The lights flickered, then went out.

Cal's chest clenched. "Was that expected, too?"

"No. Lights are out all over the ship." The glow from Alanna's screen lit up her face. "Looks like we still have comms, though." She tapped her panel. "Ethan, what's going on?"

"Alex is working on it." He grunted.

"What's wrong?" Cal asked.

"It's just getting a little hot down here."

Hot? That didn't sound good.

The enforcer ships spun toward the *Star Renegade* and throttled toward them.

"Can they see us now?" Cal asked.

Ty's fingers flew across his panel. "Sure looks like it."

"Is it getting warm in here?" Dania asked.

Cal wiped the sweat from his brow. He'd hoped he was just getting nervous.

Ethan's voice blasted over the speakers. "Cal, the engines are overloading!"

What the hell? "Can you stop it?"

"Alex is trying to disengage the tech!"

Cal looked at Alanna. "Will that help?"

"I don't know." She frowned. "Wait." The lights in the room came up.

The heat still pressed in on all sides like they were sitting inside an oven.

Cal hit the comm. "Talk to me, people. What's going on?!"

Ethan's voice came over the speakers. "The tech is disengaged, but it's glowing like a freaking sun!"

Alanna stood and shouted at the ceiling. "That's why we put it by the airlock. Eject it!"

"I can't get near it!" Ethan screamed.

Dania shouted into the comm next to her station. "Alexander, put it out the airlock."

"I think I can control it," the enforcer said. "I can stop the reaction if I just—"

"Don't even try," Dania shouted. "Get it off the ship. That's an order!"

Orion's voice came over the speakers. "*Star Renegade,* what's going on?"

The ship hummed, and a round, metal container cascaded into space.

Dania moved to the nav station. "Orion, we ejected a piece of technology from engineering in the rear of the ship."

"I see it."

"I need you to contain it. Cool it if you can. It may explode."

Five blasts of energy shot from one of the enforcer ships.

"They're going to destroy it!" Ty said.

Dania held up a hand. "No. Those are containment nets."

Cal cringed. He'd seen those nets used on a pirate ship once. Luckily, he'd been on the ship that had escaped.

Alanna tapped on her screen. "It's cooling. Whatever they did, it worked. The tech is shutting down." She sighed, sitting back. "It's done. I guess space cooled it off. We're in the clear."

Ty shrugged. "Well, it worked, kinda. Right? I mean, it was a successful test."

Except for the part where it had nearly exploded.

Orion's voice blasted into the room. *"Star Renegade,* I expect a full report in five minutes."

Cal had worse things to worry about than an overbearing enforcer. "Shut him off. I'm the one who wants a report." He tapped the comm. "Ethan. Alexander. What happened?"

"We're not sure, but we'll figure it out. There's a solid computer chip on that thing that works a lot like human tech. It will tell us what went wrong."

"Is it safe to bring that thing back on board?" Cal asked.

"Yeah, sure. As long as we don't turn it back on."

Cal didn't want that thing anywhere near his ship. It had caused far too much trouble over the past few months. Unfortunately, it was their best chance of getting through the blockade.

The goal was still to treat as many of the enforcers as possible, give Orion a better ship than the *Renegade,* and get lost in the stars. If they played all their cards right, Orion would pick up the enforcers he'd left on Kirato as soon as he found his missing princess, and the colony would be safe again. That was only possible if the enforcers never got close enough to Stanley's trading area to see anything illegal, though.

He closed his eyes and sighed. As usual, there were far too many 'what if' possibilities in this plan, but it was all they had.

"Bring the tech back on board, but I want a containment field around it and keep it by the airlock, just in case."

"Roger that."

Dania frowned, looking out at the enforcer ships

hovering with their noses pointed at the *Star Renegade*'s bridge. "I can't believe you're bringing that thing back on the ship. What are we supposed to tell Orion?"

"The truth, that we need to disappear if we want to complete our mission." There was no reason to tell Grumpy that his mission was decidedly different from Cal's.

He rubbed the back of his neck. All their plans seemed scatterbrained on the surface. This one was no different. So why did he have such a bad feeling about this one?

He needed to stop dwelling on what could happen and make sure the right things *did* happen. And right now, that meant finding a way to hide the *Star Renegade* from enemy eyes.

"Do you really think disappearing is enough?" Dania asked.

He started walking toward the exit. "We're a small army, and we need any advantage we can get." With any luck, that advantage wouldn't end up getting them all killed.

CHAPTER 34
ALANNA

ALANNA STOOD in the center of lower engineering, rubbing her arms to ward off a phantom chill. The new cloaking drive sat right up against the airlock with metal straps around it, ready to whisk the tech back into space at any moment.

Orion had taken the news of them building a cloak with his normal stony-face countenance. Then he'd ordered them to continue their research, and to *not allow the ship to explode*.

One thing Alanna loved was constructive advice. At least he was leaving them alone at the moment, which probably had more to do with fear of this technology than trust in their skills.

Alexander paced the far wall, stopping every few feet to look at Ethan's legs sticking out from beneath their ominous creation. She understood his worry. Less than five hours ago, that tech had nearly destroyed the ship, and now Ethan was poking it with a screwdriver.

Ethan eased out from under the tech. "You two built this thing pretty solid. I have to say I'm impressed. Every inch of the outer casing is just as clean and untarnished as it was during our last inspection."

"It may be solid, but it's not good enough." Alex strode toward him. "Do you have any idea why it failed?"

"Sure do. It looks like you both spent a lot of time reinforcing the main frame—which I can't blame you for doing, since this thing seems to have a mind of its own." He tapped the edge of the screwdriver on the surface. "What none of us thought about was reinforcing the seals."

Alex's brow furrowed. "We used engine-grade soldering alloy. That can withstand anything."

"Those alloys can withstand anything humanity and the Kevers could dream up." He pointed the screwdriver at the tech. "This is partly manmade, but the innards and the brain are the makings of our friends the Carteks." He pushed off the floor and stood. "I think what we need here is a chromium and gold alloy, strengthened with Lucerne ore."

Alanna placed her hand on the tech. The surface was slick and cool, just like when they'd worked on it. "Won't gold get hot?"

Ethan nodded. "That's why we use the Lucerne ore. It'll stop the gold from melting."

Alanna took her hand off the tech. "And the chromium will make it nearly impenetrable."

"You don't have Lucerne ore." Alexander pointed at the computer screen behind him. "It's not in your manifest."

Ethan puffed out a laugh. "This is a smuggling ship. Cal doesn't even know half the stuff I have."

"I wouldn't have even thought of chromium." Alanna lowered her eyes. "I should have asked you before we sealed it."

He smiled at her, but his expression didn't have his usual cocky glee. "No worries. I'll help remove what's left of your seals, and we'll get this working again." He looked in Alex's direction, then back to Alanna. "You know what? I'm kinda hungry. Do you want to go get something to eat?"

She shook her head. "No. I want to get started on removing the seals."

His gaze trailed to Alex again, then back to her. "You sure?"

"Yeah, go ahead. We're good."

"All right, then." His lips thinned. "I guess I'll bring back the supplies we need after I'm done."

Alexander narrowed his eyes as Ethan scaled the ladder. "He doesn't like me."

Alanna bit back her grin. They hadn't announced their relationship, but the crew could probably tell what was going on. Even though she'd explained to Ethan countless times that she thought of him as a brother, he'd never given up hope that she'd fall for him.

He'd understand in time. She just wished she could find a way to make it easier on him.

"Let's get to work." She grabbed a laser chisel. "This is probably going to take a while."

Alex grabbed his own tool and moved to the other edge of the tech. "I'm sorry I didn't realize that the seams wouldn't hold. I should have thought of that."

"Everyone makes mistakes."

"I don't." He frowned, as if considering that.

"It's all part of being human. We'll both sure as heck check for things like that in the future, right?"

"Of course."

"Then we've learned from all this. My mother always says: *Mistakes make the best life lessons.*"

Alex smiled. "Your mother seems quite wise."

"You bet she is. She made me the woman I am."

He bowed his head. "Then for that, I am eternally grateful."

Alanna's cheeks heated. Even the smallest, sweet comments seemed compounded when they came from Alex. Everything about him seemed like *more.*

It was strange, but a good kind of strange. She'd never felt cherished before, like someone in her life would actually die for her. Well, maybe her mom and dad, but that didn't count.

Every other relationship in her life had been fake. People always seemed to want something from her. Heck, the last guy she'd loved had sold her out to pirates for her jumping ability. If it weren't for Cal agreeing to help her, hiding her family from the pirates, she'd probably still be stuck in an endless loop of petty larceny. Before coming to the *Star Renegade,* she hadn't believed she could trust anyone.

Another shiver ran down her spine. Alexander wasn't really a member of the crew. He hadn't officially stated that he wasn't going back to his prince. Come to think of it, he hadn't mentioned it at all lately. Was that because he couldn't lie? Did he maybe still plan on returning? Could he be hiding the truth simply by not saying anything at all?

She closed her eyes and took a deep breath. She needed to push her past out of her head. Alexander was an enforcer, but he wasn't like the others. Even Dania said so.

Still, she'd feel better if he actually looked her in the eye and told her he was staying. That was a tough ask, though, and she knew it. Maybe, if she was lucky, she could steer the conversation in a way that would help him make the decision on his own.

She chiseled the edge of the sealant. "So, do you miss home at all?"

"Do I miss not having the freedom to spend time with friends, not eating and sleeping when I want, and not making technology that nearly explodes, killing us all?"

That was an odd way to end that thought. She leaned around the tech to look at him.

He smiled before looking back to his work. "There are parts I miss. Despite the limitations, it was my home."

But it wasn't his home. Not really. He'd been kidnapped and forced to be something he wasn't. But it was probably not the best time to start that argument up again.

Maybe she needed to focus on freedom. The best way to do that may be to gently remind him of who had taken that freedom away. "What about your prince? Do you miss him?"

His brow furrowed, and he stopped working on the seam. "At times I do. It's small things."

"Like what?"

He shrugged. "Well, it certainly would be easier to remove this sealant if I were fully charged. I've never been afraid of using up my power before."

"But you're stronger than Dania. You seem to be doing fine."

His lips thinned. "I'm not stronger than her. I've just adapted differently."

Differently? Was he ashamed of himself for adapting? If so, why?

The conversation seemed like it bothered him, though,

so maybe it was better if she deflected a bit. "What else do you miss about home? I've never been to Keveron."

His gaze seemed far off. "I felt like I belonged there. It's hard to explain."

But from what Doc said, he may have been programmed to feel that way. If that were so, would he ever feel at home on the *Star Renegade*?

Her heart clenched. Was it maybe something more than that? "Did-Did you have a girlfriend there?"

He huffed out a laugh. "No, that would be quite frowned upon. We are at our sponsor's beck and call every moment of the day."

"Well, it's not like you slept with him. You had to have *some* time off."

One of the machines in the wall whirred twice before settling.

Alanna stopped chiseling and looked around the tech again. "Alex?"

His brow had furrowed again, and he looked at the floor.

"Are you okay?"

Another smile appeared on his face, but this one seemed forced. He started chiseling his own seam, but he didn't answer.

He. Didn't. Answer.

"Alex?"

He glanced at her. "There were things about Keveron that I prefer not to discuss."

Wait. What? Her stomach sank. *Every moment of the day…*

She placed her laser chisel on the floor. It was well known that Kever princes and princesses took sexual favors from humans. They were celebrities, of sorts, and there were more than enough people willing to do anything to get close to someone with that much power. But when the Kevers were home, away from adoring fans… "Alex, did you and your prince have an intimate relationship?"

His eyes turned wild, and maybe angry, before he closed them and turned away. A chill ran over her skin. She placed her fingers over her lips. "D-Did he force you?"

His gaze whisked back to her. "No. Of course not. An enforcer would do anything their sponsor asks. No matter what."

Sweet stars! She tried to form words, but nothing came out.

Alexander held up his hand. "Don't judge like that. Kever culture is very different from what you're accustomed to. It's not right or wrong. It's just…*different*."

What did that even mean?

She stepped closer. "Were you able to say *no*?"

He looked down again. "It never occurred to me to try. One never questions their sponsor."

Her throat constricted. How was that any different than being forced? It was no better than having a gun to his head.

But still, he seemed to be defending this monster. Were his ties to this bastion slug still that strong? In the back of his mind, did he still love that conniving, self-serving slime trap without question?

She took another hesitant step toward him. "If he were to show up again, would you say *no* now?"

He placed down his tool and walked over to her. "I will always love my prince, but what I feel for you is different and stronger in many ways." He looked down again. "If I were able, I would say *no*."

"If you were *able*?"

He nodded.

"*Are you* able to say *no* to him? Ever?"

He drew in a deep breath and released it slowly. "No, I cannot."

She rubbed her face with her hands. Bile built at the base of her throat.

His jaw tensed as he shoved the chisel into the sealant. "Don't look at me like that."

"I'm not looking at you like anything. I love you. I'll always love you. I'm angry."

"Why? This changes nothing between us. We've both had pasts."

"I'm not angry at *you*. I'm angry at *him*. What he did to you was wrong."

Alexander placed his chisel down. "You don't understand. He cares about all of us. He…"

"Stop defending him! He stole you from your parents. He messed with your head to make you do whatever he wanted, and then he surgically altered you to look the way he wanted." She grabbed her temples, took two steps away, and then turned back to him. "And then he took advantage of you." She stormed toward him, grabbed his shoulders, and shook him. "You should *hate* him."

Alexander closed his eyes. "I know."

"Then why don't you hate him?"

"I can't. And I never will."

CAL SCALED the last few rungs of the ladder and stepped onto the main deck, heading toward the med bay. His skin crawled, and he found himself looking over his shoulder, making sure none of the enforcers had followed, despite them still being secure behind the barrier. Orion had finally stopped demanding his own room and free run of the ship, but his constant questions and glaring, convicting eyes were starting to weigh heavily on Cal. The sooner he got them off the ship, the better.

He stepped into the med bay. "You wanted to see me?"

Doc pointed at one of the beds, where Rachel was handing one of the enforcers a cup of water. "Not me, but our friend here asked to speak to you."

The enforcer took a drink and handed the cup back to Rachel. "You're Espinoza?"

Cal folded his arms, ready for the normal verbal barrage of enforcer hate. "I am."

"I've been listening to your doctor, and the conversations over the comms. I understand that the experimental technology overheated your systems."

"Yeah. So?"

"I think I can help." He tried to stand but swayed.

Rachel grabbed him and eased him back to the bed. "Whoa there, soldier. You're not cleared for duty yet."

Cal folded his arms. The last thing he needed was another enforcer poking around. "We don't need your help. I've got people working on it."

"You have people who are not adept in alien configurations."

"And you are?"

"I would not say *adept*, but I am familiar. Zindiria has always had an interest in the technological advances of the Carteks. She assigned several of us to study ships that had been captured." He held out his hand, offering a handshake. "My name is Hendry."

Cal looked at his hand before meeting his gaze again. "You've worked on this kind of tech?"

Hendry's face remained placid as he lowered his hand. "Possibly. I don't know what you've managed to procure through your illicit channels, but chances are the basics would not be different from what I've already studied."

Cal stared at him. For some reason, this seemed too good to be true, and it had Orion written all over it. "You're actually offering to help?"

He lifted his chin. "I am."

"What's in it for you?"

Hendry blinked, flinched, and looked down. It seemed weak for an enforcer...even one in as bad a condition as him.

He looked up. "I will help you, if you tell Commander Orion that I am not improving."

Did Cal hear that right? "You want us to lie?"

"You are smugglers. My understanding is this comes easily to you."

"Maybe. The question is: Why?"

"I want to serve my sponsor. If I return, Orion will no doubt stretch the boundaries of my abilities once again, and this time, I may not survive."

"I thought there was honor in dying for your princess."

"There is. But using us in this way is not her directive. It is Orion's. The high prince ordered him to find his sister at any cost. Zindiria would understand the consequences and never give such an order. Her enforcers have meaning to her. She would not sacrifice us unnecessarily."

"You don't think she'd want to run her people to the point of death, even to save her life?"

He looked down again, maybe contemplating that question. "I think she would find another way." He looked up. "But no matter. My goal is to stand at her side again. She will heal me. But I have to live long enough to give her that chance."

The sincerity in the enforcer's eyes was surprising. Somehow, his drive to get back to his princess was so strong, it was allowing him to ask Cal, a smuggler, to lie for him. Then again, it could also have been a side effect of Doc pumping artificial pathogens into his system for days.

Hendry was a rare success story. They'd already lost four enforcers who had been too far gone to treat. Hendry hadn't looked much better than the ones who'd died. Could he have been so drained that the pathogens gave him free will faster than Alexander and even Dania?

Cal would probably regret this, but he wanted to be frank with this guy. "We have no intention of saving your princess."

"That makes perfect sense. It would be foolish of you. This isn't your problem."

Doc's eyes widened. He looked from the tray of pathogens, to the enforcer, and back again.

Hendry barely blinked, even in acknowledgement of an act of defiance.

"You're okay with that?" Cal asked.

"Orion will find her. I have no doubt." He looked at the unconscious enforcer in the bed beside him. "I only ask that you drop me and Bleven off at a station where we can rest comfortably until we can reunite with her."

"You mean *hide*."

"Enforcers do not hide." He looked at his friend again. "But in this case, I can see how it may appear that way."

Interesting. Very, very interesting.

Cal puffed out a breath and dragged his fingers through his hair. He was probably going to regret this.

He turned to Doc. "Tell Orion that both these guys took a turn for the worse, and we have no idea when they'll be able to return to his suicidal lineup."

Rachel clapped her hands. "Yay! I love having new friends around."

Cal headed for the door. Hopefully, these new friends wouldn't bite him in the ass.

The door closed behind him, and Cal leaned on the wall, taking a deep breath. He probably should have talked to Alanna and Alexander before making that deal. If Ethan could figure out the problem, there would be no reason to involve an enforcer. Still, for some reason, he wanted to help the ones who were sick. Every time one of them cracked a little, it gave him hope that maybe the whole damn system could be dragged down.

Not that he wanted to be the one to do it. He had far too many problems of his own.

Bootsteps slammed on the floor tiles, and Alanna stormed around the corner. Her eyes were ablaze, and her cheeks were redder than her pink-tipped hair.

She stopped a few feet from him. "I am *so* angry!"

Cal laughed. "I can see that."

"Goddammit, Cal, I'm serious!"

Whoa. Did she just...*curse*?

Cal held up both his hands. "I'm sorry. I've just never seen you this mad before. What's wrong? Is it the tech?"

"The tech? Who gives a shit about the tech!?"

Okay, double-whoa. Two curses in fifteen seconds? "Hold on."

Cal took her arm and gently led her down the hall to the lounge. Luckily, it was empty.

He closed the door. "What's going on?"

She paced in front of the window, dragging her fingers through her hair. "We knew that prince was a jerk. I just had no idea how much of a jerk he was."

Okay, good. At least the problem wasn't with someone in the crew—and her language was coming back to an almost-like-Alanna squeaky-clean level.

She'd already known that Prince Geron had modified Alexander and Dania to make them into enforcers. That was bad in itself...but this seemed like something more.

She stopped and turned toward Cal. The heaviness in her heart showed in her eyes. Whatever this was, it had touched her soul, and suddenly, he wanted to punch someone for hurting the sweetest, kindest person he knew.

He took a steadying breath. "What is it?"

She pointed out the window. "That prince forced himself on Alexander."

"Forced himself?"

She grabbed her temples again and growled at the ceiling. "Cal, you know what I mean. Please don't make me say it out loud!" Tears welled in her eyes. "He asked for favors, and Alexander couldn't say *no*. Doc explained once that enforcers are compelled to do whatever that stinking prince asks like zombies." Her lower lip started to tremble, and she bit it. "He used his influence in the worst possible way."

Holy hell. Cal rubbed his forehead. "And I'm going to guess you told him you were angry, and he defended the prince."

"Yes! He's not even capable of being mad at him. I don't know what's more disgusting, using Alexander like that, or the mind control." She wiped the tears from her eyes.

Cal shifted his weight. If Doc were here, he'd probably hold her and whisper sweet things until she stopped crying. Peter just had a way with people that Cal could never quite emulate.

If this were Ethan or Ty, Cal would just punch them in the arm and tell them life sucked and they needed to focus and get a hold of themselves. But he'd been around the galaxy enough to know not everything was that easy. Especially for Alanna.

She turned from the window. "I'm sorry. This is bringing up all these feelings I thought I'd gotten over."

"What do you mean?"

She rubbed her shoulders. "When I was with those pirates, I hated stealing stuff for them. They were just in it for the money, and they didn't care who they hurt."

"That wasn't your fault. They were threatening your family."

"I know that, but I still had a choice. I could have walked away." She sighed. "I just keep thinking about Alex. He complied without question, but was he dying inside, just like I was?" She looked at Cal. "He didn't have the choice I did, and that's killing me inside."

"Alanna, this isn't your fault. You didn't do this to him."

"I know. It's just that everyone on this ship means so much to me, and I hate it that that slimy prince hurt my friends. Alex and Dania deserve better."

A chill rolled over Cal's skin. "What do you mean by that?"

She looked down. "He said something that made me think it wasn't an isolated case." She bit her lower lip again. "When he was defending that prince, Alex said, 'He cares about all of us.'" She gulped. "That made me wonder about Dania."

Cal ground his teeth. When he and Dania had been kissing, she'd pushed him away. She'd raised her hands and asked him not to hurt her.

Cal had frozen, wondering who could possibly have hurt an enforcer so bad that she would have flinched. Heat rolled over his skin. He spun, slamming his fist on the door mechanism and storming from the room.

The answer to his question was simpler, and more horrible than he'd ever imagined. There was only one person capable of hurting an enforcer. Someone stronger than her.

"Cal!" Alanna called from behind him.

He stopped at the main juncture and punched the wall. His knuckles stung. He drank in the pain. Relished it.

He had enforcers in his cargo hold.

He had a piece of alien tech on his ship that could blow up at any moment.

He had enforcer ships flanking them at all times.

And a commander whose only goal was a mission that would probably get them all killed.

He had a thousand monumental things to worry about.

But none of them mattered more than the anger coursing through his veins.

He continued down the hall until he'd reached the crew quarters and banged on Dania's door.

Alanna flew around the corner and skidded to a stop, her eyes wide when she saw where he stood. "What are you going to do?"

He tried to keep his voice level. "I'll know when she opens the door."

The door slid open, and Cal walked through.

Dania frowned. "What's wrong?"

"Everything."

She closed the door. "That's a pretty big word."

"This is a pretty big problem."

"Okay. Did Orion do something?"

There was no use in dragging this out. His fingers dug into his palms, and he needed an answer before he punched something else. "Did your prince take advantage of you?"

Her eyes widened. "What do you mean?"

"Did he ever hurt you?"

She flinched—less than the first time, but it was definitely there.

"Answer!"

She blinked, gaping. "Not intentionally, no. He would never hurt me."

"Either he did, or he didn't."

She lowered her eyes. "This isn't something we need to talk about."

"I think it is."

She shook her head, not raising her eyes. "It doesn't matter."

"How can you say that?"

Dania looked up. "I'm not going back to Keveron, Cal. I can't, and I won't. What happened between me and Geron is in the past."

The knife in his chest twisted. "So, you *did* sleep with him?"

She sighed. "He needs protection at all times of the day. That was an easy way to be protected at night."

He dug his fingernails deeper into his palms. "But it was more than sleeping, wasn't it?"

She took a step toward him. "I can never expect you to understand what it is to be an enforcer—what it's like to be owned by someone and worship them at the same time."

"You worshiped him, and he took advantage."

She turned and looked at her reflection in her mirror. "I never felt like our relationship was wrong, and I still don't." She spun to Cal. "But that doesn't mean I want to go back. I love it here. You and this crew, this ship, are everything to me. But..." She closed her eyes and rubbed her face.

The knife in his chest twisted harder. "What aren't you telling me?"

"The emergency feeding he sent me solidified my worst fears." She looked back to the mirror. "Even though I'm free, and I don't need to be fed anymore, I can still feel his pull, like my body yearns to be with him."

Cal cringed. Just the thought of her yearning for anyone else made him want to scream. He took a settling breath. "Doc explained that you're all like junkies needing a fix."

She nodded. "If he comes for me, I'm not sure I'd be physically able to say *no* if he demanded I return to the fold."

"You said *no* to him once." And then she'd shoved the *Star Renegade* and herself down a black hole to get away from him.

She shook her head. "I didn't say *no*. I gave in, but they were already attacking. I was going to return, but I used the last of my energy to push the *Star Renegade* to safety, and to save Alexander."

"Then you passed out and you got sucked into the black hole, too."

She nodded. "If that hadn't happened, I would probably be hunting you down right now."

"Well, you're not. You're here."

"And I want to stay here. But I'm terrified he'll find me. Orion already tracked us down. It's only a matter of time before Geron does, too. And once he's back, Alexander and I will lose all the choices you've given us. We'll return to being his pawns."

"That's slavery, and slavery is illegal, even in the Bane world. The whole poaching thing is what brought you to us in the first place."

Her eyes reddened before they filled with tears. She covered her face with her hands.

Crap. Maybe barging in here half-cocked and ready for a fight had been a bad idea. These were memories she probably didn't want to dredge up, and here Cal was, dredging away without thinking about how she'd feel.

"Stars, I'm sorry." He gathered her in his arms. "I screwed this up. This is not the way to be supportive."

"You didn't say anything wrong."

"Well, I sure as hell didn't say anything right." He tilted up her chin so she would look at him. "I can't stand knowing that someone hurt you. I want to kill him."

"You can't say that. And you *definitely* can't say that in front of Alexander or the other enforcers."

Of course not. Threatening the royal family was a crime punishable by death. No one cared what atrocities the Banes committed on their own time.

She placed her hand on his chest. "Please, promise me."

"*Someone* needs to hold them accountable."

She opened her lips, like she was about to say something, but then closed them and turned away.

"You were going to defend him again, weren't you?"

"It's not my fault. I wish you could understand."

He tightened his grip on her. "I'm trying. It's just hard. I want to keep you safe from everything. I know you don't need protecting, but I can't help it."

"It's who you are. I know."

He caressed her chin. "I'm going to keep you away from the Banes."

She stepped away, rubbing the back of her neck. "I'm not sure that's even possible."

"What does that mean?"

"He's done things to me that I can't run from." She looked down again. "I'm not sure I'll ever be normal."

Cal shook his head. "You're stronger than you know. I've watched you evolve. You're fighting him."

"I'm not sure I'll win."

Cal leaned down and kissed her. Dania's lips parted and she clung to him, accepting the small token of how much he wanted her, before he broke the kiss.

"I think you already have won."

She smiled, and for a moment, the crazed alien tech, the missing princess, and the enforcers all disappeared. The world became right again—

Until she frowned. "I wish it were that easy."

"Why do I feel like you're about to drop another bomb on me?"

Her lower lip trembled. "I'm afraid that if I were ever in the same room with Geronagain, I'd *need* to go back. I don't want to, but his power might be too strong and..." Her eyes teared up again.

Every time he thought he'd found a breakthrough, something else popped up. He needed to handle whatever she was about to tell him better than he'd managed the last nugget of horror. "What is it?"

"If Geron took me back, he could make me kill you and everyone in this crew and I would have no way to stop myself."

So, they were back to square one...the same threat as when she'd first stepped on board. "Then we keep running. We keep one step ahead of him."

"We might be running for the rest of our lives."

He pulled her close again. "So be it. You and Alexander are part of this crew now. We're all on the run anyway. What's one more prince to worry about?"

She nodded, but a deep-seated fear still hung inside her eyes.

One thing she'd said was true... If those enforcers could

track them down so easily, the prince might be able to do the same, even if Kile tried to help keep him off their backs. The clock might be ticking, and he needed to be ready to run—but he couldn't do that with a cargo hold filled with enforcers.

CHAPTER 36
CAL

CAL STOPPED PACING when Ty entered the lounge and took his seat at the end of the table. Dania sat across from Alanna, with Alex and Rachel to her right, and Doc and Ethan on the other side of the table beside Alanna. They all stared at him.

After all the extra baggage unloaded in the past few hours, he didn't blame them, and most of them didn't even know the new details... Not that the exploding tech and the enforcers weren't enough to worry about.

Cal leaned on the back of his chair. "Status report on the tech."

"Hendry has been great." Ethan leaned his elbows on the table. "We were already working on containing the heat, but he had some great ideas to keep the temperature at a more stable level."

"Does that mean it's safe?"

Ethan grimaced. "I don't know about *safe*, but I feel good about it. But... I felt good about it the first time, too."

"I want to finish the seals," Alanna said. "Better safe than sorry."

Cal nodded. "I think we're all in agreement with that. How long?"

"Another day, I think."

That would have to do. Cal looked at Ty. "Any news on finding me a ship?"

"Big-ass cruisers aren't really a tradable commodity. People who have them don't give them up."

"Being hard to find has never stopped you before."

Ty shrugged. "I made a quick call to Port Walker. Glenn said *his interest was piqued.*"

That was good news. "Does that mean he's sending one?"

"In Glenn speak, either one is on the way, or he has a lead. Who knows? The guy will never say anything that could get him arrested on an open comm."

Which was smart. If anyone could find a ship, it would be Glenn. He certainly had the connections. But Port Walker was on the other side of the galaxy. What were the chances his lead was closer than Glenn was?

"We need that ship. We're coming up on Z8. If we can get through the blockade and get the supplies Doc needs for the pathogens, I want to treat everyone we can and get those enforcers on another transport as soon as possible. Then we disappear before they get a chance to get their bearings." He looked at Alanna and Ethan. "Speaking of disappearing, we should do another test. Preferably without nearly dying this time."

Ethan tapped his fingers on the edge of the table. "I hate that I don't understand that thing from guts to outer casing, but everything Hendry showed me panned out. The formulas are solid. I think we're okay. I'm ready to test as soon as the seals are done." He looked at Alexander.

"I agree," the enforcer said. "I asked Hendry questions and got irrefutable answers. His logic is sound, and I have no reason to believe he is serving an agenda contrary to our own."

"I agree," Dania said. "He wants to see his princess again. He's on our side, at least for now."

Cal tapped the back of his chair. They were relying on the word of an enforcer. Cal was never one to trust an enemy, but if this guy couldn't lie, and Dania and Alex trusted his word, that had to be good enough. "Okay. We disappear. We get the supplies, and hopefully, we'll have a ship once we get out to unload the enforcers on." It wasn't a foolproof plan, but it would work if Glenn pulled through.

"What if Orion doesn't like the other ship?" Alanna asked.

Cal looked at Ty. "He'll like it, right?"

"I told Glenn we'd be willing to owe him big time. I mean, I didn't give him any details, but I think he gets that it needs to be princess-worthy."

Alanna sat back in her chair. "I'm just afraid that Orion might lash out on the people of Kirato."

"I doubt it," Doc said. "To be honest, I think the enforcers who are there are probably stranded in the outer rims until their princess comes to get them, or her ship is fixed. They'll need to play nice if they want to eat."

The problem was, even a handful of enforcers on the planet could find any number of illegal things at any moment. Cal would have to come up with a way to get them off Kirato, but he had to focus on one problem at a time.

He gripped the back of the chair. "We're coming up on the blockade tomorrow night. Let's be ready."

CHAPTER 37
CAL

CAL KEPT his breathing steady as Orion's star skipper disengaged from the *Star Renegade* and joined the other ships in space. Luckily, the commander had agreed that there was no way to hide the fact that Orion and his buddies were enforcers, or he'd have sent a military escort down to get the supplies. Even the enforcers had to admit it was unwise for the king's elite police force to attempt trade in the pirate sector.

Cal gripped the arms of his command chair as the three enforcer ships cut their engines and let the *Star Renegade* drift away. Any other day, he'd be making a run for it while their guard was down. His motto had always been to stay as far away from enforcers as possible. He missed those carefree times. Running was a hell of a lot easier than helping them.

Orion appeared on the screen. "The enforcers on your ship are more than prepared to deal with you should you default on our arrangement."

Arrangement? What arrangement? This guy had delusions that Cal had actually agreed to their demands. Up until now, they'd at least been going to the same place. Now that they were here, the real fun would begin. Just how much fun remained to be seen.

Cal tapped the comm. "Their job is to stay put and not be seen. If anyone finds enforcers on our ship, they'll hit us with enough artillery to destroy a small moon."

The commander's brow quirked. "Keep to the plan, Mr. Espinoza."

The screen blanked out.

Ty maneuvered the ship away from them. "Do you actually know what the grand plan is he keeps talking about?"

"I don't even think he knows what the plan is. He's being cryptic so he can charge us with insubordination and execute us when we're done."

Ty snorted a laugh.

"It's not funny." Alanna shifted at the comm station. "Who knows what those enforcers are really planning out there."

"All they care about is getting to their princess," Cal said. "Nothing's changed."

"Not until we get them that shiny new ship, at least." Ty tapped the controls, and the stars in the viewscreen shifted to the right.

Cal nodded. Whatever ship Glenn sent them had better be enough to make the enforcers forget all about the *Star Renegade*.

"We're sure the tech is fixed, right?" Ty asked.

Alanna grimaced. "I sure hope so."

They both spun toward her. "You *hope* so?"

She continued tapping on the screen in her console. "It will work." Her lips kept moving like a silent prayer, though. That couldn't be good.

Cal hit the comm to the engine room. "Ethan, that tech is strapped to the airlock, right?"

"You bet your ass it is. Any sign of a spike in temperature, and it's gone."

Alexander's voice came over the comm. "Hendry and I have been over the specifications twenty-six times. The modifications are more than adequate to contain any anticipated fluctuations."

Any *anticipated* fluctuations. If they'd anticipated it might explode the first time, they never would have turned the damn thing on.

"We're approaching the 'now or never' zone." Ty pointed out the window. "In three minutes, they'll be able to see us."

Cal tapped into the ship-wide comm. "Okay, people, hold on tight. We're about to go dark."

"Ready?" Alanna asked.

No, but Cal took a deep breath and nodded anyway. He may not have committed to that princess, but he had committed to getting the supplies to save as many of the enforcers as they could. That meant getting through the blockade—and to do that, they needed to disappear. "Let's go."

The floor hummed slightly as the lights dimmed. Orion's voice came over the comm. "*Star Renegade*, we confirm that you've disappeared." There was a slight grunt, like he was warring with himself...maybe over one of those ridiculous programming things they weren't able to get around. "If you manage not to explode, I expect you will be sharing that technology with your king."

Yeah, like that was going to happen...

Cal tapped the comm. "We're going radio silent. See you tomorrow."

The lights in Alanna's console cast a sallow glow over her features. "Everything looks good. The tech is running only ten degrees higher than its resting state." She smiled. "Looks like we did it!"

Yes, but the question was: Would the Carteks be able to spot their own tech? "Everyone, stay on your toes. We have no idea what we're about to run into."

"We should be getting a visual any second now," Alanna said.

Ty pointed out the window. "There it is."

A grid of stars laid out before them...a perfectly symmetrical weave of pinprick lights.

Cal leaned closer to the glass to take it all in. The grid spanned high and wide, as far as he could see, like someone had thrown a lighted quilt over the wide expanse of space...or maybe a net. "How do we get through that?"

Alanna's fingers flew over her panel. "Working on it."

"It's massive," Ty whispered. "But why out here?"

"Z8 isn't the most reputable place, but there is a lot of artillery in the pirate sector. My guess is they're stopping the Banes from tapping into the stockpiles of highly illegal resources out there."

"But cutting them off like that will keep the legal supplies out, too. There's not much agriculture in that system," Ty said.

Cal nodded. "I don't think there's *any*." Which meant right now, the people of Z8 were facing the same fate as Kirato, although these worlds had a lot more resources to work with.

Alanna snapped her fingers. "Found it!" A red circle appeared on the viewscreen. "There's your entrance."

Ty squinted at the glass. "That wall is solid. There's nothing there."

"Oh, it's there, all right. It's big enough for a royal cruiser to get through. It's just dwarfed by how big the blockade is."

Cal rubbed his chin. "I don't like it. It's too confined." He pulled up the information Ty had purloined from Orion's datastores. "Are we sure this thing is as big as we thought? Maybe we can get around it. It can't go on forever."

Ty scrolled through readings on the screen in his console. "Not forever, but it looks like it will take at least a week to get to the closest edge."

And Orion's fuse would burn out long before then.

Cal looked at Alanna. "Can you jump us around it?"

Her eyes widened. "I'm not sure what jumping would do to the tech."

Ty spun his chair toward them. "Not only that, but it would leave a jump signature. We might as well be wearing a homing beacon." He turned back to his station and tapped on the screens. "We can't even make better time by punching our engines or they'd see our energy traces."

And every moment they sat out there was more time for them to be discovered…stealth tech or not.

"We could always back off and head to Themyscira," Alanna said. "It's close enough, and they had the supplies we needed last time."

Themyscira *would* be easier…

"I wouldn't go near there." Ty leaned his elbow on the edge of his console. "Rumors say their military could rival

Earth's. They have to know this blockade is outside their doorstep. Chances are they'll be itchy enough to shoot anything that comes too close."

Alanna slumped. "Doc also said that we'd cleaned them out of supplies last time. A lot of this stuff is pretty hard to get." She lowered her eyes. "Sorry, it was a silly idea."

"No ideas are silly." Cal looked back at the blockade. They'd both made good points…which left their only viable option behind a nearly impenetrable wall.

Alanna put another red circle around the break in the barrier, making it look like a bullseye. "That's our ticket through."

Cal rubbed his face. He hated it when they needed to choose between a bad and a worse option. "Okay, take us closer and get a good look, but be ready to run if we need to."

Ty snickered. "One thing I am always ready to do is run."

The pinpricks of light got bigger as they approached the grid. Each light was a ship, maybe half the size of the *Star Renegade*, all linked by either some sort of cable, or a laser framework. "That's the biggest spiderweb I've ever seen," Ty said.

Spiderweb…that was a good analogy.

"The break in the wall is still clear." Alanna zoomed the image on the main screen.

Any of the ships around that opening could be surveillance stations. Maybe all of them were.

Ty glanced at Cal. "Do we slide on in like a ventilation slug?"

Cal puffed out a breath. This had to be the dumbest thing they'd ever tried. However, if they got caught, and

Rgrythei's contract was still due, he had more than enough enforcers to pay off the Carteks. Not that he'd actually do that...but it was an option if the lives of his crew were at stake.

He dearly hoped it wouldn't come to that. "Let's go."

Ty focused on the target as the lights from the blockade lit up the bridge. "Here's where all that daredevil flying you're always complaining about will come in handy."

With any luck, Ty's skills would be enough to get them through undetected.

A chill ran down Cal's spine as a few small skipper crafts moved from ship to ship on the grid. "Why can't they see us?"

"The tech should be changing constantly, reflecting what they would expect to see on our hull. If they're looking right at us, they'll see a shadow, but if not, we'll look like a scattering of stardust."

"Let's hope the guard is taking a bathroom break," Cal said.

Ty frowned. "Do Carteks even pee?"

Cal glared at him, and Ty shrugged before focusing on the grid again.

The lights glowed, pulsing on all sides as the *Star Renegade* passed through hundreds of ships. The blockade wasn't only long, but thick. There must have been tens of thousands of ships in the weave.

"No signs of any changes in the pattern of the grid," Alanna said. "Just keep it slow and steady."

"Yes, ma'am." Ty pressed forward, slowing as two ships crossed their path, leaving a hangar on one side and docking at another.

"It's like its own space port," Alanna said.

Cal nodded. When Orion had mentioned the war, he'd used the word *blockades*—as in plural. How many of these megaliths were out there?

"Coming up on the other side," Alanna said.

Ty stared straight ahead until the *Star Renegade* floated into clear, normal-looking stars. He whistled a long tone. "That's how it's done."

Cal tapped him on the back. "Keep it slow and get us to the trade center. We need to get in and out while luck is still on our side."

"You got it, boss. Slow and steady wins the race."

Hopefully, slow and steady would win them a ridiculous amount of illegal medical supplies.

Every time they had a close call, Cal swore that he'd take the *Star Renegade* somewhere safe and land the ship forever. His crew deserved a good, quiet life.

He smiled, imagining Dania pruning tomato vines while Cal pulled weeds beside her. They could grow all their own vegetables and herbs and create their own recipes. They wouldn't have to run anymore.

It was just a dream…but a nice dream. He'd give that to her if he could.

Ty pointed at the screen. "Doc's coordinates are taking us to that planet, southern hemisphere, quadrant two."

"Let's turn off the cloak so we don't suddenly appear and scare them."

"Roger that."

Their destination appeared as a tiny blue-and-green marble in space, growing larger as they approached. The last time they'd been in this sector, there'd been thousands of ships. It was eerily quiet for pirate central.

"Incoming transmission," Alanna said.

Cal wasn't surprised. He hit the comm. "This is the *Star Renegade*. We'd like to land and give a few fair trades."

A thickly accented voice sounded through the speakers. "*Star Renegade*, how be it that you gets past the blockade? How do we know you canna be trusted?"

Ty hit the comm. "Because we're the *Star Renegade*. We're more trustworthy than half the scum on your planet, and you know it. If you want us to move on and trade elsewhere, we got no problem with that."

Cal raised a brow at him, and Ty shrugged. The kid usually flashed a silver tongue in situations like this, but when talking to pirates, maybe it was best to act a little like a pirate.

The voice returned. "*Star Renegade*, pleasa send the coordinates ofa your trade location."

"Let's hope this doesn't backfire." Ty entered in the location.

A tone sounded. "You be cleared to land, *Star Renegade*. Do nota deviate from course. As you canna expect, everyone be a little bitsa jumpy these days."

"Understood." Cal pushed out his chair. "Here we go. Let's try to make this as smooth as possible." Which meant they needed to get out of there without anyone shooting at them. No problem.

ALANNA TOOK a deep breath as Ty maneuvered the *Star Renegade* to the south side of the planet. The sun bathed the bridge in natural light, and it was almost as if she were able to smell fresh, non-recycled air even within the ship.

She grabbed her bag and headed down the ladder to the lower deck.

Dania, Alexander, and Cal already stood at the opening to the cargo ramp.

Alexander leaned toward Cal, like he was trying to make a point. "Dania does not need to be here. I'm more than enough security for you and the doctor."

Alanna held back a snicker. It sounded like she'd walked into a typical *Star Renegade* testosterone-fest.

She stepped off the ladder. "I asked her to come. We're going to grab a few parts for maintenance, and it's safer to trade in groups."

A smile appeared on Dani's lips as Alanna moved beside her. They both folded their arms and stared him down.

Alexander gaped. "There's no need for you to leave the ship, either. I can get any supplies you need."

Was he serious? "If this is a chivalry thing, you better get over that real quick, mister."

"It's okay," Cal said. "It's always better to show numbers. Five is a safe number to watch each other's backs."

Even with five of them, Alanna wasn't sure they'd look menacing enough to help them avoid trouble, but they needed Ty at the ready to take off, and Ethan ready to burn the engines. And the last thing they needed was to worry about what Rachel might say to the wrong person, so five would have to do.

Dania glared at Alex. "I'm not fragile. You can treat me like any other member of the crew."

"I know you're not fragile, but you're unpracticed in combat."

Alanna's eyes widened just as much as Dania's. Alexander definitely needed to learn to sugarcoat things a little.

Dania's nose flared. "I am a general. How can you say that?"

Alex held up his hands. "I meant you are unpracticed without your power. Do you even know how to use a weapon?"

He kinda had a good point, but the darkness clouding Dania's eyes told Alanna this was an argument Alex wasn't going to win.

Dania lifted her chin. "I'm going."

Doc scampered down the ladder and jumped from the last few rungs. "All right. I have a supplier willing to chat. It looks like he has what we need."

Cal looked toward the rear of the ship. The enforcers were safely stowed in the back of the cargo area, but he probably still wished there was another door to leave the ship from in order to keep them as secure as possible.

Alanna couldn't blame him. She didn't like that there was nothing but a wall and a containment field to keep the enforcers hidden from prying eyes. She'd traded on this planet before. This was the one place in the galaxy where the people she'd dealt with were actually worse than the men who'd held her captive.

Ty's voice came over the comm. "All-righty. Ethan and I will keep the pre-flight pre-flighty just in case things go the way they always do."

"Let's hope they go right for a change," Cal said.

"Roger that."

The doors started to open, and Cal glanced at his landing party. "I know Alanna wants to get supplies, but we need to stay together. We'll get Doc's supplies first, and if all goes well, we'll stop for maintenance stuff, and if we're lucky, a little food. It's just not worth the risk of separating."

Alexander stepped between Alanna and Dania. "Agreed. I'll keep them safe."

Alanna slapped his shoulder. "Quit the noble protector act. We're a team. You're here to help all of us." Hopefully, he'd listen. The last thing she wanted was for him to let his feelings for her jeopardize the mission.

Cal's cheek ticked. She hadn't been completely open about how far things had gone between her and Alex, but Cal wasn't a fool. He knew that if they faced danger, Alexander would shelter Alanna and Dania first. Which probably meant that Doc and Cal would be fending for themselves, but that shouldn't worry him. They'd faced worse than this with nothing but their own smarts for years.

Cal started down the ramp. "Let's go."

Men in green coveralls waved them forward with orange glow-lights as Ty retracted the landing platform, sealing the *Star Renegade* from anyone who might be nosey enough to take a peek on board. The sunlight warmed Alanna's cheeks, for real this time. She would have liked to take a few moments to breathe natural air before they were herded into a building and down a long, metal hallway that didn't feel all that different from a ship.

Alanna switched her bag from one shoulder to another. "This is nothing to worry about. It's actually a friendlier welcome than I've seen in the past. They must all be very worried about the Carteks sitting right outside their borders."

The few people they did see backed away, pale-faced. Did the colonists think they were Cartek spies? Had the Carteks maybe sent representatives to the planets, or beaten them into submission?

These people weren't all that innocent, but it still sucked to see them so scared. No one should have to live in fear, especially on their own home world.

They continued through a small courtyard with sparsely stocked trading tables before their escort stopped at a modest, dented aluminum door. It opened before they could knock, and a small, balding man with grease-stained hands ushered them inside.

He shook each of their hands. "My name'sa Gilden. I musta say I wasa surprised to hear I had a customer. Not too many of those these days."

Doc moved to the front of the group. "Did you get my list?"

"Yesa, I did. Interesting. Most interesting."

"Can you fill the order?"

"Of course."

The two started exchanging big words that Alanna was fairly certain were made up, when Doc gaped. "You want *how much?*"

Gilden shrugged. "It'sa tough these days. Blockade inflation."

"That's three times the going rate for these supplies."

"To get here, you run the blockade, no? That meansa you are either crazy, or desperate." The trader held up a vial of clear liquid. "You needsa this. For what, I don't care. But you may be my only customer for months. A man's got to feed hisa family."

Doc lowered his eyes and turned to Cal. "Even pooling all our funds, we don't have enough ducets."

Alanna's heart dropped. They'd brought extra ducets for food and maintenance supplies, and even *that* wouldn't cover what the trader wanted for the supplies? Normally, they'd just move on to the next trader, but everyone on this planet was equally strapped for trade. If this was like any of the other pirate sites she'd traded on through the years, they all knew each other. If they left here, either no one would trade with them, or the prices would go *up.*

Cal looked at Alex, then Dania. His gaze stayed on her for several seconds before he turned to Doc. "Can you get enough to save our guests already in the med bay without tapping into the stash you have for Dania and Alexander?"

Dania rubbed her shoulders. "If they're the only ones treated, Orion will take Hendry back."

"Not to mention that all the ones in the cargo hold will die." Alanna shivered. Hendry had been nearly unconscious and barely breathing when the other enforcers dropped him off like a piece of trash. Every few days another enforcer suffered the same fate. It wasn't fair.

Doc placed his palms together, as if pleading with the trader. "What's the cost for half the supplies?"

Gilden smirked, only lowering the price by a fraction. Alanna didn't expect him to budge much. He had little to lose, and too much to gain. They were going to have to choose which enforcers lived and which died, and that was wrong in so many ways.

She shifted her weight, and the items in her bag clinked against each other. Her multi-tool, a small weapon—hidden in case they had taken everyone else's away—and her toy box.

Her heart sank. The gun and the tool would be meaningless to this guy, but the toy box was like nothing anyone had seen before. It created things from nothing. Yes, they were only illusions, but unlike virtual reality, the box changed everything around them and anyone in the room could see it. It really was like magic.

Alanna reached into her bag, her heart twisting as her fingers gripped the box.

She'd had the toy for so long, kept it hidden, just like she was supposed to. In many ways, it seemed like a part of her.

She dropped it back in her bag. The toy was her last memento of her childhood. She couldn't part with it.

Doc leaned closer to Cal. "I can dip into the supplies for Dania and Alexander. If I take six months' worth, I may be able to save half the others."

Cal frowned. "Then what happens in six months when you have no more for Dania? What are the chances we'll have any better luck next time?"

Doc looked down.

Alanna's stomach clenched. There were three options…

They could let the enforcers die: not good.

They could save some, putting Dania and Alexander at risk: also, not good.

Or Alanna could offer the one thing of value she had in the world to trade.

It shouldn't have been a hard decision, yet it was. She reached back into her bag and grasped the box. It was just a thing. A toy. Yet at the same time, it was so much more.

Just the thought of giving it up made her want to run and hide, but it was just a memory. It wasn't worth keeping if it could save one life, let alone many.

Her hands trembled, and she took a deep breath. "I have something I'm willing to trade, but I'm only willing to take all the supplies we originally asked for."

Gilden perked up. "I am an honest trader. As long as it's wortha my price, I am willing to consider."

Her throat constricted as she drew the toy box out. "This is priceless."

Alexander straightened, shifting his weight, looking from the box to Alanna.

She turned away, focusing on the trader before she changed her mind.

Gilden frowned. "Whatsa that?"

Alanna took a steadying breath and stared at her ultimate treasure, maybe for the last time. She concentrated, and two butterflies crawled out from beneath the box and took flight.

Gilden snorted. "Thatsa cute, but hardly priceless."

Alexander stepped beside her. "That's only the beginning." He touched the box and the room around them slipped away. Cal cursed and Doc cried out as a disk appeared under their feet, and they hung in space, staring at Saturn's rings.

Gilden whispered a few words in another language. "Howsa that work?"

"Would you like to try it?" Alex said.

The man nodded with wide eyes.

"What's one place you've always wanted to see?"

Gilden bit his lower lip. "A beach. An ocean."

Alexander looked at Alanna before he handed the box to the man. "I only need to think about what I want to see."

Alex gripped her hand and held his other hand palm out toward the box. His skin warmed, as space faded away, replaced by sand, a sparkling sun, and waves rolling on the water.

"Incredible!" Gilden said.

Yes, it was incredible. Alanna had hoped that one day Alexander could show her how to conjure more than butterflies, but she supposed that would never happen now.

Doc gaped, looking at the ceiling. "That might be the coolest thing I've ever seen. It changed the whole room!"

Alex grabbed the box from Gilden, and the vision winked away. "I trust this is worth what you asked?"

Gilden nodded. "Yes, yes. Take it all!"

Alanna took the box from Alex and gripped the memento to her chest as the others gathered the supplies. She closed her eyes, remembering countless days outside conjuring butterflies with her mother. Those had been simpler times.

She was supposed to keep this box a secret, but lives were at stake. If she could save someone, even an enforcer, her mother would be proud. At least, she hoped she would be.

Gilden reached for the box. "All I need to do is think about what I want?"

Alanna smiled. Butterflies took flight around her again.

Alex held out his hand, and Alanna placed the box in his palm. Part of her wanted to snatch it back—say this was a mistake, but she couldn't be selfish. Saving people was far more important than memories.

Alex gave it to the man. "You won't be able to use this when we leave."

He wouldn't? Alanna's sister could never get it to work, but Alanna had certainly never had a problem with it.

Gilden frowned. "It needs to recharge?"

Alanna shrugged. "Sometimes I need to wait a few days before it will work again." It was the truth. Sometimes it seemed like the box got tired if she used it too much. She never did understand fully where the power came from. Was that what Alexander had meant when he'd said the trader wouldn't be able to use it?

Gilden stared at the box like it was gold, and each member of the crew left with a bag around their shoulders.

Alanna sniffed, wiping her eyes. She'd kept that box beside her for so many years, and now it was gone. It was like losing her family all over again.

Alex placed his arm around her shoulder. "I know that was hard, but I'm sure your mother would approve."

Alanna hoped so.

Dania grabbed Alanna's arm and tugged. "We need to go." She glanced at Alexander. "I don't know where you got that *demori*, but there's no way that man will be able to activate it."

Alex smirked. "I told him as much. It was a fair trade."

Alanna moved beside Doc. "Will the supplies be enough?"

"I won't know until I analyze the grade. He didn't have time to cut it with inferior product, so I have high hopes."

Alanna nodded, glancing back to the trader's door. Her gut clenched. She needed to believe that the supplies would be worth her loss.

A light tone sounded, and Cal lifted his comm band. "Ty?"

"Cal! We've got—"

Cal stopped walking and stared at his wrist. "Ty, you cut out. You've got what?"

The sound of generators and people talking in the streets filled the area.

Cal looked up. "I think my comm went dead."

"Let me try." Doc raised his wrist. "Ty, what's up? You cut out."

The hair on Alanna's arms stood up. She looked over her shoulders, but none of the locals seemed to be paying them any mind.

Doc tapped his wrist again, and Cal's comm band pinged. "I got through to you. The problem must be on Ty's end."

Cal grimaced. "That can't be good. Let's get a move on." He picked up his pace.

Alanna adjusted her bag and started walking faster. "So much for getting maintenance supplies."

Cal kept walking. "We'll come back once we know everything is okay."

The problem was, things weren't okay, and they all knew it.

DANIA GLANCED AT ALEXANDER, but it seemed like he was trying to avoid her gaze. The appearance of the *demori* had barely even fazed him, other than a slight change in temperature that suggested he'd been concerned for Alanna. Had he given it to her? If so, why? And where had he even found it?

As soon as they got back to the *Star Renegade*, she'd need some answers. One simply didn't walk around with a power-focusing tool in their carry bag.

Alanna's cheeks reddened as they walked quickly through the streets. Ty's voice had been elevated, and the communications cutting out was concerning. However, technical problems were not uncommon for the *Star Renegade*. In the pirate sector, though, caution was always justified.

Cal's pace slowed as they reached the landing area. Across the platform, several men walked around the base of the *Star Renegade*.

Cal held up his hand, stopping everyone's gait.

Peter shifted, his temperature spiking and sweat glistening on his temples.

"Why can't we ever get a break?" Cal directed them behind a line of cargo staged by the entrance.

Alexander pointed to the right. "Three guards there, fully armed. Four more in the overheads."

Dania glanced up. How had she missed that? Were her senses and training dulling along with her powers?

"More hiding to the left." Cal motioned with his chin. "Looks like we've got a good, old-fashioned ambush."

Peter rubbed the back of his neck. "For medical supplies? If they wanted this stuff, they could have stolen it from that guy before we even got here."

"More likely, they found out about the enforcers." Cal turned to Alexander. "Let's keep things quiet and power-free as long as we can. If we're lucky, maybe we can still walk out of here."

Alexander nodded, but the edges of his hair had already lifted. To human eyes, it could easily be assumed to be static electricity, but Dania could feel the slight hum of power beneath his skin.

Her stomach churned. The only thing Dania could still do was sense temperature fluctuations. Why could Alexander so easily grasp his primordial energy when she'd lost almost all traces of her own power? It made no sense. After not being fed for so long, he should have been just as weak as she was.

Cal pulled something out of his pocket and handed it to Alexander. "Here. Tie down that hair. I'd like to keep you a secret as long as we can."

Alexander considered the black band for a moment before wrapping it around his hair in a sloppy knot. It changed his entire appearance, making him appear no more ominous than any other member of the crew.

Cal locked eyes with Peter, Alanna, then Dania. "You're my backup. Hopefully, we won't need you. Be ready." He tapped Alexander's shoulder. "You're with me."

They both flicked a quick glance in Dania's direction—Cal's expression dark and demanding, Alexander's diffident as they strode toward the ship.

Dania's gut clenched. She should have been the one standing beside Cal. She was a general.

Dania gritted her teeth and squeezed her hands into fists—a muscle memory preparation to take on the power of her prince. Of course, nothing happened.

From the moment she'd woken up on Keveron, she'd been primed and trained to use her power. She'd been described as an *elegant weapon*. A *beautiful horror*. And now she was cowering behind shipping containers.

She lowered her eyes. Cal had been right to take Alexander. She was less than a shadow of what she'd been, at least in a combat situation. Freedom, she'd found, had a price. She was just a member of the crew now. Nothing more.

Ty appeared in the *Star Renegade*'s bridge window. Cal gave him a curt nod as Ty held both hands on his temples and puffed out his cheeks. Movement behind the pilot told her Rachel and Ethan were also on the bridge. The pirates must have cut off their transmission when they'd tried to warn Cal of the ambush.

Alanna moved beside her, pressing cool metal in her palm. "The safety is off. Just point at what you want to shoot and pull the trigger."

Dania nodded, placing the gun beside her hip as the

doctor pulled his own weapon out of his bag. Cal strode confidently forward, but she imagined he had a firearm at the ready. Alexander obviously needed no weapon, even if he was low on power. The pirates still had them outnumbered, but with any luck, they wouldn't have to fight.

One of the pirates stepped forward, rubbing his gray stubble with grease-stained fingers. He pointed his other thumb over his shoulder. "This your ship?"

Cal stopped walking. "Yeah. Care to step aside?"

The man's smile didn't reach his eyes as he glared at Cal. "You flew right through the blockade. How?"

Cal's shoulders visibly tensed. "Good flying."

"Bullshit." The man sneered. "You got tech. Whatever it is, we want it."

"It's not for sale."

"We ain't *asking*."

All the pirates drew weapons at the same time.

Cal kept his breathing level, but she could sense his blood pressure rising. "Things are bad enough in the galaxy. We don't need to be fighting amongst ourselves."

The pirate leader sneered. "We don't need to be keeping secrets, either."

Cal's stance remained rigid. "I'm going to tell you again. Step aside."

The pirate snorted. "You be a bit outnumbered. You ain't in any place to make demands."

A flash of light blasted from the pirate ranks, lighting up the space between Alanna and Dania.

"Oww." Alanna hissed through clenched teeth, grabbing the side of her face.

Peter spun, pulling her down while Cal ducked, firing his weapon into the rafters. Alexander raised his arms, and the pirates around the *Star Renegade* lifted from the ground and flew to either side of the ship.

Dania gaped. How had he done that?

"Enforcer!" someone yelled from above, and laser blasts and bullets rained down on the deck.

Peter appeared at Dania's side, pointing his weapon over the top of the containers, laying cover fire over Cal. Dania blinked, shaking out of her stupor, and drew her own weapon, aiming wide around Cal.

Alexander spun, wild-eyed as he raced back to the cargo containers. He held out one hand and Cal lifted onto his feet. Blasts of laser fire bounced off an invisible shield around them as Alexander jumped over the containers and slammed to the ground behind her.

"Alanna!" Alexander gathered her in his arms.

Cal rounded the corner and cursed, crouching beside them, looking at Alanna with concern in his eyes.

"Stop it, both of you." Alanna held her cheek, blood oozing from her fingers. "I'm fine."

Alexander kissed her deeply, and Dania gasped. She'd known they were involved intimately, but she'd never seen such a show of affection from her friend. The band slipped from his hair and his long locks took flight as he drew his thumb along Alanna's cheek, not breaking the kiss.

He didn't need to wipe away the blood for Dania to know the cut would be completely healed.

Peter tapped Alexander's shoulder. "While that's probably the most romantic thing I've ever seen, and I'm totally jealous...can we save this for when we're back on the ship?"

Three shots exploded on the wall behind them.

Alanna pushed Alexander away, breathing heavily. "I

told you I'm fine." She touched her cheek. "See? It's not even bleeding anymore."

Alexander smiled before he turned to Cal. "I can throw a shield around us. We can walk right onto the ship."

Another day, a shield would be no problem, but Alexander's sallow skin showed clear signs of needing a feeding. In his condition, he shouldn't have even been able to levitate those men. She was surprised he was even able to help Cal make it to cover.

Cal frowned at him. "You sure? You don't look so good."

"I'm an enforcer. I can create a simple shield."

Dania inched up on her knees. "I'm not sure you can."

Alexander licked his lips and glanced at Alanna. "I'll be okay in a moment." He turned to Peter. "Please help her get to the ship."

"I told you I'm okay!" Alanna sat up, then fell back.

"Whoa there, girlfriend." Peter grabbed her. "Let's take things slow. You know how you like to use yourself for target practice."

Alanna rubbed her head. "Not intentionally."

Alexander held up his hands and the sound of the gunfire muffled as a shimmering barrier formed around them. "Let's go."

Peter helped Alanna to her feet, and Dania grabbed her other arm.

"I'm okay," Alanna insisted again, yet she stumbled.

Cal held his gun to the side as he circumvented the cargo containers. The air blurred around them as bullets and lasers bounced off.

He reached out, and the shields sizzled at the edge of his fingertips. "Can I fire through this?"

Alexander flinched as a blast landed near his face. "I'd rather you didn't try."

Alanna groaned as she leaned on Peter and Dania. She'd been right that the hit she'd taken had been only a graze. Why was she so weak?

More pirates entered the landing area. Their shouts sounded far away through the swirling energy of the shield.

As they neared the ship, the landing platform came down. Ethan and Rachel stood in the opening and fired over the top of Alexander's shield. Several of the pirates dove for cover, and Cal picked up his pace.

Alexander's skin grew pale again, and his steps seemed labored. Dania let go of Alanna's arm and reached for him just as the shimmering bubble around them fizzled, and her friend fell to one knee.

Cal cursed, grabbing Alexander's arm as they ran up the ramp. A spray of laser fire shot past them, scorching the outer hull.

"The shield is down!" a pirate yelled behind them.

"Come on!" Peter grabbed Alanna and helped Dania drag her up the ramp.

Cal let Alexander go as the rest of them boarded. "Seal the ship!"

Alexander slipped to the deck, breathing heavily and holding his chest as the ramp closed behind them.

Rachel laughed, holstering her weapon. "Well, that was exciting."

Cal reached for the rungs of the ladder. "Doc, you good?"

Peter waved him on. "Yeah, yeah, let me do doctor stuff. You do the *saving us* stuff."

Alanna crawled to Alexander's side. "What happened?"

He coughed and winced, like breathing hurt. "It wasn't enough."

Alanna smoothed back his hair. "What wasn't enough?"

He placed his hand on her cheek. "I'm sorry." His eyes fluttered closed, and he slumped back to the deck as the floor rumbled beneath them.

Rachel placed her hands on her hips. "Well, that sucks. At least he got you all out before he finally ran out of juice."

Alanna wiped tears from her eyes. "We aren't out yet." She looked at Dania. "The blockade." She blinked like she was having trouble seeing.

Dania stood. Alanna was right. The pirates wouldn't simply let them fly away, and Alanna looked too tired to jump them. Unless the pirates gave up, allowing them to cloak, there would be no way to get through that wall of enemy ships.

CHAPTER 40
CAL

Cal slipped into his chair. "Report."

Ty's hands flew over his console as the *Star Renegade* took flight. "Lots of bad guys with guns."

"Just like every other day. Let's get out of here."

"On it."

The clouds filtered past until the fluffy wisps melted into a deep, endless black mottled with twinkling stars.

Ty glanced up. "We have incoming. I guess our friends still want to party."

"I hate it when the host doesn't let you leave."

"Very inconsiderate. Can I assume that Alanna won't be joining us for this little soiree?"

Cal shook his head. "I'm not sure what happened. She may have hit her head or something. She didn't look good."

"She'll be all right. She's a tough cookie. I'll do my best to make our girl proud."

Five ships appeared on Cal's scanner. "Here comes the unwelcome committee."

"And me with nothing to wear." Ty banked up as a spray of artillery bounced off their outer plating.

The ship rattled.

Cal held on to his armrests. "That wasn't pleasant."

"They're being very uncooperative. What ungracious hosts."

Cal frowned as two ships charged them from either side. "Are these two pulling a kamikaze maneuver?"

"Hold on." Ty pulled up.

Cal closed his eyes as the stars shifted down suddenly. He knew there were no g-forces in space, but seeing the movement was enough to make your head believe there should be.

The *Star Renegade* rattled as the two ships hit head-on behind them and exploded.

Ty glanced at the sensors. "Those had to be drone pilots. If the rest are the same, I'll have no trouble out-flying them."

The door slid open behind them, and Dania entered the bridge. "They're being quite tenacious, aren't they?"

Cal adjusted the screen width. "They know we have a way past the blockade. I can't say I blame them for wanting it. They're going to die out here without supplies."

The ship rattled again, and Ty spun them around a skipper craft.

"I have an idea." Dania sat at Alanna's station. "Engage the cloak and head for the blockade."

"That's crazy," Ty said. "The pirates already know we're here. They'll be able to trace our engines."

"That's what I'm hoping for."

Cal looked past Ty to the nav station. "What are you thinking?"

Dania poked the nav screen like she was looking for something. "The pirates will chase us at full throttle, most likely shooting erratically, trying to hit what they can't see."

"And?"

"And the Carteks won't think to look for a cloaked ship. Once we're in range, all they'll see is a mass of pirate ships heading for them, firing weapons."

So the Carteks would think the pirates were attacking...

Ty snorted. "I'm not sure if that's brilliant, or suicidal."

Cal had to agree, but most of their plans sounded suicidal these days.

Dania met Cal's gaze. "This will work."

The certainty in her eyes was enough to make him believe her. She'd looked so lost out on the platform—a fraction of the woman he'd grown to care about. Now she was strong and commanding, very much the calculated general. He smiled, realizing how much he'd missed her fire.

He turned back to the screen and hit the comm. "Ethan, how do you feel about engaging the cloak without Alexander and Alanna?"

"Umm, I'd feel better if they were here."

"They're both in the med bay by now. Can you handle this on your own?"

Another blast lit up the screen before them.

"Yeah, I'll be okay. The worst that can happen is I shoot the thing out the airlock."

"Except we can't do that. We need the cloak to get through the blockade, so do everything you can to keep that thing running cool."

"Roger that." He cursed before the line went dead.

"How will we know if we disappear?" Ty asked.

The lights dimmed. The floor beneath their feet rattled.

Cal looked out the window as the firing stopped. "I'm going to take that pause as a sign we just dropped off their radars."

Dania placed Alanna's earpiece in her ear. "They're doing a lot of screaming out there. A few are saying there's no jump signature." She stared at the floor, holding the earpiece like she was listening. "One of the ships is saying to just fire where we last were." She looked at the main screen. "A voice is calling for them to scan for heat signatures."

"Just as we expected." Cal hit the comm. "Ethan, I know you're busy, but give me a boost on the engines." That would give them more than enough heat to follow.

Ethan's voice filled the room. "I want a raise!"

Cal tapped off the comm as the energy stores in his panel increased. "Let's go!"

Ty punched the engines.

Cal's gaze carried over the *Renegade*'s stats. There was a slight drag in the heating system, and the shields' numbers were fluxing a little more than he was comfortable with, but so far, they were okay.

Dania knitted her brow as she scrolled through something on the nav panel. "I'm not sure, but if I'm reading this right, there are a lot of ships following us."

Ty kept his eyes focused on the main screen. "Do you see a red icon in the top corner and a blue one right below it?"

Dania nodded. "Yes."

"Press blue, then red. It'll give you a red line on the screen."

"I see the line."

"That's the visual proximity marker for the blockade.

Once the pirates cross that line, the Carteks will be able to see them."

The shields bottomed out. Cal wished he could help Dania, but there weren't enough hands on the bridge. He gritted his teeth as he reverted power from the lounge and upper storage to bolster the shields. Any small tweaks he could manage up here would leave Ethan more free to handle the big stuff.

Dania gulped. "Okay, they're going to hit the red line in five. Four. Three. Two. One."

Sprays of artillery from the chasing pirates shot past them, some just grazing the surface as the blockade came into view.

Another blast skipped past Cal's screen. "Have every one of those shots missed us?"

Dania flipped through the screens on her panel. "I'm not seeing any alarms for damage. Maybe the pirates don't have heavy weapons?"

Or they were afraid to waste them when there were far larger problems on their doorstep.

The bridge brightened as the blockade came to life, flooding space with wide beams of light.

Cal cursed under his breath. "If one of those light beams hits the *Star Renegade*, will they be able to see us?"

Ty banked up and over one of the search beams. "Alanna said it was like wearing mirrors, so I'm going to act like a light beam would reflect right back at them and scream *'there they are!'*"

Ships burst from the Cartek grid, heading straight for them.

"Hold your course!" Dania tapped on the console.

"They're not coming for us. They're focused on the pirates."

Cal looked past Ty's shoulders again. "How can you be sure?"

Her gaze met his—clear, demanding, and beautiful. "Instinct."

A former general was the best instinct he could ask for.

He patted Ty on the back. "Keep going. Let them fly right over us."

"I'm more worried they'll fly right *into* us."

Cal ducked as the first Cartek ship shot over them, then the next, until all they were staring at was the blockade.

Dania beamed. "It worked! The pirates are running, and the Carteks are chasing."

Hopefully, the squids would back off, and the planet wouldn't pay the price.

He needed to worry about his own people now, though. "Slow it down just enough to make the engines less noticeable."

Ty grimaced. "We went through pretty slow last time."

"Yeah, but they weren't spooked last time. I want to get out of here as soon as we can, but quietly."

Ty squinted at the screen. "Dania, can you mark the exit on the screen for me? All I see is a wall."

Dania rubbed her chin. "No. Sorry. I don't know how."

"You're doing fine," Cal said. "Just let us know if any ships are heading for us." Cal stood and pointed at the window. "There's a break in the pattern right there."

"I see it. Damn, that's easy to miss."

"I think that's by design. Slow and steady, my friend."

The sparkling grid got larger on the screen.

"The Cartek ships are turning back," Dania said.

"They're flying at low speed, so it looks like they're just breaking off their attack and leaving the planet alone. There's no sign they've seen us."

That was good news for them, and it also meant the Carteks had spared the colony. At least Cal didn't have any innocent blood on his hands.

The lights in the grid pulsed. Every third orb-like ship spun in place with no visible link to the other ships. The technology to keep a grid like that together was way beyond anything Earth or the Kevers had come up with yet. How had the Banes ever managed to overwhelm the Carteks enough to drive them out of their territory?

Ty slid the throttle back, and the ship started to coast. "Here we go."

The lights on the grid lit them up on all sides. Dania stood and approached the screen.

She gripped the back of Ty's chair as the lights reflected in her eyes. "There's so many of them."

Cal nodded. He had the same concern. If they'd constructed this blockade without any resistance, what was stopping them from blocking off any of the major trade colonies?

The rumble beneath their feet stopped, then started again.

Cal tapped the comm. "What was that?"

"Sorry!" Ethan's voice filled the room. "It's back on now."

Was he talking about the cloak? "Are you saying it was off?"

"Only for a second. The energy matrix blipped."

"What the hell is a *blip*?"

"It was off, and now it's on. I'm sorry. I'm winging it down here!"

A light beam shot from one side of the tunnel to the other. Then another beam appeared.

"They saw us." Dania sprinted back to the nav station.

Ty moved up and over a light beam. "I don't think so. There aren't any ships coming at us. Maybe they just saw something out of the corner of their eye, and they're not sure?"

Could they get that lucky?

Cal called up the emergency ship system override, then hit the comm. "Heads up, people. I'm shutting down everything but the cloak, life support, and Ty's station. I don't want to take a chance they'll pick up any of our instruments if they run a scan."

"Good call," Ty said. "I'm going to coast as much as I can."

Cal pressed the button and the screen went black. Of course, that left Ty blind. "You're good, right?"

Ty grimaced. "I'd rather be able to see, but I think the sensors are doing a good job. It's better than something going wrong and them looking right into the deck from a window right beside us if the cloak blips again."

Cal gripped his armrests. Once again, he was risking the lives of his crew on an alien technology that worked only when it wanted to. He missed the quieter days, when all they'd needed to worry about was local police and the occasional enforcer.

Beside him, Ty's hands hovered over his panels, sometimes gripping the manual throttle control. The kid had talent. Piloting a ship was as easy as walking for him, and Cal was grateful he was on board. Cal needed to see where he was going to be able to fly. Looking at sensors, and piloting by *feel* was never something he'd gotten the hang of.

Ty breathed a deep sigh, dragging his fingers through his hair. "We just left the blockade and entered free space."

Cal let out a long breath before tapping on their controls. "I'm doing a scan to make sure they're not still suspicious."

Ty nodded. "I'm just going to keep coasting. That was a little too close for my liking."

"That makes two of us. Keep running dark and don't change anything until we're sure we're in the clear."

"Hate being blind, but I hate being dead even more."

Dania walked over to Ty and squeezed his shoulder. "That was amazing piloting."

"Gee, thanks, Mom."

She cocked her head. "*Mom?*"

Ty held up his hands. "Just a joke. Sorry."

She seemed to consider that before turning to Cal. "I tried to gather readings on the interior of the web before we went dark. The information might give us some insight on how the Carteks got that many ships out here, and how they built such a massive wall so fast."

"Good idea. Do you think that's information your buddy Orion can bring back to the king?" Cal certainly didn't want to get anywhere near the military, but any information they gleaned could have the ability to tip the balance of the war.

She nodded. "He would, but he can't do anything until he finds the princess. His programming won't allow it."

The enforcers would have to save one life before they

could save millions. Kevers and their priorities never failed to astound him.

Ty frowned. "Something looks weird on the scopes."

Cal checked his own readings. "Define *weird*."

"Bigger than a chair cushion?"

Cal adjusted the power settings. "Dania, I'm sending you just enough power to do a quick scan. See if we're out of range of the blockade."

Her face glowed as her screen came to life. "Yes, we're outside the red line, so I think that's good, but Ty's right. There's something in front of us."

Great. The last thing they needed to do was drift into space junk while they were floating blind.

Cal retracted his emergency overrides. "Returning all systems to full power."

Ethan came over the comm. "I've got lights. Does that mean I can turn the cloak off?"

"Hold on a minute," Cal said as the lights brightened on the bridge.

The screen before them cleared, revealing a wall of metal a few hundred meters in front of them.

Cal grabbed the arms of his chair. "What the blazes?"

Ty cursed as he engaged the engines and pulled the ship up. A scraping sound filled the bridge before they broke free. The floor rumbled and the lights dimmed before brightening again.

Ethan's voice came over the comm. "Like it or not, we just lost the cloak. Did we hit something?"

A spray of light slammed into the *Star Renegade*, shaking the bridge.

"It's a cruiser," Dania announced. "Heavily armored."

"And they don't look too happy to see us." Ty banked around several fighter ships exiting the cruiser's hangars.

The floor shook again. "Fly away from the damn wall of metal, Ty!"

"I can't. They're spitting out a crazy number of ships. They're everywhere!"

"Hold on." Dania tapped on her screen. "Shoot. Wait. Sorry." She scrolled again, her brow pinched in concentration. "I think there's something wrong. Those ships are launching in tandem and then passing us by. It's just that there's hundreds of them, so it feels like an all-out attack."

Cal stared at the chaos of ships flying past. "Why send hundreds of ships but not attack?"

Dania gaped, turning to Cal. "There's a huge heat signature coming from both rear engine compartments."

"What?" Cal and Ty said at the same time.

"They're not attacking. They're evacuating. That cruiser is going to explode."

Cal looked out the window before snapping out of it. "Ty, get out of here!"

Dania held her forehead. "Now there's a red light flashing, but I'm not sure what it is."

Cal sprang from his chair to look over her shoulder. "That's a priority transmission. My private and very secret channel."

"Could the cruiser have hacked us?" Ty asked.

"Not likely. The only place that code exists is in my head." Cal tapped his code sequence into the nav station.

A message popped up.

Do-Not-Jump

That was cryptic.

He put a trace on the transmission and Walker Station's callsign came up.

Ty pulled up and over a group of skippers as one fired on them. "I got a clear path out. I'm punching it."

"Wait!" Cal walked to the window. Three more skippers left the cruiser before the space around the massive ship became clear.

A blinding light blasted from the rear of the cruiser.

"It's exploding!" Ty leapt from his chair.

Cal flinched, covering his eyes, and then relaxed when his muscles realized he wasn't dead.

Ty held both sides of his head, breathing heavily. "What just happened?"

"There's another coded message." Dania rubbed her face. "This one is audio video." She tapped a few keys. "I think this will send to the screen."

The window blinked, faded to black, and then Glenn's smiling face appeared. The lights above him reflected off his balding scalp and made his cheeks glow pink.

"Cal, Cal, Cal." He waved a French fry at the camera. "I sent a text first because it would get to you faster. I trust you didn't allow Alanna to jump you to safety. If you did, hightail it back to where you started." He shoved the fry in his mouth and held both hands to his sides. "One A1 grade cruiser as you requested. Fully loaded, and recently abandoned by its crew." His brow furrowed and he leaned closer to the camera. "Nasty thing, subatomic engine particle leaks. Impossible to fix, and the ships always blow up." His smile was devilishly smug. "Thank goodness you're there to salvage that wreck." He leaned back and folded his arms. "I will expect payment next time we see each other. But I know you're good for it, my friend." The screen faded out until the stars and a massive ship filled the screen once again.

Dania stared at the screen, dumbfounded. "How did he know where we'd be?"

Cal snorted. "I learned a long time ago not to underestimate the power of Glenn."

Ty released a deep breath. "That ship is a little bigger than I think we had in mind."

Cal nodded. "Definitely, but as long as it's big enough to house all the enforcers, that's all that matters." He looked at Dania. "Let's get in touch with Orion and let him know he doesn't need the *Star Renegade* anymore." He was more than ready to leave the enforcers, and this war, far behind him.

DANIA WALKED past the blast-marked walls in the hallway, heading to the rear of the *Star Renegade*. Orion's pending arrival was more likely to complicate things than make them easier, despite having a new ship to give him. It was more than possible that Orion's secondary programming would kick in, and he'd call for the crew's execution once he realized he didn't need them anymore. She needed to concentrate on him and his enforcers, doing everything she could to keep her new family safe. That wasn't the only thing on her mind, though.

No matter how hard she tried, she couldn't get over the sight of Alexander raising his arms back on the planet and the pirates flying out of the way. Before stepping foot on the *Star Renegade*, seeing any of her people doing something so simple wouldn't have fazed her. A year ago, she would have been able to do the same with barely a thought, but now she was no better than a human—which was what she wanted, but the sensation of the primordial energy coursing through her cells and shooting from her hands was hard to forget.

She'd expected Alexander would experience the same deterioration, but every time she thought his power had depleted, he once again did something that should have been impossible in his condition.

Dania was learning to be a part of the crew, and her freedom was more important to her than nearly anything. She'd be lying if she said she didn't miss the ease of her power, though. She'd felt useless in that ambush, and seeing Alexander flex his strength made her feel inconsequential. *Small.*

Granted, Alexander was nowhere near as strong as he had been. If he were, he wouldn't have lost consciousness, but if Dania could regain even a fraction of her strength, as he had, she could be a far more valuable member of the crew.

Dania pushed through the med bay door. The bright lights made her squint as she stepped inside. Alanna handed a cup to Peter before stepping away from Alexander's bed.

"You look better," Dania said.

Alanna nodded. "I told them all I was fine. I don't know why they're acting like I was sick."

Brave words, from a woman who could barely stand the last time Dania had seen her.

Peter placed the cup in the recycler. "She seems fine. She took a long nap and woke up a little dehydrated. Not even a sign of concussion."

Dania sat on the edge of Alexander's bed. "How're you doing?"

"Better." He glanced in Alanna's direction. "I've had good care."

Peter came over and shined a light in Alexander's eyes. "That's an understatement. As soon as Alanna woke up, she was over here taking care of him. I had to keep dragging her back to bed."

The recycler went off on its own, and a towel landed on top of the clean cup.

Rachel's eyes widened before she grabbed the towel. "I did that."

Dania frowned. Had she?

Alexander pinched the area between his eyes. "May I return to my room?"

"I gave you a pathogen treatment while you were unconscious. I'd like to keep an eye on you for a little longer."

Dania inched closer. "Alexander…?" How could she bring this up without sounding needy or resentful?

"You're wondering about the power."

Dania looked up. Alexander's penchant for reading her thoughts certainly hadn't waned. But maybe this time, it was for the best. "What you did on that planet…"

"Should be impossible." He rubbed his face.

Peter tapped on a data pad. "From the way your cells are regenerating, it looks like your natural pathogens levels were elevated again, but you depleted them with all that fancy mojo." He pointed to the IV bag. "The synthetic pathogens I just gave you should stick with you longer, since you can't use them to access your powers. After a few treatments, you should be as good as Dania."

Dania shifted her weight. "But do you know why his natural pathogens keep…" How should she say it? "Waking up?"

Peter placed the tablet down. "No clue, but we did see your powers manifest a few times after I thought they were gone, too. It might be something we never figure out."

On the other side of the room, Alanna placed a cloth on an enforcer's forehead and tucked in their blanket.

Dania smiled. "She gives so much of herself to help others."

"You have no idea." Alexander looked down. "Did you spend a great deal of time with Alanna before I arrived?"

Dania nodded. "Yes. She's my friend. When I first arrived, she had a way of making me feel more at home, like I belonged here."

Alexander pursed his lips. "I bet she did."

What did he mean by that?

He dragged his fingers through his hair and looked at Peter. "I would really prefer to go to my room."

"Let me get one more treatment into you, and then you can sleep all you want."

"Shouldn't you be saving the treatments for the others who are sick?" Alexander looked back to the beds, where several enforcers still lay.

Peter grimaced. "I have enough set aside for both you and Dania. I'm making more for our friends, but the crew voted that you two were our priority."

"I wasn't included in that," Dania said.

"Because we all knew that you'd vote to save others before yourself. The vote was unanimous anyway, so we would have overruled you."

Was she supposed to feel comforted by that, or insulted? A smile touched her lips, answering her own question. For the first time in her life, she was surrounded by people who cared about her. But at the same time, she had the new experience of having something to lose, and that scared her more than the impending war.

CAL HAD SPENT most of his adult life trying to avoid enforcers. Talking to Orion, even over comm channels, still grated against every instinct that told him to run far, far away.

He couldn't wait for all of this to be over. Closing his eyes and breathing slowly, he hit the control to open the med bay doors. In the back of the room, Hendry and Alanna looked over the vials dropping into the machines. The recovering enforcer had a knack for science. If they were lucky, maybe he'd agree to help treat the other enforcers rather than hiding from Orion until his princess was free.

Alanna moved about the equipment, the dark circles under her eyes the only sign of her ordeal. Alexander sat on the edge of a gurney with Dania and Doc beside him. Cal had an odd sensation that he'd walked into an uncomfortable conversation, which was probably normal when Alexander was in the room.

Cal stepped inside. "How's everyone doing?"

"Alanna's good to go," Doc said. "One more treatment

for my boy Alex here, and then he'd like to rest in his room."

Cal grimaced. It was good that Alexander felt comfortable enough that his quarters felt like home. The trouble was, Cal didn't know how long that would last, and Dania seemed more and more attached to her friend...not to mention Alex's growing relationship with Alanna. Cal was going to have enough problems with the enforcers. He needed everyone to have their wits about them and not be worried about losing someone they cared for should Alexander choose to leave.

Orion, as always, was the wild card. He and the rest of the high prince's enforcers still had more than enough power to cause headaches for Cal and his crew.

Cal probably should have cut and run. The enforcers in the hold were still confined. In time, maybe they could have figured out how to force them off the ship and have Alanna jump the *Star Renegade* to the other side of the galaxy before the enforcers had time to regroup.

Dania stood, frowning. "What is it?"

Cal shifted his weight. He hated that his concerns were always so obvious to the people he cared about. "Ethan rigged a clone pilot to the cruiser so it will follow us. We're on a course to meet Orion."

"Wasn't that the plan? Why do you look worried?"

"I'm worried he might show up with a ship full of nearly dead enforcers." Truth was, from what they'd seen, a load of new patients was more than likely. Those small ships had no medical facilities. If the enforcers Orion had taken with him were collapsing, he'd probably just pile them on top of each other in the rear cargo compartments.

Doc pointed to the back of the room. "I've got every station making pathogens, but the formula takes time."

"I realize that, but we can't get rid of Orion until he has a ship filled with conscious, breathing enforcers." Cal rubbed his eyes. "I just have a bad feeling."

"Well, let's do everything in our power to keep that bad feeling from happening."

"That's the goal. We need to keep Orion happy until we can make a break for it."

Alexander shifted on his pillow. "You plan on running."

Cal nodded. "The first chance we get. You're welcome to stay if you want, but I understand if you want to go with them to save that princess."

Dania's eyes grew wide. Cal knew she would have preferred a slow introduction to the idea, but with Orion and his enforcers on the way, they didn't have time for handholding.

Alexander looked back at Alanna, then rubbed his face. His eyes were red when he drew his hands away. "I think I'd like another pathogen treatment before I'm asked to make that decision."

Peter nodded. "You got it. One dose of liquid freedom, coming right up."

Cal tapped Alexander's shoulder. "Happy to have you." And oddly enough, that was true. Things would be much easier if he stayed, and although Cal hated to admit it, he'd grown fond of the guy.

Alex grabbed Doc's arm as he started heading for the supply area. "After this treatment, I want you to give my pathogen rations to those who are sick."

Doc raised a brow. "You sure?"

Alexander eased back onto the bed. "You're making

more. I trust the treatments will be there when I need them, but now, there are others whose lives depend on it."

But Alexander's life obviously didn't. He only wanted the treatment to keep his mind on track to freedom, which was encouraging.

In the back of the room, a bright smile burst across Alanna's face as she handed Doc a vial. She knew this meant Alexander wanted to stay, even if he wasn't quite able to voice a commitment yet. Cal found himself smiling as well. Alanna was the nicest person he knew, and she deserved to be in a relationship where she wasn't being preyed upon for her abilities.

Now they simply needed to figure out a way to escape Orion once Cal gave him a ship that might be able to give the *Star Renegade* a run for its money.

———

Cal tapped his fingers on the wall behind him, doing his best to calm his nerves as Orion's ship docked alongside the *Star Renegade* and sealed to the cargo entrance.

He reached down and adjusted the weapon in his boot. Doc had given it to him when Dania had first arrived. It was supposed to take out an enforcer at close range. So far, they hadn't had a need to test it. He hoped that day would never come. Still, he'd slipped it into his boot every day, just in case.

The seals hissed, and Cal grabbed a metal handle on the wall as a chill settled over his skin. Before he'd started dealing with enforcers, he'd never received guests in space. They'd always landed before taking on passengers. This should have been old hat by now, but each time that door opened, he still expected the vast void of space to suck him out.

The rumbling of the ship outside abated, and a tone sounded.

Ty scrambled down the ladder and jumped off the last few rungs. "Relax, boss. The sensors won't let you open the door if the seal isn't secure."

Cal shook his head. Ty and Ethan had told him to trust the sensors on more than one occasion, but he wished he could get confirmation from a breathing human being that the seal was intact before putting the *Star Renegade*—and everyone inside—in danger.

Taking a steadying breath, he pressed the release button and the door slowly opened.

Orion glared at him as he stepped on board. "Is there a reason I was kept waiting?"

For three seconds? "I'm sorry. As you're always pointing out, I'm just a useless human."

"*Useless* is an incorrect assumption, at least in the realm of the immediate future." He took three steps toward the glowing shield keeping him and the other enforcers from accessing the rest of the ship and looked over his shoulder. "Take me to your medical bay."

"Why?"

Orion frowned, as if annoyed by the question. "I would like to see the enforcers being treated."

Cal folded his arms. "I told you, Doc likes space to work, and there's not much to see. I just came from there."

"I require the services of those who have been there the longest. I will be bringing more enforcers for treatment, so I'll be requiring the use of their beds, anyway."

That meant more nearly dead enforcers. Cal hated it

when he was right. Still, he'd made a promise to Hendry, and he'd prefer to keep it, if he could.

Ty stepped beside him. "We've already got a few weak enforcers on this level who Doc is keeping an eye on. He's planning on treating them as soon as he's able."

The shield shimmered as Orion moved closer to the outer edge of the enclosure. "The deteriorated enforcers on our ships are in more significant need, I guarantee it."

Cal gritted his teeth. "If you stopped forcing them to use their powers to the point of collapse, you wouldn't be in this position."

"The only one in a position of any negative relevance, Mr. Espinoza, is you. Now, do as you are told, or face the consequences."

Ty's ears turned red. "You know what? I think the words you were looking for were, 'Thank you very much for that fantastic ship you gave us, Captain Espinoza. We are forever in your debt.'"

Orion narrowed his eyes.

Cal stepped a little closer to provide a buffer between Ty and the enforcer.

His first mate was right, though. Orion had spent a significant amount of time on the new cruiser before returning to the *Star Renegade*. "Did you at least like the ship? It's big enough to carry all your people as well as transport your smaller ships in its hold."

Orion glanced down at the small computer band on his wrist and tapped on the screen. "It is more than adequate for our needs."

Ty shifted his weight. "And here, again, is a rousing opportunity to thank the lowly humans for their help."

The overhead comm pinged, and Alanna's voice filled

the cargo bay. "Umm, Cal? We just got a deposit into our expendables account."

Cal looked at Orion as Ty walked to the wall and tapped on the computer pad.

The enforcer's expression remained stony. "The high prince does not take kindly to being in anyone's debt. The deposit your navigator mentioned will more than cover your expenses and the cost of the ship you procured."

Ty cursed. "Cal, there's over ten million ducets in there. That's enough to… hell, I don't even know what to do with that kind of money."

Cal's stomach turned. For ten million ducets they could feed Kirato for twenty years and still retire on Earth.

The tides had certainly turned. Suddenly, he was now in a place he never expected to be…in the Banes' debt.

He'd have to move all that money to safe, untraceable accounts. Calvin Espinoza paid off his debts, dead or alive. In the likely event that he wasn't able to escape the executioners when all this was over, he needed to make sure enough of that money got back to Glenn to pay for the ship —even though he'd obviously stolen it—and the rest got to Stanley and Mel on Kirato.

Orion continued to glare. "Now that these trivialities are taken care of, take me to the med bay. Now."

Ty moved back to the computer and tapped on the comm. "Doc, Orion wants to come and see how his enforcers are doing."

Something scratched and dropped on the other side of the comm. "No, thank you. We're already too crowded."

Orion sneered. His hair took flight. "Take me there. Now!"

Ty held up his palms. Don't get your socks all tied in

knots. We're going." He leaned back toward the comm. "Hear that, Doc?"

The comm went dead. Hopefully, that meant Doc understood he had less than a few minutes to figure this out.

Orion waved at the cargo bay door. "Fallon, enter." A male enforcer, broad like Alexander but a few inches shorter than Orion, stepped through. Two unconscious women in soiled and burned opalescent uniforms floated behind him, their silver hair lax and hanging toward the floor.

Orion pointed Fallon to the ramp along the wall. "Take them to the medical bay."

Cal hated it when someone else gave orders on his ship. Still, he stepped to the comm panel. "Ethan, bring down the shield. We have two more enforcers we need to take to Doc."

The shimmering walls around them blinked out, and the enforcer headed up the ramp with the limp bodies floating behind him.

Ty's lips thinned as he watched them head up to the next level of the ship. He'd probably had the same thought Cal had. The sick enforcers needed Doc to survive, and Orion was smart enough to realize this, even if he wouldn't openly admit to needing the help of a human. What that meant for the *Star Renegade* remained to be seen.

CAL STEPPED BACK as Fallon placed one of the two unconscious women on a gurney. Rachel ran to the patient and placed a stethoscope on the woman's chest as Doc started working on the other enforcer.

"Holy heck!" Rachel threw the stethoscope on a table. "Someone, get me a crash cart!" The gurney height lowered as she placed one hand over the other and started chest compressions.

Had the woman's heart stopped beating? Had Orion really worked another enforcer to death?

Alanna ran to the back of the room and returned with a silver box on a rolling cart.

Rachel counted, throwing her whole bodyweight into her task. She glared at Orion. "You're supposed to bring them to us still breathing!"

Alanna opened the box and pulled out what looked like two flat, metal paddles with handles on them. "Peter, I'm gonna need help here!"

Doc gave his own patient an injection. "I'm coming!"

Rachel grabbed the paddles. "I got it."

Doc took a vial from the back of the room and filled a syringe.

Cal gaped. They all moved so fluidly, like this happened every day. The expressions on their faces told another story, though.

The enforcer who'd brought the patients in stood like a guard at the door, while Orion strolled through the med bay, looking unconcerned that Rachel, Alanna, and Doc were trying to save that poor woman's life.

"Clear!" Rachel placed the paddles on the woman's chest, and the enforcer's body jolted. Rachel cursed and recharged the paddles. "Again!"

Orion walked over to a bed where Hendry lay with his eyes closed and breathing with a gentle cadence. Enforcers couldn't lie, so Hendry wasn't feigning sleep. Doc must have given him some kind of sedative to make him look sicker than he was. His buddy Bleven was still genuinely unconscious in the bed beside him. Orion's nose flared. He'd probably been counting on two more volunteers to work to the death.

How in Saturn's rings could this guy sleep at night?

Rachel shocked the woman's heart again, then stepped back, taking readings.

Alanna took over the chest compressions as Doc stuck a needle through the bag hanging next to the patient's bed, and a blue liquid streamed from the bag, down a thin tube, and into the enforcer's arm.

Rachel grabbed the paddles. "Let's jolt her one more time."

Alanna stepped back, panting like she'd just run laps around the ship.

Rachel yelled, "Clear," placed the paddles on the

patient, then read the machine as a shrill tone filled the room.

"No!" Alanna started chest compressions again.

The tone continued to bounce off the walls, and Rachel stepped back, wiping the sweat from her forehead with her arm. "That's all I got. We didn't get to her in time."

Alanna continued to compress the enforcer's chest. "No! Don't give up on her!"

Rachel grabbed Alanna's arms and gently pulled her away from the bed. "Honey, she's already gone."

Alanna sobbed, walking to the back of the room, holding her hands on her temples.

So that was it…one more dead. When was Orion going to learn that even enforcers had limits?

Doc sighed and pulled the sheet over the woman's head. Another life wasted. And for what?

Orion snarled. "This is highly inconvenient."

"Inconvenient?" Doc pointed at the deceased. "How do you think she feels? Did she have a choice to allow herself to get this drained? This is murder in my book. You're breaking your own king's laws."

"Careful with your accusations, little man." Orion's eyes narrowed. "You are not in any position to…"

"Bullshit!" Doc pointed to the other beds. "These people are dying, and it's your fault. I can't believe this princess would be okay with so many people giving up their lives just to figure out where she is."

Cal gaped. He'd never seen Doc this angry. Part of him wanted to step between them as a buffer, but Doc was right, and the commander needed to hear this.

Orion cocked his head. "Her enforcers are tools. She

would expect them to be utilized in any means necessary to ascertain her location."

"Then all of you are more screwed up in the head than I thought."

Orion loomed over him. "You have one job: to treat the enforcers I bring you. I expect casualties, but you are to keep the losses at a minimum."

"Oh, well, it's okay then, because *you're okay with losses.*" Doc's face turned crimson. "Do the enforcers you're still torturing on your ship know that, or are you telling them that once they collapse, I'll be able to treat them? Because if you're telling them that, it's an outright lie, and from what I understand, enforcers can't lie."

Cal moved a little closer, but the commander remained surprisingly calm for all the outright insubordination being flung at him.

Orion's eyes narrowed. "It isn't a lie. You are treating them."

"Do they know how many are dead or in a coma?"

Orion stared at him. His deep grimace gave them their answer.

Doc fisted his hair. "I can't make pathogens as fast as you're bringing in patients. At this rate, more than half of them are going to die. Are you okay with that?"

Orion's lips thinned, looking over the filled beds in the medical bay. "If you can't save them, then your trip into the larcenous sector was a waste of time."

Doc huffed a laugh. "It wasn't a waste. If you get them to me still breathing, preferably walking…hell, even stumbling, I may be able to help them."

Orion nodded. "I agree."

Doc gaped. "You do? You mean your arrogance is going

to let you understand that these people's lives have value? Why don't I believe that?"

Orion's hair took flight. "You are beginning to annoy me."

Cal's hand flexed, ready to grab the weapon in his boot.

Doc laughed. "*I'm* beginning to annoy *you*? Well, dammit, I'm annoyed that you're bringing me patients who are beyond saving. You call yourself a leader? You're not. You're a tyrannical dictator. What you're doing is wrong!"

Orion snarled. "You will back down. You will continue to treat those who falter. While you were wasting your time with pirates, we successfully pinpointed the location of the princess."

They had?

Cal's stomach tightened. He'd hoped they would have more time.

The commander looked over those in the beds. "The state of the survivors is concerning, though. Those who are able will continue to direct us only if needed. That should decrease the number of new patients. Your job from here on out is to strengthen the remainder so they are able to assist in Zindiria's extraction."

A chill ran down Cal's back. If anything, the pathogens would weaken the enforcers. Maybe Orion didn't understand or wasn't able to fathom that. They would be healthier, but healthier meant less enforcer power than they were accustomed to.

Orion turned to Cal. "You will take all supplies needed to treat the enforcers and transport them to the infirmary on my new cruiser. Your impertinent excuse for a doctor will continue treatment from there."

Doc backed away. He knew just as well as any of them

that as soon as they found that princess, his services would no longer be needed, and his death sentence was just as final and iron-tight as Cal's.

Cal grit his teeth. "Like hell. You can't have any member of my crew."

Orion looked bored. "Mr. Espinoza, you don't have a choice."

Cal pointed at himself. "I do have a choice. There's no way…"

Doc cried out as his feet left the floor. His floating body slammed against the ceiling, and he grunted with a wince.

"Let him go, you oversized bully!" Rachel punched Orion three times in the shoulder before she, too, lifted into the air and flew across the med bay, crashing into the rear wall.

Alanna gasped, holding her hands over her mouth. The enforcer by the door had one palm facing Doc, and the other on Rachel, meaning Orion could still eviscerate anyone in the room without breaking a sweat.

Cal stood frozen, not wanting to do anything to give either enforcer a reason to hurt anyone he cared about.

Orion stepped toward him, his expression as flat as ever. "Once the medical supplies are transferred, you will see to it that the cloaking technology is removed from your ship and installed on mine. I expect a successful test in ten hours."

Cal gulped. If the enforcers had Doc *and* the cloak, then the *Star Renegade* and everyone on the ship would no longer be intrinsic to saving the princess. The enforcers would fall on their secondary programming…which meant they all had ten hours to live.

Above, Doc's wide eyes locked with Cal's. Peter was

always the one to come up with a plausible solution based on science and statistics. Cal didn't have either of those to work with. Cal dealt with luck and instinct, and half the time, his plans backfired. But if they were all going to die anyway, he'd take any chance he could find to save his crew.

He drew in a long, deep breath. He needed to keep his calm so his temperature didn't change. "Everything in this room is really technical equipment. It will take longer than ten hours to safely transfer and set up."

That part could have been true. He actually had no idea.

He turned to Alanna. "Didn't Alexander tell you that he'd melded the cloaking technology permanently to the *Star Renegade*? Ethan joked that trying to remove it would destroy us *and* the tech."

Now *that* was a complete lie...but one that only required a *yes* or *no* answer. Alanna's emotions always showed on her face, and the enforcers would no doubt pick up on the lie if they focused on her long enough.

She stared at him for a moment before she gulped and nodded.

Good enough. But now he needed to keep them all alive.

He held her gaze. "Can you widen the spread of the cloak so it can hide both the *Star Renegade* and the cruiser?"

Her eyes widened again, and Cal slowly nodded to her.

Follow my lead. Say Yes, Alanna.

She blinked, glanced at Orion, and then nodded to Cal. "Yeah, I think so."

Cal spun back to Orion, placing the focus back on himself. "That means we can leave right now. Alexander can work on expanding the cloak while we are en route, and Doc can keep on working to save your enforcers from the facilities he already has set up here. It's the most efficient option. It will get you to your princess faster."

Orion's gaze remained stony.

"Why wait ten hours when we can start moving now? Transporting personnel and supplies between ships means stopping and starting. Even you have to admit this would be more efficient."

Orion continued to stare, probably trying to find a hole in Cal's plan. He wouldn't have to look far. There were tons of holes, and all of them in the enforcer's favor. The only thing this plan bought the *Star Renegade* was more time.

Orion nodded to the other enforcer before Doc and Rachel eased back to the floor. Doc held his chest, breathing heavily. Rachel rubbed the back of her head, glaring but keeping silent for maybe the first time in her life.

"I find your solution agreeable, Mr. Espinoza. Your king appreciates your sense of urgency." He began walking toward the door and waved for Fallon to follow him. "See to it that any weakened enforcers are brought here for treatment immediately."

The door closed as they left, and Ty's voice came over the comm. "I'm watching them, boss. I'll make sure they don't steal the fine china before they leave."

Cal looked up at the camera. "Thanks." He turned to Alanna. "Do you really think you can expand the cloak?"

She shrugged. "I honestly have no idea."

"Grab Ethan and get to work. I'll have Alex join you as soon as he's feeling better. We're definitely going to need a wider range on that cloak to buy us time."

If expanding the cloak didn't work, Orion might get

creative on how to reach his goals. Luckily enough for the *Star Renegade*, the cruiser's docking ports were only large enough to accept small skipper ships, like the ones Orion had arrived in. That meant Orion couldn't force the *Star Renegade* into their cargo hold for a better chance of the cloak working on his own ship. This left Cal somewhat free to make a break for it as soon as they could...if they ever got the chance.

CHAPTER 44
DANIA

DANIA STARED at the dents and pocks in Cal's door as she knocked for a third time. Why wasn't he answering?

She moved down the hallway and tapped on the comm. "Ethan, Cal's in his room and not answering the door. Can you open it for me?"

"I can, but I shouldn't. You know, privacy and all."

Dania sighed. Things had been easier when she was a general and could order people to do what she wanted. "Have you, or anyone else, seen Cal since yesterday?"

There was a pause. The engineer was most likely asking Alexander and Alanna if they'd seen Cal since he'd asked them to expand the cloak.

Ethan's voice returned. "Umm, no. We haven't seen him."

"Don't you find that odd?" Dania tapped her fingers on the edge of the comm panel as static hissed over the line. "Ethan, please unlock the door."

"Yeah, okay. Just don't tell him it was me."

Dania returned to Cal's door and knocked again, just in

355

case. After a moment, she placed her hand on the access panel, and the door slid open.

Light shone in from the hallway as she stepped into the room. The lights were off, and even the computers in the walls had been shut down, leaving the space completely dark.

She held her hand on the control by the door. "Lights, increase by twenty percent."

A soft glow filled the room. Cal lay in his bed, turned away from her. He sighed and shifted his weight. She didn't need enforcer powers to sense his agitation.

Dealing with emotions hadn't been part of her training, though. At times like these, she deeply wished it had been.

Cal shifted on the bed. "Your buddy Orion was going to kill my crew."

"Did he say that?"

"He didn't have to."

That was probably true. Alanna had relayed the conversation to Dania, and it seemed more than likely that Orion was separating them for swift and orderly execution for the myriad of crimes they were more than guilty of. The only thing in question was…would he have counted Dania as one of the condemned, or dragged her back home to face the Banes? The latter would be decidedly worse than a quick death.

Dania sat on the edge of the bed. "Hiding isn't like you."

"Doc gave me something for a headache and said to lie down. I just haven't felt like getting back up." He rolled onto his back, his white T-shirt stretching over his chest. "They all depend on me. They trust me, and I don't even know why."

By 'they,' he must have been referring to the crew. If so, all of the things he'd said were true, but it was odd that the inflection of his voice sounded like this was a negative.

"They trust you because they know you care about them. They're not just a crew to you."

"I know, but I'm so afraid that I'm leading them past the point of no return."

"You're not forcing any of us to stay. We want to be here." She lay beside him and placed her hand on his arm. "For the past few months, I've been feeling like I have something to lose for the first time in my life. This is my family, and I'm willing to fight for it."

He turned toward her. "Even if it means fighting enforcers?"

"Yes." She blinked, startled at how quickly the answer came to her lips. Probably because it was true. She'd be at a severe disadvantage if forced to face Orion, but she'd do everything in her power to protect the people on this ship.

In many ways, that made her much like the troubled man lying beside her. As an enforcer, she would have seen his love for his crew as a weakness to use against him. But now she understood this was anything but a weakness. If anything, it made them all stronger. What they had here was worth fighting for, no matter how insurmountable the foe. That's what had made this ship so difficult to catch all these years.

He ran his fingers along the side of her face. The sensation was oddly soothing.

"You're an incredible person, you know that? And I'm incredibly lucky to have you." He kissed her cheek, then leaned away. "Was that okay?"

She nodded.

"Good." He returned and kissed her lips. He moved slowly, his touch soft and warm, before he drew away again. "How about that?"

Dania smiled. "That was nice."

He moved closer. "Remember, I would never hurt you."

"I know."

Heat seemed to roll off him as he moved closer, his breath warm on her lips. "If I make you uncomfortable in any way, let me know, and we'll stop, okay? You're in control."

Dania appreciated the sentiment, but her cheeks heated. She'd run from him the last time they'd gotten close. She hated herself for that, but sometimes human emotions were too hard to control.

"Hey." He touched her chin, lifting her eyes toward his. "We do nothing unless you want to."

Dania laughed, but she wasn't sure why. None of this was funny. She hated that he was worried about being close to her.

She touched his cheek. "I want to." Leaning up, she placed her lips on his, and Cal pulled her closer. His touch was slow, tentative, but at the same time desperate and needy. She deepened her kiss, wanting him to feel as safe with her as she felt with him.

His hand roamed down her face and neck, and over her shoulders before settling on her back. "Are you still okay?"

She nodded, finding his mouth again.

His palm moved over her shoulder again and settled just to the side of her breast. "Is *this* okay?"

"Yes," she whispered into his mouth. She wanted to tell him all of it was okay, that he didn't need to treat her like a glass ready to shatter, but in many ways, she knew that wasn't true, no matter how much she wanted it to be.

She sighed, her skin coming alive as his fingers kneaded and his thumbs drew circles. She combed her fingers through his hair, each sensation spreading warmth through her in ways that seemed wrong, but also more right than she'd ever dreamed.

He kissed her lips and cheek. "Do you trust me?"

"Of course."

He continued to kiss her as his hand skated over her hips and between her legs. His palm moved over the fabric as she tangled her fingers in his hair. This trust, this *closeness* was something she'd never known existed, and now she wanted it more than anything. He kissed her cheeks, her temples as his hand continued to rub, the friction creating heat and an odd pressure between her legs that made her breath hitch.

Cal kissed her again, and her body came alight. Tension rose up her spine then shattered. She gasped, breaking the kiss and tightening her grip on him until it subsided. Her breaths became shallow, and her hands trembled. She was oddly aware of every sound, and the mild scent of pine and sage filling the room.

"Shh." He kissed her forehead and cheek. "Just relax and ride it out."

Ride it out? What did that even mean? "I'm-I'm not sure what just happened."

But that wasn't completely true. She understood that there was a reason her soldiers had sought human company after missions. For a brief period when their power had started to wane, and before they returned to their sponsor to be fed, they'd been able to open themselves to their human sides, including desire.

This was the sensation they'd sought...a sensation that had been stolen from her.

"Was that your first time?" Cal asked. "Sorry for asking, but you look so surprised."

Her cheeks heated. "Yes." She'd never even considered spending time with humans before. The idea seemed so pointless.

"Hey." He cupped her cheek. "That's okay. It's nothing to be embarrassed about." He smiled. "There's lots of things I'd love to show you, but I don't want to rush it. We'll take it slow, okay?"

She nodded, her cheeks burning hotter. Every time she learned something about being human that she'd never experienced, she felt like a child. She hated that she'd been sheltered from all the things the Banes thought would make her a less valuable soldier.

Her stomach tensed, and a deep pressure pressed against her temples. A small point in the back of her neck burned. Her mind whirled, and the pleasant sense of relaxation and complete safety started to drift away.

No! Tears gathered in her lashes as she balled the sheets in her fists. She closed her eyes, willing the shunt to disengage, even though she knew it was fruitless.

"Dania?" Cal's voice seemed far away, like he was speaking over the comm.

She gritted her teeth. This was *her* experience. She owned it. It belonged to her, and she refused to allow Geron to strip it away.

The tension abated, and she opened her eyes.

Cal stared down at her, frowning. "Are you okay?"

Of course, she was okay, but—why was she lying on his bed?

Dania sat upright, glancing around the darkened room.

She'd asked Ethan to unlock the door. She'd stepped inside. Cal had mentioned being worried about the crew.

And then what?

Cal touched her arm. "Dania, it's me. You can trust me. Remember, I won't ever hurt you."

Hurt her? "I know that. I just..." Just what? She blinked, looking around. A sinking feeling came over her, like she'd lost something.

But what?

Dania turned to him. "I-I don't know why I'm lying in your bed."

His eyes widened. "What?"

"I remember walking in, and then I was lying beside you."

"You...don't remember anything else? None of it?"

The sinking feeling deepened. She reached behind her and rubbed the base of her neck. What had Geron stolen from her this time? It must have been incredibly important, something that he'd deem unacceptable for a general.

She gaped. "Were we just intimate?"

Cal closed his eyes and looked down. "Yeah. You—really don't remember?"

She rubbed her hands over her shirt and pants. "I'm still clothed. I don't understand."

"Do you know what foreplay is?"

The definition rolled through her mind. Ever since Alexander and Alanna had become a couple, she'd dreamed of sharing intimacy with Cal. Now, apparently, she had, but the memory was gone. "What did we do?"

He laughed, rubbing his face. "I'm sorry, but now I'm the one who's a little confused."

She reached for him. "Please don't think this is your fault. I have a chip of some kind in my neck. Alexander called it a shunt."

"A what?"

"It's one of the ways Geron controlled me. It stops me from thinking about or seeking anything that might bring me joy." She lowered her gaze. "And apparently, it makes me forget if I do experience something special." Her heart sank. Maybe she'd never been happy enough for it to engage in that way.

Or maybe it had...and stolen other memories that she'd never be able to retrieve.

"Why would he do that to you?"

"To keep me focused. To make me a better leader." And it had worked. Dania had been ruthless—more ruthless than she cared to admit. She rubbed her face. "I can't believe he still has so much control."

"Can we take it out?"

She lowered her hands. "I asked Alexander to remove it, but he was hesitant. I'm not sure how much of his reluctance is medically warranted, or if it's simply him not wanting to go against Geron's wishes."

"Some friend he turned out to be."

"Don't think that. It's not like he has a choice. Until he's completely free, he can't help himself."

"Then I'll *make him* help himself. He agreed to take the pathogens. He was even aware enough to ask for another treatment before he agreed to stay on board. If he cares about you, he'll help fix this."

"But what if he can't?" She touched the base of her

neck again. It tingled, like it had been hot, but grew colder. "He said removing it could hurt me. I might have to live with this for the rest of my life."

"Hey." He traced his fingers from her temple to her chin. "Then we'll just have a whole lot of wonderful firsts."

Cal's gaze latched on to hers, his eyes intent and focused. He meant every word, and a new warmth swirled through her. She'd love all those firsts, but she'd love them more if she could remember them.

He dragged his fingers through his hair. "Dammit!" He stood and started to pace the room. He cursed again, looking down.

"What is it?"

"I want more than anything to yank Alex away from engineering and drag him to the med bay, but I can't." He looked up. "I want to fix this for you, but we still have Orion to deal with. I need to make sure everyone is safe first, but then we're getting that thing out of you." He sat next to her, kissed her temple, and pulled her close. "I want you free of that prince once and for all."

Free... It sounded like such a wonderful dream, but she feared that dream had ended the day her parents handed her over to the Banes.

CHAPTER 45
CAL

CAL SAT BACK in his command chair, staring at the front of the cruiser drifting far closer to the *Star Renegade* than he would have liked. Ty rubbed his face, his gaze flitting from his console to the ship outside.

Alexander had requested that the two ships drift as close as safely possible for the start of the test on the expanded cloak. *Safely*, apparently, was in the eyes of the people with the bigger ship, who wouldn't be damaged if anyone miscalculated.

The windows in the cruiser were dark, looking no different from the rest of the ship. Not being able to see their command deck left an itchy sensation crawling up Cal's spine, like knowing he was being watched, but unsure from where.

Alanna ran onto the bridge and slipped into her seat. "Okay, I guess we're as ready as we'll ever be."

The team had been studying scanner data from when the Carteks had threatened Rachel's home planet of Ephershia. The cloud of ships traveling cloaked had been like nothing Cal had ever seen, either the sheer numbers, or the technology hiding them. Being able to cloak multiple ships at once could tip the balance of control in the galaxy.

Cal leaned back in his chair to look around Ty. "What are the chances of this working?"

Alanna tapped on her keyboard. "Ethan studied the patterns of the Cartek cloud while they were still traveling under the cloak. Alexander analyzed the frequencies bouncing off the different sectors and came up with a few theories about why they moved in erratic patterns."

"Was that supposed to mean something to us simpletons?" Ty asked.

She looked up. "I glued their findings together and broke it down to a much smaller scale, as in two ships rather than hundreds. It'll work." She smiled. "It's exciting. I kinda feel like Doc executing a master plan."

Alanna had always been the optimist in the group, but she was also meticulous. If she thought it was safe enough to test, that was good enough for him.

Hopefully, they wouldn't have to eject the tech again, especially after convincing Orion it had been permanently attached to the *Star Renegade*.

Outside the ship, the cruiser still loomed, the commander inside still ready to execute them all. Orion probably figured that if the *Star Renegade* exploded, that he'd just use the massive ship Cal had given him to plow through any resistance.

Cal hated knowing that he and his crew would be nothing more than collateral damage if this mission went wrong. Still, there was one fully charged enforcer in his cargo hold, and enough weak ones to do far too much damage for them to run and hope for the best. He needed to find an opportunity to get rid of their unwanted passengers and make a run for it.

Cal sat up and stretched his back before glancing at Ty. "Ready for the worst?"

"You know me. I'm always ready for the worst."

Too bad that was a learned trait. It seemed they rarely got a break.

Cal tapped the comm. "Okay, everyone, here we go. As usual, we have no idea what's about to happen. So hunker down and be ready." He nodded to Alanna. "Let's do this."

Alanna turned the comm dial on the wall next to her. "Ethan, are you with me?"

"Gotcha, beautiful. Your boy Alex is standing guard over the tech, holding up his palms. Not sure what that's all about, but I know better than to ask questions. We are ready to disappear on your command."

Cal opened a comm to the cruiser. "We're engaging the cloak. Hold your position." Which sounded redundant, since their drift hadn't faltered more than a centimeter since they'd been floating in this tight formation, but better safe than sorry.

"Okay." Alanna closed her eyes and took a deep breath, shaking out her hands before placing them on her dashboard. "Here we go."

The floor hummed and the lights dimmed.

Orion's voice blasted over the comm. "*Star Renegade*, if you have jumped your ship, the enforcers on board have been directed to..."

"Keep your pants on," Ty said. "I take it you can't see us?"

The ship loomed before them. Cal could almost sense Orion's glare.

"No, I cannot."

Ty laughed. "That's kinda crazy. What are they...like, a hundred feet from us? We could almost spit at them." He shrugged. "You know, if our spit wouldn't turn into instant ice crystals that would probably shatter on their hull."

"Guys, can you be quiet for a few minutes?" Alanna's screen cast a green glow on her face, accenting small lines in her brow. "This is the first time we've done this. I'm a little nervous."

Ty spun back to his station. "You got it. One quiet Ty, served up nice and silent."

Alanna bit her lower lip. "Here we go. I'm expanding the cloak."

The floor vibrated again before settling. Outside, the right of the cruiser faded, becoming stars. The patterns swept from right to left, wiping over the surface of the cruiser until it was erased from existence.

Ty cursed, gaping.

Cal gulped. Even though he'd known it was about to happen, being prepared and actually seeing a ship that large disappear were two completely different things.

Ty burst from his chair and hugged Alanna. "You did it! I mean, I never had a doubt...but you did it!"

Cal tapped the comm. "Orion, we have a successful test. Not only are you invisible to the eye, but we're only registering heat from your engines. If we didn't know you were there, you'd be invisible."

"As are you." Orion's voice sounded annoyed, despite the success. "This technology is valuable. Once the princess is extracted, you will surrender your ship to your king for further study."

Cal tapped the comm, leaned his head back, and laughed.

Ty returned to his seat. "Can I give him the finger?"

"You might as well. He can't see us."

Coordinates scrolled across Cal's panel.

The external comm connected again. "*Star Renegade*, we have forwarded you the coordinates of the princess. We will leave immediately."

"Hold on!" Alanna looked through the viewscreen, as if talking to the invisible ship. "We need to test how far we can separate and stuff. We don't know all the parameters of holding the cloak."

"We do not need the cloak at this moment. Keep it engaged, and we will test the distance limitations en route. We leave now." The comm cut off.

Ty shook his head. "Nothing like discussing the best possible options and coming to a mutual agreement."

"That's not the way enforcers work." Cal called up the coordinates and scanned the star map. "There's no planet there, and no space stations close. It's just space."

"A ship, maybe?"

"Could be a moving target. That may be why he's so insistent on leaving now."

Hopefully, the ship didn't have a jumper, because there was no way they were reaching those coordinates in the three-minute window where they could trace a jump trajectory.

For now, he needed to focus on the only facts they had: the location.

He sent the coordinates to Ty's panel. "Let's get moving and test the cloak at different distances. Note if the cruiser pops into existence, or if you get echoes of their presence other than the heat from their engines."

"On it."

The cruiser picked up speed, and the *Star Renegade* kept pace. Now that they understood how well the Cartek cloak worked, they had to take into consideration that for all they knew, they were racing right into an invisible blockade. If the Carteks had the princess, they had to know the king would come for her eventually, and they'd do everything in their power to keep her. Still, the big question was: Why? They weren't known to take prisoners. Then again, the king's daughter was a pretty big bargaining chip if they wanted the Banes to back down.

"Slow down a bit," Alanna said. "I'd like to test the range of the cloak."

Ty eased back on the speed. "Your wish is my command, m'lady."

The cruiser popped into existence faster than Cal had anticipated. "How far away are they?"

Alanna pursed her lips. "Not far at all, but farther than I expected." She frowned into her screen. "That's why the cloud that attacked Epershia was so dense. The ships needed to stay that close to remain hidden." She looked out at the cruiser. "It's also why the ones that raced ahead to attack suddenly appeared. Not all their ships have this technology."

Probably because it blew up so easily.

Alanna tapped on her panel. "I'm sending the distance parameters to the cruiser."

Cal sighed. "Okay, let's catch up with them. Right now, they're a big, glaring target."

Ty increased the speed. "Send me the parameters too,

please. I'd rather not fly within ramming distance if I don't have to."

"Sending now." Alanna leaned back and smiled when they moved within the distance she'd prescribed, and the cruiser disappeared. "That's handy. I didn't have to re-initiate anything."

Cal zeroed in on the princess's coordinates. It was one of those black-space regions. There wasn't even a close trade route. How were they supposed to find anything out there?

He rubbed his eyes and gritted his teeth. How were they supposed to find anything out there...*without* draining all the princess's remaining enforcers?

Alanna's login pinged on his screen as she accessed the same information. The lights on her dashboard shone in her eyes as she stared at her screen.

"What do you think?" Cal asked.

She leaned back, still focused on the monitor. "There's a lot of ghosting in the area around the pin. It could be engine discharge, or maybe residual weapons fire."

"You think the ship was destroyed?"

She shook her head. "No. There's a void in the center. I think the ship is floating without engines. It's just like when we turned everything off to avoid the scans when Dania's prince was looking for us."

So, this princess was inside a ship, and the ship was understandably hiding.

The problem was, no matter where the princess was being held, this would be a military maneuver. The enforcers' habit of hitting a ship with overwhelming force wouldn't work if they wanted to get her out alive. "We need more information."

"And a plan," Ty said.

Yes, they definitely needed a plan. Getting Orion to agree to anything that might be safe for the *Star Renegade* crew, though, was unlikely.

Cal opened a comm to engineering and the med bay. "Crew meeting in engineering in fifteen minutes. It'll be tight down there, but we all need to talk, and Ethan needs to keep an eye on the tech."

How he was supposed to come up with a plan with nothing but a pin on a star chart, he didn't know. But as usual, they needed to be ready for everything.

CAL STARED at the dented metal encasing the tech that had almost destroyed his ship. It seemed so unassuming. He had faith in his people's work, but hopefully, Hendry had found a way to keep the monstrosity running cool, and they wouldn't have to test the new seals they'd put in.

Ty and Alanna talked amongst themselves, looking at an engineering screen in the wall while Alexander and Ethan monitored the tech. Their focus in the face of so much uncertainty continued to astound him.

The door slid open and Doc, Dania, and Rachel stepped in. The door bounced once behind Rachel before closing.

Her cheeks heated, and Alexander glared at her as she passed him.

What had that been all about?

Doc strode directly toward Alanna and Ty. "Did we miss anything good?"

Alanna turned from the screen. "Ty and I have been playing with the data we have and matching it up against the defined lack of presence in the center of the space marked with a pin."

"What's a *lack-of-presence*?" Rachel asked.

Alanna pointed at the screen. "The hole is shaped like a class 4 freight and personnel hauler." She turned and looked at each of them. "It's a tank, and a big one."

Rachel walked up to the screen. "That makes sense. Their hulls are really thick. If they were floating, they could have all their power and facilities running inside, and they'd still be undetectable."

How in the name of Saturn's rings did she know that?

She spun, looking at each of them. "What are you all looking at me like that for? I know stuff, too."

Ethan looked over his shoulder. "You *do* tend to be a wealth of very unexpected knowledge. I'm still baffled to find out you're a med tech."

She scrunched her nose at him before turning to Cal. "My family settled on Ephershia when I was eleven, but before that, I grew up on a tank. It was our world, so they taught us about the ship in school, just like you all probably learned about the planets you were born on."

"That could be helpful," Doc said. "These were mass-produced, using the same diagrams for over twenty years. Every ship is supposed to be identical." He pursed his lips. "Unfortunately, the engineer got pissed at the company making them and destroyed all the diagrams. Which means we may have trouble piecing together a viable schematic."

Rachel slipped her hands into her pockets. "I can probably help. I mean, as kids, we got pretty creative to keep from getting bored. We used to play hide and seek all over the ship, from the engine room to the freight compartments."

"That sounds dangerous," Doc said.

She shrugged. "Any excitement on a freighter was a bonus. All we had to look at day after day were metal walls."

Ty called up a picture on the screen. "This is noted as the most detailed map of the two main floors. It's not complete, though."

Rachel stepped closer to the screen. "Yeah, this top one is the living area, and the bottom is where the cargo was staged. Ships could pull up and attach to ports on the cargo level, but not the crew level."

"Which means we can't dock there." Cal rubbed his chin. "That's where they'd be looking for us."

"I have an idea." Ty spun to Rachel. "What did you do with your trash?"

Her eyes widened. "There was a waste management dock."

Ty zoomed in on the map. "And where was that?"

Rachel pointed to a spot in the rear of the ship.

Ty nodded. "If a trash hauler can attach there, then a ship as small as the *Star Renegade* can, too. If Rachel can help prompt the system to lock on to us, we can walk right on board through the trash chute."

Doc smiled. "Ty, that's actually genius."

"Umm…" Rachel scratched her head. "I'm not sure how to do that. We never actually had a trash pickup."

Ty frowned. "How is that possible?"

She looked up at the ceiling. "Okay, okay, I know it's wrong, but we all just piled our trash into the airlock. No one wanted to pay for the actual trash hauler, so when it got full, we just shot it into space."

"But that doesn't mean all these ships did that." Doc

tapped his lips, looking at the screen. "Trash haulers come in more sizes than I can count. They must have some sort of gel-connection system."

Ty rubbed his hands together. "Which would fit nicely over our cargo bay. And we're invisible to the eye and to radar, so they won't see us coming or going. It's almost too easy."

Cal had to agree. "And it's on the opposite side of the ship from where they'd be expecting entry." And most likely, it wouldn't be heavily guarded, if guarded at all.

Cal tapped Ty on the back. "Good job."

"The question is: Then what?" Doc asked.

"Orion probably plans on taking his strongest in there for a quick extraction," Dania said. "But we'll need to talk him into adding some of the princess's enforcers to the team." She looked up at the schematic. "If she's on that ship, they'll be drawn to her. It's the same principle that led him to this location in the first place."

Cal turned to Doc. "How many of her enforcers will be able to make the trip?"

"Maybe five. To be honest, Hendry is in the best shape."

"He'll help," Dania said. "His goal was to get back to his princess. If she's in there, he'll probably be first in line."

Cal nodded. "Okay, good."

Ty pointed at dark bars drawn over the schematic's corridors and near the doors. "What are these?"

Rachel sucked in her upper lip as she looked at the screen. "We used to call them *shifty walls*. I think they were emergency airlocks, or security measures. We had fun finding ways around them."

Finding ways around them? "How?"

"We were bored kids who made our own fun. We scrambled through the vent systems. Sometimes we would come out the other side, disengage the doors, and then disappear back into the vents just to drive the crew nuts." She giggled. "Ah, those were fun times."

She certainly *was* a wealth of unexpected information.

"How big were the ventilation tubes?" Doc asked.

Rachel shrugged. "Some of them were huge. Grown-ups could get inside to do maintenance. But others only the little kids could get into."

That didn't sound good. "How many of the smaller vents did you need to get through to unlock the doors?"

She grimaced. "A lot."

"Can't enforcers blast right through those?" Ethan asked.

Ty zoomed in on one of the doors. "Depends on how solid they are. If this mock-up is to scale, that thing is ridiculously thick."

Dania frowned. "There are few things that an enforcer can't eventually get through, but significant defenses can slow them down." She looked down. "If we get trapped, and they unload considerable amounts of artillery in an enclosed area…"

Cal sighed, rubbing his head. "It would be very bad. I get it."

"Just because the doors are there doesn't mean they'll be locked," Ty said.

Cal started to pace. "No, but if they're trying to keep a princess extra safe, or double-confined in case she and her nearly insurmountable power got free, they would more than likely be locked."

Doc rubbed his chin. "Not to mention, we do have a

bad habit of triggering alarms or nearly getting caught. All they'd need to do is slam all these doors down and we'd be trapped."

Cal's stomach sank. There was no way he was putting his crew in that kind of danger. All Orion needed was the *Star Renegade*'s cloak and the ability to board the ship holding his blasted princess. Maybe the commander and his supercharged ego would be more than happy to enter the ship all by himself.

Alexander stepped away from the screen he'd been monitoring. "Cal, there's no way Orion will enter that ship on his own. He'll research the vessel just as we have. He'll realize those security measures may pose a problem, especially when we're unsure of Zindiria's condition."

Cal frowned at him. "How did you know what I was thinking?"

"I'm an enforcer." He turned back to the schematic. "My assumption would be that he already knows of Miss Quirky's background and plans on recruiting her for the mission."

She folded her arms. "What if I say *no*?"

"I believe last time you and Orion disagreed, you were thrown across the room and the doctor treated you for a mild concussion."

"Yeah, that wasn't fun." She rubbed the back of her head. "Please don't let him take me, Cally. I don't like this new commander. He kinda scares me. He's nothing like my Big Guy."

Doc placed both hands on her shoulders. "We'll figure it out."

"No one is taking anyone off this ship without my

permission." Cal tried to sound surer about that than he felt. If Orion grabbed Rachel, none of them would be able to stop him.

Alexander turned from the screen. "Miss Quirky has demonstrated a tendency for insubordination. My assumption is that he would also require the assistance of her captain to keep her in line."

"Hey!" Rachel pointed at her chest. "Nobody keeps me in line!"

Alexander quirked a brow. "Thank you for making my point."

Rachel's face reddened, and Cal stepped between them. "Okay, so we'll get in front of Orion's inevitable orders by offering Rachel's services."

She paled. "But…"

Cal held up a hand. "I'll be there to make sure he doesn't toss you against any walls."

She folded her arms. "And just how are you going to do that?"

Cal looked at Alexander. "I'll need your help."

Alex nodded. "My programming is still pulling me to do everything in my power to free the princess, so I'd need to come either way."

Dania stepped forward. "I'd like to help as well. I don't have power, but I still have tactical training."

Unfortunately, Cal had seen her cave once already when she'd tried to command an aerial battle. Would she be any better on foot?

Alexander glared at Cal before turning to his former general. "It's a good idea. It will also put you in a better light with Orion."

Why did she need to be in a better light with the commander? He'd rather Dania were safe on the ship.

Dania's eyes lit up, though. She'd lost so much in the past year. He didn't want to make her feel any more unimportant than she already did.

"Okay." Cal turned to Doc. "I need your big brain to come up with a way to get to that princess that doesn't lead to any of us ending up dead."

Doc drew in a deep breath and puffed it out slowly as he scanned the schematic. "Let's start with those emergency doors. We need to have a plan to get around them that doesn't involve children."

Rachel shrugged. "Well, Ethan is probably the scrawniest of us all, but I think even he's too big to get through. I mean, I was around eight when I stopped being the one to slip through and unlock the doors."

Ethan spun from his console. "Did she just call me scrawny?"

Doc tapped his finger on his lips. "It's suicide to go in there knowing they can trap us so easily."

Alexander folded his arms and stared at Rachel.

"What?" she asked.

Alexander's eyes narrowed. "It would be quite helpful in this situation if someone on the crew was even smaller than our engineer."

Ethan held out both hands. "Hey! I'm not *that* small."

Rachel lifted her chin. "I don't know what you're talking about."

"I think you do."

Rachel spun to Dania. "Alex has power, and he's not telling you where it's coming from."

Dania frowned. "What?"

Alexander pointed at Rachel. "Enough deflecting. Is your stowaway in this room with us?"

Cal's eyes widened. "Stowaway? What the hell are you talking about?" He looked at Doc. "Have you registered a separate heartbeat on board?"

Doc shook his head. "Nothing outside the guests in the cargo bay."

"Because there's nobody to scan!" Rachel headed for the door, but Alex grabbed her arm. "Let me go!"

He pulled her back. "If Orion forces you on that ship and those walls come down, the Carteks will drop enough firepower in the corridor to kill all the enforcers. Do you really want to take the chance of being caught in the crossfire?"

Rachel sniffed, looking down. "Don't do this to him. This is a big job, and it'll be dangerous."

"I think you don't give him enough credit. He's been on this ship for months without detection." Alexander drew her closer. "Is he here?"

Cal took a settling breath. "I would very much like to know what you're talking about."

Alexander looked over both his shoulders. "If you're here, I hope you understand that Ms. Quirky may be put in danger. She's been protecting you, and I have a feeling that you're intelligent enough to understand what we've been talking about."

Cal held his breath. There was no one else in this room. Had the enforcer lost his mind?

Alexander crouched and stared at...*nothing*. "Incredible." The enforcer smiled. "I can barely see you."

"Because there's nothing there," Ethan said.

Rachel sniffed again, wiping her nose. "We're caught,

Max. It's okay. Show yourself."

Cal gaped as the air in front of Alexander blurred. The tiles and Rachel's legs moved like a printed picture waving in the breeze, before shaking into... Were those *eyes*? Glossy, gray fur materialized over a thick, round body. The eyes blinked as four clawed hands tapped on the floor and a long, fluffy gray tail swirled in the air before settling around the feet of a creature that looked like a cross between a fox and a lemur.

Alanna covered her mouth with her fingers. "Oh my gosh! That's the smaller animal we picked up with the cave boar when we saved Alexander."

"No way," Ethan said. "They both went down the ramp. I saw them leave the ship."

Cal rubbed his temples. The last time he'd seen the creature, it had been scampering up the broken ramp while the pregnant boar was hanging below. They'd been so worried about saving the female that they'd lost track of the other one. He sighed and looked up. "This thing has been on my ship all this time?"

Rachel straightened. "He's housebroken. Uses a toilet and everything. I taught him."

"That's not the point, Rachel."

"I think he's cute." Alanna crouched beside Alexander and waved. "Hi, Max."

Great. Now they had a mascot.

"Please don't make him leave, Cally." Rachel scooped the creature off the floor. "He's sweet and nice and super smart."

Doc looked the creature over. "The camouflage ability is amazing. How intelligent is he?"

"Why does it matter?" Cal asked.

The creature jumped from Rachel's arms and scampered up the legs of Ethan's station.

Ethan held up his hands. "Hey, be careful there."

The animal scratched at the pad on the tabletop, and the words "I HELP" appeared on the screen.

Cal gaped. "Did that thing just type?"

Rachel folded her arms. "I told you he was smart. He picked up basic English from all of us, and then I taught him to type so we could talk. He's a really fast learner."

Doc nodded. "That makes sense. The colonists couldn't control them. They said the creatures got around all the traps they set. They probably had no idea that they were dealing with intelligent life."

Max's tail curled up and down behind him. He looked at Cal and waved, just like Alanna had.

Cal rubbed his face. His temples started to throb, and he took a few deep breaths. This thing was probably the cause of all the ship malfunctions.

If this animal was as smart as he seemed, they probably hadn't been malfunctions at all, but their new friend getting to know his new environment.

"Okay." Cal pointed at Rachel. "We're going to talk later about honesty on this ship. I don't like secrets. Consider this your one and only warning."

She nodded.

He turned back to the creature. "Max is your name?"

"I named him," Rachel said. "He seemed to like it."

Max sat up on his hindlegs and wiggled his nose at Cal. He was actually kind of cute. Cal blinked away the thought. If this creature was staying on this ship, and he was as smart as the rest of them, he had to pull his weight.

Cal motioned to the schematic. "Max, if Rachel tells you

how to get through the vents and how to get those doors unlocked, can you do it?"

Max looked at Rachel, then nodded.

"I can shout through the vents and tell him what to do. That's how we older kids trained the smaller kids when we got too big to get through ourselves." Rachel picked Max up and cuddled him into her arms again. "Are you sure, little guy? I'll be so worried about you."

Max made a chittering noise and rubbed his muzzle against her cheek.

This day just got stranger and stranger.

Cal rubbed his eyes. "Okay, Rachel, give him as much instruction as possible before we get there." He still couldn't believe he was placing all their lives in the paws of an animal, but he'd learned not to underestimate anything in this galaxy. It was arrogant to think that humans, Kevers, and Carteks were the only intelligent races in the universe.

Ethan leaned against his workstation. "Are we really trusting Max can do this? I mean, unlocking a door could be complex."

Max jumped out of Rachel's arms, scampered across the room, and jumped into a bin of parts. He clambered inside before popping out with some sort of plug, running across the room, and placing it into a slot in the wall beside the surveillance station.

Ethan gaped. "That's actually right." He looked at Max. "Have you been watching me?"

"He likes machines and stuff," Rachel said. "He drops things sometimes, but he tries to be careful." She turned to Doc. "He can do it. I mean, I'm afraid for him, but he can definitely do it."

Cal ran his fingers through his hair. "All right. So, the team will consist of whatever enforcers Orion wants to bring, plus Rachel to give directions, me to protect Rachel from the enforcers, Alexander for friendly muscle, and Max to get through the vents if needed." He turned to Ethan. "I'd like you there in case we run into any tech related issues."

The engineer chewed the inside of his cheek. "You got it, boss."

Cal walked over to Alanna. "I need you to stay behind. Help Doc prep the med bay in case we have injuries, and then I want you to get some sleep. There's a good chance we might need you to jump us out of here."

She nodded. "I can do that."

Ty folded his arms and leaned against the wall. "Let me guess: *Ty, you keep the engines hot and ready to blast out of here. Chances are we'll be running for our lives.*"

Cal smiled. "Exactly. Ethan will get them prepped for you before we leave."

Doc raised his hand. "If Alanna is sleeping, and Ty has his hand on the throttle, that leaves me to keep watch over an alien technology that has a penchant for exploding."

Alanna rubbed her shoulders. "Ethan has a bed in Engineering. I can sleep there."

Ethan cocked his head. "That's like half of my wildest dreams coming true." His brow shot up. He looked at Alex, then spun back to his workstation, probably wishing he hadn't said that right in front of the man currently living out Ethan's wildest dreams.

Alexander folded his arms and glared at him, but Alanna squeezed the enforcer's arm and smiled. Alex nodded and returned his attention to the stowaway.

Doc stared at the metal casing around the tech. "It's not a bad idea. I can keep an eye on the readings and wake her if it starts to get hot."

Again, it wasn't the best plan, but they had limited resources. They needed to help get the princess. It was the only way to get the rest of the enforcers off the ship.

Ethan turned from his screens again. "You do all realize that the big hole in this plan is that if we succeed, we'll be transporting a real-live Bane on the *Star Renegade*. I mean, I'm all for getting Her Highness off our ship and onto that cruiser the second we can...but we're talking about a princess. I mean, enforcers are bad enough." He held up both hands to Alexander. "No offense. But this is an actual full-blooded Kever."

"We have no choice," Dania said. "If the cruiser is too big to dock, we'll have to transport her. We can only hope she'll be grateful, and feel secure enough surrounded by her enforcers, that she won't realize she's on a smuggling ship until she's already safe on Orion's cruiser."

Cal nodded. "Which means we need to make sure every unfriendly enforcer goes with her." He looked at each of them. "The second she's off the ship, we jump." He pointed at Alanna. "And then we jump again. And again. And again if we have to."

She paled, then nodded. "I got it. Lots of rest required." She turned to Doc. I'm going to need help with that. I'm not sure I'll be able to sleep with all this going on."

Doc nodded. "I have an idea."

The plan sounded solid, but they still needed to sell it to Orion. Max stuck his nose up and squeaked.

"Orion will accept the plan," Alex said. "Everything about it is in his favor. We just have to be very cautious about casually escorting all of them off the ship with the princess or they will know we are about to run."

Cal nodded. That part might be even harder than saving the princess.

CHAPTER 47
DANIA

THE TENSION in the cargo bay seemed to press in on all sides. Dania stood tall next to Cal, trying to form a united front.

Orion glared at Cal. "I ordered Dania and Alexander to report for duty. I will accept Ms. Quirky for her proposed knowledge of the vessel, but the rest of you will return to your stations and await further orders."

Dania held her stance rigid and her head high, taking the command position despite her lack of power. "I've fought in close quarters with this crew. They are resourceful, and good with weapons. The Carteks will be expecting enforcers, not humans." She held Orion's gaze, keeping hers as stony as his. "If the enemy has devised a way to harm enforcers, the human members of the team will prove invaluable. I agree with this plan, and this is the plan we shall use." Technically, she was a general and outranked him, but Orion had more than enough primordial energy coursing through his veins to overrule her, and they both knew it.

She held herself steady. If she dwelled on the reality of

389

her situation, she might falter and lose any semblance of authority she still had.

He continued to stare her down, his pupils dilating and contracting as he mulled over the plan. Even he had to admit the strategy was sound.

The enforcer Orion had chosen to be his second on the mission—Fallon, the one who'd apparently thrown Peter and Rachel across the med bay a few days earlier—lifted his chin. "The humans will be a liability in battle. They will probably fall with the first round of weapons fire. We cannot waste time protecting more than the one we asked for."

Rachel shifted, obviously uncomfortable with being considered *the one they'd asked for*.

Orion glanced at Cal, and a slight smile touched his lips. "Human casualties aren't a concern. We just need to get Alexander and Dania to Zindiria. Once we get to her, getting out won't be a problem."

Dania's brow pinched before she regained her stony enforcer countenance. Orion didn't consider her as the same liability as the humans? Surely, he had to understand how limited her abilities were. But also, why was he more concerned with getting in than he was with getting out?

The commander's gaze carried to her. "Don't look so bewildered, Dania. Zindiria, even if she's been mistreated, will have no problem bringing you and Alexander back to a formidable strength. Even if her enforcers are still weak, four capable enforcers are more than enough to walk off that ship unopposed."

Dania's stomach sank. Zindiria shared the same blood as Geron. Dania knew it was possible for members of the same family to feed each other's enforcers. But what would that mean for her freedom?

Cal glanced at her, a note of panic in his eyes. They'd come so far—could they be walking straight toward her inevitable end?

Alexander stepped forward. "Dania has approved this plan, and she is still my general. There is no reason not to comply. We're bringing the humans."

She was glad for the vote of confidence, but her heart rate increased, and she grew slightly dizzy. Did she really want to be a part of this mission anymore?

Ty's voice came over the comm. "Okay, team. I'm easing toward the trash chute. Just keep in mind that if their bio-gel doesn't latch on to us, we're not going to be able to open the door or you'll all get sucked out, so sit tight until I give the all clear."

Dania shivered. That was a sobering reality. She'd faced similar danger many times, but her programming, and the power surging through her, had always kept her focused. In some ways she'd been aware of the danger, but she'd never cared. Part of that was conditioning, but the larger part was probably that she had nothing to lose but the respect of her sponsor, which one achieved by facing danger and squelching it with the swiftest, most powerful blow possible.

The ship jolted and Dania grabbed Cal's arm to steady herself. Her cheeks heated as she flicked a glance at Orion. Thankfully, the commander had been looking in the other direction. He'd see reaching for the help of a human as a lack of strength on her part.

Cal squeezed her hand. "We're okay."

She nodded but didn't meet his gaze. If Orion planned

on having her fed, they were far from okay, and Cal knew it. Still, they'd proposed this plan, and they needed to see it through. Hopefully, they'd be too busy getting Zindiria off the ship for her to do much more than touch her and Alexander. How much power that would pass from her to them, though, Dania wasn't sure.

Ty's voice filled the room. "Wow. It actually worked. We have a viable seal." The comm cut out, then came back. "Now, no one really cares if the trash can breathe, so when you step on board, the oxygen level will be low. You'll only have air from the *Star Renegade* until the outer hatch closes and the inner door opens to give you access to the ship. So don't panic."

Ethan huffed. "Easy for him to say."

A burst of static sounded over the comm before Ty's voice returned. "I'm going to stay right here, though, with the seals engaged, so if you're running on the way out, just blast through the inner door if you need to."

Cal hit his wrist comm. "Good work. Remember to keep those engines hot."

"Happy princess hunting, boss."

A hiss filled the room as the seals disengaged. The stench of rotten meat and vomit slapped Dania so hard, she stepped back.

"Ugh!" Ethan put his hand over his nose. "That's just not okay."

Orion and Fallon stepped through as soon as the door had opened, unfazed by the bags, boxes, and debris scattered in the tube. Had she been able to ignore such vile smells when she'd been an enforcer?

She tried to take a steadying breath, then gagged.

Cal's hand appeared on her shoulder. "Shallow breaths."

She nodded, but that was easier to say than to do.

Fallon kicked a bag out of the way as he and Orion reached the airlock on the other side. Dania had hoped for more fully fed enforcers on this mission, but on this, Orion wouldn't waver.

He'd left two enforcers on his cruiser, and one on *the Star Renegade* 'to keep the ship safe,' although Dania was fairly certain the enforcer's true purpose was to report back to Orion if Ty veered from the plan. What they thought Peter, Alanna, and Ty would do on their own, she wasn't sure.

Hendry looked over his shoulder at Dania before he followed, along with nine other pale enforcers whom Peter had cleared for duty.

Dania grimaced. She would never have allowed those enforcers on a mission. They were obviously hindered by their health. Then again, their only function was to point. She supposed as long as they were able to walk, they could lead them to Zindiria.

Alexander's hair took flight as he held out his hand, directing Dania and Cal to enter the ship with Ethan and Rachel. It had been decided that he would take up the rear to add a level of protection to the human members of the boarding party.

Dania's stomach churned as his hair floated about him. Rachel had quite boisterously implied that Alexander knew why his power remained so much more viable than her own. Dania had felt trickles of her energy return from time to time, but it had been months since she could harness the power and control it.

His eyes met hers, and he took her hand. "We're going to get out of this, and then we need to talk."

Had he read her thoughts? He probably didn't have to. Alexander knew her better than anyone. If he *did* know why his power was more stable than hers, there must have been a good reason he hadn't told her. Alexander was analytical and researched everything before making a decision. He must have thought there was danger in the answer, either for herself or maybe those around her.

Her chest clenched. Alexander didn't scare easily. Whatever he had to tell her may have consequences more far-reaching than facing a powerless future, or walking into a room with a princess who may be able to give her the strength she so badly wanted but was terrified of regaining.

Dania took a settling breath. Was it really possible that regaining her strength would turn her back into the monster she'd once been? Did primordial energy erase *everything*? Her stomach hardened. She knew the answer. She just desperately wanted it to be untrue.

They stepped off the ship just as the inner door opened, and Orion and Fallon left the trash chute. The scent of rotten meat and spoiled milk filled the air.

Rachel covered her nose. "I don't remember it smelling so bad in here."

Dania held her breath as she continued through to the ship. Orion and the other enforcers had fanned out on both sides of the empty hall. Metal walls and floors stretched in each direction, a cold, harsh setting after living in the *Star Renegade*'s warmth.

Rachel took a deep breath and smiled. "Ah, home sweet home."

Fallon scowled. "This is not the vessel on which you were born."

Rachel shrugged. "It could be. Who knows? Sure feels the same."

Something warm and fuzzy brushed against Dania's leg, and Rachel looked down before bringing her attention back to the hall. They'd decided not to tell Orion about Max. It was still somewhat disconcerting that even the enforcers, with their elevated senses, could not detect him.

Ethan looked up and down the hall. "It's dry in here. Really dry."

"Your point?" Orion asked.

"My point is that the Carteks are called 'squids' for a reason. They have tentacles, and my understanding is that they prefer a moist environment."

Which may have accounted for the lack of resistance. Maybe they'd only humidified the forward section of the tank. Still, an itch crawled up Dania's spine. If she'd had power, she'd draw the primordial energy and hold it just beneath her skin, ready to set free.

Hendry headed to the left. "I'm feeling drawn this way."

Cal rubbed Dania's back. "You sure you want to go?"

Sure? No, not sure at all. But she already looked so weak in everyone's eyes. She needed to regain a modicum of respect. She could still lead people. Her experience as a general had value, even without her power.

She forced a smile on her face. "Yes. Let's go."

The group followed Hendry down the hall and through what seemed like endless silver corridors. Nothing had been done to make this vessel anything someone would want to call a home. How horrible it must have been for children to grow up in an environment like this.

Ethan pointed to a groove in the ceiling. "Here's one of those doors."

The enforcers walked ahead as Rachel rapped her knuckle on a metal weave over an opening in the wall. "Here's a vent. As kids, we'd just pop these out and crawl inside." She pointed farther down the hall. "See, there's another one down there. They all connect."

"But how do you unlock the doors if they come down?" Ethan asked.

Rachel tapped a panel on the wall. "There are controls behind these panels outside every other door."

Making each set of doors an effective trap. "And there's definitely a vent between each one?"

Rachel nodded. "In my ship there were."

Hopefully, Doc was right, and the design had stayed the same over the years.

One of Zindiria's enforcers grabbed the wall beside him. "I feel strange, like the pull to my sponsor has shifted."

Hendry started to run. "He's right. She's moving away from us."

Had the Carteks discovered their presence? If so, why weren't they attacking?

The hallway ended at a large, metal door with another corridor on the left and right. Hendry slapped the door controls, but nothing happened.

The enforcer spun toward the group. "She's still moving away, but she was just behind this door."

How were they moving a Bane being held against her will that quickly? Certainly, Zindiria would be fighting them, especially if she could sense her enforcers so close. She must have been incapacitated, if not completely unconscious. Even then, how would her captors be moving her so fast?

Dania turned to Ethan. "Can you get that door open?"

The engineer pulled a screwdriver out of his bag and pried the touch panel off the wall. "Give me two minutes."

Hendry shook his head. "They're moving her at great speed. You don't have that long."

An air intake panel hummed a few feet to the right of Ethan. Dania glanced at Rachel and then pointed at it.

Rachel frowned before her eyes widened and her lips formed an "O." She yanked the webbed panel off the wall and waved her hands, whispering. Tiny taps sounded from within as Max's claws scampered through the vent.

"What is that sound?" Fallon sneered, walking toward the opening.

Rachel held up a palm. "Keep your shirt on, Ugly. The vents always tick like that."

Dania smiled. The human ability to lie with such ease was fascinating. Luckily enough, Orion and Fallon were too preoccupied to check her temperature.

The hallway around them heated as balls of energy formed in Orion's hands. "I thought you were an engineer. Work faster."

Ethan shook his head. "I'm trying, I'm trying."

Hendry smashed his fist into the door. "Break it down!"

"Stand back." Fallon raised his hands and balls of green and blue fire swirled in his palms.

"Hold on!" Ethan screamed, just as the doors sprang open.

The engineer gaped, shrugged, then picked up his tools as the enforcers ran inside.

Cal grabbed Dania's shoulder. "Stay back. I don't want you anywhere near that princess."

Alexander stepped beside her. "I have a bad feeling there's no reason for either of us to be concerned."

Rachel held out her hands and a gray fluff of fur jumped into her arms. "Good job, little guy." She stroked Max's fur before the animal shook and faded back into nothingness.

Ethan put his last tool in his bag. "I would have gotten it eventually."

Rachel patted his copper curls. "Yeah, you would. I have no doubt." She turned away from him and rolled her eyes.

Within the room, Hendry picked something silver off the floor. "She was here. I could feel her, I swear it."

Orion bore down on him. "Where did they take her? Which direction?"

Hendry shook his head. "The feeling is far away and moving too fast. She's no longer on the ship."

Dozens of bootsteps echoed through the metal halls, coming from both the left and right.

"Ambush!" Dania raised her hands, calling on her power, but nothing came.

Alexander pulled her back into the doorframe and sent a jolt of energy down the hall that exploded amid cries of alarm. *Human* cries of alarm.

DANIA WANTED to shove Alexander out of the way, but he'd been right to pull her back. She leaned out and shot her weapon to the right while Ethan shot to the left.

Cal pulled the laser pistol from the back of his pants. "Those voices don't hiss like Carteks."

As far as Dania knew, Cal had been the only one to actually speak to a Cartek and survive, so she appreciated his agreement with her assessment.

Not that it mattered at the moment. Whoever was attacking, they held a significant tactical advantage that she needed to alleviate.

Dania called over her shoulder. "Rachel, which is the fastest way back to the *Star Renegade*?"

"Back the way we came."

Dania looked straight out the door and down the hall they'd come from. There weren't any weapons firing from that direction, but they'd gone through several of the airlocks that could be manually slammed closed. And this time, the tank's personnel had been alerted of their presence. The lack of munitions from that direction most likely meant that was the way the enemy *wanted* them to go. Falling into a trap was definitely *not* ideal.

Rachel twisted the ends of her hair. "We can also go left. It'll just take a little longer."

Orion stormed toward them. The air wavered around him as a shield materialized, and the laser fire bounced back down the hall toward whoever was shooting at them. He shoved Hendry against the wall. "Which way did they take the princess?"

Hendry gaped.

Cal stepped between them. "Hey! Lay off. He already told you she was gone."

The commander pushed past Cal and leaned close to Hendry's face. "Which way?"

Hendry pointed to the right, where most of the firepower came from.

Orion glanced at Fallon. "Come. We need to get to Zindiria before they get her off the ship." They pushed through the door and sprinted down the hall, Fallon throwing blasts of energy in front of them.

"Stop!" Dania shouted. "We need to stay together!" She hated to admit it, but with Alexander weakening, she needed their primordial energy.

A blast of laser fire sliced through the air inches from her face, and she moved back inside.

One of Zindiria's enforcers glanced at Hendry. "They're right. There's still a chance we can save her."

He and five others ran down the hall behind Orion and Fallon. The remaining three crouched closer to Hendry, like injured children looking for safety.

Dania rubbed her forehead. How was she supposed to

get her friends out of this without the fully charged enforcers?

Hendry drew in a deep breath. "They're wasting their time. She's already gone."

A blast hit the wall beside him before Alexander held up his hands, creating a shimmering barrier.

"I can shield us," he said. "But I won't be able to fight."

"I'm happy with the shield." Ethan rubbed the top of his head. "I think I got singed a few times when we were out in the open."

Three more blasts hit Alexander's shield and bounced back as he and Dania moved into the hall.

Orion, Fallon, and the others turned the corner at the end of the corridor. They were gone, and so was Dania's chance to save her friends. At least no one was shooting at them from that direction anymore, but would that be enough?

Cal tugged Alexander in the opposite direction. "Come on. Keep us shielded until we have a clear run to the ship."

"But...!" But what? Dania had no idea what she'd intended to say.

How had she lost control so quickly? She used to simply *think* what she wanted, and her people obeyed in an instant. Words were hard. Words could be ignored.

Cal skidded to a stop and spun back to her as a blast ignited over their heads. His expression was stern, focused, before his eyes widened. He looked over his shoulder, then back to her.

Dania's cheeks heated, but she understood him taking point. Without her power, Cal was the better choice to lead them. Maybe Orion had been right to overrule her.

She strode forward, but her eyes burned. Every time she

thought she'd found her place, she was reminded about how much she'd lost, and how much she needed to learn before she could be a valuable member of the crew.

"Dania, wait." Cal grabbed her arm and pulled her into a hollow in the wall, probably meant to allow large pieces of cargo to pass pedestrians in the hallway. "I'm sorry."

This was foolish. They needed to keep moving. "It's okay," she whispered, not meeting his gaze.

The others ducked into the same hollow, Alexander keeping his shield up as sprays of firepower sparked across the surface.

"It's not okay." Cal's expression softened as he met her gaze. "That was force of habit, and it was wrong of me. This is your mission. What do you think we should do?"

Dania's heart raced. His eyes were focused on her, unwavering despite the blasts hitting the shield and bouncing off the ceiling.

Ethan fired down the hall twice, glanced at Dania as if awaiting orders, then fired again.

Rachel whispered, "It's okay. We're not gonna die. We really, really won't." She looked at Dania. "Right, Dani?" She gulped as she pet an invisible Max in her arms.

Alexander's expression remained focused on his shield, very much the soldier awaiting orders.

Dania straightened, nodding to Rachel. They hadn't given up on her. The only one who'd given up on her was herself.

Tension built in her shoulders. She knew better than to give in to these feelings. Fear and doubt were part of humanity. Overcoming that doubt was what separated those who followed from those who led.

Another blast scattered over the shimmering screen as

Dania raised her chin. "I think you're right. We take advantage of Alexander's shield until we reach the end of the hall." She glanced at her friend. "Then Alexander will take a tactical position and fend off the attack while Cal and Ethan take point to get the rest of the team around the next bend." She pointed to the next intersection. "We need to reevaluate our position and tactical advantages at each junction, due to the unpredictability of our adversaries."

Cal glanced at the next intersection, then at the team, and back down the hall again. He nodded at her, suppressing a grin.

Her chest fluttered. She shouldn't have cared that he was impressed with her solution, but she did. For some reason, she'd never felt so alive. But now she needed to keep them all that way.

Dania grabbed Hendry. "Let's go."

The weaker enforcers followed without complaint, although a few of them looked like they were ready to give up. Maybe they had been running on the hope that the princess would return them to health. Now that hope was gone, leaving them just as sick as ever.

Cal and Dania aimed their weapons and shot forward while Ethan and Rachel shot behind them. Alexander's shield swirled, allowing friendly fire out, but beads of sweat ran down his temples. He was losing concentration as well as strength. She shouldn't be relying on him so much, but she had no choice.

As they reached the next intersection, the halls changed from dark gray to harsh black. A spray of firepower came at them from the left, plus behind them. A blast exploded over Dania's head and Alexander waved his arms until the shimmering wall engulfed her. Another blast came from behind, hitting one of Zindiria's enforcers in the back. Hendry grabbed for him as he fell, but the enforcer slammed to the deck, staring at the ceiling with lifeless eyes.

Dania grimaced. "Leave him. There's nothing you can do for him now." She flinched, hearing the sound of her previous self—the general who'd never worried about casualties—but it was the truth. Even at his full strength, Alexander couldn't reverse death.

Hendry backed away, his eyes wide before a stony enforcer countenance returned.

Was that the first time he'd seen one of his brethren die? Or maybe, more likely, that was the first time he'd cared. Dania understood. She wished she could tell him it would get easier to see his friends fall to enemy fire, but that would have been a lie.

They ran down the empty hall to the right, Alexander holding out his arms to keep the bubble of energy around them, illuminating the inky-black walls.

"I can't hold this much longer." He blinked, his hands shaking.

A blast slammed through his shield. Ethan hissed, grabbing his arm right before another enforcer fell to the ground.

Alexander grimaced. "I'm not sure what they're using against me, but they're slicing holes in my shield. It's some sort of new technology."

Dania pulled him to another small cargo divot, not large enough to shelter them, but just enough to allow Alexander to refocus his shield on a smaller area.

Rachel pointed forward, holding her other hand on top of her head as a few sparks scattered through the shield above her. "Up ahead, we need to take a left. That will take us to the crew quarters and common areas. The right is a dead end."

Another bolt sliced through Alexander's shield, barely missing Dania's shoulder. "How long is the hall to the left before the next bend?"

Rachel twirled her hair into a knot. "Long."

Not the ideal answer, but not unexpected judging by the layout of the other hallways. If they headed left, their attackers would follow. Even shooting blindly, their assailants would eventually get enough blasts through Alexander's shields to take all of them down. "How deep is the hall to the right before it ends?"

"It's only about ten feet long, I think. I'm not sure. I was a kid when my parents got transferred. Everything looked bigger back then."

Ethan cringed away from a blast. "You're not seriously thinking of running straight into a dead end, right?"

Dania stared into the corridor, looking for other options, and finding none. "They know we're here. Unless they're completely inept, they'll be preparing an ambush. If we enter the longer hall unprepared, we may find ourselves trapped between two enemy lines with no shelter. We need to get our backs against a wall to see if we can slow our pursuers down."

Cal leaned closer, stopping Ethan before he could argue. "Dania's right. We definitely need a more defensible position. Ten feet will give us shelter and a corner to shoot around."

Dania ducked as another spray of sparks singed her skin. She also needed to give Alexander a chance to rest. He wouldn't be much good to them if he passed out.

She tugged Cal's shoulder. "Let's go. Cover each other."

The blasts increased as they left the divot and sprinted for the next junction. Pausing had probably been a mistake. Their attackers had gained too much ground, but she needed to learn to take the time to get input and give verbal orders. It was inefficient, but she needed to learn to deal with her new reality.

As they slipped around the bend, the third enforcer fell. An old-fashioned grappling hook shot from down the hall and wrapped around his leg. His eyes widened before he was dragged away into a spray of smoke and weapons fire.

"No!" Hendry started after him.

Cal drew him back. "That's not Carteks. It's slavers."

"Slavers?"

Cal's lips thinned. "The hook. Pirates would have just fired kill shots."

Dania frowned. How would slavers have the power or wherewithal to capture a princess? Zindiria's power would have been insurmountable to a human.

Unless they had Palian steel. Was that the real reason the king had ordered all deposits of the material destroyed? Could the power-absorbing metal incapacitate Banes as well as enforcers?

Alexander kept his hands lifted, ready to ward off the next attack as everyone leaned against the walls, some gasping for breath.

Ethan dragged his fingers through his hair. "This was a mistake. We're backed into a corner."

Possibly, but this was better than being taken out one at a time out in the open. These insolent slavers were using them for target practice.

Dania held her hand on Alexander's back. He'd grown

pale over the past few minutes. This alcove wasn't much, but it would give them a few moments' respite.

She holstered her weapon. "We're not backed into a corner. We're regrouping. Alexander needs to rest."

Alexander's eyes widened as he glanced at her. He was probably used to her running her enforcers into the ground, not worrying about their health. Then again, with his healing capabilities, she'd rarely been concerned about casualties. Too bad her friend was working on the last of his strength.

She turned to the crew. "Cal, Ethan, and Rachel: Take turns firing down the hall we just came from. We don't want them catching up to us or we *will* be trapped."

Dania looked down the long hall they needed to traverse to get to the ship. Rachel had been right—the span to the next juncture was just as long as the last one, and this hallway seemed devoid of cargo divots to hide in. However, there was a wide vent panel close to the floor.

Dania waved Rachel closer. "There's another vent halfway to the next intersection. Can we use that to our advantage?"

Rachel grimaced. "Not that one. We're still in the cargo staging area, so that won't go anywhere helpful. But if we can make it to the end and go right, we'll enter the blue section. There's an air-return shaft that will run along the edge of the crew quarters and take us almost all the way to the trash chute."

Cal shot twice then looked over his shoulder. "Can we all fit through the air return?"

Rachel gulped. "I can't remember."

Dania stared at the lighting system. "Are those Teresian glow panels?"

Rachel looked up. "I have no idea what a Teresian glow panel is."

Ethan inched back after firing his weapon to look down the hall. "Yeah, Dania's right. Yikes. Everyone, keep your weapons pointed low. Those things were pulled from freighters years ago. They have a bad habit of exploding when they get hot."

But maybe they could use that to their advantage.

Dania gauged the distance to the next juncture. It would only take a few moments at a full sprint, but they'd be out in the open again. And the possibility of facing resistance at the next junction was high.

Still, some chance was better than no chance, and if they were lucky, Rachel's invisible friend might be able to help them. "Is Max still with us?"

The floor blurred, and a chittering sound filled the alcove.

Good. They might need him.

Either way, they couldn't stay here. Dania rubbed Alexander's back. "Are you okay to keep shielding us while we advance?"

"With the way they keep breaking through, I wouldn't count on it. Either it's their technology, or I'm in very bad need of a feeding."

Dania's stomach sank. A year ago, she would have pulled him to her and transferred her excess energy. That was her function: to direct her people and disseminate Geron's primordial energy as needed. Once again, she was reminded of how she'd become something *less*.

But she could still direct. She needed to be the general she'd once been. It was their only chance of survival.

"Then we have a new strategy." She straightened. "Use

lethal blasts of power to cut off their attack until we're safely at the blue section."

That would expel a great deal of energy, but they'd also gain speed—and probably see fewer casualties if they could put the pirates on the run, rather than running themselves. It was what enforcers were trained to do. Unfortunately, Alexander, like herself, had developed the complication of having someone new in his life who was worth living for.

She stepped beside him, holding up her weapon as she faced the others. "Alexander will go on the offensive. We won't have the advantage of his shield, but with any luck, the fear of primordial energy will be enough to slow them down." She looked at Cal, then back to the crew. "When we step out of this hall, they're going to release everything they have on us. Alexander will hold them back while the rest of us pass behind him." She looked at Ethan. "Then Cal and I are going to shoot the lights."

The engineer's eyes widened. "You're kidding, right?"

"No. It's my understanding that there will be a five-second pause before the chemicals ignite and explode."

"It'll be more like four seconds."

She looked at Cal, then Alexander. "We'll need to time this perfectly. It'll increase our chances of getting down that hall without being shot."

Ethan rubbed his face. "This is insane. I mean, brilliant, but insane. It's going to get really hot in that hall."

Dania straightened. "I intend to be halfway to the end before the lights explode." She pulled Hendry to his feet. "We're getting out of here. Now."

Alexander took a deep breath and stepped out of their hiding place. When enemy fire rattled through the hall they'd come from, his hands ignited, throwing small balls of fire at their attackers while the rest of them ran past. It was less of a defense than Dania was used to, but it would have to do.

Ethan, Rachel, Max, and Hendry bolted down the hall.

Dania aimed at the lights. "Now!"

Dania and Cal fired, and Alexander sent a final blast at their attackers before sprinting down the hallway beside Cal and Dania.

A bright light flashed, and a fiery hum filled the hall with a roar rather than an explosion. Dania's hair matted with sweat as the temperature spiked.

Cal cursed as the heat rolled over them in waves.

"Keep moving!" Dania sprinted for the next bend. That fire would slow them down only as long as it burned, which, if she remembered correctly, was about five minutes, leaving more than enough time to escape.

She skidded to a stop at the start of the blue section as laser fire shot through the hall from her right, blocking their way to the air return shaft.

Cal cursed. "Rachel, can we go left instead?"

"Not if we want to get back to the trash chutes."

"We can't allow them to herd us away from the ship." Dania leaned around the corner and shot the vent opening directly beneath the sign that read, "Blue Q1." The webbed cover fell off and clanged to the floor. "Rachel, did you explain to Max how to open and close the airlocks?"

She paled. "Yeah, but—"

"Don't argue." Dania looked at the ground. "Max, where are you?"

His tail appeared first, then his nose and eyes.

Dania wasn't sure she'd ever get used to that. "I shot

open the vent. Get in there and see if you can shut one of the airlocks. Maybe we could use them in our favor."

Rachel gaped. "Those are *lasers*. You can't send my little buddy out there!"

"Spray cover fire," Dania shouted. "They can't see him. That should be enough. Go!"

She and Cal started firing. Max's gray hair faded to nothing as he scampered around the bend.

"What if he closes the wrong airlock?" Cal asked.

"Then we'll improvise. It's what smugglers do." She ducked as sparks scattered over her head. "An insolent captain taught me that."

Cal puffed a laugh as he shot past her. "You've been spending far too much time with Ethan."

Alexander called from behind them. "The fire is already burning out!"

So much for their short reprieve.

A loud boom echoed through the blue hallway, and the lasers stopped.

Cal peeked out. "Let's go!"

They sprinted around the corner and Dania skidded to a stop. The door had slammed down right behind the pirates who'd been shooting at them. Two men faced the massive partition, shouting at each other. Three bodies lay on the floor, their midriffs and legs hidden beneath the airtight barrier as blood spread across the tiles.

"Ew." Rachel covered her mouth. "I think I'm gonna puke."

The two living pirates spun from the massive, metal wall, their eyes wide before a push of energy from Alexander slammed them against the metal barrier where they fell, unconscious.

Dania nodded. That had been a good decision on Alexander's part. A minimal use of power that had still stopped the attack.

The ceiling rumbled. Alexander grabbed Rachel, pulling her forward as another door slammed down right where she'd been standing, sealing them off from the rest of the pirates.

Rachel patted different parts of her body as if making sure she was still in one piece. She spun toward Dania. "That was a little too close."

Dania nodded, gaping. She'd told Max to drop only *one* door!

"Okay, how is this better?" Ethan slammed his fist against the barrier.

Cal lowered his weapon. "Because, they can't shoot at us anymore."

Dania supposed that was a bonus, but these walls were impenetrable by design. They were trapped.

Alexander eased to the floor, his breath labored. She placed her hand on his shoulder. "You did well. Rest while you can."

A black, wiggling nose appeared in the vent before Max jumped out and landed on the floor.

Dania crouched beside him. "Please tell me that you did that on purpose. We can't get out."

He ran in circles, stood on his hindlegs, and pointed at the vent.

Everyone looked at Rachel.

She glanced at the small opening in the wall. "I hope you're trying to tell us we can get through there."

Max stamped his feet and then scurried back into the vent.

Dania took that as an affirmative. It would be tight, but they could fit through the opening. Hopefully, the tubes were as wide as the entrance.

Rachel tied her hair back into a ponytail. "Okay, just like old times. Anything is better than being stuck in this box." She crawled into the vent, followed by Hendry, then Ethan and Cal. Dania and Alexander took up the rear. Grunts and groans added to the sound of sliding as they made their way through the tube.

Shouts carried through the vent walls, possibly pirates who were stuck in the halls between the partitions Max had dropped around them.

The duct angled up, and the space narrowed. Dania's shoulders brushed against the walls as she dragged herself through.

"We're not going to be able to get much farther," Rachel called from the front.

Which probably made Alexander being positioned in the rear a good call. His wide shoulders may have stopped all of them from getting through. She cringed. How could she consider anything about Alexander possibly getting stuck as a positive?

"The little guy just jumped out," Ethan called from ahead of them.

Dania tried to look over her shoulder out of habit more than being able to see. "Can you get a little farther?"

Alexander grunted. "I'll make do."

If 'make do' meant he'd use his powers, then she needed to get out for her own safety. Even at partial strength, a blast of energy from Alexander could break a human in two, and she knew Alexander would rather be stuck forever than take a chance of hurting her.

CHAPTER 49
CAL

DANIA CRAWLED out of the air-return and into Cal's arms with dust in her hair and grim determination in her eyes.

He smiled. "I bet you were never trained to crawl through the bowels of a ship."

She adjusted the gun in her belt. "Definitely not."

One of the airlock doors stood firm beside them, closing them off from the other side of the corridor they'd just been in, but the hall was otherwise clear.

Rachel scratched her fingers through Max's dust covered head. "Good boy." She looked at Cal. "Told you he was smart." The animal's fur changed, the top blending with the dust and his body matching Rachel's clothes. Within seconds, she was petting what appeared to be nothing unless the animal moved.

Distant shouts sounded from the other side of the airlock. Cal had to admit, catching the pirates in what should have been their own trap had been brilliant on Max's part.

Dania pulled Cal away from the vent. "Stand clear."

"Why?"

The wall beside them shook like a small explosion had happened inside, before Alexander pulled himself out of the vent. Dust and dirt clung to his hair and clothes, making the normally impeccable enforcer look just as disheveled as the rest of them. Cal had barely made it through the small tube. He hadn't considered that Alex may have to blast his way out.

They were all a dirty mess, but at least they were free. Now they needed to find their way to the *Star Renegade* before the pirates figured out what had happened to them and crawled into their own air vent.

Cal turned to Rachel. "Which way to the trash chute?"

"We're about mid-ship." She pointed down the hall. "We need to go down there and to the left to get to the back."

"Let's get going, people. I don't want to be anywhere near here when the pirates figure out how we got out of their trap."

They were going to have to get on board the *Star Renegade* and blast off as soon as possible. The pirates knew they'd somehow snuck onto their nice, safe, impenetrable tank. If they were smart, they'd be scanning the outer hull trying to figure out how the *Renegade*'s crew had boarded. Cal's team needed to get to Ty and disengage before the pirates discovered the small, inconspicuous smuggling ship attached to their refuse port.

Unfortunately, that meant they wouldn't be able to wait for Orion and the other enforcers, but that was their own fault for taking off and ignoring Hendry's warning that the princess was already gone.

Cal turned the corner and walked right into the barrel

of a gun. The weapon fired, and the boom filled the hall. A high-pitched scream scorched his ears. Maybe Rachel. The sound reverberated as he waited for his body to hit the floor.

Cal took a deep breath.

He…*wasn't dead.*

Cal blinked, the barrel of the gun coming into focus—not aimed at him, but just over his head.

The barrel lowered, and Chris Columbus glared at him. "What did I tell you about watching for crow's nests?"

Cal coughed on his next breath and looked over his shoulder, where a body hung from a chair mounted near the ceiling, still holding a charged plasma rifle glowing and ready to fire.

Chris holstered his gun and folded his formidable arms over soiled tan military fatigues. "Did you forget everything I taught you?"

Fireballs filled Alexander's hands as he stormed toward Cal's unexpected savior.

Dania jumped between him and Chris, holding up her palms. "Wait!"

Alexander's hands still swirled with flames. "That is a criminal. A murderer and a pirate."

"But he just saved us."

Alexander's gaze was stony. "That is Chelsea Colombina. They are wanted for three counts of murder and more counts of piracy than I care to list."

Chris raised his hands slowly. "My name's Chris Columbus."

Alexander's eyes narrowed. "Changing your name does not hide your crimes."

Cal held up his hands, mimicking Dania. "I was wanted for murder too. I still am."

"You did not kill anyone."

"But I'm still wanted for murder, right?"

Alex's lips thinned. "Absolutely. You know this."

"But you haven't executed me for murder. Dania didn't execute me, either. Why?"

"Because you did not commit the crime you were charged with."

Cal held his hands a little higher. "Okay. Now just consider that for a moment. Did you see Chris commit a crime?"

"Chelsea Columbina."

"Okay, did you see Chelsea commit a crime?"

"Of course not."

"Then can you consider that maybe he's just as innocent as I am?"

Alex glared at Cal. The truth was that the enforcer was well aware of all the crimes that Cal had *legitimately* committed. He wasn't sure how the Banes' programming worked, but he needed to tap into whatever it was that allowed Alexander to forgo judgement on Cal.

"Alexander." Dania pulled down his arms. "Comply. This man's past is questionable, but he's helped us before. He could prove valuable to our escape."

Alexander grumbled something under his breath before the fireballs winked out.

Chris whistled. "Calvin Espinoza: the enforcer whisperer." He pointed to Dania and Hendry. "Did you do that to these two, also? 'Cause that's a nice trick."

Cal shoved him. "Cut the crap, Chris. What's going on?"

"What's going on is you all just walked into a trap. The slavers were counting on the princess's depleted enforcers coming for her. They expected them to be easy pickings." He pointed his chin at Alexander. "And a lot of them were real happy to see this one. There are still a few collectors bidding in case he's caught again." He turned back to Cal. "Your enforcer friend is worth a small fortune."

A deep growl eddied from deep within Alexander.

Chris held up his hands. "Hey, don't kill the messenger. It's not my fault you're so pretty." He rubbed his palms together and looked over the group. "How are you planning to get out of here, anyway? The bossman is pulling out his hair trying to figure out how you got in without being detected."

Cal narrowed his eyes. He trusted Chris, but only so far. "Let's just say we need to get to the rear of the ship."

Chris's eyes widened. "Huh. Just as resourceful as always, I see. I probably don't want to know."

With the smell down there? "Believe me, you don't."

Chris waved them to follow. "If you head down this hall, you'll be clear until the end. There's another crow's nest at the corner." He looked at Cal. "Try not to be an easy target this time."

Cal's blood heated, but Chris was right. Cal had been so centered on getting out, he'd forgotten to be careful. "And after the crow's nest?"

"That's when things are probably going to get exciting. There's a couple of enforcers down there reigning hell on everyone. Friends of yours, I take it?"

Cal pursed his lips. "Not by choice."

Chris looked at Alex and Hendry. A small smile played on his lips. "We definitely need to get a brew after things settle down. I think this is a story I gotta hear." He waved them on. "How about I provide a little distraction at the next corner?"

"That would be appreciated."

Ethan grabbed the plasma rifle and hung it over his shoulder before following.

They walked to the end, and before the bend, Chris placed two fingers in his mouth and whistled. "Don't shoot. Friendly incoming."

Cal pressed up against the wall as his friend walked out into the open.

Chris held up his hands. "Any signs of the intruders?"

A voice answered. "Not this far. I heard that…"

Alexander leaned out, holding up his palm. A loud thump echoed through the hall.

Cal moved behind him to see a body face-down below a crow's nest seat.

Chris stepped back. "You'll do *that* and you're accusing *me* of murder?"

Alex started walking in the other direction. "He's fine. Just a few broken bones."

Chris glanced at the pirate's still body. "How do you know?"

"I'm an enforcer."

Rachel tapped Chris's shoulder. "You'll get used to that. This one tends to not kill people. He's weird in that way, but it's kinda helpful, too, because we're all not, you know…dead. Which I kinda like, I ain't gonna lie."

Chris rubbed the back of his neck. "Yeah, not dead is always a good thing."

Cal moved beside him. "*Chelsea?*"

Chris looked down and laughed. "Yeah, I never really

felt like a Chelsea. Leaving that name behind was freeing in so many ways."

Too bad he'd had to become a pirate to do it. Then again, Cal had landed as a smuggler. He supposed no one planned this kind of thing.

Cal tapped his back. "Because you're a Chris. It suits you."

A door opened at the end of the hall, and shots rang out. Cal dropped to the floor, firing. Chris fell to one knee beside him.

Rachel gasped, and Hendry pulled her down, dropping on top of her.

Alexander sent a fireball into the doorway and the hall grew silent once again.

"Hendry is bleeding!" Rachel cried. "And he's kinda crushing me!"

Cal and Ethan slid the enforcer off her while Chris and Alex held point on the door. Hendry's already pale skin had grown ghostly white. Blood streamed from the top of his head, and from his hip.

Rachel wiped her nose. "I-I think he saved me."

Hendry winced. "You are valuable to the mission. Your knowledge of the ship is necessary for our escape."

"Aw, you say the sweetest things." She placed pressure on the wound.

Alexander crouched beside them, placing a hand on Hendry's head. When he drew his hand away, Hendry's wounds continued to glisten with blood.

Cal's eyes widened. "Can't you help him?"

Alex closed his eyes. "I'm too weak. If I do, I may not be any use to the rest of you."

"Leave me," Hendry said. "I am expendable."

Rachel slapped his shoulder. "No, you're not! I'm the only one who's expendable here." She frowned. "Wait, that's not right, either."

"No one's getting left behind." Cal frowned as a small puddle of blood pooled beneath Hendry's hip. Hopefully, he hadn't just unintentionally lied.

Rachel pointed at Cal. "Get that look off your face, Cally. He saved me. We're not giving up on him."

"I got him." Ethan slipped his arm under Hendry's shoulder, and Cal helped lift him to his feet.

Hendry coughed. "This is an inefficient use of resources."

Rachel slapped him again. "Shush, you. No talking unless it's constructive."

Dania got beneath Hendry's shoulder. "I'm not as good with weapons. I'll help him."

Hendry frowned. "A general never sacrifices themselves for their soldiers. A soldier should support their general."

Dania glanced at Cal. "Well, I've learned that a lot of things enforcers do are ill-advised. Let me help you."

Chris gaped, then looked at Cal. "I definitely need that drink. How the heck did you get through those thick, enforcer skulls?"

"It's a long story."

The sound of weapons fire came from down the hall, followed by a cascade of loud, stomping boots.

Chris pulled Cal in the opposite direction. "Can't wait to hear it, but let's get you out of here first."

"Wait!" Rachel shuffled after them. "That's the wrong way!"

"Doesn't matter. There's no one shooting down here!"

Chris rounded the corner and skidded to a stop at a dead end not much deeper than the last alcove they'd hidden in.

Rachel folded her arms. "Told you!" A blast of liquid fire melted the wall behind her, and she ducked, holding her head.

Ethan cursed, grabbing his arm as he dropped his weapon to the ground.

Rachel put pressure on the wound. "I got you!"

Ethan hissed.

"Oh, stop being a big baby."

Ethan had been splashed with the splatter of a plasma rifle. Those things shot liquid hell. Cal doubted he was being a big baby.

Dania eased Hendry to the floor. Blood stained her pants from where he'd been leaning on her. That wound had to be bad. Rachel was right. He'd probably saved her life.

Another blast hit the wall beside them. Straight-line weapons couldn't reach them in this nook, but the pirates were probably counting on the very effective plasma splatter. If they shot enough times, they might be able to disable everyone in this alley without walking down the hall and being picked off by Cal and his people on the way.

Rachel pulled Ethan back as a small drip of plasma ate through the flooring.

Dammit! We need to get out of here!

Cal's comm band pinged and Ty's voice came over the small speaker on Cal's wrist. "Boss, we've got a problem."

Was he serious? "No more problems! We're already pinned with injuries."

"Sorry, but Doc just intercepted a comm. It's not

Carteks you're dealing with in there, but pirates. This was all a trap to catch enforcers."

Cal ducked as another blast rained sparks over them. "This is *not* news."

"Okay, but what might be news is that the pirates were in cahoots with the squids all along. The Carteks funded the whole damn thing."

Cal glanced at Chris, who just shrugged. As usual, he'd probably followed a paycheck, not asking where the money had come from.

Cal tapped the comm. "Do you have any good news?"

"I wish I did, boss. It looks like the Carteks decided to cancel their deal with the pirates and screw them royally."

Cal rubbed his face. He didn't like the sound of that.

"Cal, they're gonna blow up the tank." Static crackled over the comm before Ty continued. "Doc translated chatter that the squids decided it would be easier to destroy it from inside rather than hitting it with a missile. Scans show three Cartek ships already docked, and the squids are flooding into the tank to fight off any pirates who might try to stop them."

Which made sense. The salvage price on a tank was enough to feed a small colony for over a year. Most pirates Cal had known were crazy enough to stay and try to save the ship rather than save themselves.

Cal leaned his head back. They were mid-ship, so they were safe for at least the next few minutes.

He rubbed his face. Tanks had gotten that nickname because they were tough. Jokes were made that they'd outlast humanity. He couldn't imagine doing anything from within that would do more than scuff the walls. "How would they destroy the tank from the inside?"

The comm crackled before Ty's voice returned. "Believe it or not, those ships are manufactured with *actual* self-destruct systems, just like in the old science fiction stories. Their hulls are too thick for them to be destroyed from the outside like normal junkers."

Ethan gaped. "A self-destruct? You've gotta be kidding me."

Apparently, he wasn't. Cal's temples started to throb. "Is that something you can stop?"

Ethan huffed a mirthless laugh. "A self-destruct is the most ridiculous thing I've ever heard of. I wouldn't even know what to look for."

Cal looked at Chris. "Do you know where it is?"

"No idea. I just work here."

The weapons fire stopped, and Chris stood.

Dania whispered something to Hendry and helped him back to his feet.

"Did they give up?" Ethan asked.

"Unlikely." Chris grabbed the plasma rifle Ethan had taken from the dead guard and walked toward the hall. He shot twice then glanced around the edge and drew back just before a blast hit him. He cursed, leaning against the wall.

"Visual confirmation," a voice shouted. "Columbus is working with the enforcers. He's cornered wi..." A gurgling sound filled the hall, followed by a thump.

Chris frowned and Cal moved closer as bootsteps came toward them.

Five large shapes turned the corner and Chris and Cal opened fire, but their shots bounced back. Plasma splattered the wall and seared through the edge of Cal's boot.

"Hold your fire!" Alex shouted.

A shimmering barrier diffused, and Orion and Fallon glared at them. Three more of the princess's enforcers stepped into view, looking even paler than they had when Cal had last seen them.

Orion glared at them. "I see you managed to get yourselves caught. How annoyingly predictable." His eyes widened as they landed on Chris.

Dania lifted a hand, while still balancing Hendry on her shoulder. "This criminal has been helping us. His sentence has been postponed."

Orion narrowed his eyes. "Your penchant for seeking the help of lawbreakers grows annoying."

"This is not open for discussion," Dania said. "The Carteks are boarding."

"So, we will annihilate them just as we annihilated any pirates we've found."

Annihilated? That may be a strong word, being that it looked like they'd lost three of the princess's enforcers in the process. Of course, Cal's team had done no better in that respect.

A mind-numbing siren filled the halls. Red lights overhead started flashing.

Rachel covered her ears. "A fire drill—are you kidding me? They're still doing these?"

Cal doubted this was a drill. He tapped his comm. "Ty?"

"Boss, the engines are lighting up on the heat sensors. I'm gonna guess the self-destruct is in countdown."

Orion snarled. "Self-destruct? What ridiculousness is this?"

Cal held his comm band closer to his mouth. "Ty, get out of here. Get the *Renegade* to a safe distance."

"Like hell, boss. My orders are to have the engines hot and heavy. I'm ready to leave as soon as you get here."

"Ty, this is an order. Get to safety."

Static came over the line. "Sorry, boss. I can't hear you."

The line crackled again before going dead. Cal was getting really tired of that ruse.

His heart rattled as he spun to Rachel. "Whoever started the self-destruct probably gave themselves enough time to get off the ship. What's the fastest way to the *Renegade* from here?"

"Back the way we came, but that's the same direction where the pirates were trying to blast us full of holes."

Cal started moving into the hall, waving the others to follow. "I'm going to guess that the pirates are smart enough to know what the Carteks have done. They're going to want to get out of here just as much as we do." With any luck that meant they'd have a clear run to the trash chutes.

Alexander appeared at Cal's side as they moved down the hall. "Orion is allowing you to take the lead."

"I guess he's learned that I deserve to be here."

"Don't flatter yourself. I think he's hoping you get killed. He's holding Dania back under the subterfuge that he's asking for her orders."

Cal looked over his shoulder. Hendry leaned against the wall as Orion spoke to Dania. Fallon had his hand on Rachel, keeping her back as well. Maybe Alexander was right.

Ethan limped toward Cal, holding a gun in his left hand, his right arm dangling at his side. The shoulder of his jacket was black and melted from the plasma splatter.

"Can you shoot with your left hand?" Cal asked.

Ethan held up the gun. "I guess we're going to find out. Just don't ask me for accuracy."

Another spray of fire crossed their path, and they pressed up against the wall.

Cal shouted down the corridor. "There's a self-destruct, and you guys are still shooting at us? Are you insane?"

A voice called from the next bend. "We're cut off from the hangars and can't get out. We know you have a ship!"

"Killing us is not going to help you find it."

The siren wailed overhead. Cal had no idea how long they had, but he did know they had no time to argue. "Let us pass, and we'll get you out."

"I have seven men."

Cal sighed. "As long as you don't mind sleeping on the floor of the cargo bay, we can fit you."

The blast of the alarm sliced through Cal's mind. White flashes danced in front of his pupils as pressure started to build behind his eyes. Now was not the time to get a migraine, but there wasn't much he could do to stop it.

The voice called again. "We're standing down. Call off your enforcers."

Cal snorted and looked at Alex. "Any chance of your friends standing down?"

Dania moved behind them. "I'm not happy about the pirates, but we need to get through."

Orion glared. "I can shield us and we can slice right through them. We're not assisting the people responsible for selling Alexander as a pet."

Alex flinched, and Dania touched his arm. "I'm not exonerating them. They'll pay for their crimes, but for now, we need to get off this ship." She glanced at Alexander. "They have technology that gets through our shields.

You've lost people, too, so you know this. I refuse to lose anyone else."

Alex grimaced. Orion and Fallon just growled.

Cal could understand Alex's reaction, but Orion and company, as usual, were just being difficult.

Dania glared at them. "You will all stand down."

None of them looked happy, but they didn't argue.

The pirates stepped into view, and Cal did the same. Both sides held weapons, just not pointed at each other.

The guy in the front gave a curt nod, shifting his considerable bulk from one foot to the other.

Stars above! It was Victor...the same guy who'd cut the deal with Cal to buy the enforcers on his ship. "You're still trying to catch enforcers?"

Victor shrugged. "The money's good." He held his arms to the side, one still holding the weapon. "I'm calling a truce, though. Nothin's worth dying for."

The sirens continued to wail.

Cal tried to look calm, despite the impending doom. "If one of you steps out of line, the enforcers have orders to execute you on the spot. Got it?"

Victor and his men nodded.

Cal looked at Chris. "These guys are your responsibility."

"Gee, thanks."

Cal waved them on. "Rachel, let's go."

The flashing lights turned from red to yellow. Cal squinted, but each flash still lanced through his pupils like a knife.

Ethan held up his hand to block the lights. "What does that mean?"

Rachel tugged at her hair. "I—um, I don't remember that ever happening."

"It can't be good. Let's go!"

Cal's vision started to blur. If he fell, Dania and Alexander would be able to get the rest of the crew out alive. The only problem was, they wouldn't leave him behind. Then they'd be stuck dragging both Cal and Hendry.

His stomach started to harden. He took deep breaths, just like Doc had taught him, but without the meds, he doubted it would work. The pressure between his temples increased. He *could not* start vomiting. He needed to keep running or they all might die here.

Someone screamed. Cal spun and realized it was several someones.

The three weakened enforcers were on the ground writhing like someone was removing their skin. Hendry knelt at Dania's feet, holding his temples and shrieking.

Orion bore down on the pirates. "What have you done?"

Victor held up his palms, backing up several steps. "Whoa there. We're just running like the rest of you."

The enforcers continued to scream.

Rachel grabbed Hendry by the arm and tried to pull him up. "Come on! We have to go!"

Victor looked up at the lights and started back down the hall. "Leave them. We're out of time."

"No way!" Rachel called. "He jumped in front of the bad guys. He saved me."

They didn't have time for this argument. "Everyone, grab an enforcer. Drag them if you have to!"

Fallon raised his hands and Hendry and another

enforcer rose from the ground. Ethan tried to lift one but cried out, grabbing his injured arm. Alexander threw the guy over his shoulder. Victor and another pirate pulled the last one by the arms. They sprinted down the hall as fast as they could while dragging shrieking, incapacitated men.

Cal tapped his wrist comm. "Ty, we've got the trash chute in sight. Be ready to go."

"More than ready."

Cal flipped off the comm. He'd tell the crew about the casualties when they boarded. Right now, they had to worry about surviving.

They squeezed into the trash chute, smashed together until the inner door closed.

"What the hell are we doing?" Victor called, trying not to press up against Fallon. "And what is that awful smell?"

Chris laughed. "You boarded through the garbage pickup? That's genius!"

The outer door opened and light from the *Star Renegade* flooded the dumpster.

Doc stood in the doorway, waving them in. "Go, go, go, go, go!"

They each grabbed an unconscious enforcer and dragged them onto the *Star Renegade*'s cargo deck. Ethan hit the door controls, sealing them off from the tank, then pressed the wall comm. "We're in!"

Cal ran toward the ladder, tapping his wrist comm. "Ty, blast through the gel seal if you have to. Get out of here!"

The ship hummed as Cal hoisted himself up the ladder. He wished he knew how much time they had. That tank was the size of a small space port, and the *Renegade* was a small ship. If that thing exploded...

A crash echoed through the ship, throwing Cal off the

ladder. He grabbed on to a rung, wrenching his shoulder to keep from falling. A dead, low rumble rolled over the hull, shaking the *Renegade* like the galaxy was ending outside.

Dammit! If the tank had exploded, there was just so much debris the *Star Renegade* would be able to outrun. They'd be ripped to pieces in minutes!

The shaking intensified. Grunting, Cal pulled himself up the ladder. He needed to get to the bridge and…

Everything grew pink and purple.

Alanna had jumped the ship! Thank the stars!

Cal breathed deeply, his vision blurring until the lights came back up.

The ship jolted, and Cal clung to the ladder as his feet slipped off the rungs. He scrambled to get back on the ladder and groaned as his shoulders burned from the stress.

Coming out of a jump could be rough at times, but that felt like they'd hit something!

"What was that?" Orion barked below.

Unfortunately, he'd need to leave explanations up to the others. Cal raced up the ladder to the main floor and sprinted toward the bridge. The lights in the hallways pierced his pupils like searchlights. He kept his gaze down, but it did little to thwart the pressure building behind his eyes. He'd promised Doc he'd go see him if he ever had even one of the five symptoms he'd experienced in the last half hour. He was just too busy saving their hides to worry about himself.

He slapped the panel and squeezed through the door before it opened. "Report!"

Ty fumbled with the controls in his dashboard. "We're caught in something."

Cal slipped into his seat. "Caught in what?"

Alanna held her head, tears streaming from her eyes. "I'm sorry. We're not far enough away."

Cal's eyes widened. Outside, massive hunks of the tank spiraled toward them.

"We need to move!" Cal grabbed the controls and pressed the ship forward. They moved a few feet, then sprang back.

Ty pulled on the manual throttle. "See? I told you."

A massive piece of the tank rocketed directly at the viewscreen.

Cal grabbed the arms of his chair. "Ty!"

"It's gonna hit!"

Cal cringed as a wall of metal filled the screen, then flashed and shattered into pieces. "What in the name of... What's going on?"

"I don't know. It looked like it hit something."

Relief melted into grim reality. If even one of those shards got through, it could pierce the *Star Renegade*'s hull.

"Get us out of here!"

Ty's hands continued to tap and sway over the controls. "Don't you think I'm trying? We're stuck!"

Cal scrolled through ship diagnostics, blinking as his eyes started to blur. "Everything looks fine. How can we be stuck?"

The doors opened and Alexander stepped onto the deck. "Did we hit something?" He approached Alanna's station. "It felt like you skipped space."

She nodded, wiping her eyes. "I did, but then I felt like I got punched in the chest." She coughed. "Like, literally. I don't know what happened."

Alexander approached the main viewscreen. "It's a web."

Cal looked up. "A what?" Clear stars shone back at him, each sparkling light lancing his brain like a needle.

Alexander pointed out the window. "It's faint, but it's there."

Cal's head started to pound, each drum slamming against his skull. He grabbed both sides of his head, taking more deep, slow breaths as bile rose in his throat. He had to keep himself together. He needed to figure this out.

Alexander's hand appeared on his shoulder. "What's wrong with you?"

"The boss gets headaches. Nasty ones," Ty said.

"That's inconvenient." Alexander's hand heated before he stumbled back, grabbing his own head.

The pounding in Cal's skull began to dull as a groaning sound filled the bridge.

Cal gulped, blinking as his sight began to return. "Is that hull pressure?"

Alexander nodded, clutching the back of Ty's chair. "The web is shrinking. It's a Cartek weapon. I've heard of it but never seen it this close." He pointed to different points outside. "The focal points are twisting. They're going to crush us."

Wonderful. How was he supposed to get out of a net he couldn't see?

Alanna wiped more tears from her eyes. "I'm sorry."

Alex crouched beside her. "Don't be. You're stronger than their technology."

She shook her head. "No, I'm not. They punched me right out of the jump."

"Only because they caught you by surprise." He took

her hand. "Now that you know they're out there, focus on a point outside the net and skip the ship right over them."

"It's all the way around us," Ty said. "We're seeing pressure on all sides."

Cal blinked a few times as everything came back into focus. "Can you blast out?"

"I tried that already. I nearly shot off our own landing gear when it ricocheted."

Alexander grabbed Alanna's face with his palms. "You need to trust in yourself. Search for the strength inside you."

"What strength?"

"The butterflies. Imagine the butterflies."

"But I don't have the toy anymore."

"You don't need it." He stood and moved behind her, holding her shoulders. "I'm here, and I can help you focus, but you need to get us out of here."

"What if they punch me again?"

Alexander leaned closer to her ear. "Then punch them back. Smugglers don't take kindly to being trapped in anyone's net." He leaned up. "You're the navigator of the *Star Renegade*. You're the reason this ship is uncatchable, and you know it."

She shook her head, choking on a sob.

Cal stood. "He's right. We'd be dead ten times over if it weren't for you."

She looked up at him, her lower lip quivering.

Ty punched the edge of his console. "Deck two is showing signs of strain. If we're going to do something, it's gotta be now."

Cal crouched at her feet and grabbed her hands. "Alexander can't lie. If he says you can get us out of here, it has to be true." He pulled her hand to his heart. "And I believe in you. We all do."

Alanna nodded and wiped her eyes as Cal helped her to her feet. She gulped, and a dial of purple-and-blue light formed at her fingertips.

"We're out of time!" Ty called.

Alanna sobbed and placed her fingers into the floating gears. The ship groaned about them and she shrieked, the sound reverberating off the walls as the air turned purple, pink, then purple again. Cal grabbed the edge of her station as a blue haze settled over them, and the air grew cool. Ty's breath puffed out in front of him in a frosty, blue cloud before the air turned purple again, then pink.

The ship jolted, and stars blurred in the viewscreen before the lights came back up.

Ty's hands flew over his instruments. "Three minutes! I'm trying to figure out where we are."

Alanna whimpered and fell into Alexander's arms.

"Breathe." Alexander eased her to the floor. "You're okay."

Cal sure hoped that was true. He crouched beside her. "That felt like a big one. I think you're getting better at this."

She laughed, then winced, holding her stomach. "It sure doesn't feel like I'm getting better at this."

Alexander ran his hands over her. "She seems fine. Just tired." But his hair still lifted, and he waved his hands like he was doing one of those miraculous healings. Either he was lying about her being okay, which he wasn't supposed to be able to do, or he was being overly cautious.

Ty sat back in his chair and puffed out a breath. "That's three minutes, and for once in our lives, there's no incoming." He spun toward them and smiled at Alanna. "Have I told you lately how incredible you are?"

She rolled her shoulder and winced. "Tell me again. It will make all these bruises worth it."

As Ty entered into a soliloquy of the amazingness that was Alanna, Cal looked out over the stars. Sometimes space looked far more peaceful than it actually was.

They'd gotten out, but just barely. And they still needed to find out what kind of weapon the Carteks had set off that had dropped half the enforcers to the ground, screaming. If the *Star Renegade* computers had picked up any data, they needed to get that information to the king.

Cal grimaced. He'd never in a thousand lifetimes thought he'd want to help the enforcers, but like it or not, they might be the only thing standing between humanity and another Cartek invasion.

CAL STOOD inside the doorway to the med bay, gaping.

They'd been hit fast and hard, and he couldn't remember ever seeing his team so rattled. Doc ran from bed to bed, injecting unconscious enforcers with what Cal guessed were pathogens. He wasn't even using the slow drip IV bags anymore.

Once he knew they were safe, and Cal had settled Alanna in her bed with Alex making sure she stayed there, a quick survey of the ship found all the enforcers in the cargo hold unconscious like the others. Most of them looked like they'd clawed at their own skin and some had slammed themselves against the security barriers so hard, they'd broken bones before they'd passed out.

Orion stood in the corner, his jaw set and a deep horror in his eyes. The full-strength enforcer he'd left on the *Star Renegade* was also being treated for injuries sustained when she'd tried to stop the others from hurting themselves. Eventually, she'd passed out from exhaustion as well.

The commander's gaze kept flitting from her to the others being treated. He knew the ramifications of a weapon that could incapacitate this many enforcers at the same time. The question was: Why were he and Fallon still standing?

Doc puffed out a breath and waved Cal inside. "We have no idea what happened. Even our old pal Bleven screamed like someone was stabbing him to death, and he was already unconscious." He dragged his fingers through his hair. "I gave them each a half dose of pathogens to try to help, but like usual, I'm at a loss."

Cal patted Doc on the back. "You're doing good." He leaned closer. "I hate to be selfish, but do you still have some set aside for Dania?"

"Yeah, but I can't make it fast enough for the rest of them. I'm not going to be able to save them all."

On the other side of the room, Ethan held his arm. "I'm hurt too, if anyone cares. A guy could bleed to death before he got any help around here."

Rachel slapped his leg with a towel. "Oh, please, you stopped bleeding hours ago."

"But it hurts."

"You're not gonna die. Get over yourself."

Cal smiled. Some things never changed.

He turned to Doc. "Make sure you get some sleep. You're not going to be any good to them if you're tired."

Doc nodded. "I have Rachel working on more pathogens. I'm thinking of giving Ethan a few painkillers and getting him to help."

Cal tapped his shoulder. "Sounds like a plan." He walked over to Orion. "Are you going to just stand here all day?"

The enforcer folded his arms. "I find myself feeling

insufficiently trained to assist." He looked down. There was an expression there—*remorse?*

Cal called over his shoulder. "Doc, do you think you could train Orion to make pathogens?"

The commander shook his head. "I cannot be an accomplice to this."

But he could watch? "How about you be an accomplice to a treatment that will keep all these enforcers alive until we can get them back to Bane space? We're not trying to free them. We're treating them. Keep that in mind." Hopefully, that would be enough to get through that blasted programming.

Orion took a deep breath and lifted his chin. "How may I assist in their treatment?"

Doc's eyes widened before he waved the commander to the rear of the med bay, where the test tubes were rising and sinking into the apparatus he'd built. Orion as another set of hands was an added bonus. With any luck he'd continue to look past the crimes and see the good they were doing.

Cal headed to the lounge and stepped inside. Chris sat at one of the tables, cradling a mug between his palms.

Cal grabbed his own drink and joined him. "Are the pirates okay with sleeping on the floor in crew storage?"

Chris's eyes rose and looked at the door, probably considering the uncomfortable accommodations across the hall. "They all agreed that would be better than sleeping in the cargo bay, where you had the enforcers. I told them we'd try to get them some blankets or something later." He took a sip of his drink. "Thanks for giving me one of the crew quarters rather than stuffing me in there with them. I think they're still a little pissed that I was helping you."

Cal shrugged. "Well, we certainly couldn't put Chelsea in there with a bunch of stinky pirates."

Chris glared. "Chelsea could kick any one of their asses."

"I'm sure that's true." Cal laughed. "But seriously. You saved my hide…again. You always have a bunk in my ship, buddy."

"Thanks, but can we please forget the whole *Chelsea* thing?"

"Aw, you gotta let me have something over you."

The comm pinged and Doc's voice filled the room. "Cal? Some of the enforcers are waking up."

Cal shot to his feet. "I'm coming."

"A captain's work is never done, huh?"

"That's pretty much true. Just keep your buddies in line for me, okay?"

Chris saluted. "Aye-aye, captain."

DANIA HELD Hendry's hand as Peter placed a salve over some of his wounds. He was awake, but his eyes were glossed over, staring at nothing.

Cal stepped inside, grabbed a chair, and sat beside her. "Has he spoken?"

"No. None of them have." She dabbed Hendry's forehead with a damp cloth while Peter moved on to another patient.

Across the room, Rachel handed Orion a test tube. He took the flask but kept looking at Hendry. Dania understood. There were far too many questions and not enough answers.

The recycler went off, and a folded towel shot out of the device and landed atop the pile. Dania glanced back to the commander to make sure he wasn't watching as the towel floated across the room and settled on her lap.

"Thank you." She patted the air in front of her and her fingers smoothed over warm fur before Max shook himself out, his coat changing to a mottled brown similar to her pants. She handed him the dirty towel, and he ran it back to the recycler.

Cal smiled. "I'm glad he found a job to do."

"I'm told everyone works on the *Star Renegade*, and no job is too small."

Cal's eyes brightened, and he leaned closer. Just being near him lifted a weight from her, like he could make anything better. That was ridiculous, of course. He was just one man. Still, she let the warmth settle over her.

He placed his hand on her thigh. "When you're done for the night, would you like to stop by my quarters? Maybe I can scrape together something to eat that hasn't been freeze-dried."

The warmth spread into her belly. How was it possible one person could make her feel so...*right*? "I think I'd like that very much."

Hendry winced and grabbed his chest. "No!" His head lolled back. "No!"

Dania grabbed his shoulders. "What is it?"

Doc ran to her side and flashed a laser on Hendry's forehead while looking at a screen. "That's good. Try to keep him talking so he doesn't pass out again."

Dania stroked the sides of Hendry's face with her fingertips. "Stay with me."

He shook his head. "It doesn't matter. Nothing matters anymore."

"Don't be foolish."

He sat up, grabbing her shoulders. "Don't you understand? Zindiria is dead."

Dania gaped. *Dead? That couldn't be!*

Orion stormed over. "What?"

Hendry released her and fell back to the bed. "I felt it. I

felt it all… The searing pain. Her scream. And then…nothing." He choked out a sob. "I can't feel her. I can't feel…*anything*."

Orion clutched his chest, backing away.

"You okay?" Doc asked.

The commander's skin paled. "I-I failed."

Dania stood. "This isn't your fault."

"It is!" He lowered his hand, backing farther away, like he was trying to escape the truth. "It was my mission to find her and bring her back to my sponsor." He took a shallow breath and choked on it. "I-I've never failed before." He slipped to the floor, holding his stomach.

Dania had seen it before, an enforcer failing and feeling the pain of not fulfilling a direct order. Few needed direct punishment from their sponsors. Their programming took care of that for them.

Another one of the enforcers woke and started sobbing.

"I'm on it." Rachel ran to their bed. "Max, get me a few warm towels."

Dania backed away, dragging her fingers through her hair. Zindiria couldn't be dead. It simply wasn't possible. She'd seen Geron angry. Two years ago, he'd lifted all the people and furniture in sight and thrown them across the room. She'd seen his younger brother punish a politician, removing his skin and melting his flesh with a flick of his wrist. Zindiria had been Prime Four. She'd been light years stronger than either of them. How was it possible that anyone could have bested her?

Cal appeared at her side. "Are you okay?"

She shook her head. "I don't know. This changes so much. I-I'm not sure what to even think."

Cal put his arm around her shoulder. "At least now we

know it's not a weapon. I thought they'd found a way to incapacitate the enforcers."

Dania nodded, but that wasn't really a comfort.

One of the royal family…was *dead*.

She'd grown up in House Bane. There were births, but not deaths. She couldn't recall ever hearing about a Bane's demise. They were the one constant in the galaxy.

And now one of them was gone.

CAL RELEASED Dania as Doc and Rachel darted about the med bay, trying to calm down their waking patients. He supposed what the enforcers were experiencing was akin to losing someone you loved… Something Cal understood all too well.

The gentle hum in the floor stopped. Had Ty cut off the engines?

He walked toward the comm and stumbled when the floor shook beneath his feet. Test tubes fell off the shelves. Max barked and ran toward Rachel.

"What's going on?" She grabbed the wall behind her as the creature jumped into her arms.

Ty's voice blasted over the comm. "Cal! Get up here!"

What now?

Cal sprinted through the door and down the hall. The silence pressed in on all sides. He rarely noticed the engines. Their gentle hum was a part of the ship—a part of his world. Now, their silence seemed deafening. As was the panic in Ty's voice. The kid could be intense, but rarely scared. And that made Cal's heart race more than the fact that they were dead in space.

He ran onto the bridge and skidded to a stop. The main viewscreen was black.

"What happened?"

"The engines shut down. I was running a diagnostic when everything started shaking." He pointed to the screen. "And now this."

Cal leaned closer to the glass. "It's on, right? You didn't accidently put it on black mode?"

"It's active. The only possible settings are a comm screen, or a window."

Cal's stomach sank. "What's it set to now?"

"Window."

So, wherever they were, there was no light, and no stars. What could possibly have happened?

"Whoa!" Ty leaned away from his station, holding up his hands. "It just changed to comm on its own. I swear, I didn't touch anything."

Ice froze inside Cal's chest as the black screen faded into stern, familiar features. Kile stared back at them, his eyes devoid of any soul.

Cal gulped. They'd given Dania's former commander a ship and sent him back to the Banes. The goal had been to get help for Kirato. At the time, it had seemed like the right thing to do. But at what cost?

After spending time with Dania and even Alexander, he couldn't fathom the possibility that humanity could be completely erased from a person, but now he was staring at that very reality head on.

He'd sent the Banes the one still-loyal enforcer who he'd allowed to have full run of the *Star Renegade*. He'd known that Kile had overstepped his bounds and learned many of the *Renegade*'s secrets. Now it seemed once again, he'd used those secrets against them.

Kile's gaze remained blank, inhuman. "*Star Renegade*, you have been forcibly powered down, and you are in custody."

Cal glanced at Ty. In custody? What did that mean?

"Mr. Espinoza." Kile's heartless gaze lanced him. "You will assemble everyone on board your ship in the lower cargo hold at the boarding ramp in eight minutes."

Cal's lips twisted. "Why, so you can execute us easier?"

"Eight minutes, Mr. Espinoza."

Cal's gut clenched. Everyone he loved was about to die.

They'd spent the last several years running. It had been fun at first, especially each time they'd returned to the cheers and smiling faces of the people of Kirato. He couldn't just order his crew...his *friends* to line up for execution.

He had to do something. He just wasn't sure what. He had nothing to use as a bargaining chip. Nothing he could offer to save his crew.

Except for one small thing. It was a long shot, but it was worth the chance.

Cal took a steadying breath. "Rachel is still on board."

The commander's countenance remained blank. His eyes narrowed slightly. "I said *everyone*."

Kile would even put the woman he cared about on the execution line? Was he really that far gone?

Ty leaned forward. "Hey, Big Guy. We're totally going to comply, but we have a lot of wounded. Mostly enforcers. None of them can even walk."

That lifeless gaze remained on Cal. "Assemble your

crew, Mr. Espinoza. You now have seven minutes." The screen went blank.

"Dammit!" Cal punched his console. Sparks shot out of the side.

Not that it mattered anymore.

Ty hit the comm. "Doc?"

"Yeah, we all heard. The audio went through the whole ship. Rachel is…not okay."

Cal rubbed his face. "None of us are. Get everyone downstairs for me."

Ty frowned. "We're not going to fight?"

Cal snorted, even though this was far from funny. "Can you get back control of the ship?"

Ty lowered his eyes. "No."

Then all they could hope for were speedy executions. Hopefully, there was still a speck of friendship in Kile that would grant them that simple kindness.

Cal reached into his boot, adjusting the placement of the weapon Doc had given him that supposedly would take down an enforcer. He'd kept it on him while Kile had been on board, then Alexander, and then Orion.

In each case, he'd only had one or two enforcers to worry about, though. Chances were, Kile had brought friends. If Cal used the weapon, he'd only get one shot. Unfortunately, that wouldn't be enough to save them.

They walked down the hall toward the ladder in the center of the ship. Cal stopped and ran his hand over one of the blast marks.

Tears welled in his eyes. The *Renegade* had earned that brand during a routine customs inspection gone bad. That had been a no-win situation as well, but at the time they'd still had their engines. Fighting had meaning. This time, there was no way to escape.

The door on his left opened, and Victor stepped out of forward storage. "That's it? You're just giving up? Where's this legendary *Star Renegade* spirit? Why aren't you blasting them out of the stars?"

"We don't have weapons. No engines. Nothing. We're caught." He heard movement down by the stairs. "Stay here. I don't think they know the eight of you are on board. If Orion asks where you are, I'll just play dumb. Kile already thinks I'm a waste of space. It may buy you some time."

"Time for what?"

Cal huffed a mirthless laugh. "I don't know. I'm sorry." He closed his eyes and looked down. The pirates would be found, eventually. Their death sentences were just as solid as those of Cal and his crew. There wasn't much any of them could do.

Victor nodded. "Good luck."

Cal grimaced and kept moving. Chris, Alexander, and Alanna approached from the rear of the ship, probably coming from the crew quarters by way of engineering. The rest of the crew filtered toward him from the med bay.

Dania ran into his arms and hugged him. "We can still fight. We can get out of this."

"No, we can't." Doc shoved his hands in his pockets. "I ran some scans. There's oxygen outside."

"What?" Ty, Ethan, and Cal said at the same time.

"We're inside Kile's cargo bay."

Dania's small frame went lax in Cal's grip. Any hope she'd had, obviously gone.

Ethan whistled. "Sounds like Big Bad came home with a big, bad ship."

Dania pulled Cal closer. "I heard his voice. There won't be any reasoning with him. If we can't fight…" Tears glistened in her eyes. Real, human tears. She was so beautiful.

Cal held her face between his hands, wiping her tears with his thumbs. "It's okay."

"No, it's not."

The pain in her voice sliced into his chest. He pulled her to him and kissed her.

He'd wanted to give her freedom.

He'd wanted to give her a real life.

Things hadn't happened the way he'd planned, but that didn't make it not worthwhile.

Cal released the kiss and looked into her eyes. "I love you. I will always love you."

She burst into tears again, and he pulled her tight against him. He concentrated on the smell of her hair, her warmth, and the way her small body felt pressed against his. If they'd only had more time, he could have given her everything.

Around them, Alanna hugged Alexander, Ty shook Doc's hand and slapped his shoulder, and Ethan held Rachel. Chris leaned against the wall, looking down, his face pale. If Max was here, he wasn't showing himself. It was oddly somber—like the day they'd all known would eventually happen had finally come.

Doc held up his datapad. "Our time's almost up."

Cal nodded and gave each member of his crew a hug. This was his family. He wanted better for them, but at least they were together, supporting each other until the end.

He stepped onto the ladder. "Let's go."

Orion and Fallon were already on the lower deck, standing against the wall with their arms folded behind their backs. It figured they'd want a front-row seat.

Cal's crew filed in behind him. Dania stood at his right, holding his hand. Alexander stood at his left, with Alanna beside him. Cal hadn't asked for the enforcer support, but he appreciated the show of solidarity.

"Should we open the door?" Ethan asked.

Ty moved behind Cal. "I don't think we have to."

There was a click outside, and the hatch opened. The cargo ramp was already down. Outside, a huge hangar held several ships the same size as the *Star Renegade* or larger. It looked more like a spaceport than a cruiser.

Dania's breath hitched and her grip on his hand tightened. He smiled at her and nodded. An odd numbness settled over him, like he was floating in a dream, as Kile stormed up the ramp with cold disdain in his eyes. Two enforcers followed him in standard triangular enforcer formation: Tall, imposing Miguel, who Kile had shot months ago and then subsequently blamed Ethan, and Shivana, who'd taken Miguel's unconscious body off of the *Star Renegade* to be treated. The two enforcers stopped on either side of the door and folded their arms.

Kile continued into the *Star Renegade*'s lower deck and stopped about six feet past the door.

Rachel sniffed somewhere behind Cal. "Big Guy!" She pushed between Cal and Alexander and ran toward the enforcers.

Kile's eyes widened slightly, barely noticeable if Cal hadn't been looking right at him. He shook his head quickly. Again, barely a flick, before he held up his hand.

Rachel's feet left the ground, her legs still running as she floated away from Kile and into Alexander's arms.

Kile's lips moved. Again, almost indiscernible, and Alexander nodded.

Cal leaned toward Alex. "Did he just say *keep her back?*"

"Yes."

Rachel struggled. "Lemme go!"

Alexander held her firm. "Stay calm."

Cal took a deep breath, mostly to keep himself from laughing. Big Bad was still in there! Despite the stony exterior, there was still a human being inside.

Cal's heart raced. They still had a chance. They still might get out of this!

Behind him, Ethan, Ty and Doc shifted, no doubt feeling the same energy. The *Star Renegade* might just squeak out of the enforcers' grip one more time.

Kile's eyes locked with his. The stare was penetrating and filled with…*regret?*

Ice coated Cal's veins once again as the commander shouted, "Clear!"

Clear? What did that mean?

Two more enforcers came up the ramp, followed by a larger figure in a navy-blue uniform. Both Dania and Alexander groaned at the same time as the figure ducked under the entrance and stepped onto the ship.

Cal's breath hitched. The air in the room seemed to thicken as the Kever man stood to his full height, easily twelve inches above the enforcers. His dark, iridescent blue-and-green skin shimmered in the low light as his green eyes scanned the room.

Dania's hand shook within Cal's grip.

"No," she whimpered, her eyes locked on the Kever.

Cal's heart sank. He knew her well enough to know that there was only one person in the galaxy she feared that much.

The man who'd taken her freedom.

The man who'd made her a monster.

Her sponsor.

Prince Geron.

———

Note from the author:

I hope you loved *Renegade Legacy*! If you're ready for the explosive series finale, order *Renegade Guardian* now!

Take me to Renegade Guardian!

—Jennifer

BONUS SCENE!

Every once in a while, scenes get deleted from books. Renegade Legacy had a scene that I loved. It always made me smile and gave a side-character a moment to shine. In the end, though, I decided to go in another direction. I'd still love to let readers see this scene as originally written, so if you're interested in reading a little "alternate way" a scene played out, it's available to my new release subscribers for free here.

https://www.subscribepage.com/s2b4f1sbbook4

ACKNOWLEDGMENTS

You may have noticed that the word "hope" appears a lot in *Renegade Legacy*. It wasn't intentional, but subliminally, the theme may have snuck in as a coping mechanism after a few very challenging years, including the 18 months it took to prepare, write, and edit this book. Writing has always been my outlet, and I hope the trials of my ragtag crew can inspire hope in *you*, if you are dealing with tragedy, illness, injuries, freak accidents, or anything else life might throw at you. (Even if they all hit at the same time.)

Thank you to *Renegade Legacy*'s developmental team, Shaila Patel, Emilee Garriss, Jenna Standage, and my son for pointing out the littlest things and helping me to make them better. And Shaila...that scene where they were running through the tank... you are such a trooper for how many times you read that. Thank you, thank you, thank you!

To my copy editor, Amy McNulty... You still added and removed commas, but I think I'm getting better. Thanks for your patience.

And my final line of defense, my proofreader, Tandy Boese...how do you find typos five other people missed?

To my family...we made it through, and we'll make it through more. You are my safe haven, my Kirato, when all the world goes crazy or crashes down around us.

To my readers...thank you for taking this amazing journey with the *Star Renegade* crew. And sorry about that ending, but you kinda knew it was coming, and I didn't want to disappoint you.

—Jennifer

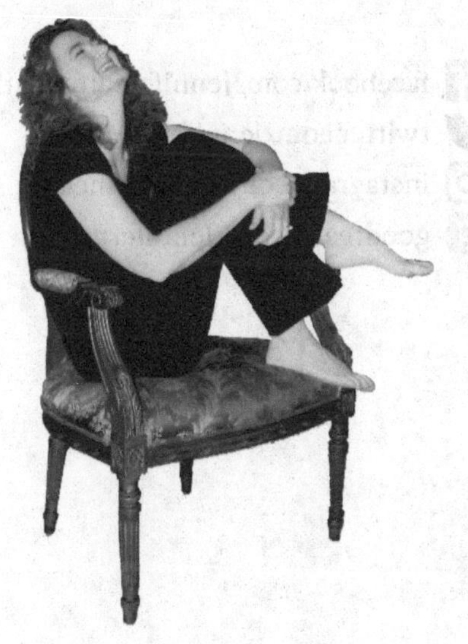

Jennifer M. Eaton hails from the eastern shore of the North American Continent on planet Earth. Yes, regrettably, she is human, but please don't hold that against her.

While not traipsing through the galaxy looking for specimens for her space moth collection, she lives with her wonderfully supportive husband, three energetic offspring, and a duo of poodles who run the spaceport when she's not around.

During infrequent excursions to her home planet of Earth, Jennifer enjoys long hikes in the woods, bicycling, swimming, snorkeling, and snuggling up by the fire with a great book; but great adventures are always a short shuttle ride away.

Read more from Jennifer M. Eaton

www.jennifereaton.com
Blog: Jennifermeaton.com

facebook.com/Jennifereaton.author
twitter.com/jennifermeaton
instagram.com/jennifermeaton
goodreads.com/Jennifermeaton

9 781949 046151